PRAISE FOR LISA SCOTTOLINE'S

*Come Home*

"This thrilling testament to a mother's relentless love may well be Scottoline's best novel to date."
—*Library Journal* (starred review)

"Three hundred pages bled through my hands and I closed the book at 2 A.M. If the sheer energy in *Come Home* could be bottled, the oil companies would be out of business. The suspense and dread build like a series of tornadoes flattening all in their path. The characters Jill, Abby, Victoria, and Sam are drawn as finely as a writer could. The pace is relentless, the twists are jaw-dropping, and then Scottoline piles ending on top of ending until you turn the last page. As I closed the novel I thought that, quite simply, Scottoline is a powerhouse."      —David Baldacci

"Just as in *Save Me*, Lisa Scottoline delivers a satisfying thriller with a family saga at its core."      —*Booklist*

"Complex family dynamics and carefully concealed secrets drive this gripping stand-alone."      —*Publishers Weekly*

"Scottoline is always awesome, but *Come Home* held me spellbound because she has such an eye for describing complicated family relationships."      —Janet Evanovich

"A gripping and compelling novel about one woman solving her ex-husband's murder and the emotional repercussions of going back into a family you no longer know. Scottoline gets all the details right, and gives all the characters flesh and blood, breath and life. This is a novel that is as full of thrills as it is full of heart."      —Kristin Hannah

*Save Me*

"Are you a good mother if you save your child from disaster? What if it means sacrificing another's child? In *Save Me,* Lisa Scottoline walks readers into this charged moral dilemma and then takes them on an intense, breathless ride where accidents might not be accidents at all. You won't be able to put this one down."  —Jodi Picoult

"Each staccato chapter adds new and unexpected turns, so many you could get whiplash just turning a page. Scottoline knows how to keep readers in her grip."
—*The New York Times Book Review*

"The Scottoline we love as a virtuoso of suspense, fast action, and intricate plot is back in top form in *Save Me.*"
—*The Washington Post Book World*

"A white-hot crossover novel about the perils of mother love."  —*Kirkus Reviews*

"A satisfying, nail-biting thriller."  —*Publishers Weekly*

"Scottoline masterfully fits every detail into a tight plot chock-full of real characters, real issues, and real thrills. A story anchored by the impenetrable power of a mother's love, it begs the question, just how far would you go to save your child?"  —*Booklist*

"An emotionally riveting novel that explores the depths of one mother's love for her daughter. Powerful, provocative, and page-turning!"
—Emily Giffin

"A novel packed with excitement and emotion, *Save Me* is a gut-clenching, heart-stirring read."  —Sandra Brown

"Heart-pounding! Scottoline provides the perfect combination of explosive action, twisting turns, and genuine emotion in this exciting novel of an ordinary mom going to extraordinary lengths for her daughter. Open up *Save Me,* and save yourself with a great book." —Lisa Gardner

"From one shock to the next, only a mom's courage and love bring justice. Nerves-on-edge, heart-pounding, and heart-wrenching, *Save Me* is thrilling and infused with love. Brilliant, I couldn't put it down." —Louise Penny

### Think Twice

"A thriller that feels like an instant classic."
—*Connecticut Post*

"So engaging [you] can't help but read it in one sitting."
—*Seattle Post-Intelligencer*

"A pulse-pounding thriller." —*Booklist*

"The intricate plot will keep thriller fans turning those pages." —*Library Journal*

"Scottoline unfolds her story in breathlessly quick cuts . . . you won't put it down." —*Kirkus Reviews*

"The perfect ingredients for gut-wrenching suspense . . . In expert fashion, Scottoline constructs the anxiety in intense emotional layers, peppering her story with humorous breaks and heartrending moments only to slam readers back into the chilling controversy without warning. Surpassing others in her field, Scottoline's *Think Twice* is everything thriller fans crave and more."
—*Suspense Magazine*

# COME HOME

Lisa Scottoline

St. Martin's Paperbacks

COME HOME

Copyright © 2012 by Smart Blonde, LLC.

Excerpt from *Don't Go* copyright © 2013 by Smart Blonde, LLC.

For information address St. Martin's Press, 175 Fifth Avenue, New York, NY 10010.

ISBN: 978-0-312-38084-7

Printed in the United States of America

St. Martin's Press hardcover edition / April 2012
St. Martin's Griffin trade paperback edition / March 2013
St. Martin's Paperbacks edition / February 2016

St. Martin's Paperbacks are published by St. Martin's Press, 175 Fifth Avenue, New York, NY 10010.

10   9   8   7   6   5   4   3   2   1

*This novel is dedicated, with deepest gratitude,
to Jen Enderlin, my amazing editor and friend.*

Physician, heal thyself.
—*The Holy Bible*, Luke 4:23


It is an old maxim of mine that when you have
excluded the impossible, whatever remains,
however improbable, must be the truth.
—Sherlock Holmes in *The Adventures of Beryl Coronet*
by Sir Arthur Conan Doyle

# 1.

Jill stopped on the stairway, listening. She thought she heard a voice calling her from outside, but she'd been wrong before. It was probably the rushing of the rain, or the lash of the wind through the trees. Still, she listened, hoping.

"Babe?" Sam paused on the stair, resting his hand on the banister. He looked back at her, his eyes a puzzled blue behind his glasses. "Did you forget your phone?"

"No, I thought I heard something." Jill didn't elaborate. She was in her forties, old enough to have a past and wise enough to keep her thoughts about it to herself.

"What?" Sam asked, patiently. It was almost midnight, and they'd been on their way to bed. The house was dark except for the glass fixture above the stairwell, and the silvery strands in Sam's thick, dark hair glinted in the low light. Their chubby golden retriever, Beef, was already upstairs, looking down at them from the landing, his buttery ears falling forward.

"It's nothing, I guess." Jill started back up the stairs, but Beef swung his head toward the front of the house and gave an excited bark. His tail started to wag, and Jill turned, too, listening again.

*Jill! Jill!*

"It's Abby!" Jill heard it for sure, this time. The cry resonated in her chest, speaking directly to her heart. She turned around and hurried for the entrance hall, and Beef scampered downstairs after her, his heavy butt getting ahead of him, like a runaway tractor-trailer.

"Abby who?" Sam called after her. "Your ex's kid?"

"Yes." Jill reached the front door, twisted the deadbolt, flicked on the porch light, and threw open the door. Abby wasn't there, and Jill didn't see her because it was so dark. There were no streetlights at this end of the block, and the rain obliterated the outlines of the houses and cars, graying out the suburban scene. Suddenly, a black SUV with only one headlight drove past, spotlighting a silhouette that Jill would know anywhere. It was Abby, but she was staggering down the sidewalk as if she'd been injured.

"Sam, call 911!" Jill bolted out of the house and into the storm, diagnosing Abby on the fly. It could have been a hit-and-run, or an aneurysm. Not a stroke, Abby was too young. Not a gunshot or stab wound, in this neighborhood.

Jill tore through the rain. Beef bounded ahead, barking in alarm. The neighbor's motion-detector went on, casting a halo of light on their front lawn. Abby stumbled off the sidewalk. Her purse slipped from her shoulder and dropped to the ground. Abby took a few more faltering steps, then collapsed, crumpling to the grass.

"Abby!" Jill screamed, sprinting to Abby's side, kneeling down. Abby was conscious, but crying. Jill reached for her pulse and scanned her head and body for signs of injury, and there were none. Rainwater covered Abby's face, streaking her mascara and blackening her tears. Her hair stuck to her neck, and rain plastered her thin sundress to her body. Her pulse felt strong and steady, bewildering Jill. "Abby, Abby, what is it?"

"You have to . . . hold me." Abby raised her arms. "Please."

Jill gathered Abby close, shielding her from the rain. She'd held Abby so many times before, and all the times rushed back at her, as if her very body had stored the memories, until that very moment. Jill flashed on the time Abby had fallen off her Rollerblades, breaking an ankle. Then the time Abby had gotten a C on her trig final. The time she didn't get picked for the travel soccer team. Abby had always been a sensitive little girl, but she wasn't a little girl anymore, and Jill had never seen her cry so hard.

"Abby, honey, please, tell me, and I can help."

"I can't say it . . . it's so awful." Abby sobbed, and Jill caught a distinct whiff of alcohol on her breath and came up to speed. Abby wasn't injured, she'd been drinking. Jill hadn't seen her in three years, and Abby had grown up; she'd be nineteen now. Abby sobbed harder. "Jill, Dad's dead . . . he's dead."

"*What?*" Jill gasped, shocked. Her ex-husband was in excellent health, still in his forties. "How?"

"Somebody . . . killed him." Abby dissolved into tears, her body going limp, clinging to Jill. "Please, you have to . . . help me. I have to find out . . . who did it."

Jill hugged her closer, feeling her grief and struggling to process what had happened. She couldn't imagine William as a murder victim, or a victim of any kind, for that matter, but her first thought was of his daughters, Abby and Victoria, and her own daughter, Megan. The news would devastate all of them, Megan included. William was her stepfather, but the only father she'd ever known. Her real father had died before she was born.

"Babe, what are you doing? Let's get her into the

house!" Sam shouted, to be heard over the rain. He was kneeling on Abby's other side, though Jill didn't know when he'd gotten there.

"William's been murdered," Jill told him, sounding numb, even to herself.

"I heard. We're not calling 911, she's just drunk." Sam squinted against the brightness of the motion-detector light. Raindrops soaked his hair and dappled his polo shirt. "Let me take her arm. Lift her on one, two, three," he counted off, tugging Abby's arm.

"Okay, go." Jill took Abby's other arm, and together they hoisted her, sobbing, to her feet, gathered her purse, and half walked and half carried her toward the house, sloshing through the grass, with Beef at their heels.

Jill tried to collect her thoughts, which were in turmoil. She'd always dreamed of seeing Abby again, but not in these circumstances, and she dreaded telling Megan about William. But as agonized as she felt for the girls, Jill wouldn't shed a tear for her ex-husband. There was a reason she had divorced the man, and it was a whopper.

And evidently, not only the good died young.

# 2.

"Come in and sit down, honey. Here, right here." Jill helped Abby to the kitchen island, catching Sam's eye. "Sam, I'll take her from here; can you get us a glass of water and some towels?"

"Sure." Sam eased Abby off his arm and hustled to the sink, while Beef danced a circle around them, wagging his tail, missing the point entirely.

"I can't believe . . . Dad's really *gone*." Abby slumped heavily into the seat, covering her face with her hands, her body wracked with sobs. "It's so . . . *horrible* . . . I don't know what to do . . . I'm not ever . . . going to see him again."

"I know, sweetie, I know." Jill sat down next to Abby and held her while she wept, and all her love for the girl came flooding back, coursing through her system, flowing warm and sure as lifeblood. "I'm so, so sorry."

"I don't know . . . *who* did this to him . . . or *why* . . . I still can't even . . . believe it's true." Abby wept, bereft and broken. "I won't talk to him . . . ever, *ever again* . . . that's not possible, that's not even . . . *possible* . . . and I don't know what to *do*."

"I know, I understand." Jill hugged her closer, trying to warm her with her body, feeling every inch like her mother, all over again. Abby's real mother had died when she was only four years old, and Jill had been her stepmother for eight years, raising Abby and her older sister Victoria for most of their childhood.

"I live at home and . . . even though Dad was, like, away a lot . . . I knew . . . I could call him . . . and ask him stuff."

"You poor thing." Jill looked up when Sam brought her the water glass and set it down on the island.

"Here we go," he said quietly, meeting her eye with concern. "You okay, babe?"

"Yes, thanks." Jill nodded, but she was fighting her own tears. It killed her to hear Abby's hoarse, choking sobs, echoing in the quiet house.

"Okay, I'll get the towels, be right back." Sam patted Jill's shoulder, then left for upstairs.

"And he took care . . . of the bills . . . and *everything* in the house . . . and I don't know how . . . to do everything . . . all by myself . . . and now . . . I'm all alone . . . like, there's no one."

"There's me, Abby. You have me," Jill said, without a second thought, and the next few words arrived unbidden, as if they'd been waiting offstage for their cue. "I love you, honey, and I always will."

"Oh, God, I love you, too." Abby looked up in Jill's embrace, her eyes brimming with tears. Mascara marred her cheeks, and the fair skin on her cheeks was mottled with emotion. "Jill, I love you, so much . . . you're my *mom* . . . and you always will be and you *always were*."

"It's okay now, honey. I'm here." Jill wiped tears and makeup from Abby's cheeks, comforting her. "Don't cry, it's okay."

"I don't know why you still even . . . love me." Abby

shook her head, bewildered. Tears spilled from her eyes. "I don't even *deserve* . . . to be here, with you."

"Of course you do, honey." Jill's heart broke for her. "What a thing to say. Of course you do."

"No, I don't . . . I don't . . . you called and called . . . and I didn't even call you back . . . I wanted to, I did, but Dad said not to . . . I was afraid to . . . he'd go ballistic if he found out . . . that's why I didn't." Abby cried, her gaze on Jill, pleading. "I'm so sorry . . . I feel so *guilty* . . . and I'm so sorry . . . I had nowhere else to go . . . I feel like such a jerk."

"It's okay, honey." Jill's throat caught, and she hugged Abby again, cradling her. "You know if I had it my way, we would've talked all the time." Jill had done everything in her power to stay in touch with the girls, but William had demanded she stop trying to contact them, even threatening her with a restraining order. She'd hired a lawyer to see if she had any legal recourse, but she didn't, and the lawyer had advised her that opposing a restraining order would mean that the girls had to testify, and she couldn't bring herself to do that to them.

"I don't know . . . how you could still love me . . . after so long, like *three years*."

"Love doesn't go away, not this kind of love." Jill hadn't seen the girls since that awful night, but the rupture still felt as fresh as yesterday.

"I know . . . I'm the one who did the bad thing . . . the way I treated you . . . you tried so hard to talk to us."

"Don't worry about it for a minute. Divorce is hard and weird, and it's not your fault, at all." Jill felt Abby's body shudder with each sob. William would have done anything to get her back for the divorce, even if it meant hurting Abby and Victoria, but she didn't want to think about him now, just Abby.

"How can you forgive me . . . I'm such a terrible person . . . and I knew if I came here, you'd be so nice."

"Honey, of course I would, and I'm glad you did, even on this sad day. Especially on this sad day. You've come . . . to the right place." Jill stopped just short of saying, *you've come home.*

"Thanks, so much." Abby burrowed her head in Jill's shoulder. "I really do love you . . . and I really missed you . . . so much . . . and I'm sorry I didn't call you back . . . I hoped you knew . . . I didn't forget you."

"I did know, and that's why I stopped, too. You know that I thought of you and Victoria, all the time."

"I never stopped loving you . . . Jill, or wishing . . . I could see you."

"I know, sweetie. I always loved you, too. You know that." Jill felt her chest tighten, her anger like a fist at the ready. She hoped William was burning in hell right this minute. It felt strange to have such hate for him and such love for Abby, both at once. "Breathe, honey. Just breathe, and I have Kleenex here. Want some? That'll help."

"Okay . . . yes . . . good idea." Abby released her, and Jill reached for the box of Kleenex, pulled out a few, and handed them to Abby.

"Here we go. Blow your nose, then have a sip of water."

"Yuck, I'm so snotty . . . I always cry like such a . . . dumb baby." Abby took the tissues, mopped her eyes and cheeks, then blew her nose noisily. "Gross."

"Here, take some more." Jill took the dirty tissues, handed Abby a bunch more, and Abby blew her nose again, then surrendered the soiled ones to Jill.

"Sorry."

"Don't worry about it." Jill handed her another few tissues, and Abby sniffled, wiping her eyes, her tears subsiding.

"I feel like such a . . . little kid."

"Everybody feels like a little kid when they cry. Ready for some water?" Jill handed Abby the water glass, and Abby took it with two hands, her fingernails polished dark purple.

"Thanks." Abby drank thirstily, and Jill appraised her with a maternal eye. Abby's eyes were bloodshot and sunken, as if she hadn't been getting enough sleep, and her dress was too thin for the weather, clinging wetly to a body that was shapely, if a little too skinny. Her dark blonde hair dripped with rainwater.

"Need more water?" Jill looked over as Sam returned with the towels.

"Here we go, babe."

"Thanks." Jill took the towels and set one on the island as Abby put the water down.

"No more water, thanks."

"Take a towel." Jill placed the towel around Abby's shoulders, rubbing her upper arms to warm her. "Better, honey?"

"Yes, thanks." Abby's chest heaved once, then again, and she sniffled.

"More Kleenex?"

"No, thanks. Whew." Abby seemed to be getting her bearings, straightening up in the seat, blinking to clear her eyes. She dried her face on the towel's edge, leaving streaks of pinkish blusher and lip gloss. "Oops. Sorry."

"It doesn't matter." Jill handed her the other towel, and Abby flopped it onto her head and twisted it into a turban.

"I just can't believe Dad's really gone." Abby sighed deeply, her lower lip trembling.

"I know, I'm so sorry, honey."

"Sorry I lost it like that." Abby shook her head, her lovely eyes shining, brown as earth itself.

"Don't be. It's an impossible thing to go through."

"Well, I'm not buzzed anymore, that's for sure."

Jill patted her arm. "Let me get you some coffee, okay? Warm you up?"

"Great, thanks."

"Still take it black?" Jill got up from the island and went around to the coffeemaker.

"Yes, like you." Abby brightened, adjusting the towel on her head. She had matured into a natural beauty, but looked more like her younger self without the makeup; she still had her large, round eyes, a small, straight nose, fair skin, and lips shaped like a Cupid's bow.

"Okay, hang in." Jill plucked a coffee pod from the bowl and popped it into the machine, then took a mug from the cabinet, slid it under the spout, and hit BREW. "How about something to eat?"

"I'd love that, if it's not too much trouble."

"Great." Jill felt better at the prospect. If she couldn't cure something, she'd cook something. "Why don't I make you some French toast?"

"My favorite." Abby managed a shaky smile, her eyes glistening. "You remember?"

"Of course." Jill smiled, then went to the refrigerator and retrieved a carton of eggs, bread, and a plastic bottle of two percent. "But the days of white bread are over. I have only whole wheat."

"That's okay. Jeez, I miss your cooking."

Jill felt her heart ease, seeing Abby recover her composure. She brought the food to the counter, and the coffee brewed behind her, filling the air with a delicious aroma. "Sam, you want some coffee or French toast, too?"

"No, thanks," Sam answered. He was leaning against the sink, his arms crossed over his chest, with Beef sitting at his side. The rain was beginning to dry on his polo shirt. They both were still dressed from their run, in polo shirts, gym shorts, and sneakers.

Abby sighed, heavily. "Dad died four days ago, on Tuesday. The cops said it was a heart attack, caused by alcohol and prescription meds."

Jill blinked. "I thought you said he was murdered."

"I think he was."

"You do, but the police don't?"

"Right." Abby straightened up, her tone newly firm. "I think they're wrong. Rather, I *know* they're wrong. You're a doctor, and you know Dad. He didn't take any prescription meds. He was murdered, no matter what the police say."

Jill cracked some eggs into a bowl, hiding her confusion. She'd never known William to take prescription meds, but she'd never known the real William Skyler. He was the ultimate con man, fooling her, Megan, and even his own daughters. "So the police say it wasn't murder. What do they think it was?"

"They say it was an accidental overdose. The cocktail, whatever that means."

"It means that certain drugs can kill you, in combination with alcohol." The coffee was ready, and Jill set the full mug in front of Abby. "What drugs did he take?"

"He didn't take them." Abby picked up the coffee and held it in two hands, warming her fingers. "The report came back today and said he had the drugs in his body, but I know he didn't put them there. He never would have, and I went on the Internet and it doesn't say those are lethal drugs, anyway." Abby sipped some coffee, then set it down, sniffling. "The cops found pill bottles in his bedroom, but I never saw them before, and they didn't dust for fingerprints like on TV, to see how they got there."

"What pills did they find?" Jill retrieved a fork and beat the eggs.

"Three bottles. Xanax, Vicodin, and one other, T-something."

"Temezepam?"

"Yes. I *knew* you'd know." Abby brightened a little.

"They're common drugs for anxiety and pain, honey." Jill drizzled a dash of vanilla into the egg mixture, veining the light with the dark, then beat it again.

"Not common for Dad." Abby shifted forward, and water dripped from a curling tendril that had escaped from the towel turban. "Plus, there was a bottle of whisky in his office, but no glass. When did you ever know Dad to drink out of a *bottle*? Never, and the drugs had to be planted there, by whoever killed him."

"What does Victoria say?" Jill picked up a pan that had been drying on the counter, cut in a pat of butter, and set it on the stove, firing up the gas.

"She says I just don't want to accept that Dad's dead."

Jill could have guessed as much. Victoria was always the sensible one to Abby's free spirit. "Couldn't she be right? It's a hard thing to deal with—"

"She's wrong, they all are. I know it, and we'll prove it." Abby looked down as Beef trotted over, wagging his tail, sending droplets flying. She rested her hand on his coppery head, where his wet fur spiked at the crown, like a doggie punk rocker. "I missed Beef, too. Remember the day we got him?"

"Sure." Jill did. It had been a cold, sunny afternoon at a golden retriever rescue in Delaware County. The three girls cooed over a passel of fluffy golden puppies, and Abby scooped up the fattest one, naming him on the spot. *This one is Beef on the hoof!*

"Where's Megan?" Abby asked, adjusting the towel.

"At a sleepover." Jill opened the bread and dunked a slice into the eggs.

"Aw, I wanted to see her. I miss her, too."

"You'll see her in the morning. Stay over with us. Right,

Sam?" Jill realized with embarrassment that she hadn't introduced them, at all. She abandoned the slice of bread. "Yikes, I'm sorry. Abby, this is my fiancé, Sam Becker. Sam, Abby Skyler."

"Hello, Abby." Sam smiled at her, with sympathy. "I'm sorry about your loss, and of course you can stay here tonight."

Abby seemed to be leaning away from Sam, almost recoiling, though she said, "Nice to meet you, Sam."

"Yes, thanks, Sam," Jill chimed in, trying to smooth over her own awkwardness. It struck her as odd that Abby and Sam had never met, as if her life had been hacked into pieces, not only the Before and After of two marriages, but the Before and Before and After, of three. She had been a widow when she'd met William, and Sam would be her third husband.

Abby kept an eye on Sam. "Not gonna lie, Sam, I feel like you're mad at me or something. Are you? Don't be mad at me, okay?"

Jill tensed, and she could smell the butter starting to burn in the pan. She hated burned butter. She turned off the gas for a moment.

"I'm not angry at you, Abby, I'm concerned," Sam answered, gently. "You drove here, drunk. That concerns me, for your sake and for the sake of others."

Jill turned to Abby, puzzled. "You drove? I thought that SUV dropped you off."

"What SUV? I parked around the corner. I looked up your address online but couldn't find the street." Abby looked down as Beef nudged her with his muzzle, his bid to keep getting petted. "I'm sorry, I won't do it again."

"I know you won't, sweetie." Jill didn't have the heart to lecture Abby, not tonight. "What did you have to drink?"

"Just some vodka and orange juice."

"Hard liquor?" Jill hid her dismay. Abby used to be so wholesome and healthy, a competitive swimmer. All the girls swam, Jill had taught them.

"I'm sorry, I know, I was upset, because of Dad." Abby stroked Beef, who rested his big head on her lap. "It's so good to see Beef again. I was worried he died."

"He's not that old, is he?"

"Sure he is." Abby patted the dog, and her wet dress gapped at the neckline, revealing a flowery tattoo above one breast. "He'll turn ten, this Valentine's Day."

"Really?" Jill tried not to stare at the tattoo, lost in time, for a moment. *When did Abby start drinking, or get old enough for a tattoo? When did Beef get so old? Where did all the time go?* Abby had arrived out of nowhere, and it was as if Jill's past had crashed her present like a house party, leaving her disoriented.

"You said you remembered, Jill. We picked him out on Valentine's Day. It was Dad's present, for you."

"Oh right." Jill had forgotten that part. She let the moment pass, eyeing Sam's back as he turned around, tore off a paper towel, and wiped his face and glasses.

"This is such a pretty room." Abby was looking around the kitchen. "It's so you, Jill."

"Thanks." Jill glanced around, too, proudly. The house was still a work in progress, but the kitchen was warm and homey, ringed by white cabinets and countertops of ivory granite veined with butterscotch. The walls glowed a golden hue, which set off a cherry dining table and kitchen island, where they all ate, used the laptop, or did their homework, like the sun to their family solar system.

"I'm really sorry about the drinking, Jill."

"I understand." Jill was curious where she got the liquor, but didn't want to torture her, not now. "I saw on Facebook that Victoria's in law school, at Seton Hall. How's she doing?"

Sam looked over, but he didn't say anything, and Jill read his mind. He was surprised that she followed the girls on Facebook. She had never told him that.

"Victoria loves law school, which isn't surprising. She was doing great, until Dad." Abby paused. "You know how she is. She'll be fine."

"You both will, in time, but don't rush it. Grief takes all the time it needs, no matter what you do." Jill knew that Victoria would internalize her grief, much like Megan would.

"She lives with some roommates, near school. I was living with Dad in town, but now I don't know what's going to happen."

"Why aren't you in college, honey? You're so smart." Jill kept her tone non-judgmental, but Abby still avoided her eye.

"I'm waitressing. I guess you saw, I started at art school but I broke up with Santos and that kind of messed me up. I'll go back someday, I know it's a good thing." Abby seemed to deflate again, her shoulders sloping and her turban sliding to the side. "Anyway, Dad's memorial service is tomorrow. They already cremated him. Victoria arranged it, I couldn't deal." Abby sighed. "Can you come to the service, Jill? And can Megan?"

"We'll see. I have to ask her. I know she'll be so sad about your Dad."

"Afterwards I can take you over to the house, and you can see what I mean. Dad was murdered, I know it."

Jill felt torn. "I can't do that, honey, especially not with Megan."

"But I'll prove it to you, I'll show you Dad's medical papers. You'll see he didn't take those drugs, there's no record of it. You know Dad used to save all his medical stuff in one place, because of his cholesterol."

Jill returned to making the French toast, while Abby

talked. William had always taken excellent care of himself. It was everybody else he disregarded, even his daughters.

"He never would have taken those pills on purpose. So he had to have been murdered, and you can help me figure it out."

"No, I can't. I'm a pediatrician, not a detective."

"You're a doctor, and Sherlock Holmes was a doctor. You told me that, remember, for that English paper? I got a B plus, because of you."

Jill felt touched. "What I said was that the author, Sir Arthur Conan Doyle, was a successful doctor, and Dr. Watson was as important as Sherlock."

"But you said that the way they solved a murder case was the same way you diagnose a disease." Abby leaned over, urgent. "Please, will you help me? We can do it together."

Sam cleared his throat. "Ladies, I'll let you two spend some time alone." He came over and kissed Jill lightly on the cheek. "Love you. Call me if you need anything." He turned to Abby, straightening. "Goodnight, Abby."

"Goodnight." Abby gave him a little wave, and Sam left the kitchen. When he was barely out of earshot, she leaned over and said, "He's kind of old for you, don't you think?"

"No. Hush." Jill saw Sam turn around, but she knew it was the liquor talking. "Now, drink your coffee."

# 3.

"I think a shower might be a good idea for you, before bed, don't you?" Jill climbed the stairs with Abby, who was still in her turban and towel.

"Yes. Clean me up and tuck me in, huh?"

"That's the idea." Jill put an arm around her, and Abby looked over, her expression sad and soft.

"Dad never got serious with anyone after you, Jill, you know. We met a few of his dates, but he didn't have a girl-friend."

"That's too bad." Jill kept her thoughts to herself. They took a left at the landing, past a lineup of candid photo-graphs of her and Megan. "Come this way. We have a guest room you can sleep in, with its own bathroom."

Abby stopped on the stair, at the photographs. "These pictures are so nice. Did you guys go to a photographer or something?"

"No, Sam took them. It's a hobby of his."

"This is the best one, of you alone." Abby lingered at one photograph, a candid taken at the Jersey shore, and Jill was laughing, her hair curling in the salty air. Sam had been trying to get her to relax, pretending that he'd dropped his camera in the sand, and Jill loved the photograph because she loved the photographer.

"Ah, I was younger then."

"You're still young, and your hair is so sexy, that way. You should wear it down all the time."

"Please. I don't have time, and it's not doctor hair."

"Remember when I was little, we looked so much alike, people thought I was your daughter? I mean, your real daughter?" Abby gestured at the photo, waving her dark fingernail up and down. "See, your nose is little and straight, like mine. Our eyes are the same shape and almost the same brown, only yours are lighter. Our hair is more different, I don't have the reddish brown like you, but we have the same exact smile. I think our smile is our best feature."

Jill managed a smile, but couldn't ignore the wistfulness in Abby's tone, and put an arm around her. "You know, I kept track of you, on Facebook. Your Dad asked me not to write you there or post on your wall, but I read your feed, all the time."

"I bet you were, I knew it." Abby smiled at her.

"I know about your cat, Pickles, and your ancient car, and how sad you were over your breakup with your boyfriend." Jill didn't add that the boyfriend looked a little rough around the edges.

"I *love* my cat." Abby smiled, more easily, and Jill warmed at the sight, happy to lighten her heart, if only for a moment.

"I can see why. He's the cutest cat ever."

"Did you see that photo of him in the laundry basket?"

"Yes, of course, and orange tabbies are my favorite."

"I know. Dad told us to unfriend you, and Victoria did, but I didn't. I just made my settings private, so he didn't know." Abby's smile faded. "I feel bad saying that about him, now."

Jill gave her a final hug. "Let's get you showered up, girl."

"Okay." Abby hugged her back, and they went to the guest room, where Jill switched on the overhead light. It flickered off, and the room went dark.

"Damn. I'll get a new bulb and some clean sheets. The last time this room was used was when Sam's son Steven visited. He's an architect, in Austin."

"So Sam lives here, with you and Megan?"

"Yes. I bought this house after the divorce, and he sold his condo in Philly and moved in."

"When are you guys getting married?"

"This summer, in July." Jill felt suddenly uncomfortable, telling her the details, and Abby smiled, shakily.

"So Steven's going to be your new stepson? Does that make this the steproom?"

Jill smiled, then the bedroom brightened from a flash of lightning, with a loud thunderclap.

Abby made a nervous face. "Do you think I could sleep in Megan's room tonight? Since she's not here?"

"Sure." Jill didn't think Megan would mind, in the circumstances. "Follow me."

"Thanks." Abby walked down the hall with Jill, and Beef stayed between them, panting and trembling, because of the storm. "He still hates thunder, I see."

"You have such a good memory, honey." Jill stopped at Megan's door and flicked on the light. "Here we are."

"*Sweet* room." Abby stood in the threshold, taking in the large room, with its white canopied bed and a pink-patterned comforter. The far wall had a panel of windows with a padded windowseat, next to full bookshelves and a matching oak desk. A bulletin board hung above the desk filled with swimming awards, team photos, and stills from the school play, as well as glossy pictures of Michael Phelps, the Phillies, and the *Twilight* crew, which Megan had cut out of magazines.

"Bathroom's to the right." Jill gestured, but Abby was already walking there with Beef.

"She was always so neat."

"She still is." Jill went to the threshold of the bathroom, and Beef settled down on the bathmat. She pointed at the shower stall, where overpriced shampoos and conditioners were lined up. "Put the caps back on, you."

"You remember the orange juice?" Abby smiled, sheepishly.

"How could I forget? It was funny." Jill smiled back. She'd taken a jug of fresh-squeezed out of the refrigerator and shaken it, but Abby hadn't put the cap back on and the walls were orange for a week. "You take a nice, warm shower, and I'll bring you some clean towels, okay?"

"Okay, thanks." Abby leaned over and kissed her suddenly on the cheek, and Jill felt a rush of emotion. It felt right to be taking care of Abby again, and at the same time, it felt strange to be taking care of Abby again. She left the bathroom, went to the linen closet, got the towels, then stopped to see Sam.

"Still up?" Jill asked, entering his home office, which was small, lined with bookshelves filled with medical textbooks and teaching awards. Sam taught at Penn's medical school and was also a researcher in diabetes.

"Just waiting on you." Sam looked up at Jill, with a worried smile. He was sitting at his old wooden desk against the window, raking his floppy hair with his fingers as he read a book online. "How's the kid?"

"Okay." Jill looked at him anew, after what Abby had said. His tortoiseshell glasses reflected two white pages with tiny footnotes, and behind them were sharp blue eyes, full of intelligence and humor. Sam was only eight years her senior, and his deep crow's feet and laugh lines only made him more handsome to her, in a lived-in sort of way. The gray in his hair reminded her of the weathered cedar of a comfy rocker, and Jill felt lucky to have him. "Thanks for being so nice to her."

"No need for thanks."

"She's upset tonight, obviously. She's really a sweet girl."

"I'm sure." Sam slid off his glasses and set them on his desk, which was clean except for his laptop and iPhone. He touched her arm. "I'm sorry about your ex's death. How are you feeling, really?"

"Honestly, it's upsetting, mainly because of the girls." Jill set down the towels and looked behind her, to make sure Abby wasn't within earshot. "Megan will take it hard, because she was so conflicted. She loved him, but after the divorce, he didn't answer any of her calls or texts. That killed her, and now she'll never get the chance to ask him why, or understand."

"I'll be there for her. We'll get through it." Sam buckled his lower lip, pained. "I was supposed to meet Lee tomorrow, he's coming in from Cleveland. But I can see him after the memorial service, if you want to go."

Jill felt touched. "But Lee's flying in just to meet with you, isn't he?"

"Yes, but I can delay meeting him. It's a death in the family, more or less."

"No, don't. Thanks for the offer, but you don't have to come. If Megan wants to go, I'll take her."

Sam frowned. "You sure?"

"Totally."

"Okay, thanks. But please, promise me you won't get sucked into this murder business. It's absurd. We both know the Internet is full of idiocy about which drugs can kill you."

"I won't get involved. The cops are experts, I'm not." Jill picked up the towels and gave him a kiss. "Gotta go back now."

"Come to bed, soon. It's late."

"I know." Jill smiled, straightening up, then left the office and went back to Megan's bedroom. The bathroom door was closed, and she knocked. "I have fresh towels, honey."

"Don't need them." Abby opened the door. Steam clouded the air, and she was wearing one of Megan's nightgowns, a red-striped Lanz, of worn flannel. "Is it okay I'm wearing this nightgown? Remember, it used to be mine?"

"How could I forget? It was so nice of you."

"It's even better than it used to be, it's so soft. Megan kept it, huh?"

"She wears it all the time." Jill smiled, remembering when Abby had given Megan the nightgown. Megan had coveted it for so long, and they'd tried to find one like it in Nordstrom's, but they couldn't. So Abby had folded her own, put it in a box, and gift-wrapped it for Christmas, and Megan had been delighted.

"God, I'm so tired." Abby padded past her and climbed into Megan's bed, and Beef bounded up behind her. The dog settled down, stretching out his tufted front paws while Abby ducked beneath the comforter. "It's so cozy here."

"Good." Jill went over to the bed and tucked Abby in, on mom autopilot. "I remember when you and Megan would get into the same bed, even though you barely fit."

"I know." Abby smiled, her breath minty from the toothpaste. "It was fun, and we would whisper so you and Dad couldn't hear. Beef used to get in bed with us, too, especially when it rained." She stroked the wavy fur on the dog's back. "I bet Megan misses those days."

"I'm sure she does." Jill sat down and moved Abby's

wet hair away from her forehead, noticing a stray streak of electric blue. "You want a towel for your head?"

"No, thanks." Abby paused. "Can I ask, what happened with you and Dad? I know what Dad said, but I want your side of the story. Why did you guys get divorced?"

"Let's not talk about that tonight, honey." Jill felt her chest tighten. If she told Abby the truth, it would make William look terrible, and she knew from her practice that kids who felt terrible about their parents somehow ended up feeling terrible about themselves. "Maybe someday, but not tonight." Jill brushed Abby's hair back again. "Blue, huh?"

"Yeah." Abby smiled softly. "Do you like it?"

"Yes, but the tattoo is another story." Jill mock-frowned. "No more tats, please. I don't have my mom powers anymore, so it's just a request."

"You'll always have your mom powers, to me." Abby raised her arms for a hug, and Jill embraced her.

"I'm sorry about your Dad. You shouldn't have to go through this."

"It's just that he looked so horrible, lying there. I found him."

"Oh no." Jill hadn't realized.

"I came home, and the house was so quiet and the cat was meowing, which she never does. I went upstairs and he was lying in bed, with the TV on. His face was all, like, slack."

Jill imagined how traumatic that would be, at Abby's age. Jill had dissected cadavers in medical school and she never got used to it. It took her months to shake the images, and some never left her.

"His mouth was open, but just hanging there." Abby emitted a new sob, her body hiccupping. "His eyes were open . . . stiff, like they were cold . . . but they weren't looking *anywhere*."

Jill held her close. She knew the unfixed gaze of the dead, but it was one thing when it was clinical, and another when it was eyes you had loved, in life. She had been there, too. One minute she'd been in anatomy class, locating the trigeminal nerve in the cheek, and the next minute, she'd come home to find another body, dead. This one, of someone she had loved, with a cheek she had kissed.

"I was . . . calling him . . . I put myself right up to his face . . . trying to get him to see me . . . but he couldn't see *anything*."

Jill was the one who'd found Gray, her first husband, lying dead on the kitchen floor. She'd tried CPR and heart massage, but he was gone, from a brain aneurysm. A week later, she would learn that she was pregnant with their child, Megan.

"I grabbed him and held him . . . and his mouth was, like, hanging open . . . and his head hung back like his neck was *rubber* . . . like he didn't even have a . . . neck bone."

Jill felt tears come to her eyes, her thoughts immersed in the past, reliving every emotion of finding Gray, the agony and the shock and the surreality. She felt terrible, mourning her first husband while Abby was mourning her second, but she couldn't help herself.

"Please, Jill . . . help me figure out who killed him . . . I can't do it alone."

"Let's not talk about it now, honey."

"Please . . . just think about it? Please?"

"I'll think about it, but just breathe for now, just breathe." Jill held Abby until she stopped crying and finally dozed off. Then Jill eased out of bed, covered Abby with the comforter, and turned out the light.

Plunging herself into darkness.

# 4.

Jill answered email from her patients, working in bed, her laptop warm on a pillow she'd set on her lap, an improvised desk. Sam slept with his back to her, Beef slumbering near his feet, and the room was quiet except for the snoring of man and beast. She felt tired but she couldn't sleep until she'd answered the questions that came in before the weekend: *how many drops in a teaspoon, do I give it again if he throws it up, it's finally yellow and that's good, right?*

She answered them all, but her thoughts kept straying to Abby, William, Megan, and Victoria. She remembered back to the beginning, the very first day when they all began, a sunny flash of beach and sand and boogie boards at the Jersey shore. She had been seeing William for a while, having met him when she worked at her old pediatric group. All but one of them were women, and William was the handsome pharmaceutical sales rep who called on them every Friday, the one they all buzzed and joked about, and some of them, like Jill, nursed secret crushes, none of them immune despite their advanced degrees, so that even their happily married office manager put up a sign in the ladies' room that read, TGIW, THANK GOD IT'S WILLIAM. He charmed them all with his dark good looks, breezy confidence, and easy smile, but more than that, he was a widower, alone with two little girls.

The hearts of every woman in the office went out to him, they all wanted to hold him, comfort him, and ease his pain, and what they didn't know about him, they filled in with their imagination, projecting onto him all kinds of qualities he'd never showed, assigning to him all of their own values and emotions, fleshing out their fantasy. He began to pay special attention to Jill, the only single doc and a widow to boot, and he struck up conversations about their mutual daughters, listening thoughtfully to her answers until his sales calls became a sort of date, with Jill putting on a little extra eye-makeup, making up a story of her own about a lonely widow and a lonely widower meeting for a last chance at love, like an announcement in the wedding section of the Sunday *New York Times,* so that by the time she and William had the girls meet each other for a day at the beach, she was stone in love.

With a fantasy.

William played his character to the hilt, and Jill marveled at how rough-and-tumble he was with Abby and Victoria, letting them jump off his broad shoulders into the crashing surf, diving under the biggest waves with them, even dunking them underwater, so different from the way Jill played with Megan, which was protective and careful, mindful always of the undertow. Megan watched William and the girls for a long time, hanging back, taking in the scene of the laughing daughters and the hunky, handsome daddy, so that by the time William turned around to grin at the fatherless girl, jerking his head back to flick his wet hair from his forehead, twisting his strong body from his tapered waist, reaching out to her a tanned and muscular arm ending in a large hand with its fingers extended, offering her a chance to be with him, the shy little girl would have begged to go.

*Come on, come in, I won't bite!*

Jill had watched delighted, seeing her daughter thrilled in the company of this unusual and exotic creature known as a man, and the five of them bobbed into the water together, Megan migrating to William, who played the father she had never known, and for her part, Jill took naturally to being a mom to the motherless Abby, who clung to her like a girl barnacle. Victoria took her time coming to Jill, always the closer daughter to her father, not wanting a rival for his attention, but she had no such problem that day with Megan, who carried with her the promise of a sibling without the rivalry.

Looking back now, Jill could visualize all of them in the water, seeing their heads from the back so that they were faceless, as if she were watching her younger self from the shore, which was exactly the vantage point her mother Conchetta had had that day. Her mother was her best friend, and the three of them—Jill, her mother, and Megan—had been on vacation when William and the girls had joined them. Her mother had always come to the beach after the hottest part of the day, sitting in her plastic lattice chair, and she'd read a book under the yellow-striped umbrella.

But this time, when Jill went back to check on her mother, her book remained unopened in her lap. Her mother had frowned up at her, her gnarled hand shading her hooded eyes, an uncharacteristic scowl replacing her usually welcoming smile, her lined features collapsing into deep, unhappy fissures, as if her very face had folded up as tight as her beach chair.

*I don't like him,* her mother had said.

Jill had been astonished. It didn't occur to her that her mother still hadn't warmed up to William. Everybody liked William, and her mother liked everybody, so it should've been a natural. Jill had asked her why.

*I don't trust him. Don't trust him. He's no good for you. He'll do you wrong.*

And Jill knew now, her mother had been right. Her mother had looked at the scene and had seen what was really happening, not the projections and the roles and the acting that had fooled Jill. Jill would turn out to be William's sucker, not his wife, and the only saving grace was that when it all came to light, her mother had already passed away. Because it would have broken her heart.

Jill blinked away tears that she hadn't realized were there, looking down at the laptop, and she found herself opening her My Pictures file and navigating to the older files. She clicked, and a photo of Abby popped onto the screen, one Jill had taken on the front steps of another house, in another town, in another time. Abby had just gotten her braces adjusted, and other kids might have whined, but Abby made the best of it, sporting red rubber bands in honor of the Phillies. She was thirteen, the same age Megan was now, still what Jill's mother used to call a tomboy. Her hair was in a messy braid, and she had on her swim-club jersey, its white letters forming a half-circle, Strafford Strokers.

Jill had encouraged her to join the school team and had loved teaching her to swim, and Abby had run to her with open arms, willing to learn anything, needing a mother like a wildflower needs sunshine. Victoria had come around only slowly, and Jill had built a relationship with her during silent car trips to the mall and awkward greetings after school plays, the cameo appearances of the suburban stepmother. Jill had saved every greeting card the girls ever gave her, and the dearest to her was a Mother's Day card from the both of them, given the first

Mother's Day after she and William were married. Victoria had handed the card to her, and it was covered with pink lace, so Jill knew Victoria had picked it out. Jill had opened it up, and she'd never forget the message, written in Victoria's perfect penmanship:

*It's official. You're our Mom now.*

Jill felt a pang at the memory, bittersweet because it had been so hard-won, and now was lost just the same, and the wound still felt acute, defying the very powers of nature, to heal. Jill knew there was no stronger bond than between mother and child, and she didn't feel like an ex-mother, nor were the girls her ex-children. She had lived long enough to learn that families didn't dissolve or reconfigure neatly, but left debris lying everywhere, and it was human debris. And sometimes, like tonight, she felt as if she were tripping over the bodies.

She pressed a key and advanced to the next photo, taken after Megan had mugged her way into the picture. She was eight years old at the time, and she and Abby had become best buddies. They could have passed for big-and-little sisters because Megan had big brown eyes and dark blonde hair, too, which she wore in a copycat braid.

Jill thought ahead, to having to tell Megan about William's death. Megan was a year old when she met William, and he'd been in her life until the divorce, when she was ten. He hadn't been especially doting or attentive, never fulfilling the promise of that day on the beach, but he'd been there, more father figure than father, and sometimes for kids, that was enough. Even now, Jill could remember trips they took as a family, one to Linvilla Orchard to pick pumpkins, or another to Great Adventure, screaming down the roller coaster. It looked like family fun on the surface, but you didn't need a microscope to see what was really going on. Jill would be having fun with the girls, and William would be off to the side, on the phone, or complaining about the long lines or the cold French fries, or withdrawn, lost in his own thoughts.

Jill hit Start Slideshow and watched Megan, Abby, Victoria, and William flash by in a continuous stream of swim meets, DQ Flurries, and guinea pigs. The divorce ended the pictures of the five of them, and the following photos were of her and Megan, like leftovers, only of family. It hadn't been an easy transition, then Jill met Sam, who turned out to be real in all the ways that William was false, and in time, the three of them had moved forward as a new family, with a second stepfather stepping into the shoes of the first stepfather, who'd stepped into the shoes of the father who had died.

Jill froze the slideshow on a photo of Sam, Megan, and Steven, who looked like a younger version of his father. Tall, lean, and brainy. Steven wouldn't replace Abby and Victoria, because nobody was ever replaced in life, no hole completely filled or loss totally healed. You didn't need a medical degree to know that the human body really wasn't stronger in the broken places. Like any bone, the cracks would always show if you looked hard enough.

"Babe?" said a voice, and Jill looked over, startled. Sam had turned over and was propped up, squinting against the lamp light. His brow furrowed, and his fine nose had two permanent pink indentations from his glasses. "You all right?"

"Sure, yes." Jill hit a key to stop the slideshow.

"What are you up to?" Sam lay back down, his eyes a calm blue now, like the sea without waves, and he regarded her with an unhurried air that told her he really wanted to know. "You upset about your ex? Or the kid?"

"Both, but mostly, I was thinking about my life."

"What about it?"

"Just that there's so much of it." Jill felt oddly embarrassed. "I have a lot of past."

Sam chuckled. "Not as much as I do."

"But my past is so much messier than yours. Two marriages, and two ex-stepdaughters. It's a mess, isn't it? Have I made a hash of things?"

"No, it's life, that's all." Sam smiled. "Is that what you're fretting about? I was worried that you'd been looking up Temezepam in the PDR online."

Jill hadn't been, but she'd thought about it. "I feel for her."

"I know you do."

"And it does seem strange, about the drugs. Not like William."

"You don't know what he's been up to the past few years."

"True."

"So?" Sam lifted an eyebrow. "If they found drugs on his tox screen, he took them."

"They could all be dissolved and put in a drink. Temezepam is a capsule." Jill knew because she had teenagers in her practice on various meds.

"You think somebody made him swallow the drugs, in a drink? He'd taste it." Sam ran a hand through his hair. "If you really want to help the kid, I'll call Sandy. She owes me a favor and she's the best psychiatrist in town."

"Thanks," Jill said, grateful. "Also, I think we might go to the memorial service, after work. Abby's the one who found William, dead. That's a trauma, and I can't just send her on her way tomorrow, alone."

Sam pursed his lips. "What about Megan?"

"She'll want to go."

"How do you know?"

Jill felt awkward, spelling it out. "I just think she'll want to go."

"Is going the best thing for her? She's only thirteen, and she'll be hurting, too."

"We should go."

"Then go, if you want to." Sam shrugged, and Jill touched his arm.

"Do you mind that she didn't invite you? I guess she felt that she didn't know you as well."

"No, I get it." Sam shifted back down onto the pillow. "Whatever you want to do is fine with me."

"Thanks." Jill leaned down and gave him a light kiss.

"It's late." Sam smiled, softly. "Come to bed."

"I am." Jill closed the laptop and set it on the cluttered nighttable, edging aside her to-be-read pile of books, a jar of Cetaphil, and her gold hoop earrings, linked together like Venn diagrams in a math textbook. She remembered helping all three girls with their math, especially Abby. She would sit with her at the kitchen table for hours after practice, their heads bent together, working the practice problems in the textbook, with a king-size bag of M&M's at hand. By the end of middle school, they'd both hate M&M's.

*I'll never understand geometry!*

"I won't get fresh," Sam said.

"Huh?" Jill asked, confused a moment, caught in mid-thought, betwixt and between.

"Trust me."

"I do." Jill smiled and switched off the lamp, and just before it went off, Beef raised his head, his eyes clouded at the edges. It struck her that the golden had lived through more of her lives than Sam had, and she couldn't imagine losing him. She reached over and patted his ample butt. "Let's have Beef in our ceremony."

"Fine with me. I thought you didn't want to."

"I changed my mind. If he jumps up on people, they'll have to deal. He's family."

"Done." Sam smiled, tugging up the covers. "He can be my best man. He's better looking than Mort."

"Aw, Mort's a sweet guy." Jill slipped under the sheets, which felt cool on her bare legs.

"Agree, but he never grew up. Not like me. I was born grown-up."

Jill smiled. It was part of Sam's charm, to her. She'd felt an ease with him from the start, which was a blind date set up by an endocrinologist they both knew, who thought Jill's bookish side would find common ground with a doctor in academic medicine like Sam, and she'd never felt more herself with any man, except Gray. She shifted over and rested her head on Sam's chest. His cotton T-shirt was soft against her cheek, with the iron-on Penn faded out of existence.

"Okay?" Sam held her close.

"Okay." Jill grew still, listening to the sounds of his heart. She listened differently since Gray had passed, hearing not the beats but between them, trying to pick up the tiny, subtler sounds that made the difference between life and death. She didn't know whether she did it because she was a doctor or a widow, or both.

"Everything's going to be all right," Sam said, reading her mind.

"How do you know? What's your proof?"

"You're asking me, seriously?"

"Yes. You're a scientist. Talk facts, not belief."

"Well, then." Sam gave her another squeeze, in the darkness. "My proof is, right now, and right here. Just *be* a minute, and you'll see."

Jill smiled uncertainly, then tried just to be, and came to understand what he meant. They were happy, really in love, a grown-up love that came from knowing and really appreciating the other person. Sam was her best friend, and she was his, and they had great kids and many other blessings. Their bedroom was large, quiet, and still. The darkness around them was as soft as black velvet, and a breeze billowed through the sheers, the aftermath of the storm. The burglar alarm was on, and the dishwasher thrummed downstairs. They lived on a pretty street lined with pin oaks, in a suburb outside of Philadelphia, which was just like all the suburbs outside all the cities all over the world.

Sam gave her another warm, cottony squeeze. "See?"

Jill felt the exact same way. "Yes. I love you."

"I love you, too. And you're stuck with me, forever."

"You, too," Jill said, after a moment.

"Now, let's get some sleep." Sam let out a final sigh, and in time Jill could feel his arms begin to slip, loosening his grip. He turned over in the next minute, and she pulled up the comforter, wondering. She'd believed in forever in her twenties, when Gray had said it, meaning every word, and she'd believed in forever in her thirties, when William had said it, lying through his teeth. But she'd lived long enough to know that forever couldn't be guaranteed to anyone. Even tomorrow couldn't be relied upon.

She closed her eyes, feeling suspended in time, between past and present, here and there, now that Abby was sleeping across the hall. Jill had thought that Abby and Victoria were a part of her past, her ex-life, that followed behind her, like a shadow, but Jill wasn't so sure of that, anymore. She was beginning to think that the past was an overlay on the present, like a transparent page in an old-school anatomy textbook. That Abby and Victoria hadn't really left her life, but had been lingering like ghosts in a familial limbo, waiting until she found them. Waiting until now.

Jill thought about getting married for the third time. She didn't have the heart to lose again, and neither did Megan. She was betting for them both, on forever. She wanted it so badly this time, and she wanted it with Sam. He was the last great love of her life. On impulse, she slid out of her T-shirt and panties, then shifted over and pressed herself against his back, feeling his warmth against her breasts, through the thin cotton. Her arms found their way around his waist, and she nuzzled his neck, kissing the hollow behind his ear, where his whiskers were rough, out of a razor's reach.

"Baby?" she breathed, a question that Sam didn't need words to answer. He stirred and came to wakefulness, shifting onto his back and reaching for her when she climbed onto him, kissing him. He tasted still of toothpaste, and his breath came quicker when she wrangled off his T-shirt and boxers, leaving the both of them naked, together, skin against skin, until they were nothing but each other, and all the clothes, eyeglasses, stethoscopes, and employee IDs had been stripped away, and the roles they played for the rest of the world had ended, and she felt as if she had been broken down like a stage set, finally becoming herself. And in that moment, she was no longer a mother or a doctor, but simply a woman, his woman.

And that was not only enough, that was everything.

# 5.

"Mom!" Megan whispered, loudly. "Abby's here! What's going on? Mom, *Mom*!"

Jill woke up to find an astonished Megan, shaking her awake. It had to be before dawn because the bedroom was still dim, quiet except for Megan, who was dressed for swim practice in her yellow Valley West hoodie. Her hair was pulled back in its doubled-under ponytail, its dry ends sprayed out, stiff from chlorine.

"Mom, *Abby's* here! In my bed! Oh my God, did you even know that?"

"Yes, I do, hi, honey." Jill rose slightly, propping herself up on an elbow. The clock read 5:15 A.M., and she didn't have to be up until seven, for work. "I didn't expect you this early. What's going on? Did Coach call a practice?"

"Yes, I have to get my stuff, but Mom, Abby's in my bed. What's she doing here? It's so weird! You know, right?"

"Yes, remain calm, and let me explain." She sat up with the grim realization that she'd have to tell Megan about William, right now.

"Why? Why is she here? I have to get in my room,

Courtney's mom is picking me up in twenty minutes, but Abby's sound asleep, in my bed! In my *nightgown*. How weird is that? So weird!"

"Relax, please." Jill inhaled, bracing herself as Sam began to stir and Beef stood up in bed, wagging his tail. Megan looked over at Sam, bewildered.

"Sam, hi, did you meet Abby, my stepsister? She's sleeping in my *bed*. In my *nightgown*."

"I met her." Sam smiled sadly, knowing that the news about William's death was coming.

"Megan, sit down, would you?" Jill patted the bed, next to Beef, who wagged his tail so hard his butt wiggled. "I need to talk to you."

"What's going on? Why is she here?" Megan sat down, petted the dog, and set her omnipresent phone beside her. "You're scaring me, Mom. Why do I have to sit down? Is she sick or something?"

"No, but I have bad news, about William." Jill prepared herself to break her daughter's heart. Motherhood was not for the weak. She put her arm around Megan's shoulders. "Honey, I'm sorry, but Abby came here to tell us that William died, a few days ago."

Megan gasped. Her hand flew to her mouth, and her eyes filmed. "Oh my God," she said, hushed.

"I'm so sorry, sweetie." Jill hugged her closer, and Megan wilted in her embrace, holding back her tears, her lips going tight over her braces. Jill's heart broke for her. "I'm so very sorry, honey."

"This is horrible," Megan whispered, stricken.

"I know, I'm sorry."

"Really, is it true? Are you sure?"

"Yes."

"I don't believe it."

"I know, I'm sorry." Jill hugged her close and nuzzled her hair, breathing in her young-girl smells of vanilla oil and strawberry-scented conditioner. "He had a heart attack, because of some medication he took."

Megan looked over, her eyes wet with tears, her brow furrowed with pain. "Like, he was allergic?"

"No, he had a bad reaction to prescription medication, which he mixed with alcohol."

"Like he had a drink and that was *it*?" Megan's lower lip trembled.

"Yes."

"Can that even *happen*?"

"Yes, it can." Jill didn't mention Abby's suspicions. It was pointless and would hit Megan like a double whammy. Beef settled down and put his head on Megan's leg, evidently getting the message, for a change.

"That's so *random*." Megan's cell phone chirped on the bed, signaling a text, but she didn't even hear it, which told Jill how upset she must be.

"Honey, I think I should call Coach Stash and tell him what happened. I'm sure he'd let you stay home from practice."

"No, don't, I can't, Mom." Megan shook her head, wiping her eye, though it quickly filled again. "I'm captain, I can't let the team down. Coach Stash is counting on me, they all are. We have qualifiers for states this weekend, remember?"

"But he'd understand, there's a death in the family."

"No, no, I can't," Megan shot back, her voice quavering. "I have to go. We were lucky to get the pool at the high school, that's why he called the practice. We have doubles today. This is our year, Mom."

Jill could see the pressure on Megan's face, and it killed her to think that her daughter's life was so scheduled that she didn't have time to cry. "Honey, I know, but this is a big deal, and you can stay home and we can talk about it."

"You have work, anyway, and I can't miss, I never miss. The team's counting on me."

"This is an exception, something he'll understand." Jill felt the conversation going in the wrong direction. They were talking about practice instead of Megan's feelings, and Sam must've had the same thought, because he shifted over and touched Megan's arm.

"I'm so sorry, kitten. This is terrible news, and I know it comes as a terrible shock."

"It is, it's so weird and horrible and random." Megan pressed her lips together, making a hump over her braces. "I know I shouldn't be upset, I mean, I hadn't seen him in so long, like, *years*."

"Of course, you're upset," Sam said, gently, stroking her arm, and Jill gave her a squeeze.

"Right, of course you feel upset and sad, sweetie."

Megan hung her head, and a tear fell on the comforter. "I shouldn't be, not really. He didn't want to see me. He didn't answer my emails, and he's only my stepfather, anyway." She caught herself, shooting Sam a teary look. "I'm sorry, I didn't mean it that way."

"I know you didn't." Sam rubbed her arm. "This is random, as you say. Nobody knows how to react."

Megan turned to Jill, blinking wetly. "How's Abby? She must be so upset. Is that why she came here? She doesn't have any parents anymore. Now she's an orphan, right?"

"She is," Jill answered, touched that Megan would even think of Abby at a time like this. Jill gave her another hug. "She invited us to a memorial service this afternoon, if you feel up to going. We can go after practice. It's at three o'clock."

"I can go, I'll go." Megan looked uncertainly from Jill to Sam, wiping her eyes. "Right? Okay? Do you guys think that's okay, or weird?"

Jill stroked Megan's cheek. "I think it's okay, and it makes sense."

Sam nodded. "Agree. I don't think it's weird, at all. I can't go with you, I have a meeting with a colleague. Your Mom said you guys can go alone, but I'll cancel if you want me to come with you."

"No, thanks, okay." Megan turned to Jill, keeping tears at bay. "Mom? Right? Do you want to go? I mean, I know you didn't love William anymore, and you got mad at him, from the divorce."

Jill gave her a squeeze. "That doesn't matter now. Of course I want to go, and I'll take you."

"I don't really know why I want to, exactly." Megan rubbed her cheeks, covering her braces with her lips again. "I just think that it's the right thing to do. Like Grandma would say, I should pay my respects."

Jill felt pleased, thinking of her mother, who had passed away five years ago. Jill still missed her, every day. "I think Grandma would be so proud of you, right now."

Megan turned to Sam, with a sniffle. "I feel so bad about what I said, it was dumb. I love you, Sam, even though you're my stepfather—oh, Jeez, you know what I mean, right?"

"Yes, and I love you, too." Sam opened his arms, and Megan threw her arms around him. He gave her a big bear hug. "I love you very, very much. We love each other, and nothing else matters."

Jill felt tears spring to her eyes. She couldn't wish for a better stepfather to Megan. Sam's calm manner was the perfect antidote to their mother-daughter drama, and he helped Megan with her homework, drove her to practice when Jill couldn't, and was even teaching her photography. Suddenly Megan's phone rang, a new Lady Gaga ring tone, and its screen lit up with a photo of Megan's best friend, Courtney.

Megan let go of Sam. "Oh, no. Mom, can I get that? She's calling to tell me they're on their way."

Jill hesitated. "Sure, get it."

"Thanks, I'll go into your bathroom. I won't be long, I have to get ready." Megan grabbed the phone, pressed a button, and left the bedroom, saying, "Court, you wanna hear something totally weird and horrible?"

The bathroom door closed, Beef went back to sleep, and Jill eyed Sam. "That was okay, to let her take the call, I figure."

"Sure. Let her talk it over with Courtney." Sam put an arm around her, and Jill felt a twinge.

"She's upset, but she's keeping it in."

"She'll process it her own way. She'll talk to Courtney and her pals on the team. Isn't that what girls do?" Sam made a talking mouth with his hand. "Yakety-yak?"

"Is it wrong to miss the days when she yakked about it with me?"

"No." Sam put an arm around her. "She's reached that age, honey. I saw it with Steve, too, but I know it's not the same as a mother and daughter. You guys are closer than we were, because of all those shoes."

Jill smiled. She knew he was trying to cheer her up.

"And to her credit, that's why she chose to go to the memorial service. She's growing up, and you take the good with the bad." Sam gave her a squeeze, and suddenly Jill realized that it had gotten quiet in the bathroom. Megan had stopped talking on the phone.

Jill rose. "Did she hang up?"

Sam looked over, and Jill heard a noise in the bathroom and knew what it was, instinctively. A muffled sob. The loss of William had just hit Megan, and she'd started to cry.

"Mom?" Megan called out, her voice choked with sobs. "I need you."

"Sure, honey," Jill called back, already on the way.

# 6.

Jill and Megan moved quickly and quietly around the bedroom, packing a swim bag for practice, while Abby made a sleeping mound in the bed. Megan was shaky and crestfallen, still recovering from her crying bout, and Jill's heart went out to her, having to function when she felt so raw.

"Megan," she whispered, by the bureau. "Did you eat? I can get you a breakfast bar, or some yogurt."

"No, thanks, I'm gonna be so late." Megan was digging in her drawer. The room was growing lighter, and they could see without a lamp. "Where are my new sweats?"

"Still in the laundry room." Jill had seen them on the top of the hamper. She hadn't gotten to the wash yet. "I'll wash them tonight, okay?"

"Okay." Megan took a bunchy set of old sweats out of the drawer, stuffed them in her gym bag, then hurried to her bathroom. "Oh Jeez," she said softly.

Jill went to the bathroom, which had been left in disarray. The shower door hung open, the shampoo lay on its side, and a pile of wet towels sat on the floor. "Sorry, honey."

"It's okay. She must've been so upset." Megan grabbed

her conditioner and shampoo and tossed them into her bag, then looked over at the bed, with wet eyes. "Uh-oh, we woke her up."

Jill turned around to see Abby sitting up in bed, raking back her long hair, and Megan heaved a little sob, dropped her bag, and hurried over to the bed.

"Abby, I'm so sorry about your Dad." Megan reached for her, and Abby raised her arms, equally teary, and the two embraced, crying and hugging each other, like two halves of the same, broken heart.

Standing to the side, Jill felt her throat catch, sad and happy, both at once. She loved seeing the sisters reunited, but not on the worst day they could share, and she thought of all the times they had consoled each other, growing up. When Megan hadn't gotten a speaking part in *Annie,* Abby threw her a pity party with a pint of vanilla Häagen-Dazs, chenille bathrobes, and an "I Will Survive" mixtape. And when a mean girl had teased Abby about her low PSAT scores, Megan had treated her to sundaes at Friendly's, with money she had earned babysitting. *Ice cream fixes everything,* Megan had said, and they had laughed through their tears. But not this morning.

Jill could hear the tremor in Abby's voice as she buried her head in Megan's neck. "I'm sorry, too, for you. I know you loved him, too."

"It's so horrible. I can't even believe it."

"That's just what I think. I can't believe it." Abby released Megan, wiping her eyes. "I just tell myself, this isn't really happening. It's not. It's not even possible."

"I know, you must be so sad, I'm so sad for you." Megan looked stricken all over again, but was trying to compose herself, wiping her eyes. "I'm so sorry, I don't even know what to say."

"I love you, Megs." Abby sniffled, sad again. "Sorry, I'm such a crybaby."

"I love you, too." Megan frowned, her lower lips trembling, seeming to cry and smile, both at once. "It's hard, I mean, he's your *Dad*."

"I know, and your Mom was so nice." Abby stifled a sob. "And you, thanks for the nightgown. It's my old one, remember?"

"Yes, sure." Megan tried to smile again, straightening up. "I still wear it, it got softer."

"I know, right?" Abby managed a smile, too. "You look so awesome, you're so skinny. Can't call you Mega anymore, huh?"

"No." Megan smiled at the old nickname.

"You have braces now? I thought you didn't need them."

"I know. My teeth shifted, doesn't that suck?" Megan touched her mouth, self-conscious. "Two more years, and this is so lame but I have to go, I have practice."

"It's okay, I know. I hated those early morning practices." Abby rubbed her forehead, and she seemed a little pale, even in the dim light. "God, I feel lousy. My head is killing me."

Sam appeared at the doorway, in his bathrobe. "Hey, ladies," he said, smiling, but it vanished when he sized up the scene. "I thought I would make banana pancakes, if anybody wants some. Abby, want to try my specialty?"

"Pancakes, yuck. I feel so sick." Abby leaned over, and before anybody knew what was happening, she was vomiting on the bed. Megan recoiled, and Sam blanched.

"Here, honey." Jill snatched up a wastebasket and rushed over, but Abby heaved again, spewing vomit on the bedclothes.

"Ugh, no, sorry, guys."

"Come on, sweetie, let's get you into the bathroom." Jill set the wastebasket down, took Abby's arm, hustled her out of bed, and got her to the bathroom just as she heaved all over her nightgown, the used towels, and the tile floor. Jill got her to the toilet, where she dropped to her knees, and Jill held her hair back.

"Mom, I'm gonna be late!" Megan called out from the bedroom. "Sorry, Abby, I have to go!"

"Hold on, honey!" Jill called back, torn. She wanted to say good-bye to Megan, to make sure she was okay, but she couldn't leave Abby. She felt ripped in half, with both girls grieving and needy, but she couldn't be in both places at once. "Just hang on one sec! I want to see you before you go!"

"I'm late, Mom, and Courtney's mom is waiting! I can't wait! Bye, I love you!"

"Oh, no." Abby began to retch into the toilet, and Jill couldn't leave her, holding her hair.

"I love you, too! Take it easy this morning! Call if you want to come home!"

"She will!" Sam called back, and Jill felt a wrench in her chest, knowing it meant Megan had left.

Abby coughed, spitting. "Please, close the door. This is so embarrassing."

"Don't worry, wipe your mouth." Jill handed her some toilet paper, then closed the bathroom door. "Be still. Let your stomach relax."

"Thanks," Abby said, thickly. She wiped her mouth. "I'm so sorry."

"Make sure you're finished. Take your time." Jill rubbed her back. "There's still some things you haven't thrown up on."

Abby smiled and let the paper drop in the toilet. "I'm done."

"Good. Let me help you up." Jill steadied Abby, flushed the toilet, and put down the lid, with a *clunk*. "Sit here until your head clears."

"Thanks." Abby sat down and put her head in her hands. "Sorry, I ruined our nightgown. Can you help me take it off? It reeks."

"Reach for the moon." Jill lifted the nightgown off and dropped it on the floor with the soiled towels. She took Megan's bathrobe from the hook and handed it to Abby. "Here, stay warm."

"I'm not a drunk girl, I swear. If I were, I wouldn't be this sick."

"I know, honey." Jill eyed Abby, straightening up on the seat. "Okay, wash up and I'll be right back."

"Okay."

Jill left the bathroom and went into the bedroom, where Sam was balling up the comforter on the bed. "How was she? Was she crying when she left?"

"She'll be fine. I gave her a big hug. I say we throw out this comforter and buy a new one."

"No, don't. She loves it, and I'm not sure they make it anymore. It'll have to go to the Laundromat. I'll take it when I get back."

"I'll do it, and by the way, Sandy emailed me to say that she'd squeeze Abby in next week, anytime."

"Jill!" Abby called from the bathroom. "Help!"

"That's great, thanks," Jill said, already hurrying back to the bathroom.

# 7.

"How are you doing, little guy?" Jill smiled at little Rahul Choudhury, an adorable one-year-old she was about to examine. She'd spent the morning treating a leaky procession of sniffles, fevers, and sinus infections, all the while worrying about Abby and Megan. They say a mother is only as happy as her happiest child, and it applied to stepmothers and ex-stepmothers, too.

"He's such a good baby," said his mother, Padma, steadying Rahul as he sat on the examining table, wobbly in his thick diaper. She was a pretty woman with a ready smile, dressed in a blue cotton sweater, khakis, and clogs. Jill would have normally worn a similar outfit, but she was dressed for the memorial service, in a dark jersey suit. Like most pediatricians, she never wore a lab coat, because children tended to associate them with needles.

"Rahul, hello, what a good boy you are." Jill wiggled her stethoscope, and Rahul's round, dark eyes focused on it so intently that they crossed slightly, under a sloping fringe of eyelashes that any woman would kill for. She kept it wiggling, initiating a tug of war with the baby, and felt satisfied when he reached out, made a swipe for the black rubber tubing, and caught it in his tight little fist. "Good for you! You're strong, Rahul. You work out?"

Padma smiled. "I hate when he's sick. I don't have time for him to be sick."

"I know just what you mean." Jill was thinking of Megan, with no time to cry. She tickled Rahul, and he giggled, drooling. "It's so easy to make a baby laugh. I should do stand-up, for infants."

Padma chuckled. "All my sons are fans of yours. Roy loves it when you ask him if he brought his heart today."

"Aww, good." Jill didn't add that joking around was part of her exam. The first thing she did with a patient was to engage him, to see if he was sick or not. One of her pediatrics professors had called it the *gestalt,* or the big picture, and her *gestalt* about Rahul wasn't good. "Now, how long did you say he'd been sick?"

"Since Thursday. It's another ear infection. He tugged at his ear most of last night, and I know, I was up, on the phone with my mother, in Mumbai. She's not feeling well."

"Oh no, I hope she feels better. You have your hands full." Jill had read the notes from the nurse, who had taken Rahul's vitals. Nothing was remarkable except a fever, at 101 degrees. Anything between 97.5 and 100.3 was normal. "When did Rahul get the fever?"

"This morning, it's new. I wanted to get him on amoxicillin before it gets worse, because I have the week from hell coming up. Two field trips, one for Roy and the other for Devi."

"Yikes. Got Xanax?"

Padma laughed, and Jill realized she'd made the joke because she must have been thinking of William. It was odd that he was taking prescription drugs, but she tried to put it out of her mind. She offered Rahul a finger in trade for her stethoscope and listened to his lungs, hearing transmitted upper-airway sounds. She checked his ears, and there was purulent fluid, or pus behind the drum.

"How's Dave?" Jill asked. Padma's husband Dave was in the Army Reserves, serving in Afghanistan.

"Fine, and he says hi and thanks for those books you sent. They all shared them. Thanks so much."

"Please, it's the least I can do." Jill looked in Rahul's nose, mouth, and throat, and they showed redness, irritation, and post-nasal drip, all consistent with a viral URI, or upper respiratory tract infection. "I give you so much credit, doing all that you do, on your own."

"Sometimes it gets to me, but most of the time, I do okay."

"I'm sure, but you can always vent to me, you know that. Email or call, I mean it."

"Thanks." Padma smiled, but Jill knew she wouldn't take her up on the offer.

"Tell me, how are the boys?" Jill palpated the lymph nodes in Rahul's neck, both the anterior and the posterior chain, and the anterior were slightly enlarged, also consistent with a URI and ear infection.

"Doing well in school, and they're brown belts, both of them."

"Wow, that's great!"

"But they miss their father, so much."

"I'm sure, poor things." Jill found herself thinking of Abby and Victoria, and how much they would miss William. She'd have to get Abby to the therapist to deal with her grief, instead of talking about murder. "I bet it's been hard on them."

"It has been, but we email and Skype, so that helps."

"That's good." Jill lay Rahul down gently and palpated his belly, liver, and spleen, all of which were also slightly enlarged, again, consistent with his little body trying to fight the infection. But for some reason, he was losing the battle, too often. It was Rahul's fifth ear infection this year and he'd also had pneumonia, which worried her.

"How old is Megan, now?" Padma cupped the back of Rahul's head with her hand. "In middle school?"

"Yes, if you feed them, they grow. Right, handsome?" Jill spoke to Rahul, and he broke into a smile, with wet lips, which showed he wasn't dehydrated. To double-check, she pinched him gently on the arm, and his skin didn't tent. "What a tough guy! No crying, huh?"

"He's the third. They learn."

Jill smiled, stroking Rahul's soft cheek, noting his color. His Indian ancestry gave his skin a glow, but she'd trained at D.C. Children's, where she'd seen kids of all races, and she thought he was febrile, feverish. "He look flushed to you, Dr. Mom?"

"He always does when he gets an ear infection. So, do you have a wedding dress yet?"

"I'm thinking a lab coat. It's white, right?"

Padma laughed. "Come on, tell me everything. It's fun to talk girly stuff. I love being a boy mom, but I wish for something with ruffles at times."

"Well, I do have a suit, a nice one." Jill palpated the axillary lymph nodes under Rahul's armpits, which were also swollen. "Megan's addicted to *Say Yes to the Dress,* so I'm failing her as a mother."

"I know that feeling. It comes with the territory."

"Ha!" Jill peeked inside Rahul's diaper, which was clean and dry. "They'll grow up and realize how lucky they were, but by then, we'll be dead."

Padma laughed.

Jill's last stop was to examine Rahul's skin, and she noticed a tiny patch on his right arm, which reminded her of something about his older brother, also a patient. "Roy has hay fever. Do you or Dave?"

"Yes, I do. Why?"

"Look at this." Jill showed her the patch. "This is eczema."

"Really?" Padma peered at it, frowning. "I thought it was a rash, or maybe poison ivy. He was playing in the grass yesterday while I weeded."

"It's not uncommon in babies, and it's nothing to worry about. But we call asthma, allergies, and eczema, the allergic triad. It runs in families, and several of them can be in the same child."

"They do, I know, in my family."

"Let me see the rest of you, Rahul." Jill examined the skin on his chest, legs, neck, and back, with its tiny scapula, like the nubs of angel wings. There were no other eczema patches. "How's he eating?"

"Not great, but not terrible."

"Drinking?"

"Okay."

"Sleeping? You said he tugs at his ear?"

"Yes, off and on, at night."

"Poor little guy." Jill looked up and met Padma's eye. "I think you're right, it's another ear infection, but he gets a lot of ear infections for a baby who's not in day care. On the other hand, he has older brothers, so I bet he gets all the colds they bring home from school." Padma's eyebrows sloped down unhappily. "Do you think he should get tubes? My brother does, and they helped my nephew."

"No, I wouldn't do that for Rahul. We used to do that more often, because of language impairment, but he isn't showing any delays. You can dress him, now." Jill went to the computer on the desk, typed her password into Epic, opened Rahul's file, and typed in her notes. Pembey Family Practice had EMR, or electronic medical records, but Jill always waited until after the exam to record her findings. She liked to look the mom in the eye and stand in front of a child, not a keyboard.

"So no tubes?" Padma asked.

"Not yet. Let me check one last thing in his file." Jill navigated to Rahul's weight chart, with its line climbing up a hill, until six months ago. He'd started life in the thirtieth percentile, but now was down to the fifth, which meant he fell off his curve. That wasn't good, either.

"So, amoxicillin?"

"Yes, since it's been over a month since the last time he'd used it, and Tylenol, too." Jill closed out the file, leaving the screen waiting for the password of the next doctor. She'd coded it as a URI for insurance purposes, but she wasn't 100 percent sure why it kept happening. The saying in medicine was, if you hear hoofbeats, don't go hunting for zebra, but Jill knew better. Zebras existed, and pediatrics was full of them. She stood up. "Let's see him again on Wednesday. I know you're busy, but I want to keep an eye on him."

"Okay."

"Also, before you leave, I'd like to take some blood." Jill didn't elaborate because she wasn't about to alarm Padma. There was a chance that Rahul had an autoimmune problem, leukemia, or lymphoma, but they were only remote possibilities. "The lab's just down the hall. It won't take long."

"Blood?" Padma's dark eyes flared. "For an ear infection?"

"Yes, I want to know why he keeps getting them, and a blood test will give me a complete picture of what's going on in his system and see what type of infection his body is fighting." Jill didn't add that the blood test would tell her how many and what type of white blood cells Rahul's body was producing, whether lymphocytes, neutrophils, or monocytes, and that would eliminate the more serious diagnoses.

"You only have to take him down the hall, and I promise Selena will make it easy."

"Okay, if you think it's really necessary." Padma pressed a strand of dark hair into her short ponytail.

"I do, and I'll call you when I get the results, probably on Tuesday. Please let me know if anything changes." Jill printed out a script for amoxicillin, signed it, and handed it to Padma. "Here we go."

"Thanks." Padma picked up Rahul's little jeans, and Jill placed a reassuring hand on her shoulder.

"I mean it, don't hesitate to call me."

"Will do. Thanks again." Padma smiled, and Jill gave her a hug.

"Love to the boys and Dave. Rahul, bye-bye." Jill caressed the baby on the cheek and left the examining room, checking her watch on the fly. Pembey Family Practice had office hours until one o'clock on Saturdays, and it was 1:15, so she wasn't as behind as usual. She needed to spend time with the patients, but it put her in constant conflict with their office manager, Sheryl Ewing. Jill hoped to leave today without seeing Sheryl because she didn't need the lecture, with the memorial service ahead of her.

She bustled to her office, thinking of William, and anger flickered in her chest, an ember that didn't need fanning. She felt hypocritical going to his memorial service when, in her darker moments, she had actually wished him dead. And if she were really honest, she wouldn't be surprised if it turned out that someone had murdered him.

Because in her very darkest moments, she would have done it herself.

# 8.

Jill drove down Route 202, heading east toward Philly, with a somber Megan in the passenger seat, her face turned to the window. Even her phone was quiet, and Jill wondered if she had silenced it or turned it off. Rain pounded against the windshield, and they passed a strip mall that used to have a huge Circuit City, which was now vacant. The only sound was the rhythmic beating of the wipers and the low rumble of the road.

"You look nice, honey," Jill said, looking over. Megan looked grown-up in a simple black dress she wore for choir concerts, with low-heeled black shoes. Her hair was still wet from the shower and gathered in a black velvet scrunchy.

"Thanks." Megan turned to her, with a brief smile, but the strain showed on her face. "Is this service gonna be weird?"

"A little, but we'll get through it."

"Will it have an open casket like Grandma's?"

"No." Jill felt a pang, thinking of her mother's wake, in the funeral home. "This isn't a Mass, it's a memorial service, in a church. A historic church."

"William didn't go to church."

"Sometimes they hold services in church, even if the person didn't go there."

"Is there something after it, like with Grandma? Do we all go to a restaurant?"

Jill realized that Abby hadn't mentioned a reception. "I don't know."

"Who else will be there, besides Abby and Victoria?"

"I don't know. I guess William's friends and maybe someone from work."

"Where did he work?"

"I don't know that, either."

Megan shook her head. "We don't know anything about him anymore, and he used to be my *Dad*."

Jill felt stricken. She knew the feeling, albeit from the other side. If it was impossible to be an ex-parent, it was impossible to have one.

"It's like he just forgot we were in the same family. Like he never even knew us, and we didn't matter to him at all."

"He didn't forget you, honey." Jill's fingers tightened on the wheel. They'd talked about this many times, but it was all coming back now, with William's death.

"Yes, he did. He didn't answer any of my emails or texts, not one. He didn't call me, not even when I got into National Honor Society." Megan's tone stayed matter-of-fact. "You tried to talk to Abby and Victoria, but he didn't even try to talk to me. He didn't even answer me, when *I* tried."

"That doesn't mean he forgot you."

"Yes, it does."

"No, not necessarily," Jill said, wanting to comfort Megan, even though she could never forgive William for cutting Megan off the way he had. If Jill hated him for one single thing, it was that, and she always would.

"Then why didn't he answer my email?"

Jill tried to think of an honest answer. "Maybe because he couldn't face his hurt, or yours. We'll never know now. But I know nobody could forget you. You're a wonderful, wonderful girl." Jill patted her leg, and another silence fell. Megan looked out the window again, her head moving slightly with the motion of the car.

"Look, a padiddle." Megan pointed at the window. "Remember when we used to play that game in the car, with Abby and Victoria?"

Jill did. A padiddle was a car with only one headlight, and whoever saw one on the road got a point. "I do remember that, but I don't see a padiddle."

"Look in your mirror. There's a padiddle behind us, one car back."

Jill glanced in the rearview, and a black SUV with one headlight was behind them. She flashed on the scene outside the house last night, when Abby had come staggering down the sidewalk. She'd been visible in the beam from a black SUV, with one headlight. A padiddle. Not that it meant anything. The world was full of black SUVs, with or without headlights, which was why Jill drove a white Volvo.

"Do you think they think about us, when they play padiddle?"

"I bet they do." Jill was remembering that the headlights on the SUV last night were boxy, but all SUVs had boxy headlights. SUVs were boxy, in general. They were practically boxes on wheels.

"Except they probably don't play padiddle anymore. They're too old."

"They still might."

"I think Abby thinks about us, but Victoria doesn't, as much. Abby loved us more." Megan turned back to Jill, her dark eyes troubled. "Victoria doesn't let herself love people a lot, you know what I mean?"

"Yes, exactly."

"Victoria doesn't love enough, and Abby loves too much. Isn't that funny?"

Jill looked over, impressed. "Well said."

"Which is better?"

"The middle. Let yourself love. Love is good. Just choose the people you love wisely. They have to deserve you." Jill heard herself pontificating, but she'd learned it the hard way. "You'll make mistakes, but that's okay."

"It is?"

"Yes, of course, it's human."

"You mean because you can always get a divorce?"

"Well, yes," Jill answered, pained. "It's not ideal, but it's the best choice, if your marriage is terrible."

"Except I didn't divorce William," Megan said, again, matter-of-factly. "I didn't divorce anybody. Neither did Abby or Victoria. The kids don't get a choice."

Jill felt a wave of guilt. "I know, sweetie, and I'm sorry."

"I didn't mean it in a bad way, I'm just saying."

"I'm still sorry, for the way it all turned out."

"It's okay." Megan reached for her phone at the sound of an incoming text.

"Don't forget to turn that off at the service."

"I won't." Megan checked the text, and a new smile flickered across her face.

"Is that Courtney?"

"No. A boy."

"Really?" Jill brightened, happy to change the subject. "Can I know more?"

"Well, he's really cute." Megan smiled, warming. "He's in one of the other clubs, the Hornets. He's one of the fastest freestylers on the team."

"Good for him. What's his name?"

"Jake Tilson."

"Did you start doodling Megan Tilson in your notebook?"

"No, Mom, you weirdo!" Megan laughed, which was the desired effect.

"What does he look like?"

"He has blond hair and it's curly, and he has blue eyes and he's a little short but I don't care. And he's really cut."

Jill laughed. "Everybody's cut at thirteen."

"No, he's *cut,* Mom. He's *ripped.* He's *shredded.* You can see his abs from across the pool. And he plays guitar. Real guitar, not Guitar Hero."

"How did you meet him?"

"I've seen him at meets but I talked to him at Courtney's party. He knows her twin brother from swim camp. He friended me after the party, and now we're texting."

Jill felt delighted. Megan needed more fun in her life. "Sounds like a modern romance."

"And guess what else?"

Jill smiled, looking over. "What else?"

"We *kissed*!" Megan covered her face with her hands, laughing.

"Good for you. So, was it fun?" Jill knew this was big news, because Megan hadn't had a boyfriend yet. She felt happy, and sad, that Megan had her first kiss, but counted herself lucky that Megan was slower than her classmates, judging from the stories she'd heard from other swim moms.

"No!" Megan slid her hands down, flushed. "It was scary and I was bad at it. He has braces, too. We were like Iron Man!"

"Aw, no you weren't."

"We *were*." Megan moaned. "It's me. I'm a bad kisser."

"You want a tip?"

"*Mom*." Megan recoiled. "It's not like the backstroke, you can't *teach* me."

"Why not? Just relax your mouth. Don't pucker up."

"Oh, this is so *random*." Megan giggled. "You have to be kidding me, right now."

"No, I'm a pretty good kisser. I've been kissing boys for a long time. I've kissed thousands. Millions." Jill's heart eased when Megan giggled again.

"Stop, no. This is gross."

"No, it's not. It's okay to like a boy, and it's okay to kiss a boy, too. Just don't lose your head."

"I won't, Mom." Megan snorted. "I'm not *Teen Mom*."

"I know that, but still." Jill knew that any teen could become *Teen Mom*.

"You're so *wacky,* Mom."

"I know, I get it from you."

Megan laughed again, then resumed texting, and Jill hit the gas, keeping her eye on the road. Traffic picked up, and she took the on-ramp onto the Schuylkill Expressway with most of the traffic. She checked the padiddle, and it was still back there, behind a white pickup, too far away to tell the make. They reached West River Drive, and she lost the padiddle in the traffic. The rain finally stopped, and they parked in a garage, where Jill cut the ignition.

"Remember, stay with me," Megan said, looking over.

"I will, don't worry." Jill managed a smile, shooing the black SUV out of her mind.

# 9.

Jill and Megan got to the church early, entered through the arched doors, and found themselves milling in the back among a small, well-dressed crowd, talking in low tones before they went to their seats. Jill didn't recognize anyone, which didn't surprise her, because after the divorce, their few friends had sided with her. She caught a glimpse of a teary Abby, accepting condolences from the guests, standing next to the rector, in his red-and-white vestments.

"Poor Abby," she said to Megan.

"I know, she looks really sad," Megan whispered back. "I feel so bad for her."

"Me, too." Jill felt a deep pang, seeing how Abby looked, lost and heartbroken in an ethereal boho dress, with heavy makeup. It made her worry about Victoria, whom she couldn't see through the crowd. "Megs, do you see Victoria?"

"Yes, you'll see her when that old lady moves. She's doing better than Abby. Look, Mom, she looks so pretty. She got highlights."

"Really?" Jill craned her neck and spotted Victoria,

standing tall in a black linen dress with pearl drop earrings. Her newly honeyed streaks were pulled back into a sophisticated twist, and her lovely face had elongated as she'd gotten older, enhancing the prominence of her cheekbones. Light, perfect makeup emphasized her hazel eyes, and she projected grace and poise, though she was only twenty-three. Jill felt a bittersweet rush of emotions, feeling love at seeing her again, happy that she'd grown up so well, but loss at all the years they could have been in touch, and pain for how she must be feeling.

"I think that's her boyfriend," Megan whispered, and Jill noticed a tall, good-looking young man in a dark suit and wire-rimmed glasses, who stood behind her.

"Think she has a boyfriend?"

"Yes, I see him all the time, on Abby's Facebook page."

Jill blinked, not surprised that Megan was checking Abby's Facebook page, too. "Let's find our seats. They're going to start the service."

"Mom, Abby just saw us, she's coming over." Megan stiffened. "What do I say to her? I already said I'm sorry."

"Say what you feel." Jill looked over to see Abby walking toward them, wiping a tear from her eye. It struck Jill that no one else was crying, or even upset, except for Abby, and that didn't surprise her, either. William had lots of acquaintances, but no real friends, which was only one of the red flags Jill had ignored. Love was not only blind, it was color-blind.

"But what *should* I say?" Megan asked, worried.

"You can say you're sorry again, that would be nice."

"Like, 'I'm sorry'? Or, 'please accept my . . . sorrow'? Or what?"

" 'I'm sorry' will do, sweetie," Jill answered, as Megan met Abby and gave her a hug.

"Abby, I'm so sorry, again, I really am."

"Thanks." Abby squeezed Megan tight, her eyes brimming with tears, then she let Megan go, turned to Jill, and practically fell into her arms. "Jill, thanks for coming."

"I'm sorry, honey." Jill embraced her, trying to will the strength from her body into Abby's.

"This makes it so real, doesn't it? Like he really is gone, and all these people I don't even know them."

"I know, sweetie, I'm sorry." Jill released her when she spotted Victoria heading for her, with a deep scowl.

"Jill, what are *you* doing here?" Victoria's eyes flashed with anger. "You have no right to be here. This is a private ceremony."

Jill froze, stricken. "I'm sorry, I thought—"

Abby interrupted, "I asked her to come, Victoria."

"Are you *crazy*?" Victoria shot back, then turned to Jill, infuriated. "How *dare* you! You should be ashamed of yourself. You know what you did to Dad. To all of us."

Megan gasped, teary. Heads turned. The rector's mouth fell open.

"Victoria, wait." Jill put up a palm, stunned. She'd never seen Victoria so angry, especially not at her. They used to be so close. "Listen to me—"

"No, *you* listen to *me*." Victoria's fair skin flushed with barely controlled rage. "You didn't love Dad, and you didn't love us, either. You threw us out!"

"No, that's not true." Jill edged away, mortified. Her face felt like it was on fire, her mouth had gone dry. She wouldn't stay another minute if it upset the girls. The crowd murmured. The rector grasped Victoria by the arm, but she pulled it away.

"Now it's my turn to throw *you* out, Jill. Leave. Go!" Victoria pointed to the door, but Jill was already in motion, turning to catch up with Megan, the two of them fleeing, their pumps clattering on the colonial floorboards.

"Jill, no!" Abby shouted, and just when Jill thought it

couldn't get worse, she realized that Abby was running after them.

"Megan, wait!" Jill called out, but Megan blew through the glass doors into the church's courtyard. Jill ran through the doors after her and reached Megan, who was crying, full bore, in the rain.

"Mom, what did I do? What did I do?"

"Nothing, honey." Jill hugged Megan just as Abby came flying out, her cheeks tear-stained, her mascara dripping black.

"Jill, I'm sorry." Abby ran headlong toward her, and Megan backed off. Jill caught Abby as she burst into new tears. "I'm so sorry."

"Abby, what's going on?"

"I'm sorry, it's my fault, I messed up. I didn't tell her, but I didn't think she'd freak out in front of everybody." Abby sobbed, shuddering. Megan stood aside, wiping her eyes, but Jill couldn't go to her, because she was comforting Abby. "Dad said you cheated on him, that you wanted a divorce, you met another man."

"*What?*" Megan blurted out.

"No, that's not true." Jill released Abby. "Abby, go inside. This isn't the time or the place—"

"Was he lying?" Abby wiped her eyes, leaving mascara smudges. "You didn't really cheat on Dad, did you?"

"My Mom would never do that!" Megan shouted. "She cried, I heard her, lots of nights! He probably cheated on *her*!"

"No, he didn't!" Abby shouted back.

"Yes, he *did*!" Megan yelled louder, veins bulging on her neck.

"Stop fighting, both of you." Jill took control, horrified. "Abby, we have to leave. Go inside. Take care. Good-bye."

"No, wait, don't go." Abby grabbed Jill's arm, her tears abruptly stilled. "Can't you just come over, like I asked?

Please, after the service? Somebody murdered Dad, and we have to find out who."

"No, Abby, I can't." Jill pulled her arm away.

"Mom, was William *murdered*?" Megan asked, her voice breaking.

"No, he wasn't," Jill answered firmly, taking Megan's hand. She could see Victoria inside the church, hurrying toward the glass exit doors. "Let's go."

"Yes, he was, Megan!" Abby called out, and behind her, Victoria was opening the door, followed by the rector. "Somebody killed him, I know it! Jill, please, help me!"

Jill hustled a weeping Megan away just as Victoria emerged with the rector.

"Please, Jill, I need you!" Abby called again, but Jill kept going.

Running from one crying child, with another.

# 10.

Jill sat across from Megan in a restaurant near the church, a small, quiet place that seated them at a table in the back. Megan had stopped crying in the ladies' room, though her eyes were still puffy and reddish, and she'd cut her lip on her braces. "Are you okay, honey?" Jill asked Megan, worried.

"Yes." Megan drank some water, crestfallen. "Victoria was so mad, I didn't mean to upset her."

"Honey, stop, you didn't do it. Victoria didn't expect us, and we caught her by surprise. She's a little crazy right now, is all."

"What's Abby talking about, that William was *murdered*?" Megan's eyes rounded, a bloodshot brown. "Was he, Mom?"

"No, sweetie."

"Why does Abby think he was?"

"She's wrong, honey." Jill shook her head. "People say and think strange things in grief. She's too upset to think straight. They both are."

Megan sniffled. "I know you didn't cheat on him, Mom."

"I didn't. I never would."

"I know, you're honest." Megan managed a weepy smile. "You don't let me sign your name to anything, *ever*. Even absence notes."

Jill smiled.

"Did he cheat on *you*?"

Jill sighed, inwardly. A couple of tourists got up from a nearby table. "I'm not sure we should get into this here and now, honey."

"Mom, I can take it. I'm not a baby."

"Frankly, it's not your business. Or Abby's. Or anybody's but mine." Jill wanted to stand her ground. It wouldn't help for Megan to know more, and it was too emotionally charged a day. "I had to divorce him, and I did, and we're better for it."

"Mom, tell me, please?" Megan leaned forward, putting her hands on the table, palms down. "William told Abby and Victoria. He thought they could handle it."

"William lied to Abby and Victoria."

"Trust me, Mom. Trust me enough to tell me."

"It's not a matter of trust." Jill tried to shift gears. "I wish we would use this day, and the fact that he's gone, to put this chapter behind us and go forward."

"We can't go to the next step until we understand this one."

Jill blinked. Either Megan had read that somewhere, or she was getting smarter.

"You told me that, last week. When you were helping me with equations. You said you can't go to the next step until you understand the last one." Megan leaned over, bearing down. "Now tell me what happened. Why did you and William really break up?"

Jill felt her resolve weaken. She spotted their waitress, coming toward them with their meals. "Hold on."

"Here we go, ladies," the waitress said, setting salads

in front of them, filling the air with the tang of balsamic dressing. They both thanked her, and Jill waited for her to leave before she spoke.

"Honey, I don't know if he cheated, and it really doesn't matter to me."

Megan's eyes flared. "Of course it does. It *should*."

"Let's keep the drama to a minimum," Jill said, though she doubted it was possible. Mothers and daughters were automatic drama, and if you add dead ex-husbands, it rose to operatic levels.

"So what went wrong?"

"We were happy for a while, but then the trouble started, and I didn't notice it at first. I ignored things, like symptoms you minimize when you don't want to change your initial diagnosis. Classic confirmation bias."

Megan nodded, used to medical analogies by now.

"You remember William, right? What was he like, to you?"

"Fun. Silly. He liked to do things." Megan smiled. "Like when he got the bouncy house, and the trampoline."

"And the red convertible. Remember that day? He took you all for rides?"

"Right. The Mustang." Megan smiled more broadly, and Jill hoped she hadn't made a mistake, having her recall such happy times, but that was the point.

"Well, somebody had to pay for all that. William made money, but not as much as I did, and he wanted that lifestyle. He wanted to buy cars and trampolines, whatever he wanted, you name it."

Megan frowned. "So what's wrong with that?"

"Nothing, but he began to run up huge credit bills and wanted to take loans against the house. I'm not a big spender, and married people are supposed to agree on things." Jill tried to explain, but it was impossible to explain divorce to a teenage girl, with a head full of *The*

*Bachelor.* "He wanted more money, so he was always investing in things. He wanted to buy into a biotech start-up, and when I gave him that, he wanted to buy a title insurance company. He was all over the place."

"So it was only about money?"

"Not only about that, but money matters."

"He was trying to follow his dream, Mom."

"Not exactly." Jill wasn't surprised by Megan's defending William, because she always did, which was why these conversations were no-win. "It's not 'follow your dream,' like *American Idol.* You can follow your dream, but you have to be practical, too."

"So he couldn't afford to pay for his dream."

"No, he didn't really have a dream. His only dream was being rich, and that doesn't count as a dream. That's just plain greed."

Megan blinked.

"Pretty soon I could see a pattern, and I knew it would never end. No matter how much money I gave him, it would never be enough. If I let him, he would bankrupt me."

Megan frowned. "So that's *it*? That's *all*?"

Jill felt her chest tighten. "One day he asked me for a lot of money, for another business venture."

"How much did he want?"

"$325,000."

"Wow." Megan's eyes flared, though Jill knew she had no idea how much or how little that was. If it was as much as an iPhone, it was a lot.

"I said no." Jill wouldn't tell her that the money William asked for had belonged to Megan. It was her inheritance, since Gray's parents had established a small trust for her after his death. Gray hadn't had any life insurance; they both thought he was too young to die, and in fact, he was. "And when I said no, he asked me to take out a loan for it, and I refused. Then he did something that broke the camel's back."

"What?"

Jill hesitated, but maybe it was time. "He used to come to the office at night and bring you. He'd wait for me, and you'd play with the toys in the waiting room, then we'd go out to dinner."

"I remember, it was fun."

"I thought he came by to see me, but he didn't. It turned out that he was stealing from my office."

Megan's lips flattened, and Jill could see hurt flicker across her face.

"Petty cash went missing, and drug samples. It took us a long time to notice, because we weren't talking to each other about it, with all the work we had to do. He did it in small amounts, especially the pads."

"He took pads? Like school supplies?"

"No, prescription pads. People sell them to other people so they can get prescription drugs, illegally."

"Really?"

"Yes. You can get as much as fifty dollars for a blank prescription, and they're usually bought by people addicted to pain meds, like Oxycontin and Vicodin. We didn't know who was stealing ours, but it was William."

Megan fell silent, wounded, for William, and Jill kicked herself for starting the story. She decided not to tell Megan about the money William had taken from her purse, or his trick of using her ATM card before she was even awake, withdrawing amounts too small to notice, until too late.

"You okay, sweetie?" Jill reached across the table and rested her hand on top of Megan's.

"How do you know he stole the pads? You could have been wrong."

Jill sighed inwardly. "No, actually, we caught him in the act."

"Really?" Megan asked, hushed.

"He was caught in the basement, taking old pads out of the box. We left them down there, out of the locked cabinet, to catch the bad guy. We even set up a hidden video camera, which was my idea. I never thought the bad guy would be my own husband."

Megan set down her fork, stricken.

"It was a terrible thing he did, embarrassing to me, and worse, it could have ruined me and all of the docs in our group. My colleagues, my friends. We could've lost our licenses."

"He didn't have to go to jail, did he?"

"No." Jill felt touched, and saddened, that Megan was still concerned for William. "The group didn't report it, out of kindness to me, but I had to leave the practice and I paid back every penny he took. I was lucky to get work anywhere else, after all the gossip. That's why I took the job at Pembey Family. They were the only ones who made an offer."

Megan blinked. "Do you think he cheated on you?"

"I don't know, and I don't care."

"*Really,* Mom?"

"Really." Jill squared her shoulders. She didn't bother to explain that the betrayal was worse. The deception was worse. That she hadn't known what was going on under her own roof, under her very nose, that was worse. "I want to be with a man I can trust and believe in. So I took some time alone, and finally met Sam. End of story. Or beginning."

Megan cocked her head, mulling it over. "I think William had a dream, but it wasn't the dream you wanted."

"Okay, we can agree to disagree on that one." Jill swallowed hard, knowing it was time to stop, if only to save Megan's feelings. The unsayable thing, the thing she was about to say next, the real truth of the matter, was that Jill didn't think William ever really loved her, he just married her for her money and to have a mother for his children. But if Jill told Megan that, then Megan would conclude that William had never really loved her, either, that he had only acted as if he had, that she had been used, too. And Jill sensed that Megan couldn't handle hearing that, despite her middle-school savvy. She was only thirteen, and inside, just a kid.

Megan was eyeing her. "What's your dream, Mom?"

Jill was happy to change the subject, and almost laughed with relief. "You," she answered.

Megan laughed, unexpectedly. "No, really."

"What? It's true. My dream is having a wonderful daughter, like you." Tears came to Jill's eyes, surprising even her, and she blinked them away. "I never dreamed I'd be so lucky. I don't know how I got so lucky."

"But for *you,* what's your dream? Like they say, your passion?"

"Other than you?"

"Yes." Megan rolled her eyes, but Jill wouldn't let go.

"Honey, someday you'll understand this, but every mother's passion is her children, and there's nothing wrong with that. People don't say it enough. I see it every day at work, in all the mothers doing everything they can to help their babies get well, in all the panicky calls and emails, in all the things mothers do for their kids." Jill thought of Padma and her three sons, and her own mother. "Women sacrifice every day for their children, and they love it. They do it without question, second nature. *That's* passion."

Megan smiled, but still looked searching. "Okay, but before me. Before I was born, what was your passion? Did you have a passion then?"

Jill thought a minute. "Okay, well, I guess I would say that my passion was helping kids. That's why I became a pediatrician. I'm a professional mother now."

Megan grinned. "Uh-oh. Watch out."

"I know, right?" Jill smiled at her, happy they were back on an even keel. "Let me ask *you* now. What's your passion? What do you love doing?"

Megan frowned, slightly. "I don't know. Is that bad?"

"No, not at all. You're still young, and you'll know when you know. Like love, because it is a form of love. It could be swimming, or becoming a vet. You're great in the school plays, and your passion can be acting or singing. *That* will be your life's work. Money isn't a life's work. Love is."

Megan sighed. "So what are you going to do about Abby?"

"What do you mean?" Jill had to switch gears.

"What if she's right that William was murdered?"

"She's not. The police say it's not murder, just a reaction to the drugs and alcohol. He had some whisky that night, and you can't mix those."

"I remember he liked whisky sometimes, he let me taste it. Ugh." Megan wrinkled her pretty nose. "I didn't know he took drugs, though. What drugs?"

"They found drugs for anxiety and painkillers."

"Was he on them when you guys were married?"

"No, I didn't think he was, but he was stealing samples and prescription pads. When I confronted him, he said he sold them, so I didn't think he was taking drugs himself. I was wrong, I guess."

"Were those the samples he stole?"

"No, he stole ADHD drugs, like Ritalin." Jill didn't have to explain because Megan knew about a scandal at the high school last year, with kids arrested for selling their Ritalin as a study drug.

"If you took those drugs with alcohol, do you get a heart attack?"

"Yes, you can." Jill picked up her fork and stabbed her salad. "It's possible, and it's not suspicious that he did."

Megan looked down at her food, untouched, and Jill could see she was struggling.

"Honey, this talk of drugs and murder is Abby's way of not accepting that William is gone. The police say it wasn't murder, and Victoria agrees."

Megan looked up, her eyes glistening again. "But I still wish you'd do what Abby wants. Help her figure it out."

"Why?" Jill asked, dismayed. "She's wrong. She doesn't know what she's talking about."

"Then help her figure that out, too. Don't you love her, anymore?"

"Yes, I do."

"She loves you, Mom. She always did. She acted like you were her real mom. She told me once, she doesn't even remember her real mom."

Jill didn't know what to say. Abby's real mother had died when she was only four, in a car accident. She'd had money, too, but Jill didn't want to go there, and this conversation was supposed to be about Megan. "Did that bother you?"

"No, not at all. You always love it when people love what you love." Megan smiled. "Like when people say Beef is cute, I love that. I hate people who say he's old or fat. Abby's a sweetie, and you know how she is when she gets an idea in her head. She's like Beef, with his sock, she never lets go. She needs us, Mom. We're her family."

"Are we?" Jill asked, feeling surprised and validated, both at once.

"Yes, sure, you can't just kick somebody out of your family. She's in my family, so she has to be in yours."

Jill smiled. She still thought of herself as Abby's mother,

but it came as a revelation that Megan thought of her as family, too.

"Mom, you say your passion is helping kids. Right?"

"Yes," Jill answered.

"So how can you *not* help Abby? She's *ours*."

# 11.

Back at home, Jill had changed her clothes and was putting fresh sheets on Megan's bed, in a house that was empty and felt that way. She had dropped Megan off at Courtney's to work on an English project until their afternoon practice, and Sam was still in town with his colleague Lee. Jill was doing laundry and other chores, trying to put the memorial service and its aftermath out of her mind, without success.

*Why did you guys really break up?*

Jill felt a twinge, missing Megan. It was too soon to be an empty-nester, but you didn't have to be a pediatrician to know that the baby birds left before they could fly. She tucked in the flat sheet and made a lousy hospital corner. She had worked in six different hospitals and couldn't make a decent hospital corner. Even hospitals didn't make hospital corners anymore. The irony was lost on Beef, who watched her from between his paws, resting his head on his dirty tube sock.

*She's like Beef, with his sock. She never lets go.*

Jill reached for the duvet cover, an old one she'd gotten from the closet. It usually took her two or three tries to put on a duvet cover, and it was a chore she hated. She'd rather change a bedpan than a duvet cover.

*Brrring!* Her cell phone rang, and she slid it from her pocket and checked the number, in the Philly area code. She answered it, "Jill Farrow."

"I'm so sorry about what happened." It was Abby, her voice thick, and Jill set down the duvet cover, feeling for her.

"How are you, honey? How was the service?"

"Um, okay. I'm okay." Abby sniffled. "I'm glad you didn't change your phone number. Am I still A on your speed dial?"

Jill felt a stab of guilt. "You were until I got a new phone, but that erases all the speed dials. Where are you, honey?"

"Home."

"Alone?"

"Pickles is here."

Jill sank onto the bed, hating that Abby was all by herself after William's service, sitting in the house they'd shared.

"Jill, I'm so sorry for what I said, accusing you of cheating on Dad. I know, deep inside, that you didn't, but Dad said it and Victoria went along, and I didn't want to think he'd lie. I mean, he's all I have. Had."

"I know, don't worry. Did you have a reception afterwards?"

"We did, but I left. Victoria's so mad at me. She's still at the restaurant. It was Brian and all her friends anyway."

"Who's Brian?"

"Brian Pendle. He was at the service. Tall and cute, with glasses."

Jill remembered. "Megan said he was her boyfriend."

"Not yet. He has a girlfriend studying abroad, but

Victoria's working on him. He's a lawyer in New York, and she's crushing like crazy on him. The more unavailable the guy, the happier she is."

Jill let it go. "Did you eat?"

"Not yet. I'll get take-out, I'm obsessed with this Chinese place near us. The one time I didn't call and order, they called me to make sure I was okay. It was the day Dad died."

Jill shuddered.

"What are you and Megan doing?"

"Everybody's out, and I'm making the bed somebody barfed on." Jill was trying to make Abby laugh, and she did, chuckling.

"Oh no, yuck, sorry. Does Megan hate me?"

"No. Megan loves you, and so do I."

Abby fell silent. "I don't mind being here alone. I have Pickles and I decided I'm going to live here on my own, from now on. Victoria says I can't do it, but I know I can. She wants to sell the house, but I want to stay."

Jill knew it was the grief talking. "It's too soon to make any decisions, sweetie. See how you feel in time."

"I can't, Victoria's already talking to the lawyer. We're in a fight."

Jill sank onto the bed. "Well, maybe she's right, honey. It costs money to live in a house. You have to pay the mortgage, every month."

"No, there's no mortgage. The house is paid for."

"That's not possible." Jill and Sam were a decade away from paying off the house, and together, they made good money.

"Yes it is, Dad told me."

Then Jill figured it had to be a small mortgage. "But you'll have living expenses. Can you afford them, waitressing?"

"I quit."

"What?" Jill checked her tone. Criticism was the last thing Abby needed today. "Why?"

"I want to find out who killed Dad. I'm going to do it, whether you help me or not."

Jill let that go, too. "What will you do for money? Did your Dad have life insurance?"

"Yes, Victoria said there was a policy for a million dollars, and we're the beneficiaries, and I saved about three thousand dollars, so I'll be fine."

Jill relaxed, reassured. She'd made William get life insurance when the girls were young, though they hadn't had a million-dollar policy. It seemed odd.

"Jill, can you tell me how to set up a budget? How to run the house, like Dad did?"

Jill saw room to strike a bargain. "Yes, but if I do, you have to do something for me. I want you to meet with a psychologist, a really great woman. "

"A shrink?" Abby moaned.

"You've had a terrible loss, and there's no shame in therapy. I had plenty after my first husband died. Give it a chance is all I ask. She'll see you anytime this week."

"Okay," Abby answered, after a moment.

"Thanks, sweetie." Jill felt a wave of relief.

"So wanna come over? You said you were alone. We can order Chinese."

"Tonight?"

"Why not?"

Jill felt her mood lift. She had answered all her patient email, returned all their phone calls, and done the laundry. She was going to take a swim, but she could do that anytime. "Okay, sounds good," she said.

But Jill didn't know what she was in for.

# 12.

It was almost dark by the time Jill got to Philly, surprised to find that William had lived in one of the best parts of Society Hill. His house was a stunning contemporary column, with a concrete-and-glass façade, and she climbed the steps in astonishment, ringing the bell. Abby opened the door in her flowing boho dress, sweeping into Jill's arms.

"Jill, I'm so glad you came."

"Me, too, sweetie." Jill let her go, gesturing at the modern façade. "This is your house? It's amazing."

"Now you know why I want to stay. Come in." Abby moved aside, and Jill followed her through an all-white entrance hall to a dramatic living room, with walls of massive glass sheets and beige leather sectionals, arranged around a state-of-the-art TV and entertainment center.

"Abby, where did your Dad work?" Jill asked, mystified. She set her purse down on the couch. "He wasn't still a drug rep, was he?"

"No, he was doing really well on his own, making investments with his friend Neil." Abby smiled, with pride. "Dad has a Mercedes, and he bought Victoria a BMW, so she could drive back and forth to visit us. He got me the old Datsun, you saw, but it was all I wanted. She's a rescue car."

Jill didn't get it. "But even if you have the money, are you sure you want to live here, by yourself?"

"I already do. Dad was on the road, sometimes four nights a week."

"Why, if he wasn't a rep anymore?"

"For business." Abby shrugged. "He went lots of places, to New York and other cities. You know how Dad was, he kept his business to himself."

Jill bit her tongue. William kept everything to himself. "So you would be here alone?"

"No, my boyfriend was here. Santos." Abby's face fell. "He helped me a lot with the house, he was older."

Jill had guessed that the boyfriend was older. Santos must have been the raggedy-looking guy on Abby's Facebook page. "How old was he?"

"Thirty."

Jill masked her disapproval, worried at how vulnerable Abby was, especially now. "Honey, I don't know if you're safe, living here alone."

"Sure I am. We have a burglar alarm, and Dad had a gun."

"He did?" Jill blinked, surprised. That would have been a new thing for William. They'd never owned a gun, at least she didn't think they did, but there was so much about William she never really knew. "But you, in this big house, honey? It's too much for you."

"Why does everybody keep telling me I can't do things, even you?" Abby's eyes turned pleading. "You never did that before, Jill. You were the one person, all my life, who told me I could do whatever I set my mind to."

"It's not that I don't think you can, it's that I don't know why you want to."

"Why *wouldn't* I want to find out who killed my Dad?"

Jill let it go, for now. "Okay, now, where did your Dad keep his bills and things?"

"Upstairs, in his office. It's really his man cave. Come this way." Abby turned and led the way to a transparent staircase leading to a light-filled hallway on the second floor, then opened a door. "Here's my bedroom. The other is Victoria's room, but only Pickles sleeps there. He likes it in the daytime."

Jill looked inside Abby's bedroom, speechless, for a moment. It was a replica of the one she'd shared with Megan, traditionally decorated with a blue hook rug, a comforter covered with forget-me-nots, and matching curtains.

"I know, it's crazy but I wanted to make it feel like home, so I wouldn't miss everything so much."

"Did it work?" Jill asked, pained.

"Kinda."

"Good for you." Jill touched her arm, realizing that the divorce had cost Abby her family and her home, neither of which could be replaced by an empty glass column, a veritable house of air.

"Here's Dad's office." Abby walked ahead, and Jill found herself in a stark, masculine office with a dark-patterned carpet. There was a black leather sofa and a side chair with lacquered end tables, and a sleek walnut desk with a black Herman Miller chair. "He paid all the bills in here, and I have to learn about that stuff if I'm going to take over. The file cabinet has lots of the old bills."

"Okay, but I have an easier way." Jill went over to the laptop. "When we were married, we used Quicken, which is a program that pays all the bills. Mind if I check the laptop?"

"Go for it." Abby stood aside, and Jill sat down at the desk and tapped a key, feeling odd about intruding into William's life. The laptop came to life with a vacation photo of a grinning William, Abby, and Victoria, and Jill cringed, looking up at Abby, to see if it upset her.

"You okay, honey? We can do this another time."

"No, I'm fine, go ahead. I already checked his email but I didn't see any hate mail, psycho girlfriends, or anything suspicious." Abby pointed to the side table. "That's where the police found the bottle of whisky. It was Glenfiddich, but there was no glass. If Dad had the killer up here, whoever it was took both glasses when he left."

Jill let it go. She scanned the Programs, found Quicken, and clicked the icon for Household Expenses, which brought a virtual check register onto the screen. "Here we are. This will tell you your fixed expenses each month, and we can make you a budget. Easy-peasy. Where did you say the old bills were, just in case we need them?"

"Here." Abby went to the file cabinet and rolled open the top drawer. "This is all the bills. I went through it, looking for clues, but I didn't find anything."

Jill let that go, too. She crossed to the cabinet and skimmed an array of files that started with AT&T Mobility and ended with Verizon. There was a file labeled Important Documents, and she slid it out and opened it. On top was the deed to the house, which was in William's name. "So the house is in your Dad's name, it will have to go through the estate. Let's check out the other drawers."

"They're empty now. Victoria took it all, for the lawyer." Abby closed the top drawer and opened the second, which was empty. "They used to have bank statements and financial stuff."

"Okay." Jill straightened up. "Okay, why don't we bring the files and the laptop to my house, and you stay with us a few days, while we get you up and running? If you have a bag or a suitcase, we'll pack it and go."

"Great, thanks." Abby brightened, then hesitated. "But don't you want to see Dad's room, where he died? Please?"

She gestured at a closed door off the office. "I kept it closed after the police left."

Jill sighed. "Why, Abby?"

"To help me." Abby begged Jill with her eyes. "I need your help, Jill. There's no one else."

"But honey, I'm not an expert. Why don't we hire a private investigator? I'll even pay for it, how's that?"

Abby shook her head. "Why? No stranger will care as much as I do. Jeez, aren't you even curious if he was murdered? You loved him once, didn't you?"

"Of course I did, but—"

"Jill, please." Abby grabbed her arm, urgently. "I just want to understand, that's all. My life turned upside-down all of a sudden, and I didn't see any of it coming. Can't you just take a look in the bedroom and tell me if you see anything suspicious?"

*How can you not help her, Mom?*

Jill sighed. She always had trouble saying no to the girls. "*Please,* Jill?"

"All right, but just one look, then we go."

"Thanks." Abby whirled around, and Jill followed her into the bedroom, which was large and modern, with white walls and a navy blue accent wall, a navy oriental rug, and a walnut headboard that matched the nighttable and a long, low bureau. On the bureau was a posed photograph of William and the girls, all of them in matching white shirts with him in the middle, his grin cocky and his eyes flashing darkly under a spray of jet-black bangs.

"Abby, I don't see anything suspicious. Can we go now?"

"Wait, listen." Abby turned, newly animated, her gaze focused. "I know there are no signs of a struggle, nothing out of order or searched, but that's not the way I think it happened."

"What do you think happened?" Jill asked, trying not to sound like she was humoring her.

"I think he'd been in his office with the killer, and they had a drink, then he came in here and . . . died. I found him here, on the left side of the bed, nearest the office door." Abby gestured, dry-eyed. "I didn't see any marks on him, like he was hit or anything."

"I understand." Jill felt her chest tighten, looking at the bed. The navy sheets were in disarray, and there was a large stain on the left. It was urine, and she shuddered.

"Here's why I think it. He had on his jeans and his white dress shirt, like he'd been out or met someone. You remember how he used to change his pants, but not his shirt?"

"Yes." Jill remembered, but she didn't want to. She just felt sad that Abby sounded so convinced.

"If he was going to stay home, he would have had on a T-shirt or something more relaxed. But he had on a white shirt, which tells me he had a meeting." Abby walked over to the nighttable, which held two pens, a car magazine, and an empty phone charger. "Also, there were three bottles of pills here and his cell phone. The police took them, but I know they weren't his pills. Look." Abby dug in her dress pocket, pulled out a yellow Post-it, and handed it to her. "I wrote down the doctor's name and number. He's not our doctor, and he's not returning my calls."

Jill took the Post-it and read it:

Dad's meds:
Vicodin, 5 mg, once a day
Xanax, 10 mg, once a day
Temezepam, 10 mg, once a day
Dr. Raj Patel # 9483636
(215) 555-2923
All were filled same day 4/12
Broad Street Pharmacy, 1200 N. Broad Street
(215) 555-9373

Jill thought a minute. "These could have been pre-scribed by a psychiatrist, and if your Dad was seeing one, he might not have wanted you to know."

Abby scoffed. "Please, he wouldn't've cared. I tried to Google the doctor, but you know how many Dr. Raj Patels there are? Also, I went to the drugstore and showed the pharmacists a picture of Dad, but they hadn't seen him before, and they were all women." Abby lifted an eyebrow. "Now, I ask you. What woman would forget Dad, only a week later?"

"It's possible, Abby." Jill didn't press the point. She was trying to forget him, years later, but not in a good way. She handed the paper back to Abby. "Here."

"Keep it. I have a copy."

Jill stuck it in her purse, which was still on her shoul-der. "You said he had a gun. Where is it?"

"Right here." Abby slid open the drawer on the night-table, revealing a black revolver. "It's loaded."

Jill didn't get it. "Honey, if someone was trying to kill him, why didn't he use the gun to protect himself?"

"What if they drugged him? What if he didn't know it was happening, and by the time he did, he couldn't do any-thing to help himself?"

"He could have pressed the alarm button." Jill spotted a burglar alarm panel on the wall, near the bed. She knew it would be there because they'd had one there at their old house, at William's insistence.

"Not if he was drugged."

"But the room is in perfect order. Didn't he fight back, at all? Your Dad was a big, physical guy."

"What if he did, and the killer put it back together, after-wards? Without fingerprints, how would you know?" Abby's tone grew stronger, more confident. "The police refused to call the mobile crime unit because they said there was no sign of a murder, so I'll investigate it myself, whether you help me or not. No matter what it takes, or how long. I'll do it."

"Why would anybody kill him?" Jill asked, trying to reason with her. "There's no sign of a robbery. Look." She walked to the bureau, where a lacquered box was open and in full view, with an array of watches on a velveteen stalk. Then she remembered that William always kept cash in his sock drawer, so she opened the top drawer, and under his balled-up socks nestled a stack of wrinkled twenties. "This money isn't hard to find, all anybody would have to do is open the top drawer. He wasn't robbed, even after the fact. Where was his wallet?"

"In his back pocket. The police took that, too." Abby frowned, frustrated. "Maybe it wasn't about money. Maybe it was personal."

"Do you know of anybody who had it in for him?"

"No. Neil called him The Mayor. Everybody loved Dad, he had tons of friends."

Jill let it go. She hadn't seen "tons of friends" at the memorial service, and there hadn't been a tear in sight. "Who's Neil?"

"Neil Straub, his business partner."

"Oh, right. Did he get along with your Dad?"

"Totally. Neil would never do anything to Dad."

"Where does he live?"

"New York, but he travels with Dad a lot."

"Okay, now, can we go?" Jill had indulged this long enough, and Abby was getting riled up, with all the encouragement.

"Wait, one last thing." Abby went to the bathroom and opened the mirrored medicine chest. "Here's Dad's Crestor. This is where he keeps his meds, not on the nighttable. Also, this prescription was filled at our CVS. Dad chats up the pharmacists, and they all love him. Proves my point." Abby turned at the faint sound of a hip-hop ringtone. "Wait, that's my phone, downstairs. I should get that." She headed out the bathroom door, then the bedroom. "I'll be right back."

"I'll come with you."

"No, wait, stay." Abby rushed out of the room, leaving Jill lingering unhappily by William's bed. She and William used to have a brass bed, and she flashed on a Sunday afternoon long ago, when they were driving in the car, dropping off the last daughter at her friend's. It was early on in their marriage, still happy times, and as soon as the car door closed, they both looked at each other across the console and realized, in the same moment, that they would have the house to themselves, like a sort of suburban miracle.

*Are you thinking what I'm thinking?* William had asked her, with a grin.

*Totally. Food-shopping can wait.*

William had hit the gas, and they raced home, flew from the car, then ran inside, not stopping to let Beef out, and William chased her upstairs to their brass bed, shouting, *Let's make some noise!*

"Oh, well." Abby was entering the bedroom, teary again, and the expression on her face brought Jill back to earth. She went over and gave Abby a warm hug.

"What's the matter, honey?"

"That was Victoria on the phone. I can't go to your house, tonight." Abby sniffled in Jill's arms. "She says I'm taking sides, or switching to the wrong side, or whatever."

"Aw, there's no sides, there never was, not to me." Jill let her go, and Abby wiped her eye.

"I know, but still, I don't want to upset her anymore. It's a hard time for her, too, and she's right, I'm not being very considerate."

"I understand." Jill used to mitigate Victoria's tendency to boss her little sister, but those days were gone. "Don't worry about it, honey. Whatever you're comfortable with, I'll do."

"I'll stay here tonight, but please, take the laptop and the other stuff. I do want to try and live here, make a go of it, no matter what Victoria says."

"Okay." Jill hated leaving Abby alone, but there was no choice. "What's in your refrigerator, sweetie?"

"Bottled water." Abby managed a smile. "And half and half, for Pickles."

"How about I go to the store for you, pick up some groceries, and drop them off? Then you can at least make yourself a bowl of cereal in the morning. You still like Special K? With strawberries?"

"You remembered." Abby smiled, more broadly. "You're such a *mom*."

An hour later, Jill was back in the car in the rain, having dropped off groceries for Abby and picked some up for herself. The traffic on the expressway heading out of the city was congested, and she inched along, using the time to return phone calls and emails from her patients. Padma hadn't called her about Rahul, and Jill hoped he was improving, but the bloodwork would be definitive.

She stewed behind the wheel, her thoughts all over the map. So much had happened, she couldn't absorb it quickly enough.

*What woman would forget Dad?*

Jill couldn't shake the question, and it wasn't the kind of thing that would get the attention of the police, even if they had followed up. You had to know William to know it was fishy. She fed the car some gas, then braked again in traffic, and the reflective letters of a sign on the overpass caught her headlights. BROAD STREET, ½ MILE.

She remembered that William had filled his scripts for the drugs at a pharmacy on Broad Street, and she wondered if she should stop in and ask. She was curious about the scripts, and Broad Street was on the way home.

*You're a doctor, and Sherlock Holmes was a doctor.*

She thought of the lesson she'd taught Abby, that all deductive reasoning was the same, a process designed to find the truth. When Jill ran a differential for a patient, she would systematically cross off diagnoses that weren't supported by the data and keep those that were, testing as she went along, until she understood what was really going on. That was the reason she'd ordered the blood test for Rahul; if his results came back normal, as she expected, she'd have ruled out the more serious diagnoses.

Jill thought about it in traffic. If she could go to the pharmacy and rule out anything being wrong with the scripts, she could put to bed Abby's murder theory. So she reached for her purse and felt around for the yellow Post-it.

# 13.

Jill cruised down Broad Street, going north in the driving rain. The boulevard bisected the city, and this stretch was lined with check-cashing agencies, empty storefronts, and used-car lots. Streetlights were broken, leaving entire blocks in darkness, and Jill tried to understand why William would have come here to fill the scripts. She saw the BROAD STREET PHARMACY sign ahead and scanned in the darkness for a parking space. One opened up suddenly, and she braked to pull into it, but when she checked her rearview mirror, something strange caught her eye.

*Mom, look in your mirror. There's a padiddle behind us, one car back.*

She blinked. There was a padiddle, two cars behind her. To double-check, she squinted at her outside mirror, and she could see the padiddle clearly, though raindrops dotted the mirror. It was two cars back, and it was also a black SUV, with the left light out and the same boxy grille, which was quite coincidental.

Jill's mouth went dry. She hit the gas, drove past the drugstore, and turned right off Broad Street. The sidestreet was skinny and even darker, lined with rundown brick rowhomes and plenty of parking spaces. She pulled over, shut off the engine, and slid down in the driver's seat to see if the SUV would follow her.

Her heart started to pound, and she felt scared and silly, both at once. Her eyes were glued to the outside mirror. A few minutes later, the padiddle appeared, driving fast. She ducked deep into her seat, let it pass, and popped up again. She couldn't see the driver, but she caught the beginning of its license plate, and the first letter was a T.

Jill told herself to calm down, trying not to jump to conclusions. There would be no reason for anybody to be following her, and it would be dumb to follow anybody in a padiddle. Then she thought again. The driver might not know he had a headlight out, and maybe he'd started following Abby, then more recently started following her.

Jill started up the car, drove out of the space, took the next right, and backtracked three blocks, heading for the drugstore. She parked, chirped the car locked, grabbed her purse, and checked around her before she got out, but the SUV wasn't anywhere in sight. She climbed out and hurried through the rain into the drugstore, more than a little spooked.

She hustled inside the bright-lit store, which was cold, empty, and dingy, with a tile floor that felt gritty under her pumps. She spotted herself on a security monitor, then hustled to the back where the pharmacy would be and got in line at the counter behind a young blonde mother, with a crying baby wrapped in a thin receiving blanket. There wasn't a pharmacist on duty, just a young male clerk with gelled hair, whose pallor wasn't helped by the fluorescent lights overhead.

"Is this a drop off?" the clerk asked the young mother, who was jiggling the baby while he cried.

"Can I see the pharmacist?"

"No, she's gone for the night."

"Then can you help me?" The woman held the baby close, but the crying didn't stop. "My little boy's teething, and my aunt said to rub brandy on his gums, but it doesn't help."

"You gotta go to the doctor. I'm not a doctor."

"I don't have one. I went to the ER, but it was too crowded. Can you just answer a question for me?"

"No, I just work here, sorry."

Jill felt torn, knowing she wasn't supposed to step in. The baby wasn't her patient, and the Good Samaritan didn't apply. But she wasn't about to let a mother and child suffer, even if the system would. "Miss, maybe I can help you. I'm a pediatrician."

"You, a doctor?" The young woman's eyes lit up, an exhausted blue, and she had a neck tattoo with her name written in curlicued script. "He kept me up all night with his crying, and I can't calm him down, no matter what."

"Let me see his hand a second." Jill checked his tiny hand, and he had a telltale rash. She didn't even have to take the baby, because when he cried, he opened his mouth wide enough for her to see a blister on his tongue. "How did he sleep and eat, today?"

"Not much."

"And he has a fever, I bet."

"Last night it was 101, and he's still warm, for sure."

"Is he urinating, wetting his diapers?"

"Sure, all the time. I keep him changed, though. Nice and fresh, all the time."

"Good for you, and it's good that he's not dehydrated. He's not teething, he has coxackie virus."

"Cock-a-what?" The mother frowned, understandably.

"It's a virus that babies get in their mouth, and it's also called hand, foot, and mouth disease. It'll go away in ten days, but don't give him any more brandy. Popsicles are great to give him fluids, and he'll feel comfier on Tylenol. How old is he, eight months or so?"

"Yes, eight months."

"How much does he weigh?" Jill couldn't tell, he was so bundled up

"Twenty pounds."

"Okay, then give him infant's Tylenol. Use the dropper inside, and give him one full dropper."

"I ran out," the young mother answered, averting her eyes.

"Let me treat you to a bottle, okay?" Jill slipped her hand in her purse, pulled out her wallet, then handed a ten to the clerk. "This is for her Tylenol."

"Okay." The clerk pointed left. "It's right there, top shelf."

"Thank you." The young mother smiled gratefully, at Jill. "Thank you so much, ma'am."

"You're welcome. He'll be fine. Hang in with him."

"Thanks again." The mother hugged the baby and hurried down the aisle.

Jill faced the clerk. "Now, I need to see the waiver book."

The clerk smiled slyly. "You a real doctor, lady?"

"Yes, now can I see the book?" Jill put down another twenty, and the clerk scooped it off the counter, then slid over the red plastic binder.

"You got it."

"Thanks." Jill flipped the pages, slowing when she got to the fifteenth, then scanned the printed names next to each customer, with their signatures. None were William, so she flipped one more page, and his name leapt out at her. **William Skyler.** Three script stickers were pasted in a row beneath the label, all filled at 12:03 A.M. The signature was so messy she couldn't even tell if it was forged.

William's handwriting was more slanted, but he could be sloppy, too, in a rush.

"Okay?" the clerk asked.

"You have a surveillance camera back here, don't you? Most pharmacies do, and you have one at the front of the store. I saw it when I came in."

"Yes, what about it?"

"I need to see the tape. For fifty bucks."

"Sweet! Meet me in aisle eleven, near the soda. The office door is right here."

"Thanks." Jill turned right, headed back toward aisle eleven, and waited by the office door. Five minutes later, Jill had paid the clerk his fifty dollars and was standing with him in a cramped, filthy office stuffed with boxes. Video equipment sat stacked on an unpainted plywood shelf, under a small security monitor. The clerk aimed a remote control at the equipment, and the screen showed people zipping around in reverse. Their faces were small, but visible, and Jill was hoping that William had filled the scripts, so she could tell Abby and end this thing.

"Keep going?" the clerk asked, turning to her.

"Yes, all the way back to the twelfth."

"You're lucky, Doc. It only goes back a week, then it erases."

Jill watched the people walking backward, at speed. The numbers of a digital clock were spinning on the screen, too fast to read. The pace of the surveillance film slowed, and the clock wound back from 2:00 A.M. to 1:00 A.M. The onscreen clerk was an attractive woman. Jill asked, "Is the clerk a pharmacist?"

"No, that's Trisha. We don't have a pharmacist on that late at night. We stay open for pickups only. The CVS down the block is twenty-four-hour, but we're not. Okay, I'll stop the tape now." The clerk pressed a button on the remote. "Is that the dude?"

The screen froze, and Jill squinted at the grainy image, unsure if it was William. His face was obscured by aviator sunglasses, and a black ballcap hid his hair and forehead. He had on a nondescript windbreaker, and he was tall and broad-shouldered, like William and five million other men. Jill gestured at the screen. "I can't tell, but how can you dispense narcotics to someone you can't see? It looks like an obvious disguise."

"You don't know the wack jobs we get in here, Doc. They don't look half as good as him."

"Can you play the film slowly back and forth, one more time?"

"Sure." The clerk did, and the man in the black ballcap went to and from the counter, in slow motion. He didn't seem to talk to the clerk more than was necessary, and he kept his head down the entire time. It wasn't the way William behaved, and it was no wonder that Trisha hadn't remembered him when Abby had asked.

Jill had another thought. If William had wanted these drugs, he could have gotten them as samples, because he knew reps at all the drug companies. So maybe the man in the ballcap wasn't William at all. Maybe he drove a black SUV, license plate T something, and didn't know his headlight had burned out. She eyed the screen, thinking of yet a third possibility. That the man really was William, but for some reason, he was disguising himself.

"Uh-oh." The clerk pointed at the small window in the door. "Customer's out there. I gotta go."

"One more sec." Jill reached in her purse, took out her BlackBerry, and snapped a picture of the monitor's screen. "Thanks."

"No problem." The clerk grinned. "Come back anytime."

# 14.

Jill closed the front door, dropped her keys in the bowl, and lugged two food bags inside. Beef ran barking to greet her, sniffing the bags, but the house was otherwise quiet. Sam's maroon Lexus was in the driveway, so she knew he was home.

"Babe?" she called out, and Sam came in barefoot from the family room, rubbing his eyes with a tired smile. He looked comfy in his T-shirt and baggy jeans, and he tucked his book under his arm as he took the bags from her and kissed her lightly on the lips.

"How are you, honey?"

"Good."

"How's Abby?"

"Fine." Jill would have to figure out when to tell him about the pharmacy. "How about you?"

"Catching up on my reading. Lee's well and says hello, and I washed the comforter, so Megan's back in business." Sam headed into the kitchen with the bags, and Jill fell into step beside him, dropping her handbag on the chair.

"Thanks. Was it gross?"

"Nah. Did you know that Laundromats have video games these days? I watched a ten-year-old save the planet." Sam set the bags on the island. "Before I forget, Katie called you. She said she left a message on your phone, too."

"Oh, thanks." Jill hadn't heard her phone ring. Katie Feehan was her best friend, and she lived nearby, with her husband Paul and three boys. "Did she say it was important?"

"She needs your help with a recipe. Something for the kids."

"Uh-oh." Jill smiled. Katie was a better friend than a cook.

"Are there more bags in the car?"

"No, just a box, with a laptop and some papers."

"Whose laptop and papers?"

"William's. I'm going to help Abby do a household budget. She's going to live on her own."

Sam shrugged. "Good for her, but with what money?"

"More than we have. It looks like William finally hit the jackpot." Jill rummaged in the shopping bags, found the ice cream, and put it in the freezer. "And she agreed to see a therapist."

"Great." Sam broke into a relieved smile. "I'll call Sandy and we'll make that happen. Where's Megan?"

"Courtney's, doing her English project." Jill unpacked the bagged vegetables and stowed them in the fridge. "I think she's milking it, don't you?"

"I don't blame her if she needs some time with Courtney. She can't be delighted with Abby after last night."

"Because of the comforter? It wasn't Abby's fault. She got sick."

"Not only that, but the way she kind of barged in, and all of a sudden, she's taking up your time. Like tonight."

Jill looked at him, surprised. "That's harsh, don't you think? I was alone, so I went over. I wanted her to come and stay a few days, but Victoria bullied her out of it."

"What do you mean, a few days?"

"I mean hang here for a little, so I could help her with the budget, and she could spend time with Megan."

"She works, though."

"She quit."

Sam frowned. "I don't know if her coming here is a good idea. Do you?"

"Sure, why not?"

"Is it a *fait accompli*?" Sam's eyes flared briefly behind his glasses. "Do I have a say? Does Megan?"

Jill didn't get it. "Megan was really close to Abby and she'd be happy to have Abby stay."

"I'm not sure you're right about that."

"I know I am. Megan told me she thinks of Abby as family."

"Megan may not understand the implications of that for the future, and anyway, do I count? Abby's not in *my* family. I don't know her. Steven never even met her."

Jill felt a tug at her heart. She couldn't say he was wrong, and she couldn't agree with him, either. "Abby's a great kid, Sam. Give her a chance."

"May I be honest, or are you going to bite my head off?"

"Be honest," Jill answered, meaning it. She hadn't seen this coming.

"You're thinking of the Abby you raised, not the Abby I met. The Abby I met drove drunk, was rude, and took over Megan's room. Is that the same Abby you remember?"

Jill felt stung, for Abby. "You can't judge someone on the worst day of their life. Her father just died."

"Isn't it likelier that she's changed? She's grown up without you, or any mother, in her life, and it hasn't done her any good."

Jill felt a wave of guilt. "That's not her fault, and I really think you're being harsh. You talked to her for fifteen minutes."

"I can tell. You can't. You're not objective. You love her."

"So what are you saying?" Jill asked, puzzled. "You don't want her here this week?"

"I think you should slow this relationship down, between you and Abby. Even between Megan and Abby. You're responding to a need, automatically, which is what you do so well. It's as if Abby's an acute wound and you're rushing to stop the bleeding." Sam kept his tone reasonable, his gaze steady. "It's what makes you a great mother, and physician, too. But you have competing needs here, and you have to weigh them carefully."

Jill couldn't agree. "You're making too much of it. How does it hurt Megan if Abby spends time here?"

"Megan's gotten used to living without her, and it took a long time. I know, I remember that time. Do you?"

"Yes." Jill nodded. Megan had gotten a little lost after the divorce, weepier and more sensitive than usual, with the familial rug pulled out from under her. "But it wasn't only about Abby."

"Either way, you're inviting Abby back into Megan's life, but it won't be the same as before. Abby isn't the same girl, and neither is Megan. Megan's grown up a lot, and these girls won't fit so well together." Sam leaned on the gleaming counter, which reflected him in a murky outline. "In fact, if you ask me, Megan's gotten stronger, and Abby's only gotten weaker."

"I don't get it." Jill couldn't deny a growing irritation, like having something in her shoe. "Abby needs a hand now, so can't we give it to her? She's so vulnerable, and anything can happen. I'm scared for her, Sam. Can't we just see her through this patch?"

Sam blinked. "How long is the patch?"

"I don't know."

"Then how do you know it's a patch?" Sam raked his hand through his hair. "I don't know where this road ends, or if it ends. This is a kid who'll need help for the fore-seeable future. She'll need therapy, love, a family, and a home. You name it, she needs it, she's a *bolus* of need." Sam cocked his head, blinking thoughtfully behind his glasses. "How will you cut her off, babe? When? It'll only get harder, you know. You're taking on a problem you don't own, and where will we be, down the line? Megan goes off to college, and we're at home with Abby? I don't want the problems of a problem child, at this point in my life."

Jill recoiled. "Slow down. We're not there yet."

"But we have to think about it, now. You know me, I'm a researcher. I know that what I do now will pay off years from now. In fact, it won't pay off *until* years from now. Everything's long-term, Jill. *Life* is long-term."

Jill had heard him say this before, to Megan. "So what's your point?" she asked, impatient.

"My point is, let's not start this process without think-ing. You have a triage mentality. You see a problem, you fix it. You go. You act."

"It's not because I'm a clinician, it's because I'm a mother. That's what all mothers do, Sam. We're practical."

"But whose mother are you? Don't slip so easily into the role of being that kid's mother."

"I used to be."

"But you're not, anymore."

"Really?" Jill's chest tightened. "What's a mother, or a stepmother? What's a family? Isn't it forever? The love doesn't stop when the legal relationship does."

"No, but the obligation does. The responsibility does."

Jill tried a different tack. "Okay, think about it this way.

Your son Steven is going to be my stepson, after we get married. I love him, and he's a great young man. Let's imagine that, God forbid, something happens to you, and I remarry, and your son Steven gets into trouble. Medical, legal, whatever. Do I turn my back on him because my new husband says so?"

"Steven's thirty years old, busy as hell, down in Texas. He doesn't need us anymore, he barely even visits."

"But he could need us, or me."

"Then you can't be there for him, not forever and ever."

"Love isn't finite, Sam."

"No, but time is. Money is. Resources are. Energy is."

"I know, but is that the world you want to live in?" Jill thought he was missing the point. "Wouldn't you want me to take care of Steven?"

"No, I still come down the same way." Sam's lips flattened to a firm line. "I'd understand it if your husband felt the way I do, which is that I didn't sign on for this. I love you and I love Megan, but I don't love your troubled ex-stepdaughter, and I don't want another kid. I'm getting out of the kid business."

Jill felt her heart sink, listening to him and seeing his adamancy. She could tell the way it was going, and it wasn't good. If she wanted her family with Abby in it, then she'd have to fight for it. And the person she'd have to fight was Sam.

"I'm older than you, and I see the light at the end of the tunnel. Steven's gone, and Megan's on her way. She'll be in college before you know it." Sam leaned over, urgently. "I'm looking forward to you and me, being alone together. No more blow dryers or swim meets."

"I think exactly the opposite." Jill felt heartsick. "I'll be sad when Megan leaves. I'm sad that she's already growing up, so fast. I never want to be out of the kid business."

"We'll be fine, you'll see. You'll love it."

"You never talked this way before," Jill said, hurt.

"I never had to."

"Are you unhappy?"

"No, I'm happy, and I'm trying to stay that way. We were fine before Abby entered the picture, just last night. We were great." Sam smiled and tried to touch her arm, but Jill found herself backing away, wishing she had a sounding board.

"You know what, I'm not that tired, so maybe I'll drop by Katie's and see if she still needs me."

"Really, babe?" Sam looked disappointed, puckering his lower lip.

"Well, she is cooking."

"Fair enough." Sam managed a smile. "She could burn down the neighborhood."

"Right." Jill picked up her handbag, gave Sam a dry kiss on the cheek, and left the kitchen. "I should be back in an hour, or so."

"Okay, drive safe," Sam called after her.

"Love you." Jill called back, and it wasn't until she reached the front door that she realized she hadn't told Sam about the pharmacy or the padiddle.

But he wasn't exactly a willing ear.

# 15.

"Sorry I missed your call." Jill followed Katie into her kitchen, which was in disarray. Flour dusted the butcher-block counter, and grated potatoes made a lopsided snowdrift on a plate, next to a lineup of cracked egg-shells, chopped onion, and a Pyrex bowl of batter. The air smelled like something good was cooking. "Yum. What's going on here?"

"Paul took the boys out to dinner, then the bookstore." Katie hurried back to the stove, her blonde ponytail swinging. Like Jill, she had on a light cotton sweater, capris, and clogs, the uniform of suburban moms. Katie picked up the spatula. "I was having an I'm-gonna-kill-my-kid moment."

"Why?" Jill asked, though she knew Katie was kidding. They'd been best friends since Penn State, and Katie had gone on to become a teacher, then an at-home mother of three sons, all under twelve years old. She always said humor and a cattle prod were her only weapons.

"Monday is International Day at school, and Robbie tells me this an hour ago, when we're gone all day tomorrow." Katie rolled her large, cornflower blue eyes. She was wholesomely pretty, with no makeup, an easy smile, and a turned-up nose under a sprinkling of soft freckles. "We're moving my mother-in-law to a retirement village. With her, it'll take a village."

"Yikes." Jill set down her purse and came over to the stove. The big Viking oven gave off a homey warmth, and she started to relax, after the talk with Sam. She felt lucky to have a friend like Katie and she could only imagine how Katie would react when she found out about William's death.

"You want soda or coffee? Or a margarita? Feel free."

"No, thanks. So what are you making? It smells great."

"Irish potato pancakes."

"Ambitious."

"*Insane.*" Katie flipped the pancake. "He has to bring in a typical food that represents his family, and you have to *make* it, so no Entenmann's."

"Uh-oh."

"Am I screwed or what? Can I just say that not all moms can cook? And what kind of time do they think we have? Should I thatch the roof next? Jeez! You know, the joke is, I assigned all this crap when I taught, too. Payback's a *bitch.*"

Jill smiled. "How can I help?"

"Just keep me company. It's good to see you. I called you to get an old family recipe of yours, for anything, but then I found this old family recipe on the Internet."

"How many do you have to make?"

"Too damn many." Katie flipped the third pancake. "There are twenty-three kids in the class, and I figure some kids will eat two, so that's thirty-three. Plus I have to suck up to the teacher, the aides, and the secretaries in the office, so that makes fifty. I bribe everybody. Elementary school is a banana republic, without the limos."

Jill smiled. "It's nice to include the office. I always did. Nobody makes them anything. They'll never forget it."

"I know. Great minds, right?"

"Here, let me help."

"Okay." Katie waved the spatula at the base cabinet. "Get another pan going. We'll get it done twice as fast."

"On it." Jill went into the cabinet, got a heavy skillet, and set it on the stovetop, then reached for the butter, glancing over. "You need to let them cook longer."

"No, I don't. This is for eight-year-olds. They eat crayons."

"You'll give them salmonella."

"You get what you pay for." Katie flipped another pancake. "I'm so glad you came over. What's shakin'?"

"Brace yourself. I have big news." Jill held the pan's handle, turned on the heat, and waited for the butter to melt, a spreading pool of gold. "You're not going to believe this, but William's dead."

"*What?*" Katie gasped. She looked over, her eyes wide, in disbelief. "William, your *ex-husband*? Are you *kidding*?"

"No, it's true."

"Hallelujah!" Katie broke into an incredulous smile. "Was it painful? Please tell me it was painful."

Jill felt torn. "I admit, I'm not crying over the man, but—"

"Look, a jig! Kiss me, I'm Irish. Happy International Day!" Katie put down the spatula and did a dance, shaking her butt. "Lordy be, what goes around really does come around. Hey, can we go dance on his grave?"

"He was cremated."

"He did that for spite." Katie made a face, scrunching up her nose.

"Come on, stop. Be nice. Abby came over with the news last night, and she thinks he might have been murdered."

"Abby was at your house?" Katie asked, suddenly growing serious. "Aw, I love that girl. How was it to see her again? How is she? Tell me everything."

"I will, but your pancake's burning." Jill gestured with the ladle, then poured some batter into the pan. "I feel terrible for the girls."

"Oh, well, okay, that *is* sad, only because they're hurting." Katie's face fell, and she picked up the spatula. "But they're better off without him, they just don't know it. He didn't really care about them. Narcissist, crook, thief, liar, sleaze, cheater."

"Cheating was unproven." Jill reached over and flipped one of Katie's pancakes. "Now, don't speak ill."

"You can't talk about William Skyler *without* speaking ill." Katie shook her head, disgusted. "I'm sorry, Jill, but he almost ruined you, and he kept those girls from you, too, after the divorce. He punished you, and he punished them, too. He used them like pawns to hurt you, and he straight-up *abandoned* Megan. I'll *never* forgive him for that, ever."

Jill tasted bitterness on her tongue. "Well, he's gone now. You want to hear what happened or not?"

"Yes, please," Katie answered, calming down, and while they cooked, Jill told her the whole story, from Abby's visit to the surveillance film at the pharmacy. Katie asked questions, Jill elaborated, and sixty-two pancakes later, the story was finished.

"You want to see the photo from the drugstore?" Jill went to her purse, slid out her BlackBerry, thumbed her way to the photo, and showed it to Katie. "Think it's him?"

"I can't see it, it's too small. Email it to me." Katie went over to her laptop on the counter near the chopped onions, and Jill emailed her the photo. They huddled around the computer while Katie opened the email, saved the photo, and enlarged it. Katie shook her head. "It could be William, but I can't tell."

"Me, neither. He could be disguising himself."

"Why would he do that?"

"I don't know." Jill dug in her purse. "Hold on, let me check something else on the web."

"What?"

"The prescribing doctor." Jill found the paper with Abby's notes, logged onto the Internet, Googled *licensing authority in Pennsylvania,* and got the website. "I have his license number, so I should be able to find his address."

"How?"

"Anybody can check the status of a doctor's license, online."

"I didn't know that."

"Most people don't. Luckily, Abby didn't." Jill found the Pennsylvania Department of State website, typed in Medicine, then supplied the doctor's name and license number from Abby's paper. She had to add a location, so she plugged in Philadelphia, then hit Search. The screen switched to a single line of text:

**Dr. Raj Patel, Lic. No. 9483636, DEA # 393484,
DECEASED, 3/9/09**

Jill felt her heart sink. "The prescribing doctor is dead, so Abby's right about one thing. This script is a fraud."

"Whoa."

"And it's not even recent, so it's not like the doc wrote the script, then died."

"Are you sure it's the same Dr. Patel?"

"Yes, it has to be. Only one doc is given that license or DEA number. They're unique." Jill shook her head. It meant that she couldn't put the matter to bed, not yet. "If it's William, he's up to his old tricks, using stolen prescription pads. But I don't know why he'd fill them himself, if it wasn't his meds."

"Wonder where he got Dr. Patel's pads?"

"He could have called on the practice in the old days,

or got them from the office trash." Jill opened the enlarged photo of the man in the black ballcap, eyeing it in confusion. "None of this makes sense. William knew enough about drugs to know not to mix them with alcohol."

"Is there life insurance?"

"Yes, for a million bucks. The girls benefit."

"We're worth more dead than alive, too."

Jill blinked, thinking. "That's funny. What if he took the pills intentionally? What if it really was suicide, but insurance companies don't always pay off for suicides. He wanted the policy to pay off, so he made it look like an accidental death? What if he staged the whole thing?"

"Why would he do that?" Katie's eyes narrowed, sharply blue. "He had money, so he didn't need it from the insurance company. Unless he doesn't really have the money, and it's all a sham."

"True, but I can't find that out. Victoria and the lawyer took his financial info, but some of it should be in Quicken."

"Definitely, if he pays his bills online."

"He didn't, at least when we were married. He said he didn't trust it."

"The pot calling the kettle." Katie snorted. "I don't see him killing himself for them. It would be a supremely unselfish act."

Both women fell silent a minute, thinking, and Jill picked at the pile of rejected potato pancakes. "I wonder if I should call the cops. Tell them about Patel and the faked script. They can check out the surveillance video."

"No reason not to call, but why would they care? It's not evidence that he was murdered, and they don't care if he committed suicide."

"The insurance company does." Jill thought of the implications. "But if it's suicide, and I start raising questions, I could do the kids out of their benefits."

"Right." Katie looked over, her brow wrinkling with new concern. "Can I ask you a question? Why do you care?"

Jill smiled, but Katie wasn't kidding this time.

"Who cares why or how William died?"

Jill answered, "I told you, Abby thinks it was murder."

"I'm asking why *you* care."

"I don't care, I'm just exploring it."

"It sure looks like you care. You're running around to drugstores and researching licenses online."

Jill realized she was right. She valued so many things about Katie, and her honesty, above all. "Okay, good point. I care because of Abby. She believes it was murder and she's going to try to figure out who did it. She reached out to me, after so long." Jill knew it now, she felt it inside. "I care because Abby does, and I can help her. She needs to get her life back on track, and she won't do that as long as her father's death is a question mark."

Katie shrugged. "Okay."

Jill smiled. "That easy?"

"It was such a good speech."

"So glad we had this little talk. Do you think I'm wrong to help Abby?"

"I don't judge you, honey. I understand why you'd want to help, and why you feel you have to."

"Sam doesn't."

"He didn't know her, and he's not a mother."

"He's a father."

"It's not the same. Sorry to be politically incorrect, but it's true." Katie ate a piece of blackened pancake. "Paul is a great father, but he got to take the kids out while I stayed behind, and I guarantee, he'll read the computer magazines while they pick out their books. He won't sit with them, helping them pick one like I would, and he won't worry if they get out of his sight. Men don't worry like we do, but we know, things go wrong."

"True." Jill saw it in her practice, when a child's eye got injured by a paintball gun, or an arm sliced with a fishing knife. She knew things went wrong, and some made wounds you couldn't suture.

"My real worry is my godchild. Megan." Katie's features softened. "You're talking about Abby's loss, but Megan lost a father, too, and William's death comes at a bad time for her, with you about to get married. And now Abby's back in the picture. Even if Megan's happy about it, it's a change. Megan's got a lot going on, for a kid."

"You're right." Jill felt a guilty pang. "It's like the King is dead, long live the King."

"Exactly."

"I guess I haven't been paying enough attention to Megan, with Abby so needy."

"It's understandable. Like my mother says, you give to the kid who needs it the most."

"What if they all need it the most?"

"Margarita time."

Jill smiled. "Sam wants to get out of the kid business."

Kate scoffed. "Gimme a break. Moms never get out of the kid business. Last time I checked, motherhood had no expiration date."

Jill laughed. "How'd you get so smart?"

Katie smiled. "Hanging around you, except for the padiddle part. First off, can I just say, I hate all car games?"

"Do you think the black SUV is following me? Or Abby?"

"No, that's totally paranoid. Don't worry about it."

"But what if the driver is the man in the black ballcap?"

"The man in the ballcap had the worst disguise ever, and anyone who would follow you in a padiddle is the worst stalker ever." Katie snorted. "Come to think of it, maybe it is the same guy, but he sucks."

"If he killed William, he doesn't."

"Tell me about it." Katie raised an eyebrow. "If he killed William, he deserves a medal."

# 16.

Jill pulled into her driveway and cut the ignition in the dark. She hadn't seen any padiddle on the way home, and she was starting to think Katie was right about her being paranoid. She got out of the car, breathing in the cool night air, damp from all the rain. She closed the door behind her, looking down at the end of the street where she'd seen the black SUV.

*What SUV? I parked around the corner.*

Jill thought a minute. She had first seen the SUV in front of the Bakers' house, but they didn't own an SUV, so on impulse, she walked down the street to the Bakers'. The lights were on inside the house, a Dutch colonial, and a flickering TV shone through the curtains in their living room, so she walked to the front door and knocked. It was answered in a minute by Janet Baker, an older woman with a round, sweet face.

"Hello, Janet," Jill said. "Sorry to bother you."

"It's okay." Janet smiled, pleasantly. "What brings you here?"

"Last night, during the rainstorm, did you have a visitor

who drives a black SUV? I saw one pull away from the front of your house."

Janet frowned, shaking her head. "Why, no. We were home alone. Just us."

"Do you know if the DiLorios did, or the Jacksons?"

"I have no idea."

"Thanks. Sorry to keep you. Goodnight." Jill backed off the steps, wondering, then put it out of her mind. It had to be nothing. She walked back down the street to her car, retrieved the box with William's files and laptop, then closed the door and went into the house, juggling her house keys, purse, and the box to open the door, which was when her cell phone started ringing, with Megan's ringtone.

"Arg." Jill clambered into the house to the sound of Lady Gaga, plunked the box on the console table, and slid her phone from her purse, pressing ANSWER. "Honey, aren't you home?"

"No, I'm at Courtney's. Can I sleep over?"

"Again?" Jill sat down in a ladderback chair, and Beef came over, wagging his tail and sniffing the box, which had a paper plate of pancakes on top, covered with tin foil.

"I know, but we're working on our English project, and we're not finished yet."

"What is this project, anyway?" Jill could hear the sound of the TV, playing in the family room.

"We're studying *Romeo and Juliet,* and we have to memorize a scene and do it for the class, so we have to practice together. I'm Juliet."

"How much longer will you take to finish?"

"A while, Mom," Megan answered, with theatrical impatience, and Jill let it go, trying to take it easy on her.

"You can come home after you finish it. I'll pick you up, whenever."

"Why can't I just stay here? Her parents are home."

"But I was hoping to see you tonight. I know it's been a tough weekend for you, and I'm worried about you."

"I'm fine, Mom." Megan sighed, and in the background, Courtney was saying something.

"I have fresh potato pancakes," Jill offered, though the days of food bribes had gone. Pizza bagels used to be her trump card. "Wait, don't you have a meet tomorrow?"

"Yes, but I'll sleep, I promise."

"Okay, you can stay, but don't make it a habit."

"Thanks. Courtney's mom will take me to the meet, if you can bring my bag. It starts at noon, at the high school. Also, did you order that book for my report?"

Jill had forgotten. "No, but I will. When do you need it by?"

"Next Monday. Courtney orders online all the time, by herself, from her iPhone. Why can't I do that?"

"Because you don't have an iPhone."

"That's not funny, Mom."

Jill laughed to herself. "I'll take care of it, honey."

"Thanks, I gotta go. Love you. Bye."

"See you tomorrow. Sleep tight. Love you, too." Jill hung up, set the phone down, and petted Beef on the head, his brushy tail awag. Sam hadn't greeted her, which wasn't like him, and she owed him an apology. She got up and went into the family room, but he'd fallen asleep on the couch, his book open on his chest and his glasses pushed onto his head, so his hair puffed through the nosepiece. The TV played on low volume, and Jill thought of the scene that Abby had described, when she found William lying in bed with the TV playing.

*Dad never filled those scripts. They were planted there by the killer.*

Jill shuddered, going to the kitchen, where she slipped Beef a piece of pancake and put the rest in the fridge. She went out to the entrance hall, got the box with the laptop and files, brought everything back into the kitchen, set it on the island, then sat down and dug in.

The manila folder on top was labeled MEDICAL INFO, and she opened it and skimmed through. It contained William's lab reports for his bloodwork, and the results were normal. The only drugs William reported as taking regularly were Crestor, 10mg, and Co Q 10, commonly taken with statins. There was no mention of any other prescription drugs, so either he wasn't taking them or he was lying.

Jill went through the rest of the files, determined they were nothing but old bills, so she closed the box and opened the laptop, plugging it into the island outlet and getting busy. An hour later, she'd gone through William's laptop, but had found nothing unusual. His email was between his golf buddies, Abby, Victoria, Neil Straub, and various women, a sharing of blog posts, articles, YouTube links, and plans for golf dates or dinners. The email was more significant for what it didn't contain rather than what it did. There was nothing about his business investments, which had to be what was paying for his house, lifestyle, and the girls.

She navigated back to Quicken and skimmed the entries, which were equally mundane, and he still wasn't paying his bills online, so she couldn't connect to his bank files. It only took her twenty minutes to make a spreadsheet for Abby, because the household expenses were so routine, and there were no other financial files. She went back to the Programs files, but the laptop had only the programs the computer came with, and not much else.

She eyed the laptop, in thought. It was almost generic, as if it had been sanitized or kept purposely clean. She went online, clicked on the online history, and it was empty, erased. She went to the deleted email file, and it had been completely emptied, too. So either William had cleaned out this laptop or someone had done it for him.

Jill tried another tack. If she worked under Abby's theory and assumed that somebody killed him, it had to be someone close to him, since there had been no sign of a struggle or break-in at the house. So all she had to do was figure out who was close to him. She went into My Computer, scanned the list of programs, and found My Pictures. She clicked to open the file, and there were three file icons, the oldest dating only from a year ago: **London trip with girls, Victoria's graduation weekend, Neil at Pebble Beach**. She skipped to the folder with Neil, to see if he was a viable candidate for the man in the black ballcap, despite what Abby had said.

Jill opened the pictures folder, and there were photos of William on a golf course with Neil, who was wearing a white Callaway ballcap and aviator sunglasses similar to those worn by the man in the black ballcap. The outfit obscured some of Neil's features, but he had a winning smile and a strong, jutting chin and he was tall and well-built, about William's height and weight. Jill clicked, and more of the file photos flashed by, but they were all taken outdoors and Neil wore sunglasses in every one, and so did William, in a few shots. She clicked a photo of them together and hit PRINT.

She went online and Googled Neil Straub, but there were no listings. She checked him on Facebook, and he was on, but he'd blocked his profile except to his friends and had no picture. She logged onto www.whitepages.com for his address and plugged in New York, but no address came up, so it must have been unlisted. Neil Straub kept a low profile, and Jill wondered why.

Just then her phone rang, and the screen flashed a number she didn't recognize. It was almost eleven o'clock at night, and it could have been a patient. She answered the phone. "Jill Farrow."

"It's Victoria. Let me speak to Abby."

"Victoria," Jill repeated, startled at the sound of Victoria's voice. She had heard it so many times before that she could've picked it out in a choir, and had, at so many school concerts, when Victoria was growing up. Victoria sang in a clear, strong alto, ringing with certainty, always pitch-perfect, more than a match for the showy top notes of the sopranos in the Stafford High Select Chorale, and her voice stood out so much for its clarity that the choir director had given Victoria a solo, even as a freshman, which had terrified the reserved young girl. That night, Victoria had called Jill from backstage, in a panic before she went on.

*Jill, I can't do it, I'm going to forget the words. I can't solo!*

*Victoria, relax, you can do it, I know you can.* Jill answered the call, sitting in the audience with Abby and Megan, at another concert that William had missed, supposedly working late.

*Where are you guys sitting? Are you in your regular seats?*

*Yes, stage left, front row. We'll be right in front of you. Just forget everything and sing, honey. Sing it out. Let everybody hear your voice. We know you're wonderful, and it's time to show everybody else.*

And after the concert, Victoria had come running, her eyes alive with pride and happiness, her arms reaching for Jill.

*I sang it to you, Jill. I sang it to you.*

"Jill, put Abby on," Victoria was saying, her voice now so cold that the disconnect left Jill shaken.

"First, Victoria, let me tell you how sorry I am about—"

"Put Abby on, please. I need to speak with her."

Jill swallowed hard, recovering. "Listen, she's not here, and I'm so sorry about your father's death, and about what happened at the memorial service. I know this is an impossibly difficult time for you, and I wouldn't have come if I had known—"

"Save it, okay, Jill? I need to speak to Abby. I know she's there. I also know you were at the house with her tonight, and I told her not to go home with you, but once again, she didn't listen. Put her on, please."

"She's not here, Victoria. She didn't come home with me, after your call." Jill moderated her tone, trying to open the door between them. She couldn't accept that Victoria was a stranger, when she used to be her daughter.

"You're incredible, you know that? Let me talk to my sister, now. Stop lying for her."

"I'm not lying. I never lied to you, honey." The term of endearment just slipped out of Jill's mouth, and she knew it was the wrong thing to say before Victoria raised her voice.

"Don't call me *honey*! That works on Abby, but not on me. Put her on, now."

"I swear to you, Abby's not here." Jill's thoughts shifted from Victoria to Abby, and she started to worry. "When did you see her last?"

"None of your business. She's probably at work, but they don't pick up the phone."

"She's not at work. She quit her job."

"She *quit*? How do *you* know?"

"She told me. Could she be on a date? She might have been last night. She was drinking when she came over."

"There's a shocker," Victoria said, drily.

"Do you know who that was? Was it Santos? Could they be back together?"

"Again, how do *you* know about Santos? Boy, you don't waste a minute, do you?" Victoria snorted. "My father just died, Jill. Can't you hold your horses before you try to worm your way back into my family?"

Jill didn't want to fight. It was bad enough that she and

Victoria were so far apart. "Do you have Santos's phone number?"

"No, he moved back to Brazil. She could have picked somebody up at random. She does that, you know. She goes out a lot, she likes to party."

Jill cringed. "On the night of her father's memorial service? She didn't seem like she was up for a party when I left her. Did you call any of her friends?"

"I don't even know her friends. They didn't even care enough to show up at the memorial service."

"Are you going to the house to check on her?"

"No, Jill. I'm not her mother, and here's a news flash, neither are *you*. Good-bye."

"Wait, please call me if you hear from her, or ask her to call me."

"Like you care?"

"I *do,* Victoria. I care about you both. Please, call me or—"

Victoria hung up, leaving Jill holding the phone, and she pressed END. She scrolled back to her phone log, found Abby's phone number, and pressed CALL. It rang and rang, then the voicemail came on, with Abby saying, "I'm having too much fun to take your call! Leave a message!" The beep sounded, and Jill said, "Abby, I'm worried about you. Please call me and let me know how you are. Victoria called, looking for you, too. Call me anytime, no matter how late. Love you."

Jill hung up, worrying. It seemed odd that Abby wasn't home tonight. Abby would have no reason to go out, and she didn't seem strong or stable enough to party. Jill thought of the padiddle. The man in the ballcap. The surveillance video. The sanitized laptop.

Suddenly, Jill didn't think it was completely outlandish that William had been murdered, then something else dawned on her, with a shock. If William had been murdered, Abby could be in danger, too. Abby lived in the same house as William. Maybe she had seen the killer and didn't know it, or overheard something or saw something else, or maybe the killer merely thought she did. Whatever William was up to could destroy Abby, as well.

*I love you, Jill.*

Jill felt a bolt of fear at the notion. She couldn't bear it if anything happened to Abby. She jumped up like a shot and went running to the family room.

"Sam!" she called out, stricken.

# 17.

Jill sat in the chair across from Sam, having told him about the surveillance tape, the forged script, and the black SUV, at warp speed. Beef slept on the rug, his back legs twitching in a doggie dream, and the TV was playing a late-night talk show, on mute. Sam had calmed her down, listening carefully to her, looking over the top of his glasses, sitting forward on the couch, resting his arms on his thighs, his concern etched into every line on his face.

Jill asked, "So what do you think, honey?"

"I think a lot of things." Sam raked a hand through his hair. A glass of soda with melted ice sat next to him on the oak end table. "I must admit, it does seem strange, especially that the prescribing doctor was dead."

"I know, right?" Jill felt a rush of validation, but an equal measure of worry for Abby.

"It's what William did to you, stealing the pads, so it suggests it was him filling the script."

"Why would he disguise himself?"

"In case someone found out it was a phony script. To avoid prosecution."

"Right. I didn't think of that." Jill rubbed her face. "My

brain must not be working, I keep thinking about Abby. Where could she be?"

"Anywhere." Sam's expression cooled, and he slid off his glasses.

"What if she's in danger? Or trouble?"

"I doubt that she is." Sam checked his watch. "It's one o'clock in the morning, and we know she likes to have a good time."

"She wasn't having a good time last night, Sam. She was in pain."

"Okay, fair point."

"I wish she lived close, I could go check on her." Jill tried to suppress her fears, but failed. "Anything could have happened to her, even in the house. She could have had too much to drink and fallen down the stairs. She's so alone. She has no one looking out for her."

"She has a sister."

"Who's in disapproval frenzy."

Sam lifted an eyebrow. "Maybe she deserves it."

"Nobody deserves it, Sam."

"People who drink and drive do."

"Don't judge her, help her."

"Stop." Sam put up both hands. "We are. I am. Could we change the subject and talk about you, instead of her? The black SUV following you, that concerns me. It might be nothing, but I'd prefer it if we played it safe."

"And did what?"

"Stay out of this. Who knows what William got himself into?" Sam frowned, deeply. "I don't think you should get further involved."

"I didn't mean to, it's just happening."

Sam pursed his lips. "The drugstore didn't just happen, Jill."

"I didn't expect the answer that I got."

"Understood. So stop, now. Tell the cops, and let them

handle it." Sam shook his head. "I don't want you in harm's way. Or Megan."

"I would never endanger Megan."

"You may have, already. You're worried about Abby's safety, what about hers or yours?" Sam gestured at the door. "You're saying the SUV was on our street, for God's sake."

"I didn't realize it." Jill felt defensive, her thoughts confused. "It might not have been the same car."

"Is it or isn't it? Why take a chance? Do you really want to bring trouble to our door, and for what? It's police business, not ours." Sam raised his hands slowly, palms up. "Why am I so involved in your ex-husband's life's, all of a sudden? Why are you?"

"I don't think of it as his life, honey. I think of it as Abby's life."

"It's the same result, isn't it? It's all about him. You're on his laptop, reading his email, trying to find his business partner. Until yesterday, your ex was dead to you. And now that he's dead, he's come back to life."

"Don't be that way." Jill could see he was hurt, even jealous, which was so unlike him. "I can't just give up on Abby."

"She's not yours to give up."

"It's a figure of speech."

"No, it's not." Sam sighed heavily, and just like that, they were at an impasse.

Jill looked around the family room, with its cheery, red-checked couch and white ginger lamps. She had picked out new furniture after she was divorced, and this house was smaller than the one she'd lived in with William and the girls. When Sam had moved in, they'd added a picture rail for his photographs and bookshelves for his collection of first editions. They'd worked together on the room, and they'd succeeded in making a new home and a new family, until now. The family room didn't define the family anymore, and Jill knew they needed to find some middle ground.

She met Sam's eye. "You're right about the police. I'll call them tomorrow. I'll tell them about the forged script and the SUV."

"Good, thanks." Sam rose stiffly, offering his hand. "Why don't we go to bed and hope that Abby's back in the morning?"

"Honestly, I know I won't sleep. I can't rest until I know everybody's safe, all under one roof."

"She has a different roof, babe." Sam let his hand drop to his side, and Jill wanted to clear the air, once and for all.

"I know that, but it seems like a technicality, doesn't it?"

"No."

"Really?" Jill didn't understand. "What if she's injured, Sam? Or missing? Doesn't that change your analysis?"

"No." Sam stood firm, straightening up. "Did it occur to you that her disappearing act could be a bid for attention? It's inconsiderate, at best. You're back in her life, and she loves it. She loves you. You heard her last night."

"I love her, too. That's real, honest emotion, not manipulation."

"Is it, on her part?" Sam cocked his head. "What was she thinking, inviting you to the memorial service and not telling her sister? She had to know there would be a scene."

"She didn't expect that reaction."

"Come on, Jill. If you ask me, the kid's acting out to keep you involved with her, taking your attention away from Megan and me."

"You? That's crazy, Sam."

"No, it isn't. I'm the guy who replaced her father. She was downright hostile to me last night."

"She was drunk, and she doesn't even know you."

"Okay, enough. I'm out of gas. I'm going to bed. Wanna come?"

"No, not just yet." Jill felt torn, betwixt and between, again. She loved having Abby back in the fold. It made her feel whole again, filling the Abby-shaped hole in her heart, like the blank cutout from a sheet of cookie dough. "I'm not tired, and I just can't go to sleep like nothing's wrong."

"One last thing, babe. Ask yourself whether you're getting involved with Abby because Megan's pulling away."

"Do you believe that?"

"Doesn't matter. What I said was, ask yourself." Sam put his hands on his slim hips. "You don't have to answer to me, you have to answer yourself. Maybe you're getting what you want, in Abby. A kid to worry about, a kid to raise. Because Megan is growing up, the way she's supposed to. Maybe you want to have a baby forever, to replace her."

Jill opened her mouth to object, then shut it. She knew he was wrong, but he had a working hypothesis, and she couldn't talk him out of it, tonight.

"Either way, I love you. Goodnight." Sam leaned over, placed his hands on the arms of her chair, and gave her a dry kiss on the lips. But when he pulled away, he didn't meet her eye, and his expression looked troubled. "I'll let the dog out."

"No, I will. You've done enough today."

"Thanks." Sam flashed her a tired smile, then turned to go.

"Love you, too," Jill called after him, listening to the sound of his footfalls disappearing. She didn't like the distant look in his eyes, one she'd never seen before, and she could feel a new rift between them, as if suddenly they were on two separate ice floes, drifting apart on a vast and frigid sea.

*Jill, I love you, so much, you're my mom.*

Jill got up and hurried into the kitchen.

# 18.

Jill crossed to the coffeemaker and popped in a pod, then set a mug underneath and hit BREW. She couldn't ignore the sensation that Abby was in trouble. Abby's drinking worried her, and it was possible that she was passed out in a club or an alley somewhere.

Jill picked up the phone and checked her messages, but Abby still hadn't called her back, so she called her again and left another message, saying the same thing. On impulse, Jill called the University of Pennsylvania Hospital in Philly, transferred to the emergency room, and asked for Abby Skyler or a Jane Doe with Abby's age and description. No luck. Meanwhile, the coffee had brewed, and Jill slid it out, took a hot sip, then called Temple and Hahnemann hospitals, but Abby hadn't been at either of their ERs or admitted.

Jill took the mug back to the laptop and moved the mouse. There was nothing more she could do for Abby right now, so she told herself to be patient. She stared at the screen for a moment, feeling the weight of Sam's words and wondering if she'd been giving short shrift to Megan. Katie had said almost the same thing, and Jill was beginning to sense a consensus. She'd have to make sure to take care of Megan, too, and even that seemed a familiar balancing act, from her days as a mom of three.

She had to get Megan that Lincoln book, so she navigated to an online bookseller, plugged *Lincoln's Ghost* into the search, and waited for the book to come up. It appeared, and she clicked SEND TO CART, but then realized she might have to rush it to make sure it got here in time, so she reviewed the order form, changed the shipping preferences, and looked at the shipping addresses, which was when it struck her.

The list contained all the people who were closest to her, both past and present. She'd never deleted the older addresses, and it still had her mother's home address and Sam's old condo address. William could have had a list like that, too, online. He used to shop online and was always sending gifts to doctors, nurses, and secretaries whose offices he called on, to grease his sales calls. Jill even knew his passwords, but she didn't need them. She had his laptop.

She palmed the mouse, went online, and plugged in the website. The flash screen came up, offering an array of new and upcoming books, and at the top, it read, **WELCOME, WILLIAM!** She navigated to My Account, which had all of his account settings, including Addresses, and the Default Address was the house on Acorn Street in Philadelphia. She clicked Manage Addresses, and a list of old addresses popped on the screen, some twenty odd long.

Jill shifted onto the edge of her seat. William had sanitized his laptop, but he'd forgotten to erase information that was stored online. The second address on his list was an apartment in Philly, to which he and the girls moved after the divorce, and after that was their old home address. Next was a string of doctors' office addresses, with the names of office managers, followed by a few women with addresses in and around Philadelphia, presumably girlfriends. There was a group of men on the list, but all of them were doctors except for the one she'd hoped to find: **Neil Straub,** with an apartment address on West 11th Street, in Manhattan.

Jill picked up her phone, called information in New York City, and asked for the phone number, but the automated voice said they didn't have the listing. She pressed 0 for an operator and reached a supervisor who looked up the number, then came back on the line, saying, "I'm sorry, we can't give out that number."

Jill hung up, with a growing suspicion that Neil and William had been up to no good. She'd found out as much as she could about Neil for now, but she could find out about the others on the address list, and maybe they would yield information about him or lead to something else. Maybe there would be some connection to Abby, or at the very least, it would give Jill something to do until she could call Abby and the hospitals again.

She printed the address list, then got to work.

# 19.

Jill woke up in front of her laptop at the island, with a shaft of sunlight coming through the windows over the sink. The kitchen was bright and still, and the wall clock read 6:15 A.M. Her first thought was of Abby, and she prayed that she'd called or texted. She picked up her BlackBerry and checked her messages, but there was nothing from Abby, or Victoria. None of her patients had called either, including Padma, but Jill wouldn't rest until Rahul's blood-work came in.

Beef came over from his dog bed, wagging his tail slowly, and she patted him on his soft head, scrolled to her call log, found Abby's number, and pressed CALL on the way to the back door, to let him out. The call rang as she unlocked the deadbolt, and Beef trotted outside, with Jill behind. It was a clear Sunday morning, the neighborhood quiet and peaceful, because it was too early for leafblow-ers and lawnmowers. Their backyard was large, a full, flat acre with a pool, bounded by a tall privacy fence. Pin oaks shaded the left end of the property, which was Beef territory.

Jill stood in the sunshine, letting it warm her and

hoping Abby would pick up the phone. She listened to the ringing, but there was no answer, so she left another message, then pressed END. She scrolled back to her call log, pressed in the number for the Penn ER, and asked again about Abby. Still no luck. She called Temple and Hahnemann, but Abby hadn't been in there, either.

She checked her phone for the time, and it was 6:35. She wanted to go to Abby's house to check on her, but she'd have to leave soon to be back in time for Megan's meet. She found Victoria's number in the log and pressed CALL.

"Jill?" Victoria answered, groggy. "Why the hell are you calling me so early?"

"I'm sorry to bother you, but I didn't hear from Abby. Did you?"

"No. You woke me up."

"I'm sorry, really. She hasn't returned my calls, and I want to check on her, but I don't have the keys. Do you know if any of the neighbors have a set?"

"I don't know, and are you *nuts*? What's your problem, Jill? Stay out of it, would you?"

Jill had expected the reaction. She kept her tone conciliatory. "I'm worried she fell down the stairs, hurt herself, or can't get to the door somehow."

"She didn't fall. She's not an old lady. Jeez!"

"If she was drinking, she could have fallen and aspirated her own vomit. It happens, Victoria. People die from that."

Victoria scoffed. "I thought you said she wouldn't go out partying last night."

Jill bit her tongue. "What if I was wrong? Do you have keys?"

"Yes."

"Will you meet me there?" Jill asked, hoping against hope. She couldn't drive to Victoria's apartment in Central Jersey and still get back in time for Megan's meet.

"Why would I do that?"

"Because you love your sister."

"Right," Victoria shot back. "I love her enough not to enable her."

Jill wasn't getting anywhere, so she went for it. "Victoria, I think a car might have followed her to my house the other night, and I think it's been following me. It's a black SUV, and the license plate was T something. Do you know it? Does she date anybody who drives a black SUV?"

"No." Victoria scoffed. "How do you know it was following her?"

"I don't, for sure, but it had one headlight. I noticed it because it was a padiddle, that game we used to play."

"You think a *padiddle* is following her? Really? Did you spy it with your little eye?"

Jill didn't know how to convince her. "Besides that, the pills that were found in your father's bedroom were prescribed by a doctor who's been dead for years. It was a forged prescription."

"Are you saying Dad *forged* his prescription?"

"Either he or someone trying to—"

"He would *never* do that. Are you crazy? Really, are you? None of this is your business."

Jill wanted those keys. "Victoria, you don't know this, but if you meet me, I can explain. He did it once before—"

Victoria gasped. "Stop it right now. Did you wake me up to trash Dad? What's the matter with you? You're a sick woman."

"Please, meet me and give me the keys, for Abby's sake."

"No, this is all about *you*. She's fine, you're the *freak*." Victoria hung up, and Jill pressed END, agitated. Beef came trotting forward, wagging his tail, and she turned to see Sam coming out the back door with a soft smile, in his T-shirt, running shorts, and bare feet. He met her and gave her a big hug, holding her close.

"Sounds like that went well," he said, sadly, and as Jill hugged him back, she felt that the tension of last night had diminished, and they were reconnecting, almost back to themselves again.

"I'd kiss you, but my breath stinks."

"Kiss me, anyway."

Jill went on tiptoe to give him a kiss. "Tastes like stale coffee, right?"

"No." Sam smiled. "Tastes like wife."

"I love you." Jill smiled back, but her thoughts returned to Abby. "Are we allowed to talk about Abby?"

"Yes." Sam smiled, crookedly.

"She's still not answering, and I want to go downtown and check on her. Megan has a meet today, and Courtney's mom is taking her. It starts at noon but I can be back in time, don't you think? She won't swim until one o'clock or so."

"Yes, and I'll go downtown with you."

"No, thanks, I can go alone."

"I wish you wouldn't." Sam's expression darkened. "I slept on it, and though I don't think your ex was murdered, I'm worried about this SUV."

"I'll keep an eye out for it. On a Sunday morning, I'd spot it a mile away, there's no traffic. Besides, Megan needs her swim bag, and if I run late, I can't get it to her."

"We can drop it off on our way out."

"And wake up Courtney's family? Their dogs bark like crazy."

"Then we can leave it at school."

"The meet's at the high school. It won't be open, and where would we leave it? They don't know her there." Jill gave his arm a squeeze. "Thanks, but it's best if you stay. If there are any problems, I'll call the police."

Sam pursed his lips "You're supposed to be calling the police today anyway, correct?"

"Yes, I will, after I check on Abby." Jill gave him a final hug and patted Beef good-bye. "I'll pack Megan's bag before I go."

"I can do it. But be careful in Philly, will you? Any sign of that SUV, call 911, then call me. Text me when you get there."

"Will do."

"Wait. What are you going to do if Abby doesn't answer the door?"

"I'll knock until she does, or I can see if her car is there, so I'll know she's home."

"You don't have a key to the house, do you?"

"No, but I hope a neighbor does. We always used to do that, just in case."

"By 'we,' do you mean you and William?" Sam lifted an eyebrow, but he smiled.

"Yes. Sorry."

"We're going to stop talking about him by our wedding, no?"

"Promise," Jill answered, and took off.

# 20.

Jill zoomed into town and didn't see any black SUVs as she hit the on-ramp toward Society Hill. She made it in no time and found a parking space on Acorn Street, cut the ignition, texted Sam that she was fine, and got out of the car. The sun slashed through the trees along the street, and a breeze disturbed the leaves of the trees, but it was too early on a Sunday morning for anyone to be out, even tourists.

Jill made a beeline for William's house, hustled up the steps, and rang the bell. She rang it again, then again, but no answer. She knocked on the door, rapping hard with her knuckles. "Abby?" she called out, loud enough to be heard without waking the entire block. "It's me, Jill! Open up!" She waited, then called out again, knocking, but there was no reply.

She peeked in the front window, edging over on the stoop, but she couldn't see anything. The window was too high in the wall, and a massive shade covered the bottom. There were no lights on inside the house, and she didn't know if Abby was home, but she knew a way to find out. She climbed down the front steps and continued down the street until she came to the break in the rowhouses. She'd lived in the city during her residency and she knew that alleys usually ran behind the rowhouses.

She took a right and hurried down the alley, which changed to a stone walkway that led to a pocket parking lot. Each house had two parking spaces, and the lot was full. There was a cheap orange Datsun parked right behind a black Mercedes sedan, and they had to be Abby's and William's cars. Jill worried anew. So Abby was home, but she wasn't answering the door? Was she hurt inside the house? Or had she gone somewhere, with someone who had driven her? Jill went over to Abby's car and peered inside. Balled-up Trident wrappers dotted the passenger's seat, next to an empty water bottle and a hairbrush. On impulse, she went over and looked inside William's car, and it was predictably immaculate.

She straightened up, then noticed something. The house had a back door, painted dark blue. She walked around the cars and down another stone walkway that ran along the back of the houses, stopping at the door with house number 363. A recycling container sat outside it, next to a galvanized trash can. She banged on the door, and called, "Abby, Abby!"

"Hey! What are you doing?" said a stern voice behind her, and Jill turned around to see an older man in a green track suit, with a newspaper tucked under his arm. He was standing in the lot, his lined brow furrowed and his hooded eyes glowering behind bifocals.

"Hello, I'm Jill Farrow, Abby's stepmother, and I'm looking for her. Are you a neighbor?"

"It depends." The man frowned, but his tone softened. "Abby's the girl who lives here?"

"Yes, that's her car." Jill gestured at the Datsun. "She's home but she doesn't answer the door. Her father, who lived here, died last Tuesday, and I'm worried about her."

"Oh, I didn't know that." The man's forehead relaxed. "My condolences. Name's Ernie Berg."

"Hi, Ernie." Jill walked over and shook his hand. "Where do you live?"

"Two doors down, on Acorn." Ernie pointed at a black Lincoln. "That's my car."

"Have you seen Abby recently?"

"No, not recently. Pretty girl, and she always waves. I'm retired, so I'm home, and I see most things on the street. I'm on the Town Watch, too."

Jill knew it was a lucky break. "How about William, then? Her father? Do you see him much? The Mercedes is his."

"I know who you mean, but he's not around that much. That night, guess it was a few days ago, the street was full of police, even the medical examiner. Quite a to-do." Ernie shook his head. "He was too young, wasn't he? What did he die of?"

"A reaction to a prescription drug."

"That's too bad. I didn't know him, but a man that young, that's too bad. I asked him to be on the Town Watch, but he said no. Said he was traveling all the time."

Jill made a mental note. "Do you know the neighbors on either side? I'm wondering if they've seen her or if they have a key to the house."

"You can forget about that. The Wilsons and the Eraskos. The Wilsons are skiing, and the Eraskos are on some college tour, with the son. He plays basketball. Heavily recruited."

Jill felt defeated, momentarily. "I'm worried that Abby's in the house and fell or something. She lives alone now that her father died."

"I'd worry, too." Ernie buckled his lower lip. "Most fatal accidents occur in the home. Might be time to go to the police. We discourage the use of 911, when it's not an emergency, and our precinct house is just a few blocks away. We're in the Sixth District."

"You think I should go?"

Ernie shrugged. "How many daughters you got?"

Jill was about to answer "three" when she realized it was rhetorical.

# 21.

Jill hustled toward the police station, which was an aging, low-rise building of nicotine yellow brick, shaped like a grocery-store sheet cake. It had a stop-time blue sign with art-deco letters that read POLICE 6TH DISTRICT, and a parking lot beside the building held a handful of white cruisers bearing the distinctive yellow-and-blue stripe of the Philadelphia Police. There weren't any cops on the street or out front, and she hurried inside the smudged stainless-steel-and-glass entrance.

She found herself in a hallway of dingy tile that ended in a forbidding steel door, obviously locked. To the right was a pay phone, and to the left was a poster that read CURFEW CRACKDOWN, then a small sliding window in a blue frame. She crossed to the window, which revealed a rectangular room barely large enough to fit four old desks of gray metal, arranged cheek-by-jowl, each with a black swivel chair. Two of the chairs were occupied by a female and male police officer, and the female looked up, rose, and came to the window.

"Good morning, I'm Officer Mendina," she said, pleasantly. Her nameplate read Veronica Mendina, and her blue shirt matched the earnest hue of her eyes. Her thick brown bangs were held off her forehead by a bobby pin. "May I help you?"

"Hi, I'm Jill Farrow, and I'm worried that my former stepdaughter is hurt in her house, or missing. Her name is Abby Skyler, and she lives on Acorn Street. Her car is there, but there's no answer at the door."

"How old is she?"

"Nineteen."

"When was the last time you saw her?"

"Around seven o'clock last night, and she hasn't returned my calls or her sister's. Her father just died, and she believes he was murdered."

Officer Mendina's eyes flared. "She believes he was? Was it ruled a homicide or not?"

"No, it wasn't, but she still believes it was." Jill realized something. "Would you be the ones who investigated it, when the police were called? His name was William Skyler."

"No, that's Central Detectives, up on 21st Street. So you say she's missing, but it's only been one night. Does she usually stay out all night?"

"I don't know, I don't live with her. I'm a mom, so I worry."

"I hear that." Officer Mendina reached under the window and pulled out a form, revealing a black Glock holstered on one hip. On her other hip was a radio, its stiff antenna sticking up like a black spire. "Now what did you say your daughter's name was? Also, I'll need to see an ID."

"She's not my daughter."

"I thought you said she was."

"No, she's my ex-stepdaughter." Jill went into her purse, got her driver's license, and slid it across the sill. "I used to be her stepmother, and both of her parents are dead."

Officer Mendina examined the driver's license. "Are you her legal guardian, Dr. Farrow?"

"No."

"Then what exactly is your relationship to the girl, again?" Officer Mendina returned the driver's license, but withheld the form.

"I'm her ex-stepmother. I was married to her father, who died last Tuesday."

"Then you don't have standing to file a missing persons. Sorry." Officer Mendina put the form away.

"Does it matter who reports it? She's hurt or missing, that's all that matters." Jill pulled a photo from her purse that she'd printed from William's laptop before she left the house. It showed all of them together, down the Jersey shore. "Look, this is us, from when I was married to her father. The long-haired one is Abby."

Officer Mendina scrutinized the photo. "Who's this other girl, the tall one?"

"Her sister, Victoria. Can she file a report?"

"No, she can't. You say the girl's over eighteen, so she's legally an adult, and it's not against the law to want to be left alone. It's only one night."

"But can you check the house? She's been so distraught since her father died, and drinking."

"I'm sorry, I can't help you. Our manpower is limited, and we can't go chasing down every nineteen-year-old who has a few beers." Officer Mendina pursed her unlipsticked lips, and Jill saw empathy in her eyes.

"But she's just been orphaned, and that's hard at any age. Are you a mother? Can't you just check on her?"

Officer Mendina paused. "Wait here. I'll talk to my supervisor."

"Thank you, I really appreciate it." Jill watched her walk back to the office and disappear out of view, and she returned a few minutes later with a shortish,

African-American police officer in a white shirt. He had wire-rimmed glasses and a serious expression, and he walked over to the window with Officer Mendina, then took the lead.

"I'm Sergeant Destin, and I'll tell you what we can do for you. I'm going to send Officer Mendina and another officer of mine to do a walk-through of the house. Make sure everything's okay."

"Thank you so much," Jill said, grateful.

"You can't file a report, but we can make sure nothing's going on inside. We can also talk to the neighbors, see if any of them saw her, and put your mind at ease. You say you don't live with her, though?"

"No, I don't."

"You have keys? We don't break in."

Jill had assumed they would, unfortunately. "I don't, but I can get you some. Gimme an hour."

"Do it, and we'll meet you there. What's the number on Acorn?"

"382."

"Okay." Sergeant Destin checked his thick watch. "Wait for us at the house."

"Thanks so much." Jill turned, slid out her cell phone, and scrolled down for Victoria's phone number as she hurried out of the police station. The call rang twice, then connected. "Victoria, it's Jill."

"Don't tell me, let me guess. Abby's over your house. Does she have her own bedroom yet?"

"She's not with me." Jill hurried toward her car, which was parked in front of the Vietnamese restaurant next door. "I need you to meet me at your father's house, with the keys. The police are going to go inside and—"

"The *police*? What do they want?"

"They're coming to the house to check it out and—"

"What are you doing? This is none of your business, Jill."

"Victoria, please don't give me a hard time. I'm worried that Abby is inside and may be hurt. Her car is there but she doesn't answer." Jill got her car key, then chirped the door open. "Just come with the keys. Please."

"I can't, I have to study."

"It can't be helped." Jill climbed inside her front seat, keeping a lid on her temper. "I know you love your sister, so please come."

"I don't need you to tell me whether I love my sister or not. I have a life, Jill. I'm not my sister's keeper."

"Victoria, if you don't come open the door, they'll break it down." Jill would tell a white lie, if it saved Abby's life. "You have to come with the keys, as soon as possible."

"Damn you! This is a total and complete waste of time." Victoria hung up.

Jill pressed END, set the BlackBerry down, and slid the key into the ignition. The engine and dashboard clock came to life, glowing a digital 8:03. She had time, but she had to hustle.

She hit the gas, took a right onto Vine Street, then headed back toward Society Hill.

# 22.

Jill stood in front of William's house waiting for Victoria, while Officer Mendina and a heavyset male cop were knocking on the neighbors' doors, asking about Abby. The block was waking up, and young couples, groups of tourists, and runners eyed the police and their two cruisers, their presence causing a commotion. Suddenly a white BMW steered onto the street and drove toward them, and Jill spotted Victoria in the passenger seat. Her friend Brian was driving, and Jill hustled toward the car.

Victoria got out when the BMW slowed to a stop, double-parking to drop her off, and her lovely hazel eyes glittered as they surveyed the street. She must have dressed quickly, but still looked put together in a white sweater, skinny jeans, and ballet flats. Her makeup was perfect, and her blonde hair twisted into a tortoiseshell barrette.

"What the hell is going on, Jill?" she asked, angrily. "This is a circus."

"I'm really sorry to take you from your studies." Jill kept her tone even, still hoping to reconnect. "If you give your keys to the cops, they can do a walk-through—"

"Hell to the *no*." Victoria turned away, hoisted her purse to her shoulder, and stalked off toward the police, and Jill fell into step beside her.

"Victoria, look, I'm sorry, but—"

"I told you, you can bulldoze your way into Abby's life, but keep out of mine. Now, don't speak to me."

Jill took it on the chin, and they both walked to meet Officer Mendina, who was climbing down the steps of a rowhouse and slipping a long white pad into her back pocket. She strode toward them, frowning under the patent bill of her cap.

"Dr. Farrow," Officer Mendina called out, with a wave. When she got closer, she said, "No one's seen the girl this week, or seen anything else suspicious at the house or on the street, except the day her father passed. Do you have the house keys?"

"Right here," Jill answered, gesturing at Victoria. "Officer Mendina, this is—"

"Jill, excuse me, I can introduce myself." Victoria edged Jill aside. "Hello, Officer, I'm Victoria Skyler, Abby's sister. I'm also a law student at Seton Hall, and I object to these tactics by the police. You have no right to break down the door to my father's house."

"Hold on a minute, Ms. Skyler." Officer Mendina raised a hand. "I'm sorry about your loss, and you have my condolences. Unfortunately, you may be misunderstanding our procedure. We're not breaking down any doors. We don't do that unless we know a crime or a medical emergency is in progress."

"I *thought* so." Victoria turned to Jill. "You told me they'd break down the door."

Jill's mouth went dry. "I'm sorry, I told you that to get the keys."

"So you lied to me." Victoria nodded, her lip curling.

"You disgust me, you know that? Didn't you say on the phone last night that you'd never lie to me? Wasn't that you? You're the one who called me 'honey,' right?"

Jill felt her face flush, embarrassed. She'd started off on the wrong foot with Victoria and she felt heartsick, wondering if they'd ever be close again. "Only because I was worried about your sister."

"She's *fine,* Jill. I know her a helluva lot better than you do. Butt out."

"Ladies," Officer Mendina said, toughening her tone, "if you want us to do a walk-through, we will. If not, we won't. Make up your mind. What's the decision?"

"No," Victoria answered.

"Yes," Jill answered at the same moment.

Officer Mendina looked from Jill to Victoria and back again. "We're here, we canvassed, so we might as well finish what we started. May I have the keys, Ms. Skyler?"

"Oh, fine." Victoria dug in a huge black purse, stuffed to the brim with a hairbrush, flowery makeup case, and an orange EpiPen, for her allergies. The sight of it took Jill back to a spring day when the girls were little and she'd taken them on a picnic to Valley Forge. Victoria had been stung by a bee, and before Jill even realized what happened, the self-possessed little girl had slipped her EpiPen from her pocket and was injecting herself with the calm assurance of a surgeon.

*Honey, you did that perfectly,* Jill had told her, afterwards. *You'd be great in an emergency.*

Victoria had grinned up at her. *I'm going to be a doctor, like you.*

Jill banished the memory as Victoria found the keys and handed them to Officer Mendina.

"Ladies, you both wait outside." Officer Mendina slid out the printed photo from her back pocket and handed it to Jill. "Dr. Farrow, before I forget, here's the photo you gave us."

"Thanks." Jill took the photo, and Officer Mendina left for William's house, meeting up with the other officer on the sidewalk in front.

Victoria frowned. "Jill, where did you get that picture? It's Dad's."

"Here, please take it, then. I didn't mean any harm. It was in his laptop." Jill didn't want to fuss anymore, especially now that the police were walking up the steps to William's house. She found herself in motion, her gut tensing at the thought of what they might find inside.

"Where did *you* get his laptop?" Victoria dogged her steps.

"Abby lent it to me. She asked me to help her set up a budget." Jill kept walking, and the officers were unlocking the front door.

"She had no right to give it to you, and you had no right to take it. It belongs to Dad."

"I'm only trying to help her." Jill stopped at the sidewalk outside the house, her heart in her throat as the police vanished inside. It killed her not to follow them.

"Please stop telling me about my own sister, whom you haven't seen in, like, forever. You're not our mother anymore."

Jill felt cut to the quick, but sucked it up. She glanced back at the house, and the front door was closed partway, with the officers inside. "Victoria, just so you know, Abby came to me, not the other way around."

"Of course she did, because she's a drama queen, and it's the only way she knows to get attention. She can't do anything right, so she does everything wrong. She can't live on her own. She's a mess, and you have yourself to thank for that."

Jill took it on the chin, wondering again, what was going on inside the house. Passersby were beginning to stare, making a pedestrian gaper-block. "Then maybe I can help her now."

"Too little, too late." Victoria shook her head. "She's manipulating you, and you're too full of yourself to know you're playing into her hands."

"That's not true." Jill edged over to peek in the window, but couldn't see a thing. "Victoria, your sister really could be in there, hurt or injured."

"No way, she's only gone one night, and she sleeps around, don't you get it? She's the crazy chick that men love." Victoria stepped closer. "All that talk about Dad being murdered is for attention. He wasn't murdered, Jill. I'm really not shocked, the way Dad died. He worked all the time, and he took meds, so what? I take them, too. It's not that bizarre."

"No one's saying that it is." Jill could hear that Victoria was feeling criticized, and it reminded her that Victoria was just as sensitive as Abby, maybe more, but would never let it show. Jill turned to her, trying to make peace. "Is that why you're so angry?"

Victoria's face flushed. "No, I'm angry because you and Abby are turning my father's death into yet another drama, and it's all about her. You should've seen her at the memorial service. She made that scene of running after you, and when she came back in, every man in the church was standing in line to console her."

Jill ignored the jealousy in Victoria's tone and pictured the memorial service, intrigued. "Does that include Neil? Did he say anything to you at the service?"

"I don't know Neil, and the service was chaos. I didn't see him or half of my friends, because of you." Victoria threw up her manicured hands. "You're making everything worse, Jill. You're making *Abby* worse. We're not yours anymore. Go home to your own family. Leave mine alone. In fact, leave now. *Go*."

Jill felt slapped. "I understand how you feel, and I'm sorry, but I'm not going, not this time. I want to make sure Abby's okay."

"She's not, and she never will be. You should've thought about that before you ditched us." Victoria's tone changed slightly, her anger giving way to the pain, beneath, and Jill realized, like an epiphany, that Victoria was feeling as betrayed by her as she was by William.

"Victoria, I didn't ditch you, I want you to know that. I never ditched you. If I had my way, I would have seen both of you, anytime, but your father told me not to—"

"Shut up!" Victoria shouted, as if newly provoked. "Can't you leave my father out of it? Will you ever stop hating on him? He's *dead,* Jill!"

Jill felt stricken. Between fighting with Victoria and worrying about Abby, her head was about to explode. She looked back at the house. She didn't know what was taking the cops so long. The crowd was gathering. Suddenly, Jill took off for the stairs to William's house. She couldn't wait another minute to know if Abby was safe. She was going in.

"Jill, no!" Victoria shouted. "Don't go in! The cops said to stay here."

Jill hit the stairs just as Victoria's friend Brian came hurrying up the street.

"Brian!" Victoria called to him. "You're not going to believe this woman! She's driving me nuts!"

Jill hurried inside.

# 23.

Jill scanned the living room, relieved to see that Abby hadn't fallen down the stairs, and everything looked as it had last night. She could hear the police walking around on the second floor, and they were talking and joking with each other, their voices echoing in the large, open house.

Jill felt a wave of relief wash over her. If the police had found anything wrong, they wouldn't be joking around. But she didn't hear Abby's voice among theirs, which left her more confused than ever. Abby's car was here, but she was gone, and Jill wondered what had happened after she'd left that night, after dropping off the groceries.

She sneaked into the kitchen, which was large and ringed with gray enamel cabinets and black marble counters. Sunlight emanated from a window that overlooked the car park, and the kitchen was clean to the point of being unused. She wondered if Abby had ordered her Chinese takeout for dinner, so she opened the chrome trash can with a step-on lid, releasing the odor of a scented garbage bag. The can was empty, and there was no take-out debris.

Jill turned and opened the refrigerator door, but it was

full of the food she'd bought—salmon, cold cuts, even
blueberry yogurt. None of it had been opened or eaten, and
it suggested that Abby had left before dinner.

She closed the door and looked in the dishwasher, but
there were no used tumblers. She noticed two bowls on the
floor, one filled with triangle-shaped kibble. She remembered that Abby's cat drank half and half, but she didn't
see the cat anywhere.

*He always hides when people come over.*

Jill went over to the bowl. It was full of half and half,
and its surface had thickened, leaving a yellowing ring
around the bowl. The bowl of kibble was also full. Just
then she heard a commotion in the living room, and it
sounded like Victoria and Brian entering the living room,
and the cops, coming down the stairs, so Jill left the kitchen
to meet them.

"What were you doing in there?" Victoria asked, frowning. She stood next to her friend Brian, who was tall and
good-looking in wire-rimmed glasses, a starchy white
oxford shirt, pressed jeans, and Gucci loafers, looking
every inch the Manhattan lawyer, on the weekend.

Officer Mendina turned to Jill, disapproving. "Dr.
Farrow, I asked you to wait on the sidewalk for your own
safety."

"I know, I'm sorry. What did you find?"

"Nothing. She's not up there, and there's no sign of anything to worry about."

"Is the bed slept in? It's the blue one."

"No, it's made and didn't look slept in."

"Is there a suitcase out, or anything?"

"Nothing like that. It all looks normal, nothing out of
place."

"When you were upstairs, did you see a cat?"

"No, she has a cat?"

"Yes, but it hides."

"Then it hid." Officer Mendina took out her long pad and slid a ballpoint pen from her shirt pocket. "Our procedure is to leave a 48A, an incident report, in plain view. It says we've been here, so when she comes home, she knows. But that's the most we can do."

"It just seems odd. She didn't eat last night, even though she told me she was hungry when I left. I went to get her groceries."

Victoria rolled her pretty eyes. "Oh, brother," she said, under her breath.

Officer Mendina cocked her head, her expression sympathetic. "Dr. Farrow, I have a twenty-year-old daughter, myself. She doesn't cook. Nobody cooks. Mom-to-Mom, don't worry about it. She'll be home when she gets home."

Jill wanted to believe her. "I'd agree if it weren't such strange circumstances, with her father."

Officer Mendina shrugged. "You still got questions, I'd take them over to Central Detectives. If there's a body on a floor in Philadelphia County, a detective gets called. Two, usually, and they work it up. Central Detectives has jurisdiction over the Sixth District, and they're the ones who decided it wasn't a suspicious death."

"Do you know which detective I could ask for, in particular?"

"No." Officer Mendina scribbled on a pad. "Whoever caught the case when the daughter called. That's what happened, right?"

"Yes, I believe so." Jill glanced at Victoria for verification, but Victoria only looked daggers at her.

"Then ask them." Officer Mendina tore off the sheet of paper, set it down on the coffee table, and gave the keys to Victoria. "Ms. Skyler, thanks for your cooperation. Looks like your sister isn't here, and I didn't see anything suspicious. Just the same, you're lucky to have somebody like Dr. Farrow worrying about you two."

"Thank you." Victoria dropped the keys into her big purse.

Jill caught Officer Mendina's eye. "Thank you for your help."

"You're welcome," she said, and the police left for the front door.

Victoria turned to Jill, frosty. "Leave. Go. Stay out of my life, and Abby's."

Jill composed herself. "I'm sorry for what happened, for everything. I was trying to help Abby, and I'd do the same for you, if you needed it."

"I won't need it." Victoria's eyes narrowed. "So now what? You're going to the police station? You're investigating my father's alleged murder? You're buying into Abby's craziness?"

"I'm going to see what I can find out in the hope it will shed some light on where Abby is. I'm not investigating any murder, I'm looking for your sister. Good-bye now, and please call me if Abby calls you." Jill started to walk to the door, but Brian caught her by the arm.

"I'm Brian Pendle, and I don't believe we've met." His blue eyes flashed behind his glasses, and his grip on her forearm felt oddly firm.

Jill pulled her arm away. "I'm Jill—"

"Oh, I know who you are." Brian's tone was calm and controlled. "Let me break it down for you, Dr. Farrow. Victoria's been through hell since her Dad's death. It's hard enough for her to deal with that and her sister, while she's in law school. I don't know what your agenda is, but you need to step off."

Jill felt taken aback. "I don't have an agenda, except helping Abby."

"Nevertheless, you don't belong. I'm an attorney, and if you keep this up, calling Victoria at odd hours and taking property that is part of her father's estate, I'll file for a restraining order against you."

Jill bit her tongue. "Good-bye, now," she said, going to the door. She wasn't afraid of restraining orders anymore. She was afraid that something had happened to Abby.

Not even a lawyer could stop a mother.

# 24.

"I'm Jill Farrow, I'm wondering if you could help me," she said to the affable detective sitting at the front desk. She'd never been inside a real squad room before, and it looked distinctly less photogenic than on network TV. Two detectives worked on outdated computers at old gray desks stacked high with files and papers, and the sun struggled through dirty windows on one wall, barely illuminating a panel of mismatched file cabinets and a cork bulletin board cluttered with Wanted posters, official memos, wrinkled cartoons, and an old March Madness office pool.

"Yes, hi, I'm Detective Pitkowski." The detective extended a hammy hand over a half-eaten Egg McMuffin, which filled the air with the aroma of steamed sausage. He was in his fifties, completely bald, with an unusually bumpy head and steely glasses that perched atop a bulbous nose. "What can I do for you?"

"It's about my former stepdaughter, Abby Skyler. She's nineteen, and she didn't come home last night. I'm worried it has something to do with her father, William Skyler, who was found dead in their home on Acorn Street, last Tuesday."

"Skyler? I know that case." Detective Pitkowski nodded, pushing up his glasses from the bridge. "It wasn't a homicide."

"Abby thinks it was. Were you the detective on the case?"

"No. And you are—"

"His ex-wife."

"Is this a joke?" Detective Pitkowski chuckled, and his pot belly jiggled, straining the buttons on his shirt, above his belt. He had on a striped tie with his white, short-sleeved shirt, and an old-school tie clip. "I got an ex who'd throw a party if I kicked the bucket."

Jill managed a smile. "No, it's not a joke. I'm trying to find Abby. Can I talk to the detective who worked on the case? Do you know who it was?"

"Detective Reed, but he's not in, and he couldn't meet with you, anyway. You're not immediate family."

"But I was."

"You're not now. Sorry."

Jill felt momentarily stumped. "My problem is that Abby has been gone all night, and she was raising questions about her father's death, so I'm worried that something bad happened to her."

"Like what?" Detective Pitkowski asked, cocking his shiny head.

"Worst case scenario, some form of foul play." Jill shuddered at the very notion. "She thought there was something fishy about the prescription painkillers that killed her father, and it turns out that they were gotten via a forged script, and the guy who filled the script was in disguise."

"Whoa, whoa, whoa." Detective Pitkowski put up his hand. "Let me ask you something. How did you find this out?"

"I went to the pharmacy and checked. Also, I think

there's been a black SUV following her lately, and maybe even me. The license plate starts with a T."

Detective Pitkowski frowned. "How do you know it's following you?"

"I saw it, twice." Jill saw his expression change to skepticism. "What do you advise I do, if she's missing?"

"She's not a missing person after only one night."

"I would agree with you, if not for whatever happened to her father. She lives with him, and if he was murdered, maybe she saw something or knows something, or the killer *thinks* she does, and that's why she's gone."

"You're speculating wildly here." Detective Pitkowski eyed her. "Tell you what, when she comes home, and I bet she will, have her come in. Detective Reed will sit down with her, talk to her, and answer any questions she has. You can come with her, if you like."

"Let me ask you this. Detective Reed took her father's cell phone, wallet, and the pills. Would he give them back to her?"

"The phone and wallet, yes."

"Would he show her your file, your investigation of her father's death, if she had questions about whether it was really a murder?"

Detective Pitkowski shook his head. "No, not even immediate family sees our files. It has crime scene photos and the like. We show that to no one."

"If she got a lawyer, could he see it? Or if she hired a private investigator?"

"No. No charges were filed, so it should never come to light."

Jill took a flyer. "Do you happen to know if Detective Reed spoke with any of my ex-husband's business associates about the case? There's a man in New York named Neil Straub whom he should call. I have Straub's address."

"Hold up, I suggest we do it this way." Detective Pitkowski slid a ballpoint from a Phillies mug on the desk. "Give me all the information you have, and I can pass it on to Detective Reed. The prescription, the SUV, the whole kit and caboodle. He'll look into it."

"Will he get back to me?"

"Only if he has a question, he will. Otherwise, he's not gonna discuss this case with you. If the daughter calls, he'll discuss it with her."

"Okay, thanks." Jill told him the story, and Detective Pitkowski listened in a professional way, taking notes and asking questions. It took about twenty minutes, and when she was finished, she hurried from the police station, checking her watch on the fly. She'd make it back just in time to see Megan swim.

She hustled to the car, chirped it open, hopped in, and started the engine, but couldn't stop worrying about Abby. Jill remembered what she'd said to her, only last night.

*There's me, Abby. You always have me.*

# 25.

Parents and kids filled the pool area, and their cheering, talk, and laughter echoed harshly off the tile walls and deck. The air was warm and thick, and the meet was already underway, but Jill had five minutes before Megan swam. She scurried up the stairs to the bleachers and spotted Sam sitting with the other swim moms and dads, Len Wynn and Rita Cohen, the McGraths, and Bill Roche and Jenny Zeleny.

"Sam!" she called out, and he turned, breaking into a grin.

Sam motioned her to come over, and Len and Rita looked up, smiled, and shifted aside to make room as Jill picked her way down the row. She sat down on the hard wooden bleacher and kissed Sam lightly on the lips.

"Hiya, honey." Jill was already sweating under her shirt, and she could practically feel her hair curl. "I made it."

"Way to go. What happened? Was Abby there?"

"No, but her car was. I went to the police, and they checked the house."

"Good." Sam nodded, his face shiny from the humidity.

"I told the police everything, but I'm still worried that she hasn't called me back."

Sam patted her leg again. "I gave Megan her swim bag."

Jill could see he was over talking about Abby. "Was Megan bothered that I wasn't there?"

"If she was, she didn't say so. I told her you went to check on Abby, and she seemed fine with it."

"Good." Jill turned her attention to the pool, which was new and Olympic-sized, to accommodate the high school. Navy-and-white tiles rimmed the edge, in Sequanic High colors, matching the floating lane dividers. The far wall was a panel of glass, and it flooded the pool area with indirect light, making bright shadows of each ripple, illuminating the chop churned up by a hundred arms and legs, like a restless sea.

Sam craned his neck at the starting blocks, where the girls clumped together, a noisy flock of yellow bathing suits and swim caps, like so many baby chicks. "Which one's Megan? I can never tell. They all look alike."

"There." Jill pointed at Megan, standing near the front and swinging her arms to keep them warm. The yellow spandex of her bathing suit outlined her skinny little body, and Jill could see her hips and breasts, formed but not fully mature, somewhere between girl and young woman.

"How can you always tell it's her?"

"It's like penguins. You know your own."

Sam gave her a sweet nudge, and they both watched Megan, who was looking up at the bleachers, trying to find them in a way that wasn't obvious.

"Hey, honey!" Jill called out, raising her hand, but Megan was still looking for her. "She doesn't see us."

"Yes, she does."

"No, she doesn't, I can tell." Jill stood up, waving her arms, but Megan had already turned away and was talking to Courtney, their yellow caps close together. Jill shouted, "Megan!"

"Down in front!" called a man behind her, and Sam turned around and shot him an annoyed look.

"It's okay." Jill sat down, and on her other side, Rita leaned over.

"He's from the Plymouth Meeting club. Want me to hit him?"

Jill smiled. "It's okay, I just like it when Megan knows I'm here. We always make eye contact before she gets on the block. It's our thing."

"She saw you." Sam patted her leg. "It's okay, relax."

Jill thought Megan looked worried as she walked toward Coach Stash. Jim "Stash" Stashevsky was only in his thirties, short but powerfully built in his yellow polo shirt and sweats. He bent over to talk to Megan, tucking his clipboard under his arm, and she listened intently, nodding as he spoke, her dark eyes looking up at him and her mouth making a stiff little line, like a dash.

Sam shifted forward on the bleachers. "You can do it, Megan!"

Jill made a megaphone of her hands. "Go, Megan, go!"

Megan climbed onto the third platform, swinging her arms, then slipping her yellow goggles down over her eyes and adjusting them on her head, her cap, and her nose. Jill knew all of Megan's swim rituals, and the time for making eye contact with Mom was over. She'd be visualizing the race, ignoring the other swimmers as they climbed onto the blocks, shaking their arms and fidgeting with their goggles.

"Go, Megan!" Jill shouted again.

"Come on, Megan!" Sam hollered, and Rita, Len, and the others cheered for Megan, because they all cheered for each other's kids. The parents from other clubs added to the chorus, hooting and hollering for their own kids.

Megan and the others took the positions on the blocks, bending at their bony knees, tucking their heads, and curling their toes around the edge. The electronic beeper sounded, barely audible above the crowd noise, and the girls shot into the air, stretching out their lithe bodies and extending their fingers and toes. For a split second, they were all knifing forward through thin air, transformed from girls into something that could fly. But Megan didn't get her typical smooth start, and she hit the water behind the others.

"Sam?" Jill heard herself say, her gaze on Megan. "Did you see that? She's off."

"She'll catch up."

"No, it's not that." Jill had been a competitive swimmer, but she didn't care about Megan's time or if she won. Megan's skinny arms started to bend and extend, but they were churning more than usual, and she didn't move through the water the way she always did. Her hands slapped the surface, and her kick was too low, not her distinctive flutter. "Am I crazy, or is something the matter?"

"No, she's fine."

"Go, Megan, go!" Jill yelled. The other swimmers stroked ahead, kicking hard and picking up the pace, and Coach Stash shouted for Megan, holding his clipboard to his mouth, to amplify the sound.

Megan fell behind two lengths, then three, and the other girls reached the wall, straining for the tiles with outstretched fingertips. Megan only seemed to slow down, losing ground.

Jill leapt to her feet. "Go, Megan!"

Sam rose. "Go, Megan!"

The man behind them yelled, "Sit down!"

They both ignored him, and Jill started to worry as Megan took a few more feeble strokes, then stopped in the middle of her lane. Coach Stash hustled poolside past the cheering teammates, and before Jill knew why, she found herself in motion, climbing down the bleachers toward the pool, pushing past the other parents.

"Yo, watch it!" one man said, as Jill moved him aside. The race continued fast and furious, the crowd kept cheering, and the teams on the pool deck jumped up and down with excitement.

"Megan!" Jill cried out, just as Megan's yellow cap disappeared beneath the water. Glare from the windows reflected on the chop, whiting out the water's surface, obliterating everything.

"Help!" Jill reached the bottom row of the bleachers, threw herself over the rail, and half stumbled and half slipped toward the pool.

Megan was gone.

Coach Stash dropped his clipboard and dove into the water. Jill dove in behind him. The water muffled the cheering, and she opened her eyes to see Megan sinking to the bottom of the pool, her eyes closed and air bubbles leaking from her mouth.

Coach Stash reached Megan first, grabbed her by the waist, and raised her head up and out of the water. Jill grabbed her other side, pushed aside the floating lane markers, and they all popped together to the surface.

"Megan!" Jill shouted, terrified. Megan remained unconscious, her head flopped over. "Get her to the side!"

Coach Stash nodded, his eyes wide with fear. The race stopped, and the cheering silenced. Kids and parents watched in shock, and a stricken Sam came running.

"Megan, Megan!" Jill shouted, swimming with Megan, and they reached the edge of the pool. The coaches grabbed Megan and lowered her onto the pool deck. One flipped Megan onto her back and started to administer CPR, but she coughed and gasped.

"Megan!" Jill climbed out of the pool and scrambled to kneel beside her on the watery deck.

"Stay back!" shouted one of the other coaches, stiff-arming Jill, but she brushed it aside.

"I'm her mother and a doctor," she said, turning Megan onto her side, letting her cough out the water. Coach Stash, the other coaches, and all the swimmers gathered around while Jill kept a hand on Megan, who was spasming with coughs. "Honey, let it come out. Cough it out."

"Mom?" Megan said, weakly.

"I'm here." Jill held her steady. "You're okay. Every-thing's okay."

Megan expelled the pool water, inhaling deeply.

"Just breathe, honey." Jill sent up a silent prayer of thanks, and Sam came through the crowd of coaches, hor-rified.

"Is she okay?"

"Yes," Jill answered, holding back tears of relief.

Later, Jill, Sam, and Coach Stash stood at the exit of the high school, where the ambulance was driving around to pick Megan up. A healthy pink had returned to her cheeks, and she was breathing normally, sitting wrapped in a yellow team towel. She'd taken off her swim cap, and her dark blonde ponytail hung down her back, its tip wet, like a brush dipped in black paint. She sipped water from a bottle, and Courtney sat next to her in a wet bathing suit and towel, providing moral support.

Jill touched Megan's shoulder. "Feel better, sweetie?"

"Yes, I'm fine." Megan glanced over her shoulder at the pool, where the other swimmers were visible through the windows. "I don't have to go to the hospital, do I, Mom?"

"Yes, it's a good idea to have you checked out."

"But can't you guys drive me, please? An ambulance is so embarrassing."

"It's safer this way, just in case."

"Do we have to? I'm fine, now, I really am."

"Let's do it this way, honey." Jill patted Megan on the shoulder.

"It won't have the siren, will it?"

"I don't hear one."

Megan set down the water bottle, then glanced back at the other swimmers again. "Court, is he there?"

Courtney nodded, and Jill realized that Megan was embarrassed in front of her new crush.

Megan looked up at Coach Stash, her eyes baleful. "I'm sorry, Coach. I let you down, and the club."

Courtney shook her head, her goggles around her neck. Her cute little mouth tilted down at the corners. "No, you didn't, Megs."

"Don't worry about it." Coach Stash shot Megan a wink, his team towel over his soaking sweats. His wet hair was a shiny black helmet. "Nice warm water, big-time pool. I felt like a swim, and so did your mother. Right, Jill?"

"Right." Jill smiled, grateful for his kindness to Megan. "You're fast, Coach."

"If I'm not, I'm fired."

Megan looked up at him. "Will we lose now, Coach? Because of me?"

"Just focus on getting better." Coach Stash patted her on the shoulder. "You're our star, Megster. You'll always be our star."

"I warmed up so well." Megan shook her head. "All of a sudden, my heart started beating real fast. It felt like I was going to die. Like it was going to jump out of my chest."

Courtney looked over at Megan. "Was it like that time we had the triple shot at Starbucks?"

"No, worse. A lot worse."

Jill already had a diagnosis, and it wasn't a difficult one. "Honey, when did it start, your heart beating so fast?"

"Before the race. My hands got sweaty, too. My palms." Megan showed her hands, palms up. "At first I thought it was pool water, but when I wiped it off on my suit, it kept coming back. It got worse when I got on the block. I thought it would go away, but it didn't."

"Could you see okay?"

"Yes."

"Hear any weird sounds?"

"No."

"Dizzy?"

"No."

"Any headache?"

"No, and when I dove, I couldn't catch my breath and my heart wouldn't stop, and then I just, I don't know, went unconscious." Megan looked down. "I drank my water, Mom, I did."

"I know, honey." Jill didn't think it was dehydration, and Megan had no history of heart problems or low blood sugar. Suddenly, an orange-and-white ambulance reversed into the driveway and braked, then the back doors opened and a paramedic sprang from inside, rolling out a gurney on wheels. The kids at the pool pressed closer to the window, and Megan groaned at the sight.

Jill helped her to her feet. "Let's go, sweetie."

Megan rose. "Thank God there's no siren."

Courtney got up, too. "I've never been inside an ambulance. I think it's awesome, Megan."

"Mom, can she come with us?"

"Sorry, I don't think that's allowed. You're stuck with me." Jill motioned the paramedics over with the rolling gurney, and Megan lay down so they could strap her in.

And just then, the ambulance's siren went off.

# 26.

Jill sat in the hard chair in the examining room, her damp clothes sticking to her body. She'd dried off as best as she could with some paper towels, and she and Sam were alone together while Megan had been taken off for tests. A fluorescent panel overhead shed bright light, and the pastel blue walls were covered with inspirational posters and state-of-the-art equipment. The air smelled of an antiseptic that did little to stop bacterial infections, many of which were spread by doctors who didn't wash their hands between patients. But that was one of the profession's dirty little secrets.

"So, what do you think?" Jill asked. "Panic attack?"

"Agree." Sam was leaning against the wall with his arms crossed. "It's been tough for her, lately."

"Yes, it has." Jill shook her head, kicking herself. "And all I could think of on the way here was Abby. I even called back a bunch of patients, and I worried about one of them, Rahul, a baby waiting on a CBC. I worried about all of them, not Megan. You can say I told you so, anytime."

"No, I wouldn't, you know that."

"Thanks." Jill appreciated him being so kind. "Panic

attacks are symptomatic of anxiety. All in one weekend, she lost her stepfather, got thrown out of a church, and was reunited with her ex-stepsister, who puked on her bed."

"Don't beat yourself up." Sam straightened up, walked over, and stroked her hair, which was finally drying. "After all, you're the mom who jumped into the pool to save her."

*Too little, too late.*

"Honey?" Sam asked, and Jill realized she'd lost focus, remembering what Victoria had said, this morning.

"Sorry."

"You were in that pool before I knew she was going under. I thought you were going to dive on top of Coach."

Jill knew he was trying to cheer her up, but it wasn't working. She felt so guilty, first over Abby, then over Victoria, and now over Megan. She'd been trying to mother all the girls and failing each of them. She didn't know how she had managed being a mother of three before, or how any mother did it, with more than one child. It wasn't just a juggling act, it was a *magic* act.

Sam touched her shoulder, gently. "Maybe we should think about making an appointment with Sandy, for Megan. Let her talk it out, explore her feelings about William's death."

"I'll think about it." Jill groaned. "I'm not only a bad mother, I'm a bad ex-stepmother."

"It's okay." Sam rubbed her back. "You want some coffee? I saw vending machines in the hall."

"I would, thanks." Jill smiled up at him, and Sam bent down and kissed her on the cheek.

"Be right back. Hang tight."

"Thanks. I really love you, you know that?"

Sam lifted his eyebrows, surprised. "What did I do right?"

"Everything. Sorry it was such a difficult weekend."

"No apology necessary." Sam flashed her a reassuring smile, then left.

Jill tilted her head backwards, against the wall. She wondered if Victoria had been right, and she had blown everything out of proportion. Maybe Abby had met a cute guy and stayed out all night. Maybe William wasn't murdered but filled the scripts in disguise, for the reason Sam had said. Maybe Abby was in denial, and Jill had jumped at the chance to get back into her life, to have a permanently needy child at home.

*We're not yours anymore.*

Jill swallowed hard. She thought of the Venn diagrams again and pictured herself stuck in the intersection of circles, a member of both families at once, conflating past and present. Katie had said that motherhood had no expiration date, and Jill had agreed, believing to the bone that it transcended everything—biology, law, even time and space.

*Abby's in our family, Mom. You just can't kick someone out of your family.*

Jill thought of what Megan had said that day, feeling the weight of her words and their truth. Jill resolved to fight harder, for her family, and she couldn't neglect Megan just because Abby was missing, especially because Megan was probably worried about Abby, too.

Jill slid her BlackBerry from her purse, relieved that she hadn't had it in her back pocket when she'd jumped into the pool. She checked it, but there were no new messages from Abby.

*I'm glad you didn't change your phone number. Am I still A on your speed dial?*

Jill scrolled to her phone log, found the last time that Abby had called her from her cell phone, and saved the number to her speed dial, under A.

Now all Abby had to do was call.

# 27.

Jill set the swim bag and purse down in the entrance hall while Beef met them all at the front door, wagging his tail and sniffing all the strange new smells. "Hiya, Beef," she said, dropping her key into the bowl.

"Hey, pal." Megan scratched the golden behind the ears. "Guess what? We lost."

Jill looked over. "Don't let it bother you, honey."

"Right." Sam closed the door behind them, muffling the noise of a neighbor's lawnmower. "Dogs don't care about winning and losing. They're too smart for that. They love you, no matter what."

"I love you, too, boy." Megan bent over and kissed Beef on the muzzle, and Sam whistled for the dog.

"Come on, Beefsteak. Wanna go out?" Sam went to the back door, and Beef trotted after him, his nails clicking on the hardwood.

"Let's eat," Jill said, going to her comfort default. "Anybody else hungry?"

"I am." Megan flashed a game smile. She looked like herself again, her eyes bright and her hair dry, in its messy braid. She'd changed into a gray hoodie and jeans at the hospital, and the ER doc confirmed that she'd had a panic attack. She hadn't asked any questions, and if it'd bothered her, she hadn't let it show. Jill was wondering if that was part of the problem.

"Megan, I'm going upstairs to change, and I'll be right back."

"Okay. I'll get a drink."

"Oh, wait, I'll get it for you." Jill started into the kitchen, but Megan waved her off with a smile.

"Mom, I can get it myself. You don't have to baby me."

"Okay." Jill checked herself. "Be right down."

"Good. Love you."

"Love you, too." Jill gave her a quick kiss, then went upstairs to her bedroom and peeled off the clammy shirt, then her jeans. She was about to toss them in the hamper, but they felt heavy, and she realized she'd left her BlackBerry in her pocket. She pulled it out and checked the messages, but there were none. She slid into her go-to jeans and a thin white T-shirt under a navy cotton sweater, then found a barrette and clipped up her wet hair. She slid the phone into her back pocket and went downstairs to the kitchen.

"Hi, Mom." Megan was writing in her binder, already doing her homework at the kitchen island. The pink troll doll that sat atop her pencil wiggled with each stroke, and her phone rested near her right hand.

"Hiya, sweetie. Why don't you put your notebook away and take a break, until after dinner?"

"I can't, I have to finish this dumb worksheet." Megan wrote in her notebook while checking her phone.

"Honey, no phones at the table, okay?"

"We're not eating yet, and everyone's texting. They want to know how I am." Megan looked up, eyes pleading, pencil poised. She had spent most of the ride home answering text messages, and Jill was guessing that the mystery boy was one of them.

"Okay, just for today."

"Thanks. Can we have grilled cheese?"

"For dinner? I could make salmon, and we have brown rice."

"Nah, I'm hungry, and I have to finish my homework."

"Do you need more time? I can probably get you an extension, if we show them the ER doctor's note." Jill realized it was the wrong thing to say as soon as she'd said it, and Megan winced.

"No, I can do it, and I don't mind grilled cheese. Is that okay?"

Sam came into the kitchen, with Beef trotting behind. "Grilled cheese is fine with me, too," he said, going to the island.

"Grilled cheese it is." Jill went to the fridge, feeling a warm rush of love for Sam. He'd eat anything to make Megan happy.

"Mom, can we put the tomato inside, like last time?"

"Sure." Jill rummaged in the fridge and retrieved a block of cheddar cheese, bread, and two tomatoes.

"Awesome." Megan filled in a blank on her worksheet, and Sam looked over her shoulder, sliding his reading glasses on.

"What're you working on, kitten?"

"Health. It's so dumb."

Sam eyed the worksheet. "Ask me about fallopian tubes, go ahead. I'm an expert. I have five."

"Eeeww!" Megan squealed, giving him a playful shove, and not long afterwards, the kitchen was filled with the delicious aroma of grilled cheese sandwiches, the merry noise of talk and laughter, and the sweet snoring of an overweight golden. Not to mention the occasional beep of a text message.

In other words, a family.

Or at least, most of one.

# 28.

Jill took her time tucking Megan into bed, because that was when they usually talked things over. She knew Megan had a lot on her mind, because she'd grown quieter as night fell. "How you doing, sweetie?" Jill asked, sitting on the edge of the bed.

"I'm okay, I guess." Megan pulled her covers up, watching Beef circle a few times before assuming his customary curl on the bed. "He's making his glazed doughnut."

"He's beyond cute."

"What a good dog." Megan patted Beef's back, where his coat curled in waves.

"He sure is." Jill moved some hair back from Megan's face, and her eyes glowed in the warm light from the lamp, on her nighttable. White dots of acne medication made a constellation on her chin.

"Did you throw my other sheets away?"

"No, Sam took them to the Laundromat. The comforter, too. Wasn't that nice of him? So I didn't have to."

Megan grinned. "Gross, right?"

"I'll say. What a guy."

"You don't always have to tell me how great Sam is. I know he's great. I love him."

Jill's throat caught. She hadn't realized she did that, but Megan was right. "I love him, too," she said, simply. "So what's on your mind? I can tell those wheels are turning."

Megan frowned, her smooth forehead creased by one tiny line. "Like, I don't know what comes after you die. What do you really think happens?"

"Really?" Jill guessed Megan was talking about William, and maybe Gray, too. "I think your spirit lives on, with God. I think all your emotion and thought and heart can't just vanish."

"Do you think somebody killed William? Courtney says there would be more evidence, like *CSI*."

Jill hoped to ease Megan's mind, not upset her before bed. "I don't know, but I told the police about it, and they're looking into it."

"You did? When?"

"Today. That's why I was late to the meet, and I'm sorry about that."

"It's okay, Sam told me. Do you think Abby's okay?"

"I'm sure she is."

"But she still hasn't called you. I saw you checking your phone, after dinner."

"I'm hoping she will soon."

"I sent her a message on Facebook, but she didn't answer yet. I sent one to Victoria, too. She didn't answer, either."

Jill hid her annoyance at Victoria. "When did you do that?"

"When I was doing my homework."

Jill let it go. She didn't like the multitasking that Megan did, but she knew it couldn't be stopped. Her own mother used to say, do one thing at a time, but those days were long gone.

"Abby has lots of guy friends on her Facebook page. I was thinking that she could be with a guy friend. Maybe she's not really gone, or missing."

"You're right, that's what I'm hoping. Don't worry about Abby. Leave that to me." Jill tugged the comforter up, and next to Megan, Beef lowered his head onto his paws, closing his eyes. "You need to get a good night's sleep."

"Am I lame because I had a panic attack?" Megan asked, after a moment.

"No, of course not." Jill kissed her warmly on the cheek. "It's been a hard weekend, with the news about William. On top of that you have homework, the meet, Abby, and your Guitar Hero. There's a lot of emotion, all at once. It's too much for anybody to deal with, even somebody as strong as you."

"I thought I was having a heart attack."

"I bet. You weren't, it just felt that way."

"I thought I was going to die. You can't die from a panic attack, can you?"

"No, of course not." Jill stroked her cheek.

"I mean, what if I die tonight? In my sleep?"

"Honey, no, that can't happen." Jill was about to launch into a medical explanation, but stopped when she read Megan's expression. Her brow wrinkled deeply, and her lips clenched over her braces, in what was becoming a nervous habit. Megan was an anxious little girl in the body of a young woman, and she didn't need a pediatrician, she needed a mom. Jill gathered her up and gave her a big hug. "Everything's going to be okay, honey. Don't worry about a thing."

"Wanna lie down with me a while, Mom? Like we used to?"

"Good idea." Jill released Megan, then reached up and turned off the light, leaving them both in a soft, velvety darkness. "Move over, okay?"

"Sure." Megan shifted over in bed, and so did Beef, which left a skinny strip for Jill at the edge of the bed, only as wide as a balance beam, but familiar to mothers everywhere.

"Perfect," Jill said, meaning it, and she hugged Megan close, feeling her body relax.

"You sure I won't die?"

"Positive." Jill hadn't realized that when Megan was asking about death, she was asking about her own. "It's impossible. Don't worry about it, at all. Okay?"

"Okay." Megan paused. "Did you really kiss thousands of guys, Mom?"

"*Millions.*" Jill laughed, and so did Megan.

Sam's silhouette appeared in the door. "What's going on in here? Sounds like you two girls need adult supervision."

Jill was about to answer, but Megan beat her to it, opening her arms to him.

"Sam," Megan called out. "Come in! Kitten needs hugs! Hugs!"

"Talked me into it." Sam walked over, piling into bed and giving Megan a big hug, and Jill watched Megan cling to him. Sam was a true father to her, not just the father figure that William had been, and it would kill Megan to lose him.

Jill had to find a way to make it work, when Abby came home.

If Abby came home.

# 29.

It was Monday morning, and Jill walked from the parking lot to the office, trying to switch mental gears. She'd worried about Megan and Abby all night, tossing and turning, but she'd have to put them to the back of her mind today. Flu season was like tax time for germs, and she'd need to focus at work. She'd called Padma about Rahul, and he was still feverish. She wished she'd ordered his bloodwork stat, just so she'd have the answer.

PEMBEY FAMILY PRACTICE, read the carved wooden sign in front of the large stone home, one of many on the street that had been converted to offices for doctors, lawyers, and accountants. Pembey was the town next to Jill's, only twenty minutes from her house, and a suburban practice had been just the ticket while Megan was still young.

Jill opened the door onto the waiting room, greeted by its freshened air and soothing blue décor. Big bay windows made it feel cheery, homey, and bright, even on an overcast day like today. Patients occupied most of the comfy blue-patterned chairs, reading magazines or typing into BlackBerrys, but none of the patients was hers. She didn't have anybody for half an hour, and she'd come in early to catch up on her charting and insurance paperwork, which was endless. Pembey Family took fifteen types of insurance, and Aetna alone was four of them.

Jill headed for the door leading to the doctors' offices and examination rooms, then spotted Elaine Fitzmartin standing at the intake window, signing in her elderly mother, Mary, who was an Alzheimer's patient of Dr. Thoma's. They were in all the time, and Jill liked them both. "Hi, ladies, how are you this morning?" she asked.

"Fine," Mary answered, turning with a sweet smile. "You look nice today."

"Thank you," Jill said, though she only had on her usual cotton sweater, khakis, and clogs. "How are you feeling today?"

"I did the crossword this morning, in pen. Do you do the crossword?"

"Not in pen, my dear. Good for you. Keep it up." Jill turned to Elaine, because she knew from taking care of her own mother that caretakers needed caretaking, too. "And how about you, Elaine?"

"We're fine, thanks. Much better now that Mom's on Memoril."

"Great." Jill didn't know much about Alzheimer meds. "And you, are you living on the edge, too? Doing crosswords in pen?"

Elaine smiled. "No, but I'm loving that book you lent me, the mystery. I can't put it down."

"Great." Jill noticed Sheryl, their office manager, eavesdropping from the file cabinets, but she ignored her. "You won't guess the ending, so don't even try."

"I always try, and I think I know who did it."

Jill smiled. "Don't skip ahead, like last time." She turned to Mary. "You're her mom. Tell her not to skip ahead."

"Oh, she never obeys me. She never obeys anybody."

"Then you raised her right," Jill said, and they all laughed. Behind them, Sheryl was motioning to Jill to finish the conversation.

"Excuse me, ladies, I've got to go. Take care." Jill opened the door into the hallway, and Sheryl swooped out to meet her, short and stocky in her blue scrubs, with bristly, short hair that was prematurely gray, from trying to control the universe.

"I need to speak with you in your office, right away."

Jill didn't break stride. "Okay, I have an idea. Why don't I invite you into my office to speak with me, right away?"

"That's not funny." Sheryl clutched a file folder to her chest.

"By the way, good morning." Jill opened the door into her office, a windowless white box that held her diplomas, licenses, reference books, and a neat desk with a struggling ficus plant. She spent as little time as possible here, preferring the examining rooms. She loved her patients, but didn't love working at Pembey Family, mainly because of Sheryl. "So what's up?"

"I need to speak to you about your stats, again. I know you're part-time, so I accounted for that." Sheryl pursed her thin lips. Her eyes were dirt brown, and she had the doughy features of a baby, without any of the charm. "I sent an email to John, showing that last quarter, you saw only between eighteen and twenty cases a day." Sheryl whipped out a printout of numbers, from the folder. "That's ten to twelve fewer than the average of all the other docs. Each doc needs to keep the schedule, and you need to see more cases a day."

"They're patients, not cases, and if you want to talk averages, their average age is two." Jill had explained this many times before. "I'm the only pediatrician here. I take longer because babies can't tell you where it hurts."

"Don't be funny."

"I wasn't being funny, just now. I was being funny, before." Jill gave up on the humor thing, and Sheryl's eyes hardened.

"The numbers don't lie. You take too long with the cases. You have to draw the line. Five minutes with each case, ten at the max, and twenty only if it's an annual. You're consistently running twenty minutes or longer, with each case."

"Sheryl, come on. Pediatricians don't work the same as adult docs, we can't." Jill had said this before, too. "Each visit, I have two patients, a parent and a child. I use the time it takes to give my patients the best care possible, and no more."

Sheryl gestured at the door. "Like with Mrs. Fitzmartin, you chat them up, don't you?"

Jill almost laughed. "Guilty as charged. I'm friendly with the patients."

"She's not your patient."

"I *like* her, is that okay with you? If I were keeping patients waiting, it would be different, but John wanted me to build a pediatric practice. The best way to grow is to provide quality care, including the relationship side. The statistics aren't the same for me."

Sheryl arched an eyebrow. "You don't follow *any* of the rules of Pembey Family, whether they pertain to a pediatric practice or not."

"Of course I do. Which rules don't I follow?"

"For starters, you answer questions by email."

Jill blinked. "How do you know that?"

"We monitor it."

Jill recoiled. "You *read* my email?"

"It's not your email, it's Pembey Family email. We own it, it's proprietary, and it's my job to monitor it."

"Since when?" Jill should have guessed as much, but somehow she hadn't. "Why do you care if I answer by email? We lose the exam fee?"

"It's a business, Jill. We don't encourage uncompensated phone or email advice. You're the only doc who gives out her intraoffice email, Jill@pembeyfamily.com, which you're not supposed to do, either. All patient email has to go to me, at info@pembeyfamily."

"Then it gets to me three days later."

Sheryl frowned. "Also, you're exposing us to lawsuits if your orders are misunderstood, or if a misdiagnosis is made because the case wasn't seen."

"I would never prescribe anything unless it was a patient I'd seen, and I don't use it for acute medical issues." Jill was so sick of hearing about lawsuits. Pembey had layers of CYA paperwork in case they got sued, and that was on top of the insurance-company paperwork. "I have to be available by phone and email. You can't tell Mom to chill out when her baby's sick."

"You're only hurting yourself, you know. Your bonus would be higher if you were more productive."

"Seeing more patients isn't necessarily more productive, and if money were all that mattered, I'd do cosmetic surgery for a living."

Sheryl's eyes narrowed. "You think everything is a joke, don't you?"

"No, I don't. I take my patients and my practice very seriously. I'm using humor to keep the mood light, and I'm failing, evidently."

"I have a sense of humor."

"Where?" Jill smiled, and Sheryl frowned.

"You act as if you're the exception."

"I am, because of what I *do*."

"Not so. You're the only part-timer we have. Why? That doesn't have anything to do with what you *do*."

"Yes, it does." Jill felt taken aback. Of all of Sheryl's complaints, she'd never heard this one before. "I do it to be home with my daughter. I love kids, even if they're mine, as absurd as that sounds."

"Megan's *thirteen,* Jill. I don't think she needs you to take her to playdates anymore. You'd be working full-time if you were committed to Pembey Family."

"I'm committed to *my* family, okay?" Jill felt herself flush. "I made a part-time deal when I got here, and I still don't get home some nights until eight."

"Every doc here works long hours."

"I'm sure," Jill said, though she never saw any of the four other docs. They all ran separate practices, and there was no time to interact with anyone except Sheryl. "But I'm the only woman, the only mom."

"So again, you're the exception."

"Yes." Jill wasn't getting anywhere. "Look, I have to do some charting, then get ready for Carrie Bryson, who'll be here any minute. She has a two-year-old and she emailed me last night, about his rash. She called the office first, for the after-hours program." Jill caught herself. "But I guess you knew that."

"Yes, and you told her that you could squeeze her in this morning. You have to stop doing that, too." Sheryl frowned. "She has to go through Donna. Donna is the appointment secretary."

"I emailed Donna and told her myself."

"That's not Pembey Family procedure. These procedures serve a purpose. If we don't know Carrie's coming in, we can't pull her file, and we can't make sure that the case is properly logged, coded, and billed."

"Donna wasn't available at midnight, when I answered the email. I know we have procedures, but they can't get in the way of the patients and the medicine. That's why we're here."

*Rring!* Jill's cell phone rang in her back pocket, and her heart leapt up. It had to be Abby; it wasn't the ringtone for Megan or Sam. "Excuse me." She reached for her phone and checked the screen. She didn't recognize the number but she wasn't taking any chances. "Sorry, I have to get this."

Sheryl was already stalking away. "Don't be long," she called over her shoulder, closing the door behind her as the call connected.

"Jill, it's Victoria, calling from home. Have you heard from Abby?"

"No," Jill answered, surprised. Victoria sounded less angry. Not warm exactly, but not as hostile as yesterday. "She hasn't returned my calls."

"Mine, either." Victoria paused. "She usually calls me back, eventually. She would have called by now, especially after the last message I left."

"Why? What did you say?"

"I yelled at her."

Jill could imagine. "Did you check the house again?"

"Yes, and I don't think she's been home. The car is there."

"How about the cat?"

"I don't know, I didn't check. I never see that cat."

Jill sank into her chair, her gaze wandering over the things in her office, ending with the miserable ficus. "Do you have any idea where she could be?"

"No, none."

"Is there anyone she would turn to?"

"Not that I know of, in particular."

"What about Neil Straub? Would she call or contact him?"

"I guess that's possible," Victoria answered, sounding encouraged. "It makes sense she'd contact him, but I don't have Neil's number or address."

"I have his address. It's in Manhattan. I can go see him tomorrow, on my day off."

"No, I can go. I'm going into the city tonight, for dinner."

"I don't think you should. It might not be safe." Jill caught herself before she called Victoria "honey." "If Neil had anything to do with your father's death—"

"That again?" Victoria scoffed, cold again. "Enough. Stop with that."

"Please, let me go instead. It can wait a day."

"Dad wasn't murdered, and Neil is his best friend. I can go see if she's there, I'm a big girl. What's the address?"

Jill told her. "Let me know what happens, okay? You have my cell number."

"Good-bye," Victoria said abruptly, hanging up.

Jill hung up. If Victoria was going to see Neil Straub, now Jill was worried about *her*.

And just like that, Jill was a mother of three, again.

Worried, times three.

# 30.

"What happened?" Jill said into her cell phone, when Victoria called back. It was after dinner, and she was in the kitchen, returning calls from patients and charting on the laptop. Sam was reading in the family room, and Megan was upstairs in the shower.

"Neil wasn't home. The guy at the desk buzzed. It's a doorman building."

"They called the apartment from downstairs?"

"Yes. It's 4-D, but he didn't answer." Victoria sounded cool, almost businesslike. But not angry, so Jill counted that as progress.

"When were you there?"

"I made them try when I got there, around six o'clock, then I went for dinner and came back later, at eleven. Neil still wasn't home, and I still haven't heard back from Abby. Have you?"

"No." Jill rubbed her forehead, slouching behind her laptop. It had been a long day at work, and she'd seen a slew of flu, colds, and sinus infections that didn't respond to antibiotics. If she could bottle the resourcefulness of a sinus infection, she could find Abby in no time. "Did they tell you when Neil's expected back?"

"No, they don't know."

"When did they see him last?"

"They didn't say."

"Did they see Abby?"

"They didn't say that, either."

"Did you ask?"

"Yes, but they said they don't give out information about the residents. They blew us off."

"Who's us?"

"My friend Brian came with me, after dinner."

"Did you tell them it was an emergency?"

"Yes, but they still wouldn't tell me anything about the residents."

"Understood." Jill felt momentarily stumped. Her gaze shifted restlessly around the kitchen. The dishwasher thrummed, and the granite countertops glistened. "The fact that Neil isn't there doesn't mean much. He could be elsewhere with Abby. So the issue is if the doorman has seen Abby, or if anybody else around the building has, like other tenants."

Victoria snorted. "They for sure won't let me ask any other tenants."

"You don't have an office address for Neil?"

"No."

"Do you know the name of his company, if he has one?"

"No."

Jill didn't like what she was thinking. Even if Neil wasn't a suspect, he could be in danger, too, if he and William had been involved in anything crooked. Either way, Abby could be in danger if she was with him.

"Jill—" Victoria hesitated.

"What?"

"I'm worried she could do something to herself, if you know what I mean."

"No. What do you mean?"

"I mean, like, suicide."

"Don't be silly. She'd never do anything like that."

Victoria fell silent a moment. "She already has. She tried it once, before."

Jill thought she'd heard Victoria wrong. "*What?*"

"Abby tried to kill herself, before."

"No!" Jill cried out, reeling. "When? How?"

"A while ago, about three months after we left the house. I was at school, and she called me and told me that she and Dad had a big fight." Victoria hesitated. "She was telling him that you guys should get back together. He said no, that the marriage was really over, and never to answer your emails. The next day, she tried to, you know, commit suicide."

Jill's heart broke. "How?"

"Pills. She took the whole bottle."

"What pills?"

"Lexapro. She was on it, for depression. She still is, that's why she shouldn't drink."

Jill didn't have to ask when Abby's depression had started, because she could guess.

"I found her. Dad had left that morning on business. I stopped home, just by chance. I thought she was taking a nap, but she wouldn't wake up. If I hadn't come by, she'd be . . . gone."

Jill visualized the scene, horrified. After a bottle of Lexapro, Abby would be almost comatose. It wasn't a suicidal gesture, it was a bona-fide attempt.

"That's why I've been so mad at you." Victoria's tone softened, just a little. "I blamed you for her trying to kill herself, and deciding to be a screw-up, the rest of her life.

If you hadn't left, she'd be fine, and I wouldn't have to act like her mom all the time."

Jill listened, and her head dropped into her hands. She never would have believed Abby would do anything like that. Abby's pain must have been so deep, like an agony.

"So that's what's worrying me, now. I try not to worry about her, and I don't want to worry about her, but I do, all the time, like if she does it again, it'll be my fault . . ." Victoria's sentence trailed off.

"I'm so sorry, Victoria." Jill's head was still in her hands, and she let all of her regret and anguish flow. "I'm so sorry for what happened to Abby, and for what you had to deal with. I never wanted it to be—"

"Whatever," Victoria interrupted, cool again. "You see the problem now. I'm not worried about somebody hurting Abby. I'm worried about *Abby* hurting Abby. That's why we need to find her, fast."

"Okay, right." Jill rubbed her face, straightening up. She willed her emotions under control. "I know what to do. I need to go back to the police and light a fire under them. It's been another whole day, she's still missing, and they should know all the facts, especially this one."

"No, I'll go instead. I can do it. It's my place."

"Can we go together?" Jill asked, hopeful. "I've been there before, and they know me. I can meet you there, it's Central Detectives, on 21st Street."

"No, I'd prefer it if you didn't go. I'll go with Brian." Victoria's tone was final, and Jill could feel her maintaining the wall between them.

"Why don't we just go together?"

"Jill, you have to respect what I'm saying. Can't you do that, please?"

"Okay, fine, if that's what you want." Jill surrendered, tired of fighting and getting nowhere. "Ask for Detective

Reed. He's the one who handled the investigation of your father's death. Detective Pitkowski is the one I spoke with, because Reed wasn't there."

"Got it."

"Please call me and let me know how it went?"

"If I have time. I have a brief due, for legal writing."

Jill bit her tongue. "Please let me know if Abby calls you then, okay?"

"That, I'll do."

"I think I'll go up to Manhattan tomorrow and stop by Neil's apartment, to see if they'll tell me anything they wouldn't tell you."

"Okay, whatever. Knock yourself out."

"Thanks, bye. Love you," Jill said automatically, hearing herself end the call the way she always used to, with Victoria.

*Love you.*

"Babe, you okay?" Sam asked, from the threshold of the kitchen.

Jill pressed END. She didn't know if Victoria heard her, or how long Sam had been standing there.

And she didn't like the look in his eye.

# 31.

"Did you say that Abby tried to commit suicide?" Sam asked, quietly.

"Yes, a while ago, after William and I broke up."

Sam padded over barefoot and cupped her shoulder. "I'm sorry, honey."

"Thanks, but it's not about me, it's about her."

"You feel guilty."

"As I should." Jill shook her head, slumping in the chair. "When we find her, I'll make sure she goes to Sandy, I swear. It's a way for me to make amends."

"You don't need to make amends."

"Yes, I do." Jill straightened up and met his eye. "She suffered after the divorce."

"They all did."

"It doesn't mean that she didn't, and in some ways, it was unique."

Sam frowned. "Was it really?"

"Yes." Jill could sense the tension growing between them, as if the kitchen had developed an atmospheric pressure of its own, brewing a domestic storm. "She tried to kill herself. Victoria didn't. Megan didn't. That's unique."

"Everyone suffers in his or her own way."

"True, but that's beside the point." Jill stood up and walked past him to the sink, where she grabbed a tumbler from the cabinet and let the door close with a *bang* that woke Beef up, blinking.

"I'm sorry," Sam said. "I don't want to fuss."

"Me, neither. Sorry." Jill ran water into the glass, turned off the faucet, and took a sip. It was warm and tasted like nothing. She tried to move past the moment. The air felt too thick to breathe. "Anyway, the problem is we don't know where Abby is, and time matters. It doesn't make sense that she's disappeared of her own volition. If she would try to commit suicide because I wasn't in her life, why would she vanish now that I am?"

"Because now she knows you're watching." Sam came over and leaned against the counter, on his elbow. "It's how she keeps your attention. It's consistent with the drunk-driving, the phone calls, the requests for help. You stay if you're needed, so she acts needy."

"I wouldn't keep ascribing so much bad motive to her, honey." Jill felt her chest tighten. "Her father, he was a schemer, but she isn't. If I can separate the two, so can you."

"But you're seeing her suicide attempt as a game-changer, and it isn't. This isn't new news, not really. We knew she was troubled."

Jill couldn't hide her irritation. "Anyway, you heard, I'm going to New York to find her, tomorrow."

"Why *New York*?"

Jill thought he said it like *Neptune,* even though they went up there all the time, for the museums. "Neil Straub is a guy who was in investments with William. He lives in an apartment in the West Village. Victoria couldn't find out much about him, but I hope I can."

"Why do you think so?"

"Because I don't take no for an answer."

"That's for damn sure."

Jill looked over, then let it go. She dumped out the water and set the tumbler in the sink since the dishwasher wasn't through with its cycle. "Abby could have gone up to be with Neil. Or he could have taken her in, even. Or he could be in danger, too."

Sam lifted an eyebrow. "Then it's not a great idea, your going there."

"I'm just going to ask a few questions, like if the doorman has seen Abby with him recently. If it seems dangerous, I'll go to the police."

"In New York?"

"Yes. They have cops there."

Sam's lips flattened. "Do you want to fight? It seems as if you do."

"No, I don't, but I just don't want to be"—Jill paused, searching for the right word—"*resisted,* at every turn. To get pushback when I'm trying to do the right thing."

"But what if I disagree that it's the right thing? I'm supposed to be a yes man?"

"No."

"Then what?"

Jill leaned on the counter, suddenly weary. "Abby is still missing, Sam. She's a suicidal girl. I'm not making something out of nothing."

"Still, it's not your problem."

"Yes, it is. I can't unknow something. I helped create the problem and I can't deny it."

"No, you didn't," Sam said, firmly.

"Then we don't agree, and in any event, who's going to look for her? Her parents are dead."

"What happens to Megan, when you're in New York?"

Jill thought it was a low blow. "What does she have to do with it? She's in school tomorrow, then she has practice. Manhattan is two hours away. I should be home by five at the latest, even if I take the train."

Sam shook his head. "I would think that after yesterday, you'd let go of this Abby thing, but you're just getting in deeper."

"I can't let it go, now." Jill raised her voice, though she knew Sam wouldn't. Whenever they fought, she felt like a screaming meemie. The angriest he ever got was a sort of scholarly consternation.

"You have to let it go. Megan needs you."

"During the day, for what? I'd be running errands, making calls, or answering email while she's at school." Jill didn't add that she'd been feeling more and more useless on her days off, like she didn't deserve to work part-time anymore, especially after what Sheryl had said.

"So we're in for the duration, are we?" Sam took off his reading glasses and tossed them to the counter, an uncharacteristic gesture.

"What's that mean?"

"It means we're going down this road. You're fully on board with Abby, and we're left behind."

"Who is?"

"Megan and me."

Jill moaned. "Oh, come on, that's not fair. I'm paying special attention to Megan after what happened, but I don't have to choose, I can multitask. Nobody's where they are anymore. I have to return calls while I make dinner. I have to answer email when I'm in the car, waiting for Megan. Every mom does it, every day. *I* do it every day."

"And what about me?" Sam's blue eyes pierced her. "Where are my wishes in your plans? Where are my concerns? Do I even factor in, or do I just keep the home fires burning while you go off on your own?"

"Do I have to get permission from you to go to New York?" Jill asked, incredulous.

"No, but you're not thinking this through, you're just reacting."

"Yes, because it's an emergency. I'm trying to find Abby. She could kill herself."

"Let's say you find her. Does she come with us to Austin, or did you forget?"

Jill had forgotten. They were due to visit Steven, this weekend. "I haven't gotten that far."

"Well, you should. You have a stepson. When did he stop counting?"

"He didn't."

"Explore this with me, then." Sam opened his hands, palms up. "Assume you find Abby. Then what? You help her live on her own?"

"I suppose so," Jill answered. Her thoughts hadn't gotten that far on that issue, either.

"You don't want her to move in with us, do you?"

Jill blinked, and Sam eyed her fixedly.

"Well?"

Jill felt her heart tug.

"Please tell me it's impossible."

"I can't."

Sam winced. "You're kidding."

"No."

"I knew it." Sam shook his head, looking away. "Why not? It's your house."

Jill didn't want to go there again. It was an old wound. "You moved in here because we didn't want to uproot Megan. You resent that now?"

"No, not at all. I'd do anything for Megan, but not for Abby." Sam's lips went tight. "Does Abby take Steven's room?"

"What do you want from me, Sam? Just forget about her? You're making me choose, her or you, is that what you want?"

"Tell you what I *don't* want. I don't want another kid, and I don't want *that* kid, in particular. You're simply ignoring my wishes, no matter what I say or do, and I don't want to be in a marriage in which my wife gets what she wants, no matter what I want."

"So don't marry me!"

"Then I won't!" Sam shot back, and for a second, the words hung in the air between them.

Jill was too angry to appease him, and their eyes met without seeing each other.

"I'll sleep at the lab." Sam turned around and left the kitchen, and Beef lifted his ears and looked bewildered at him, then back at Jill.

Jill felt anguished tears come to her eyes, but blinked them away.

# 32.

Jill stood in the backyard with Beef, her arms folded across her chest, trying not to think about Sam. He hadn't called or texted, and neither had she. She didn't know if he'd really meant what he said, and she didn't know if she did, either.

*Then I won't!*

She bit her lip, wondering if they were going to fall apart, dreading she'd been right, that forever was impossible. She found herself back on the night her marriage to William had ended, when she'd confronted him about the theft. They were alone upstairs in their bedroom, and she'd hoped to ask him about it calmly, but as soon as she mentioned the script pads, he'd flown into a rage like she'd never seen from him before.

*How dare you accuse me! How dare you! You disgust me!*

Jill had gasped, frightened. His face had gone bright red. Veins bulged in his neck and forehead. He was spitting mad. She didn't know what he would do. *We have a videotape,* she said, and that was all she got to say. William had raced from the bedroom and down the stairs, Jill terrified at his heels, not knowing if he'd hurt the girls or what he would do. *No, William, stop, please, we can talk about it!* She hadn't seen this coming, this violence. *Don't hurt them, don't hurt them!*

William had raced into the family room, where the girls were watching TV and doing homework on their laptops, in sweats and flannel pajamas, bowls of microwave popcorn at their sides, with Beef eating fallen kernels off the rug. They looked up as their parents ran into the room, crazed and screaming, Jill pulling at William, the three incredulous girls, their mouths horrified circles, like silent screams.

William yelled, *Abby, Victoria, get up, get your coat, we're leaving! Right now! Get the hell up!*

*Dad, what?* Victoria shook her head, terrified and stricken. *No! Is this a joke?*

Abby burst into tears. *No, I won't, I can't! No, Daddy, no! Jill, Jill? Why? We live here!*

*GET UP, GIRLS! NOW!* William grabbed Abby by her shoulder, ripping her pajama top, her favorite pair, covered with cartoon tabby cats.

*DADDY?* Abby shrieked, terrified, and Victoria fled the family room, her laptop falling to the floor.

*Mommy, Mommy!* Megan had run howling to Jill's arms. *Mommy!*

*William, no!* Jill had shouted at him, shielding Megan with her very body, wishing she could run after the girls but Megan was shaking, clinging to her, screaming and screaming. William had yanked Abby away, dragging her, hysterical, to the entrance hall, throwing his daughters out of their own house, grabbing the car keys on the way, slamming the front door.

*BAM!*

In a matter of seconds, the family had been blown apart, like a bomb exploding in the family room, and all that was left was Jill and Megan weeping, collapsed together on the floor, and Beef barking and barking, running back and forth, alarmed and not knowing why, so freaked out he ignored the popcorn, spilled in bowlfuls on the rug.

Jill wiped a tear from her eye, coming back into the present. She refolded her arms, hugging herself, breathing in the night air. It was cool out, and the darkness above took on a softness, with the stars obscured. Crickets kept up a constant chirping, and bats squeaked noisily behind the louvered shutters of the house.

Beef lifted his muzzle, turning toward the pool, and she looked over, but couldn't see what had drawn his attention. The flagstone deck was slick from the humidity, and the pool looked black, without the light on. She always opened the pool early and heated it because she loved to swim, but she hadn't gone for a night swim yet. She could use one, now. Her last was last summer, with Sam.

*I'll sleep at the lab.*

Jill went over to the pool, found the outlet hidden near the steps, and flicked on the light. It transformed the pool into a glowing turquoise rectangle, like a blue topaz in an emerald cut, a "dinner ring" her mother used to called them, wistfully. She remembered the day she'd bought the house, happy to be able to afford an in-ground pool. She'd grown up using the public pool, in much humbler circumstances, her father a draftsman and her mother a nurse.

On impulse, she slid out of her sweater and khakis and let them drop to the flagstone, which left her in a bra and panties. It was the same thing as a bathing suit, and nobody could see through the privacy fence. She stepped into the pool and stood on the top step, getting used to the cold water, like the old Italian grandmas at the Jersey shore. Beef trotted over, standing on the deck and wagging his tail, and she petted his head, staying in the moment. Just her and a dog and the water. No men, no kids.

She waded into the shallow end to her waist, gasping at the sudden chill, then she plunged underneath, stretching her fingers ahead of her, feeling the cold everywhere at once, as she held her breath and plowed under the water, driving a wedge, then she was off.

She swam freestyle, her favorite stroke, and tried to focus on technique, bending and extending her arms, keeping her elbows high, holding her head down, in line with her spine, then rolling to catch her breath and pointing her toes to the back of the pool. She was breathing hard in no time, her body remembering its job even though her lungs weren't as able, and she reached the wall and did a flawed flip-turn, then slipped through the water again, rolling left, then right with each stroke, trying to streamline her body, ignoring the raggedness of her breath and the ache in her arms. Her college coach used to say that nothing trains you for swimming but swimming, and he'd been right, though she kept on anyway.

Jill swam, letting her body feel its own way and find its natural rhythm. She heard the gasp of her own breathing, and she tried to maintain the pace, taking the fewest strokes because it would make her faster, striving for economy of effort, matching the gliding motion she visualized as she swam. She focused with all of her being, exerting muscle, heart, and mind, feeling the sheer physical pleasure of the water sliding against her breasts and tummy.

She hit the wall again, did a better flip-turn, and powered forward, fingertips reaching and legs fluttering until her body finally found its stride, slipping through the water at speed, her brain focused only on her swimming, like a meditation in motion, and she hit the wall again, then again, swimming one lap, then the next, effortless as a jet at cruising altitude, until she exhausted herself, when she stopped, her heart thundering, floated suspended in the pool, then holding on to the jagged edge of the thick flagstone and climbing out, gasping for breath but feeling better. Cleansed, relaxed, new.

Beef barked at the fence, standing up, his tail straight out, and Jill hoisted herself out of the pool, turning to see where he was looking, but there was nothing there. The neighbors, the Weitzes, weren't in their driveway, and the neighborhood had gone to sleep.

"Quiet, Beef, no!" she said, her chest heaving from exertion.

Beef ignored her, barking and bounding to the privacy fence, as if someone were on the other side, and Jill rose to a crouch, dripping wet, beginning to wonder.

Beef barked and barked, the hair rising on the back of his neck, and before Jill understood why, she was scooping up her clothes, instinctively covering her body with them, feeling exposed and vulnerable.

"Beef, come!" Jill shouted, hurrying toward the house. Maybe she was being paranoid and maybe she wasn't, but she had to get inside.

Jill tore open the door and scooted into the house, dropping the clothes and hiding behind the door, but she couldn't leave Beef out.

"Beef, *come*!" she called, with fear in her voice, and Beef came running to her, his tail between his legs as he bolted inside the house.

Jill slammed the door closed behind him, locked it, and twisted the deadbolt, then hurried to the burglar alarm pad and pressed STAY, listening to the beep of its exit delay, staying close to the wall, trying to hide from the windows, dripping water onto the hardwood floor, spooked.

And wishing she knew what was on the other side of that fence.

# 33.

"Megan, hurry." Jill didn't want to miss the train to New York and hurried to the car under a clear, morning sky. Megan inched along, texting with her head down, her knapsack and swim bag hanging in the crook of her arm and banging against her legs. Jill unlocked the car, put her purse inside, and climbed in, starting the engine. "Megan, *today*."

"Chill, Mom." Megan opened the passenger door and tossed her bags onto the floor, then climbed into her seat, phone in hand. "We've got plenty of time."

"No, actually, we don't." Jill could have launched into a lecture, but Megan had already returned to texting, absorbed. "What's going on, if I may ask?"

"Just Courtney," Megan answered, head down, and Jill steered down their street, waving to Janet Baker, who was leaving for work.

"Oh. I thought it was Guitar Hero."

"No." Megan looked over, frowning. "Mom, is Sam coming home? I heard you guys fighting, last night. Then he left."

Jill almost braked in surprise. Megan didn't need that

kind of stress, especially now. "He slept at his lab, and he'll be back tonight," Jill answered, though she wondered if that was true. She hadn't heard a word from Sam, nor had she sent him one.

"He doesn't like Abby, does he?"

"He will when he gets to know her."

"No, he won't. I get it. She's changed." Megan checked her phone, which chimed to signal an incoming text. "I like the old Abby better than the new one, too. But I know the old one's in there, somewhere, if that makes any sense."

"It does." Jill cruised down the street, joining the line of traffic heading to work, all the drivers sipping travel mugs of fresh coffee and making their first phone calls of the day, like a parade of distraction.

"I don't want anything to happen to her."

"Me, neither, and it won't."

"Do you think she's, like, a runaway?"

"Honestly, no. It's all right." Jill patted her leg. "Tell me about you. What's up today?"

"I have a French test."

"Oh, Jeez." Jill was a little out of touch. Normally they went over her French vocab together. "You ready?"

"Did Abby run away because of Sam?"

"No, not at all, and she didn't run away. Like we said, she could be with a date, and we're doing all we can to find her. Victoria went to the police, and they're handling it. Don't worry about Abby."

Megan fell silent, looking down at the phone. "She was embarrassed that she barfed on the bed. Maybe if I was nicer about it—"

"No, that's not it," Jill interrupted, to nip that thought in the bud. "It was nothing you did, and she didn't run away. I don't know where she is, but she'll turn up. Honey, please try and put her out of your mind."

"But if she's like a missing person, like on TV, we have

to hurry." Megan's forehead wrinkled. "They say you only have forty-eight hours, Mom."

"Don't worry," Jill said, with more confidence than she felt, and Megan's phone chimed again, but she ignored it, her gaze searching.

"I went to the stair, I listened. What if she hurt herself?"

Jill sighed inwardly. "Okay, she tried to do that once, a long time ago, but there's no reason to think she will again."

"You think she could. You told Sam you're worried."

Jill tensed, busted by her own daughter. She wasn't sure what to say. "Just because I worry doesn't mean you should worry. You know I worry too much."

"But remember Josh's sister?"

"Abby won't hurt herself, not again." Jill cringed. A classmate of Megan's had a sister in ninth grade who'd committed suicide, and it had generated a candlelight vigil, an assembly, and a memorial garden, the public-school protocol for grief-management.

"But she *could* do it. She's drinking too much, and her Dad just died."

"Stop, enough, she'll be fine, and the police will find her," Jill said firmly. She had to get this out of Megan's mind, but she knew that wasn't possible.

"If the police will do it, then why are you going to New York?"

"I can do my part, too." Jill honked the horn. The car in front was going too slowly. "A friend of William's lives there, and he might know where she is. Now, tell me about this French test. Is it vocab?"

Megan's phone chimed again, another text coming in, but she ignored it. "Mom, I heard what Sam said last night, that he'd sacrifice for me but not for Abby. Did he say that?"

"Basically, yes." Jill hit the gas, hiding her dismay.

"I love him." Megan checked the phone as another text came in, then she thumbed in a response. "You guys are going to make up, right?"

"I hope so." Jill looked over, and a frown crossed Megan's downturned face. "What's going on?"

"Nothing." Megan pressed her lips over her braces, typing away. "When William was the dad, Abby was the first choice. But now that Sam's the dad, I'm the first choice. I kinda like being the first choice."

Jill hid her dismay, wondering if she'd ever be able to navigate the waters of her own family. She could swim in a pool, but they were an ocean, where the currents crossed and collided with each other, flowing too deep to be seen from the surface.

Megan halted her texting and looked over. "Is that a bad thing to say? That I like being first?"

"No, not if it's true," Jill answered, eyeing the red light.

# 34.

Jill looked through the smudgy glass window of the cab, and a warm day in Manhattan whizzed past. Cars, vans, and bicycle messengers clogged the streets, and filling the sidewalks were Asian tourists, a pierced gaggle of hipsters, and a brace of bright young men, puffing away on acrid cigars, their ties flying. Mostly everyone talked into a cell phone or a Bluetooth, all of them hurrying, smoking, and eating on the fly, their lives lived in fast-forward. A cacophony of honking, shouted epithets, random laughter, and the throbbing bass from a passing radio wafted through the window, though Jill had silenced the news video that played in the cab, hoping to be alone with her thoughts.

*I went to the stair, I listened.*

Jill checked her BlackBerry for the umpteenth time, for a call from Abby. There were no red asterisks by the phone icon, indicating a missed call, and she put her phone back into her purse. She hadn't heard from Sam, either, though she'd thought about calling him, but didn't. On the train, she'd ended up in the quiet car by accident, but it gave her time to think. She didn't know what she would say to him, nor what she wanted to hear. She was old enough to know

that soft words wouldn't smooth over the situation, and a
very real disagreement divided them.

*That's no way to run a marriage.*

Jill shooed Sam's voice from her head, eyeing the sky,
where a pale sun hung like an afterthought, nature herself
taking a backseat in the city. The cab turned onto the West
Side Highway, the six-lane highway that ran along the
Hudson, and a helicopter flew over the river, pitched forward like a top-heavy bug. On the New Jersey side, the
old-school painted LACKAWANNA sign contrasted with the
stylish neon W HOTEL sign, glowing red even in daylight.
Air thick with garbage and gas odors blew inside the cab,
and the humidity made Jill uncomfortable in her navy
linen blazer, khaki pants, and a white shirt, with her hair
pulled back into a simple ponytail. She was dressed to talk
her way past the doorman, a mom on a mission. More ac-
curately, an ex-stepmom on a mission.

*What if she hurt herself?*

Her gut tensed as the cab left the highway, made a few
more turns through a fashionable warren of West Village
streets, and pulled finally onto West 11th. They bumped
over the cobblestones on the street, which was lined with
ritzy apartment buildings, many modern, and all glass.
Tall, skinny trees, boxed in by wrought-iron fences, threw
scant shadows on sidewalks that had been hosed clean, still
drying in spots.

"This is it," the cabbie said, and Jill grabbed her purse,
slid the money from her wallet, and handed it to him
through the plastic window.

"Thanks, keep the change." Jill got out and took stock
of the building. It was shorter and smaller than the modern
ones, classy in an old Knickerbocker way, with art-deco
fluting over the entrance. She walked to the door, pushed
through, and scanned the lobby, which was long and nar-
row, with a black-and-white tile floor. Brass sconces flanked

a black security desk, and the doorman looked to be in his sixties. He was tall and lean, with frizzy gray hair, wire-rimmed bifocals, and a navy blazer that looked unfortunately like Jill's own.

"Nice jacket," she said, walking over.

"It looks better on you," the doorman said with a polite grin. His black nametag read MICHAEL, and a *New York Post* lay on his desk, open to the sports page. "How can I help you?"

"I'm looking for a man who lives here. Neil Straub."

"Mr. Straub? He's not in."

Jill was ready for that. "When did you see him last?"

"Sorry, but we don't give out that information."

"I know, but this is an emergency. I'm Jill Farrow, and your name's Michael?"

"Mike Moran, yes."

"Mike, please help me, if you can. Neil is a good friend of my ex-husband, who just passed away last Tuesday, leaving two daughters. One of them is missing, and I'm trying to find her."

"That's too bad." Mike frowned, with genuine sympathy.

"Her sister Victoria came here yesterday, looking for her and asking about Neil Straub. Do you remember her?"

"No, I wasn't here. It was my day off."

"I see." Jill reached in her purse and withdrew two photos she'd printed. The top one was a recent one of Abby, from William's computer. "This is my stepdaughter, Abby Skyler. Have you seen her? She could have come to visit Neil."

"Hmm." Mike took the photo, eyeing it. "I haven't seen her. Mind you, I see a lot of people in this job, but I tend to remember."

"So you don't remember seeing her?"

"No."

"Who covers the desk on your day off?"

"There's three of us, and we rotate. I'm day shift, Tuesdays and Thursdays, and we split the night shifts, plus we got the weekends."

"So when would the night-shift doorman come on?"

"Leon comes in at five."

"Do you have his phone, so I can call him?"

"No can do, sorry."

"How about his address, and I'll look up his phone number?"

"No, sorry." Mike buckled his lower lip. "I'd like to help, but I can't give that information out. If you stop back at five o'clock, you can ask him then."

Jill thought a minute. It made sense that the day-shift doorman hadn't seen Abby. She'd gone missing on Saturday night, and maybe that was when she'd come up. "Okay, maybe I will. Do you think Neil, Mr. Straub, will be back by then?"

"I doubt it. He travels a lot."

"What does he do? Something financial, right?"

Mike hesitated. "Yeah, but you didn't hear it from me. I shouldn't have said what I did. Keep it to yourself, okay? I need this job."

"Sure."

"Mr. Straub is a nice guy, and rules are rules. The board takes them very serious."

"The board?"

"The co-op board. They run the place." Mike handed her back the photos, but the bottom one fluttered to the desk. It was the one of Neil and William in sunglasses, on the golf course in Pebble Beach. Mike picked it up. "Oh, there's Mr. Straub. Musta been younger then."

"Yes, by a few years, I think."

"Looks that way." Mike chuckled, handing her back the photo. "But he's gotta lose that shirt. I mean, pink?"

Jill didn't get it. In the picture, Neil was wearing a navy blue polo shirt, and William had on a pale pink one. "What do you mean? Neil's not wearing pink."

"Sure he is." Mike pointed to William. "I'm not color-blind, and this is pink."

"Yes, the shirt is pink, but that's not Neil."

"Yes, it is." Mike tapped William's face with a bitten-off fingernail. "This here is Mr. Straub."

Jill didn't understand. Mike was pointing at William's face. "That's not Neil Straub. The other guy is."

"I know Mr. Straub when I see him, and the guy in pink is Mr. Straub."

Jill put it together, hiding her astonishment. "You mean Neil Straub is William Skyler?"

"I don't know what you're talking about." Mike handed the photo back. "All I know is, the man in the pink shirt is Neil Straub. I know the man, I talk to him all the time. He's lived here, like, three years, in 4-D."

"Thanks." Jill put the photo in her purse, struggling to get her bearings. So William had another identity, a double life as Neil Straub. She wouldn't have guessed as much in a million years. William was a con artist, but this had to be his sickest scam ever, because he'd deceived his own children. Abby couldn't have known or she would have told Jill. Jill's next thought was that William's double life could be connected to Abby's disappearance.

"Excuse me, hold on." Mike's attention shifted to the elevator as it *ping*ed, and its doors opened, revealing an attractive woman, well-dressed in a white pantsuit, carrying a purse, a cell phone, and a large cardboard box.

"Mike, honey," the woman called. "Can you give me a hand, please?"

"Sure thing, Belle," Mike called back, coming around the desk and taking the box.

"Wait, Mike, please." Jill followed him. "Who's the other guy in the photo, wearing the navy shirt?"

"I have no idea," Mike answered, over his shoulder. "Belle, where do you want the box?"

"On the desk, temporarily." The woman eyed the lobby, annoyed. "My client isn't here yet? Sheesh! I hate it when people are late."

Jill couldn't let it go. "Mike, please, just one last question."

Mike walked back and set the box on the desk, then turned to Jill with a frown. "What?"

"Is there anyone who runs the building, like a super I could speak with?"

"Only residents speak with the super," Mike answered, his tone newly official, but the woman lifted a perfectly penciled eyebrow.

"Why, dear? Are you interested in a unit? It's wonderful building, and I used to live here myself. I can show you an apartment that's very special. In this market, it's a steal." The woman thrust out a manicured hand. "I'm Belle Kahan, with Prudential."

Jill had nothing to lose, and everything to gain. "You know, I *am* looking for an apartment in this building."

Mike turned, pursing his lips tight. But he said nothing.

# 35.

Jill walked into a large, empty apartment, with two tall windows that overlooked the Hudson River. She scanned the view, her thoughts in tumult. It boggled her mind to think that William had lived in this very building, as Neil Straub. She had a zillion questions, but the only one that mattered was Abby.

"Quite a view, eh?" Belle asked, gesturing at the windows. "It doesn't get better than this."

"It's great." Jill managed a smile. "What can you tell me about the building?"

"It's a co-op, very exclusive, very fiscally responsible. It's well-run, and smaller than others on the street, only forty units. Are you working with a Realtor?"

"Not yet."

"I'd be happy to work with you. I know this building and the entire West Village, like the back of my hand. I live on Horatio now."

"I like this building." Jill remembered the doorman saying that William's apartment was 4-D. "Have you sold other apartments in it?"

"Tons. What do you do?"

"I'm a doctor," Jill answered, and Belle's eyes lit up.

"Wow! Who doesn't want a doctor in the house? You'll pass the board with flying colors."

Jill was wondering how William had passed a co-op board, with a false identity. "I've never applied to a co-op building before. What information do you have to show them?"

"Everything and then some. Tax returns and bank statements, and you need to get two recommendations and references, besides a letter from your landlord saying you're paid up. Are you currently renting in the city?"

"No." Jill still didn't get it. If William had to show that much information to the board, he'd have a whole separate identity set up with a bank. "How careful is the board? Not just anybody can get in here, can they?"

"No, but you'll do fine. This board isn't as power-crazy as the ones on the Upper East. It's much more laid back, downtown." Belle flashed a lipsticked smile. "You're engaged, I see. Nice ring. Are you scouting for both of you?"

"Yes." Jill managed a smile.

"Good for you. This building has a really nice group of residents. Very chummy, because it's so small. They have parties on the roof deck every Fourth of July, to watch the fireworks."

Jill got an idea. "Funny, I saw someone in the lobby the other day, whom I think I know from college. Neil Straub. Tall, good-looking. I think he lives in 4-D."

"4-D?" Belle paused, thinking. "Oh, right, he's a subletter. I don't know him, but I sold that apartment a few years ago to a couple from London, and they moved back home. There's only a few subletters in the building, and the board likes it that way. Don't have the same controls, with a subletter."

"Do subletters have to get board approval?"

"No."

Jill thought it explained how William had gotten past the board.

"I know who you mean." Belle leaned over, in a cloud of flowery perfume. "He's quite the ladies' man. My best friend still lives in 4-A, and we see what goes on with him. He keeps busy, if you know what I mean."

Jill did, unfortunately. "He hasn't changed since college, huh?"

"They never do, girlfriend. Like the kids say, he's a *playa*."

"I guess he never got married."

"I've see him with the same girl a few times, but I doubt she knows about the others."

Jill doubted it, too. "What does she look like, this one?"

"Thin, blonde, and young. What else?"

"What does he do for a living, do you know? He used to be in the pharmaceuticals business."

"Don't know, but it's something that makes a lot of money. He drives a big Mercedes. Silver. I know because he took my parking space once."

"Doesn't the building have parking?"

"Yes, but it costs extra. He was out front, unloading."

"Where's the garage, and how does the parking work? Are there numbered spaces?"

"Yes, all marked by the apartment number." Belle gestured behind her, to the north. "The garage is at the back of the building. Sometimes it's easier to drop off your bags, then go park. Now, shall I show you the kitchen?"

"Yes, thanks." Jill learned nothing more and spent the next half-hour being led around an apartment she didn't want, trying to piece together a puzzle she hadn't seen coming. She bid Belle good-bye, left the apartment building, and stood on the sidewalk, revising her plan. It wouldn't make sense to come back at five to see the night-shift doorman. He wouldn't recognize Abby because she undoubtedly hadn't been here.

*The garage is at the back of the building.*

Jill walked to the end of the street, heading for the garage, curious if William's car was there. Runners trotted past her toward the river. She took a right onto the West Side Highway, and traffic had picked up, *whoosh*ing loudly in both directions, uptown and down. She turned right onto the next street, a skinny sidestreet of cobblestones, and kept walking.

Midway up, Jill found a gate over a driveway, which had to be the garage to the building. There was a door next to the entrance, and she made a beeline for it. She tried the knob, but it was locked. She glanced behind her, to make sure no one saw her, when suddenly, she spotted a black SUV, parked at the curb behind a row of others, on the West Side Highway.

Jill froze. The SUV hadn't been there before, or she hadn't seen it. It looked like the same model as the padiddle that had been following her. The headlights were off because it was daytime. She couldn't see the license plate. Sunlight glinted off its chrome grille, and a man sat behind the wheel, a still figure in shadow.

Jill told herself to stay calm. It would've been impossible to follow her here, so it probably wasn't the same car, but there was only one way to find out. She turned on her heel and walked toward the car. Suddenly the black SUV's engine roared to life, the SUV reversed, cut the wheels, and started to wedge itself out of the parking space.

Jill broke into a run, almost tripping on the cobble-stones. It couldn't be a coincidence. The SUV had to be leaving because she was coming. She reached the line of parked cars just as the SUV pulled onto the West Side Highway, heading uptown. It had a Pennsylvania license plate that read TJU-something.

"Wait!" Jill yelled, on the run. "Stop! Help!"

And before she realized what she was doing, she was running down the West Side Highway after the SUV.

# 36.

"Stop that car!" Jill screamed, frantic. Heads turned. Runners stopped running. A cyclist braked, putting down his cleated shoe.

Jill ran as fast as she could. Her legs churned. Her arms pumped. Her flats slapped the sidewalk.

The SUV veered to the middle lane but couldn't go forward. The cars ahead of it were stopped at a red light. Crosstown traffic flowed onto the highway, in force. There were traffic lights at almost every block, and it was the only thing that gave Jill a fighting chance of catching him.

She ran harder, almost colliding with an older man walking a poodle. She kept her eyes glued to the SUV driver. He was looking this way and that, his head swiveling left and right. He was blocked in and knew it.

A moving van pulled out of the cross street and stopped, blocking traffic. The light turned green, and the SUV and the other cars started honking.

Jill raced ahead, gaining ground. Only half a block separated her from the SUV, then less. The moving van would go any second, pulling onto the far side of the highway, heading downtown.

Jill tore down the sidewalk, glanced behind her, and ran into the street like a madwoman. "Don't hit me!" she screamed, putting her hand up.

The red Saturn behind her braked, then started honking. Van and limo drivers looked over, angry. "Honk!" blared a tractor-trailer, startling her.

Jill struggled to keep up her pace. Her breaths were ragged. Her thighs burned. She closed in on the SUV. Eight cars, then seven, then six. She was almost there. The Saturn hung back, honking.

The moving van inched forward. The SUV honked and honked, still blocked.

Jill tried to run into the middle lane, but a battered pickup wouldn't let her in, roaring past her as if she'd been in a car.

"Stop that car!" Jill shouted. The SUV still couldn't go. Her lungs were about to explode. Sweat poured into her eyes. Her purse swung wildly at her side. She clamped it down with a hand.

She burst ahead, closer to the SUV. There were three cars left between them, then two, then one.

Suddenly the moving van cleared the lane. The SUV accelerated and switched into the fast lane.

Jill couldn't keep up. The SUV found open road and was getting away. Her heart thundered. Her legs wobbled. She stumbled, almost falling.

The Saturn driver leaned from his window. "Get outta the street!" he hollered, waving at her.

Jill threw her purse at the SUV in frustration, hitting the back just as the driver took off, cut the wheel, and jumped the median, making a daring U-turn and zooming down the other side of the highway, going downtown.

"Move, lady!" the Saturn driver yelled.

Jill hurried to the curb, then doubled over, trying to catch her breath. A police siren blared behind her, but it sounded too far away to get here in time. She straightened up and watched a minivan run over her purse and Black-Berry.

Cars and trucks *whoosh*ed past her, and the police siren sounded closer. She blinked sweat from her eyes and spotted the NYPD cruiser, driving toward her.

She stuck out her hand to flag it down.

# 37.

Jill sat in a hard chair beside Officer Mulvane's desk, and he was just finished typing his report on an old computer, with a grimy keyboard. The Greenwich Village precinct house had the same desks, mismatched file cabinets, and cluttered bulletin boards as the police station in Phila-delphia, except for the moving tribute in its entrance hall, where six gleaming bronze plaques on a tan marble wall memorialized its six officers who gave their lives on September 11, 2001. Jill had paused at the memorial, say-ing a silent prayer.

"Okay, that's about it." Officer Mulvane hit a key and the form printed at a cheap desk printer with a Yankees sticker. He was a beefy cop in his thirties, with bright blue eyes, a ready smile, and thinning blond hair. He extracted the form, picked up a pen, and handed both to Jill. "Wanna give me your John Hancock?"

"Sure." Jill skimmed the typed portion, which was her account of what had happened, then signed it at the bot-tom. Her flattened purse sat on her lap, and her BlackBerry was road kill, but she felt more like herself, having washed up in the ladies room. "So what do you think, Officer? Can you help me find Abby?"

"Here's how it goes." Office Mulvane eyed Jill, pursing his lips. "I'd like to help you find your kid, I mean, your ex's kid, but we don't have jurisdiction. If your ex was murdered in Philly, it's a Philly case. If the kid went missing in Philly, it's a Philly case. Here, take this back." Officer Mulvane handed over the photo of William and the mystery man in the blue shirt. "Neither of these guys are known to us, much less a Known Wanted. I can't run a check on them using the images alone."

"Thanks." Jill stuffed the picture into her broken purse. "But here's what I don't understand about jurisdiction. My ex is renting an apartment a few blocks from here, under a fake name, with fake identity. Doesn't that give you jurisdiction?"

"No. Your ex-husband could be guilty of fraud in connection with the apartment, but not all fraud is criminal." Officer Mulvane nodded hello at another cop passing his desk, a radio attached to the cop's thick belt and flopping against his side. "If your ex-husband entered into a contract with the co-op membership under a false name, it's not enough to involve NYPD."

"But what if he's impersonating someone? Isn't that criminal?"

"Criminal impersonation is somebody pretending to be somebody famous, to get favors or money. Like we got a guy, he's in here all the time, pretends he's Robert De Niro to get a free meal." Officer Mulvane picked up a Styrofoam cup of coffee with two thick fingers, as if he'd crush it otherwise. "Your ex-husband isn't doing that."

"So you need jurisdiction—"

"No," Officer Mulvane interrupted, setting down his cup. "I don't *need* jurisdiction. I can't act unless I *have* jurisdiction. I'm not looking for things to do, I got plenty."

"Okay, what about the fact that I think I'm being followed by a black SUV, on the West Side Highway?"

"You don't have any real evidence that you are, and you don't know it's the same car."

"The license plate has the T, and he drove away when he saw me coming."

"Dr. Farrow." Officer Mulvane smiled, sympathetically. "Don't take this the wrong way, but I saw you, and you looked drunk and crazy. No wonder the guy hightailed it. And lots of plates start with T."

Jill tried another tack. "What if I were a friend of Neil Straub's, and I come to you and tell you that he's missing. I tell you he lives a few blocks away and I'm worried about him. What if he's dead in his apartment, right now? That would be criminal, and you'd have jurisdiction, right?"

"Right, but that's not what you said."

"It could be." Jill saw her opening, but Officer Mulvane frowned, shifting heavily away from her, in his chair.

"It isn't. I stopped for you because I thought you were a knucklehead about to get run over."

"Now you know I'm a knucklehead trying to find my daughter." Jill managed a smile. "You want me to go out, come back in again, and tell you the new story?"

"It's not a game, Doc."

"I know, and I'm not playing. I really need help. No one's looking out for Abby but me. You understand, you have a child." Jill gestured at the photo on his desk, of an adorable little boy in a blue baseball uniform, resting a bat on his shoulder. "What if your son were out there on his own, after you were gone?"

"Oh, don't do that to me." Officer Mulvane looked pained, and Jill thought of the 9/11 memorial in the entrance hall. She realized that cops went to work every day, knowing that they might not come home. She flushed, feeling terrible.

"I'm so sorry, Officer. That was thoughtless of me."

"Don't worry about it." Officer Mulvane sighed. "Okay, you win. There's one thing I can do for you, in these circumstances."

"Thank you so much," Jill said, grateful.

# 38.

"They've been up there forever, haven't they, Mike?" Jill paced the lobby in William's building, waiting for Officer Mulvane and his partner, who were upstairs with the super, a bald and surly little man named Ivan Ronavic.

"No. You need to relax." Mike peered at her over his glasses. He was sitting at the desk, turning a page of the newspaper. "It's only been twenty minutes. They'll be down soon."

"I wish I could've gone with them."

"You heard them. No way. The cops aren't even allowed in the apartment, they gotta wait in the hall while my boss checks it out."

"Is Ivan your boss?"

"Yes." Mike chuckled. "You asked him so many questions, I thought he was gonna hit you."

Jill snorted. "I've met surgeons with less ego."

Mike laughed. "He didn't like you much, either."

"Ask me if I care. I should fix him up with *my* boss, Sheryl."

Mike cocked his head. "You're a doctor. You shouldn't have a boss."

"That's what *I* think." Jill let it go. "You've seen the apartment, right?"

"Yes."

"What does it look like?"

"Not for me to say. You've gotten me in enough hot water for one day."

"Sorry." Jill felt a guilty twinge. "I can write Ivan a letter, apologizing."

"Nah, don't worry about it. It's good to shake things up. Get's so quiet around here."

"I wonder what's going on up there." Jill sank onto a cushioned bench, suppressing her anxiety. She felt so out of touch without her BlackBerry and wondered if Abby had called her or Victoria. Or if Sam was home from the lab, Megan had had another panic attack, or Rahul's bloodwork had come back. Jill stood up and started pacing again.

"Here they come." Mike rose, and the elevator *ping*ed. Jill got to the elevator as its stainless steel doors slid open, letting out Ivan, Officer Mulvane, and Officer Yokimura, his talkative young partner.

"Well?" Jill asked, and Officer Mulvane smiled in a reassuring way.

"Nothing to worry about, and your kid isn't up there. It's all in order. Clean as a whistle."

"What did you see? What does it look like?"

"It's a typical guy apartment."

Officer Yokimura added, "A typical *rich* guy apartment."

Officer Mulvane didn't comment. "There was nothing suspicious. Ivan did a walk-through, answered all our questions, and told us what we needed to know. Neat and clean. Refrigerator empty except for water and beer. Stack of newspapers and bills on the table."

"What name's on the mail?"

"Neil Straub."

"No other?"

"No."

"Except for Current Occupant," Officer Yokimura deadpanned.

"Any mail from a business, like one he owned?" Jill asked.

"Not that Ivan noticed."

"What's the oldest date on the mail, do you know? Or the oldest newspaper?"

"About a week ago, that Ivan saw."

Jill turned in frustration to Ivan, who had walked to the front desk. "Can't you please tell me more about him, like what you have on file, from when he subletted?"

"No, I can't." Ivan's thin lips made a flat line. His wiry frame seemed lost in his blue jumpsuit, and he had mournfully dark eyes. "Like I told you, I do what the board president tells me. He's not givin' out any info without a warrant."

"But Neil Straub is only a subletter."

"Makes no never mind."

Jill turned back to Officer Mulvane. "We can't get a warrant?"

"No. No probable cause. No crime. No nothing."

Jill knew when she'd lost a fight. "Was there any sign of a woman living with him, like things in the bathroom, medicine chest? Or stray jewelry? He has a young blonde girlfriend, and it would help if I knew her name."

Officer Yokimura grinned. "Hell hath no fury, eh?"

Jill turned to Officer Mulvane. "Well?"

"Ivan did see some things that belonged to a woman. Clothes in the closet, that sort of thing." Officer Mulvane crossed to the front desk. "Hey, Mike, how does the mail get upstairs?"

"When the resident is out of town, we bring it up every

few days. We always do that for Mr. Straub because he's usually gone so long, it clogs up his mailbox. About ten percent of the building is absentee; they got second and third homes in Florida, or they're foreign. We're white glove here. Bring up the dry cleaning, water the plants, too. Whatever they need, we do."

Officer Yokimura smiled. "Must be nice."

Officer Mulvane asked, "When was the last time Straub was here?"

Mike consulted a log book on the desk. "I found the entry, when you were upstairs. Last Monday, he left at 10:20 A.M. I was on the desk, I remember, because I filled in for Enrique. He didn't say when he'd be back."

Jill felt her gut tense. Monday was the day before William died. Neil Straub wouldn't be back, because William Skyler was dead. "Was he alone?"

Mike hesitated.

Officer Mulvane asked, "Was he?"

"Yes," Mike answered.

Officer Mulvane patted the desk, as a farewell. "Thanks for your trouble."

Jill came over. "Officer Mulvane, can we check out his car, too? I just want to see if it's here." She'd asked before, but maybe he'd forgotten. "He has a silver Mercedes, but we can't get into the garage unless they let us in."

Ivan looked over at Jill, annoyed. "You're an instigator, you know that?"

Jill smiled at him. "Hardly, but are you single? Because I've got the girl for you."

# 39.

Jill felt her eyes adjust to the darkness as she walked past one expensive sedan after another, their chrome fenders gleaming under the low lights in the garage ceiling. Reflective numbers painted on the concrete floor behind each car bore an apartment number, and they were at 4-B.

"Hey, Doc." Officer Mulvane turned to Jill as they walked together with Ivan and Officer Yokimura. "You understand, we can't search his car without a warrant."

"I know. I just want to see if it's here."

"Fine. Then we're done."

"This is it." Ivan stopped, gesturing with his jingling keyring at a silver Mercedes that sat in one of the parking spaces assigned to 4-D. The other space was empty, and William's car had a New York license plate, JU 5359. Jill took a pen out of her bag and scribbled the number on a scrap of paper, since she didn't have her BlackBerry to take a picture.

"We done here?" Ivan scowled.

"Yes, thanks," Jill answered, but she stepped over and peeked inside the car, which had a light, clean interior. William always kept his cars clean, then Jill remembered that he also always kept a spare key under his car's back bumper.

Officer Mulvane peered into the car, too. "Looks kosher to me."

Officer Yokimura snorted. "Looks *awesome* to me."

Jill's thoughts raced ahead. "Well, thanks, Officers. I really appreciate your time."

"No worries." Officer Mulvane put a hand on Jill's shoulder. "I wish you luck with your kid. She'll be fine, you'll see."

"Thanks, I hope so."

Ivan gestured. "Come on, folks. Wild goose chase is over, I got things to do," he said, and they all turned to follow him, with Jill a step behind, pretending she'd gotten something in her shoe.

"Oops, a stone," she said, but she hooked a finger inside her flat and pulled out the small innersole in the back of her heel, which had an adhesive bottom.

Ivan led them to the exit door, which he opened, and Officer Yokimura went through. Jill hung back, expecting Officer Mulvane to go next, but he turned to her.

"Ladies first," Officer Mulvane said, with a smile.

It caught Jill off guard, and she had to think fast. "Damn, I was trying to check out your butt."

"I still got it, eh?" Officer Mulvane burst into easy laughter. "Tell my wife that."

"She already knows it. Now, work it!"

Officer Mulvane wagged his butt in a comical way as he went through the door, and Jill stuck the gluey bottom of her innersole on the doorjamb, blocking the lock, then closed the door.

"Thanks for all your help, Officer Mulvane," Jill said, as they walked together down the street toward the West Side Highway.

"Sure thing. I'm sure your kid will show, sooner or later.

Hell, at that age, I was up to no good. Take care, Doc."
They reached the West Side Highway, where Jill waved
good-bye to them.

"See you. Thanks again!" Jill raised her hand to hail a
cab, standing in almost the same spot where she'd seen the
black SUV. The shards of her BlackBerry couldn't be far
away.

"Take care!" Officer Mulvane called back, and the three
men took a left, walked back down the street, and disappeared around the corner.

Jill kept her hand out, stalling until the police cruiser
steered around the corner and took a right onto the highway. She waved to the police as they drove past, and when
they were out of sight, she turned around and scooted back
up the street to the garage. She yanked on the door, which
opened easily because of the innersole, then she ripped
it off the jamb and hurried to William's Mercedes. She
didn't know what she'd find, but she wasn't going home
without trying.

She reached the car, ducked down to feel under the
bumper, and found the spare-key box. She slid open
the tin lid, took out the big black key, and aimed it at the
trunk, chirping it unlocked. She opened the trunk and
looked inside. Nothing. It was massive and looked clean
as new. She felt around the black interior to make sure,
but there wasn't anything inside or hidden. She closed
the trunk, then hustled to the driver's side and slipped
into the seat. It was dim inside the car, but she didn't want
to turn on the interior light, in case someone saw her.

She eyed the interior, and it was immaculate, smelling
faintly of Armor All, a car fetish of William's. She looked
in the door's side compartment, but there was nothing in
it except a pack of gum. She opened the lid of the center
console, and it contained only a pack of Kleenex and a
navy plastic envelope, which she picked up and looked

inside. It held the car's registration and proof of insurance. NEIL STRAUB, both read, and the address was the apartment building. She looked down at the signature on the registration. *Neil Straub,* it read, but it was clearly William's handwriting. Jill stuck the papers into her flattened purse, then reached over and pressed the button to open the padded glove compartment, where she spotted the glint of a gun.

Jill reached inside and pulled it out, dismayed. She'd never held a gun before, and this one was black, compact, and lethal, with cross-hatching on the handle and a small trident on the side. Beretta, it read underneath. She'd never known William to have a gun, but now he had two, and she wondered why he felt the need for so much protection. Her gut told her that his double life had to have played a role in what happened to him, and she prayed that whatever he was doing hadn't jeopardized Abby, too.

Jill put the gun back in the glove compartment, which contained nothing else but a thick owner's manual, so she shut the compartment's door. She turned around and checked out the backseat, which was clean. There was nothing on the floor in back, either. She turned back, eyeing the dashboard, which had an array of smooth buttons, giving her an idea. She plunged the car key into the ignition and twisted it on, and the dashboard came alive.

NAVI, read one button, the navigation system. She pressed it, and it brought up a list that started, ADDRESS ENTRY. She scanned the list until she got to ADDRESSES FROM MEMORY, scrolled to highlight the selection, then pressed. There were no listings, not even HOME.

Jill didn't believe it for a minute. William loved gadgets, and it seemed unlikely that he'd never used the GPS system. She glanced at the odometer, which glowed 30,393 miles, a lot of driving to not use a GPS for. She strolled down to LAST DESTINATIONS and pressed the button. NONE, it read.

Jill thought about it. There must have been a way to wipe the memory from the GPS system, and if so, William must've done so. She wondered why, stumped. She inhaled, thinking. Then she breathed in again. Armor All wasn't the only smell in the car. There was a sweeter scent, then Jill remembered his girlfriend.

She shifted over the console, climbed into the passenger seat, and flipped down the makeup mirror. There was nothing stuck underneath. She checked out the compartment on the passenger side door, and hit paydirt. The compartment had stuff in it, but she couldn't see what it was in the poor light.

She scooped the stuff out and arrayed it on her lap: a Laura Mercier lipstick, an eyelash curler, a black tube of violet-scented hand cream, and a white plastic bag from Sephora. She opened the bag, but it was empty, and she assumed it had contained the makeup, bought on the run. In the bottom of the bag were receipts, and she pulled them out and read them. One showed cosmetics and beauty supplies, for a total of $136.98, and the other was the thin receipt from a Visa customer copy.

Jill's gaze shot to the bottom of the receipt, where it had been signed by the customer.

*Nina D'Orive,* it read, in a lovely, flowing script.

# 40.

Jill emerged from a cab at Penn Station, eyeing the rush-hour crowds. If the black SUV had followed her to William's apartment, it could follow her here, and she scanned the cabs, limos, vans, and cars all around her. She spotted three black SUVs but couldn't see the drivers, and it made her nervous. Worse, she wasn't any closer to finding Abby, and what she'd learned about William made her heartsick, for Abby.

Jill hustled to the curb, threaded through the commuters flooding into the station, boarded the escalator on the run, and kept moving. She hit the ground floor running and made a beeline for the ticket booth in the back, but the line was too long. She hustled to the ticket kiosk, eyeing everyone around her with suspicion; the burly man in a suit that strained at the seams on his upper arms, the sleepy hipster with the oversized black glasses and guitar case, the young woman in an unseasonably heavy sweater, who seemed to watch her every move.

Jill didn't know whom to suspect, so she suspected everyone, then it dawned on her that there could be more than one person following her. They could be working together as a team; in fact, they had to be. There was no way one person could have followed her from her car to the train to the apartment building. She glanced over her shoulder as the ticket printed out, but suddenly people starting surging in three different directions, regrouping as quickly as a school of tropical fish.

"Acela to Washington, D.C., with stops in Newark, Princeton, North Philadelphia, Philadelphia," blared the loudspeaker.

Jill joined the crowd surging forward, then squeezed her way into a human funnel as each passenger showed his ticket to the conductor. She filed in behind an older woman as the escalator carried them down to the bowels of the station, where she hurriedly boarded the train and took the first empty seat, next to another older woman, who immediately pulled out her knitting.

Jill set her purse on her lap and looked out the window. The train was still boarding, and all she saw on the platform was darkness broken by an array of shifting shadows. She closed her eyes, and a wave of exhaustion washed over her, born of anxiety and fear. She flashed on Abby's face and prayed she had called her phone or Victoria's, or had finally come home.

Jill kept her eyes closed as the train started to move. She didn't feel safe enough to fall asleep, but the car began to rock slowly back and forth. She forced her eyes open and found herself resting her cheek in her hand while the noise and chatter of the other passengers grew distant. In her mind's eye, she could see Abby, younger and grinning until her rubber bands showed, then Abby morphed into Megan, who morphed into Rahul, and all of the children became one, and they were all happy and whole and healthy, living without danger, disease, or death, rocked in her loving arms, back and forth, forever and ever.

And in the next minute, Jill had fallen asleep.

# 41.

Jill got home to a house quiet except for Beef, who barked his way down the stairs, in excitement. She knew Sam was home because his car was in the driveway, but he didn't greet her. "I'm home!" she called out, hopeful.

"Up here!" Sam called, from upstairs.

"Be up in a minute," Jill called back, relieved they were on speaking terms. She set down her purse and keys, patted Beef on the head, then hurried into the kitchen to check her messages.

She went to the wall phone, picked up the receiver, and pressed the number code for her messages, but they were all telemarketers, not Abby, Victoria, or any of her patients. She hung up, went to her laptop and moved the mouse to wake it, then logged onto her email, skimming it quickly. Again, there was nothing from Abby or Victoria, but there were two emails from patients. She read them quickly, but they could wait for an answer. She checked for Rahul's results, but they hadn't come in yet, which concerned her. Her appointment with Padma and Rahul was tomorrow.

Jill went to the stairs, anxious to see Sam. She didn't know how he'd react to her knowing about William's double life, or how she would tell him. It struck her that she hadn't felt so awkward about seeing him since their first date, years ago. She climbed the stairs, thinking about it. She'd finally felt ready to go out again, but had been on one bad blind date after another, putting herself out there, keeping her chin up through the heavy drinkers, the men still in love with their exes, and men who expected her to sleep with them on the first date, since they were both adults now. She'd almost lost heart the day she'd arrived at the restaurant, early as usual, and spotted Sam already sitting at the table, wearing the plaid tie he'd told her he'd have on, and the thing that gave her a spark of hope was that he was reading a book.

*Sorry I'm late,* Jill said reflexively, slipping her shoulder bag on the back of the chair and extending her hand like it was a job interview.

Sam smiled, rose, and shook her hand. *You're not late, I'm early. I'm always early.*

Jill smiled, sitting awkwardly, then she noticed the title of the book. *Angela's Ashes,* by Frank McCourt, which was one of her favorites. *I love that book.*

*Me, too. I'm re-reading it. It's so beautifully written, and it reminds me of how lucky I am in my life. How much human beings can endure and still survive.*

Jill felt exactly the same way, but didn't say so, thinking it would sound too cute. *So, well, hello, Sam Becker. You're in diabetes research? How wonderful.*

*Thank you.* Sam closed the book and set it aside. *But I don't think of what I do that way. That permits the disease to define me and my work, and I concede nothing to the disease. I'm trying to beat the disease.*

*So then what do you do? How do you define your work?* Jill felt awkward again, like she'd stuck her foot in her mouth, though Sam's smile was even warmer.

*I'm not in diabetes research, I'm in people research. I*

*research people, to help them fight disease, so that some-*
*day they'll live happy and healthy lives. They deserve that*
*chance. At the very least, to survive.*

Jill nodded. *Like the book, I guess.*

*Yes, right.* Sam blinked. *I never made that connection,*
*before now. Thank you.*

Jill smiled, flattered. *That's what books do, isn't it?*
*That's why I love to read. They bring us closer to our-*
*selves.*

*And closer to each other.* Sam smiled, then laughed,
flushing. *Wait, hold on. That's not a line or anything. I*
*hope it didn't sound that way.*

*No, not at all,* Jill assured him, meaning it, but she
didn't add that she'd liked the sound of it, and when he'd
said it, she'd felt a little thrill, a flash of emotion too small
to warm her heart, but enough to fill it with light, and that
was how she came to think about Sam himself, after she'd
gotten to know him and had fallen in love with him, that
his soul filled hers with light, and always would.

Jill was standing at the threshold of their bedroom, and
Sam was packing his black rollerbag, which lay open on
the bed like a thick book, one side filled with folded shirts
and slacks, and the other with shoes. She stood at the
threshold as if it weren't her bedroom, too. "What's this?"
Jill asked, her mouth dry.

"I'm going to Cleveland." Sam looked up, his eyes cool
and distant behind his reading glasses. He was still dressed
from work, in a blue shirt, loose striped tie, and Dockers.
"Lee got sick and I have to help present his paper."

"Oh." Jill wasn't sure what to say. "It's a conference, so
you'll be back when? A day or two?"

"No." Sam picked up a sneaker from the floor and
wedged it inside the bag. "I thought I might get a jump on
it and go see Steve."

"But that's this weekend."

"Come on, Jill." Sam stopped fussing with the sneaker and met her eye. "We both know you're not going to Austin if Abby's still missing, and I assume she's still missing or you would have called me. Am I right?"

"Well, it's true, if she's still gone, I'd feel funny leaving—"

"That's what I thought. So why should I fly home for one night, then leave for Austin alone?" Sam zipped the black netting over his shoes. "Megan's at Courtney's, and she's fine. She called you, but you didn't call back, so I told her it would be okay to sleep over. I thought it made the most sense for tonight, since I had to leave."

"I dropped my phone, sorry."

"Don't worry about it." Sam closed the top of the suitcase, then zipped it, which for some reason, was never a good sound.

"Sam, I'm sorry. This is so crazy what's going on, with Abby gone. I found out William had a double life, a secret identity in New York."

"Really." Sam picked two novels and his electronic reader off the bed, then slid them inside the exterior flap of the suitcase and zipped it closed.

"I went to the New York police but they—"

"Stop." Sam picked the suitcase off the bed, set it on the floor, then brushed off the comforter. "I have to catch a plane, and I'd prefer it if our last words to each other weren't about your ex-husband."

"Okay." Jill sighed, resigned. "So you're still angry."

"No, I'm not angry, I'm unhappy." Sam hesitated, softening. "This conference comes at a good time, doesn't it? Let's use the opportunity to go to our respective corners and think things over. We're in trouble, the two of us."

Jill hated to hear him say it. "No, we aren't."

"Yes, we are." Sam picked up the bag and walked to the door, giving her a dry peck on the cheek. "Abby came to us out of the blue, a curve ball. Let's see what we both want from the future, given the new normal."

"What's that supposed to mean?"

"Babe, we've gone over and over this." Sam set down his bag.

"Are we still engaged?"

"Honestly, I don't know. You should answer that for yourself, and I'll answer it for myself, and we'll talk when we get back."

Jill felt like crying, but she couldn't pinpoint why. Heartbreak. Anger. Fear. Sadness. All of the above. "Really?"

"Really."

"But what about Megan?"

"She doesn't have to know. Don't tell her."

Jill tasted bitterness on her tongue. "We can't disagree without breaking up?"

Sam picked up the bag. "We can't go forward without agreeing."

"And you're punishing me until I agree."

"How am I punishing you?"

"Withdrawing, leaving."

"No, no." Sam shook his head. "I have a job to do, just like you do, and this makes the most sense to me. I don't want to hang around like a puppy dog, waiting for you to come home."

"But you're not."

"Yes, I am." Sam started to go, and Jill felt a twinge of anger.

"This isn't what I want."

"Yes, it is." Sam turned at the head of the stair, in front of his lineup of photographs, all of them taken in happier times. "It must be, because it's the logical result of what you're doing. You couldn't have set it up any better."

Jill was suddenly tired of his research jargon. "Not everything is a controlled experiment, Sam."

"Then choose."

"What?"

"Choose now. I can tell you, now, that I don't want to parent Abby, in any way, shape, or form."

"She's *missing,* Sam. Can't we stay in the present?"

"Can't we plan, for the future?" Sam frowned, deeply. "Think ahead to when she comes back, or you find her. Tell me how you're going to replace the father and mother she lost. Explain how you're going to shore up a troubled kid who's already tried to kill herself once. Choose, now. Last chance. Pick that family, or this one."

"Why do I have to choose?" Jill asked, agonized.

"You just did," Sam answered, turning away.

# 42.

Jill felt empty and hurting, disconnected, loosed from her moorings. But she had to make herself act, given that Abby was still missing. She changed quickly into comfy jeans, a sweater, and loafers, and went downstairs. She thought she should go back to the Philly police or touch base with Victoria, but she wasn't sure which to do first.

She went to the phone in the kitchen and pressed in Megan's number. The phone rang, and she sat down at the island, tugged the laptop over, and moved the mouse to wake it up. Her email server popped on the screen, and she scanned her email again to see if Rahul's results had come in, but they still hadn't.

"Mom?" Megan said, when the call connected. "Why are you calling from the house phone?"

"My BlackBerry's broken."

"Is that why you didn't get back to me? I called and texted, so don't get mad."

Jill could hear the attitude in her tone. "So what's up? You guys having fun?"

"No, working on this dumb project. Did you find Abby?"

"Not yet, but don't worry about that. Did you eat?"

"Yes, Courtney's mom made lasagna."

"Yum." Jill's stomach growled. "Wish I were there."

"Sam said I could stay over, even though it's a school night."

"I know, but let's make this the last time, okay?" Jill knew she had said the same thing, just yesterday or so.

"What's the big deal? We're working, Mom."

"Don't be fresh. How will you get to school?"

"Carol can take me."

"Since when do you call her Carol? Call her Mrs. Ariz." Jill adored Courtney's mother, Carol, and they'd been friends since the girls made the club swim team, years ago. "Be sure to thank her for me. She's doing a lot of the driving lately."

"She doesn't mind."

"Why don't I take you both to school, then she can pick up, since I can't?"

"She's *fine* with it, Mom."

"Okay, but what are you going to do for clothes? I can bring you some fresh ones, then take you to school."

"Mom, no." Megan sighed, in an exaggerated way. "I borrowed some from Courtney, and Sam brought me some, too. He was coming home early to pack for his trip, so he brought over my stuff."

Jill rubbed her face, sick at heart. She couldn't imagine telling Megan that their engagement was off. "I really wish you were home."

"I'm fine here."

Jill sighed. "Goodnight, then. I love you."

"Goodnight. Love you, too."

"Fine, and don't forget—" Jill started to say, then the line went dead. She pressed END and called information for Victoria's phone number, because it was in her Black-Berry, now defunct. She waited for the call to connect, and while it rang, she logged onto whitepages.com and plugged in Nina D'Orive, then New York.

"Jill?" Victoria answered. "Did Abby call you?"

"No, didn't she call you?"

"Oh, no." Victoria still sounded remote, but distinctly worried. "Now, this is really scary."

"I agree. I'd have called your cell, but my BlackBerry's broken." Jill read the laptop monitor, and the website had found three Nina D'Orives. She clicked on the first one, and it showed a Nina D'Orive at 335 Winding Way, Scarsdale, but her age was listed as sixty-seven. Jill eliminated her, surprised the website even gave ages. "What happened last night, at Central Detectives?"

"Nothing. Neither Detective Reed or Detective Pitkowski were in, so we left a message to call me."

"Did they?"

"No."

"We have to go back there."

"I'll go again, but what's new? Nothing."

"Not exactly." Jill had decided on the train that Victoria was old enough for the truth about her father. "I did learn a thing or two in New York that might help them."

"Like what?"

"It's a long story, and I'd rather tell you in person." Jill clicked on the next Nina D'Orive, who lived at 701 Young Street, Albany, and she was forty-five. It was unlikely that William would be dating somebody who lived so far upstate, so she eliminated that one, too. "Just meet me at Central Detectives, would you?"

"Sure. I'll leave now."

"Good. See you there, out front." Jill hung up and clicked the final entry. Nina D'Orive, Apt 2F, East 94th Street, in New York. Her age was thirty, which would be more William's taste, and Belle Kahan, the Realtor, had said that the girlfriend was young.

Jill felt her heart beat faster and clicked on the high-lighted name. A grid popped onto the screen, showing D'Orive's last known work addresses. The most recent was Pharmcen Pharmaceuticals.

Jill hit PRINT, jumped up, and went to get her bag.

# 43.

Jill, Victoria, and her friend Brian Pendle sat across from Detective Ronald Hightower, who was a tall, fit, African-American in his forties, with short hair, knowing brown eyes, and a brushy mustache. Detective Pitkowski wasn't in, Detective Reed was on vacation, and Jill was starting to think that Central Detectives was a group practice. She asked, "So if Detective Reed is on vacation, do you handle the case?"

"No, I don't. There's no case to be handled. We investigate homicide, and William Skyler's death wasn't ruled a homicide." Detective Hightower had retrieved the file, and it lay open in front of him, on a desk that looked neat, with squared-off stacks of notes, files, and papers. His phone message slips were arranged in layers, each overlapping the next, like napkins at a reception, and his manner exuded professionalism as he turned to Victoria. "Ms. Skyler, I'm sorry about your father's passing. Don't think me hard-hearted, but it's not police business."

"But Detective, doesn't my sister being gone make a difference to you? It's not like Abby not to return my calls for this long." Victoria leaned forward urgently, looking more dressed-up than usual, with a black blazer over her white sweater and skinny jeans. Her hair was in its usual twist, her makeup was perfect, and she had on her pearl earrings. "Abby thought Dad was murdered, and I didn't agree, but now I'm wondering. What if Abby found out something, or saw something? They lived together, and who knows?"

Jill knew it was time for the truth about William's double life. She hadn't told Victoria and Brian outside, when they'd met, because it hadn't seemed like the place and time. Now it was, and Jill wished she could soften the blow for Victoria, but there was no way. "Detective Hightower," Jill began, "I have new information for you. I'm concerned that Abby's disappearance is related to a Neil Straub, whom William said was his business associate, in New York. Well, he isn't. Today I learned that Neil Straub and William Skyler are one and the same person."

"*What?*" Victoria turned to Jill, her bright eyes narrowing. "What are you talking about? That's a *lie*!"

"Are you crazy?" Brian frowned, stiffening in his striped tie and gray suit as if he'd come from the office.

"Dr. Farrow, what do you mean by that?" Detective Hightower asked, so Jill told them everything and showed them the photo of William with the man in the blue shirt, his Mercedes registration, and Nina D'Orive's home address. Detective Hightower took notes, and Jill could see his concern growing. Victoria's expression went from disbelief to disillusionment when she saw William's signature on Neil Straub's car registration. After Jill finished, she looked over at an anguished Victoria.

"I'm so sorry you had to hear all this, honey. I know it's confusing, and strange."

"Dad would never—" Victoria started to say, stricken, then stopped herself, her expression darkening. She shook her head, aghast. "I just don't understand. This makes no sense. I don't know why he would do this."

"I know, I'm sorry." Jill felt the urge to touch her but didn't know if it would be welcome. "I'm as shocked as you are. We can't know everything about our parents, Victoria."

"But *this*? A secret life? An apartment in the city? Double cars and everything?" Victoria's manicured hand flew to her forehead, rubbing it and leaving pinkish streaks. "*Dad* is *Neil Straub*? That's *unreal*!"

"I'm sorry, Vick." Brian reached over and touched Victoria's shoulder, his eyes an agonized blue behind his wire-rimmed glasses, and Jill could see how much he cared about her, which made Jill like him better.

"Victoria," Jill said, softly, "your Dad must've gotten mixed up in something that made him want to disguise his identity, but let's not dwell on that, now. The important thing is getting Abby home." She turned to Detective Hightower. "I'm hoping that William's girlfriend, Nina D'Orive, might have some idea where Abby is. Will you go and question her?"

"Correct, or NYPD will. We'll have to iron out the jurisdictional issues." Detective Hightower's dark eyes softened. "Given these circumstances, I agree that Abby's disappearance is concerning, and we'll take it up with Missing Persons."

"Thanks so much." Jill almost cried with relief.

"Yes, thanks, Detective." Victoria nodded, still upset. "I appreciate it. Abby's my only sister, and we're all we have . . ." Just then, a cell phone started ringing, and Victoria reached, embarrassed, into her large black handbag. "Sorry, I forgot to silence my phone." She pulled out an iPhone, and her eyes widened when she saw the screen. "Oh my God, it's Abby!" Victoria held up the phone, which showed a photo of a grinning Abby. "What do I do? What if she was kidnapped or something?"

"Answer it." Detective Hightower rose and hustled around the desk. "Put it on speaker."

Jill's heart started to pound. "Can you trace it somehow, Detective Hightower?"

"No." Detective Hightower waved at two other detectives, who were talking near the file cabinets in the back. "Guys, quiet a minute!"

Victoria hit the ANSWER button. Jill leaned over to listen from the left, and Brian leaned from the right, with Detective Hightower in the back.

"Abby?" Victoria answered the phone, uncertain. "Is that you? I have it on speaker because . . . my hands are full."

"Hi, girl!" Abby said. "What's up?"

Jill couldn't believe her ears. It was Abby, and she sounded happy and carefree.

Victoria frowned, shaking her head in confusion. "Abby? Are you okay?"

"Oh, I'm fine, sorry."

"Really, you're fine? No one's making you say this?"

Abby laughed. "What? Are you kidding?"

Victoria's mouth dropped open. "This is really you? And you're fine? I've been worried sick about you! Why didn't you call me back?"

"I know, I should have called, I'm sorry." Abby groaned. "But I knew what you'd say and I didn't need you to yell at me."

Jill sat, stunned. It didn't sound as if some bad guy was holding a gun to Abby's head, making her say these things. Brian leaned back, pursing his lips. Detective Hightower straightened up, waved the other detectives back to work, and strode to his chair, his lips tight.

Victoria said into the phone, "Where are you? What are you doing?"

"Jeez, sorry, I met someone."

"Who?"

"A guy. His name's Brandon, okay? He's in the TV business and he was in town, scouting locations. He has an *amazing* apartment here, so we flew out and—"

"Flew where?"

"L.A."

"*Los Angeles?*"

Jill couldn't process it all fast enough. Brian folded his arms, his annoyance plain. Detective Hightower bent over his desk, writing notes in the file.

Victoria's fair skin flushed with new anger, and she set the iPhone down on the desk. "Abby, are you *kidding* me right now? I thought you were dead."

"I'm really sorry, I am." Abby sounded genuinely regretful. "I've been so upset since Dad died, and I think I need a break, you know, to sort things out. Brandon said he can get me a job as a P.A., which means production assistant. I might come home in a week or so. I can't decide when—"

"I cannot *believe* you played me this way. What the hell is the matter with you? We're at the police station, they're about to call Missing Persons. Jill's here, too."

Abby gasped. "*Jill,* for real? Oh, no. I'm so sorry, Jill!"

Jill leaned toward the phone. "Abby, what's going on? Why didn't you return my calls?"

"I did, today. I left a message, but you didn't call me back."

Jill flashed on her mashed-up BlackBerry. "My phone broke."

"Jill, I'm so sorry, but you'd love Brandon. He doesn't think I should live alone in the house, either. He says I need to start over and take responsibility for myself. That's what you said, too."

"I'm just trying to understand what's going on with you. This is such an about-face. And how old is Brandon, anyway?"

"Older than me, but don't worry about it. I feel so much better now, and you helped me, too. I'll see you when I get back, and we can catch up. Please don't be mad at me."

Victoria snatched the iPhone from the desk. "Abby, *I'm* mad at you. When are you gonna grow up? Dad *died*, then you vanish? Do me a favor, will you? Stay in L.A. *Live* there with Brandon. You're a selfish *bitch*!" Victoria hung up, jumped to her feet, and turned to Jill, red-faced. "You got me into this! I told you, I told you, I *knew* it! I should have listened to myself!"

"Honey, please, relax." Jill reached for her arm, but Victoria edged away, holding up both hands.

"Back off! And for God's sake, I'm *not* your 'honey'!" Victoria shook with anger, and Jill thought she might faint.

"Let me get you some water."

"No!" Victoria shot back, then exhaled, seeming to catch herself. "I'm sorry, Jill. I'm sorry. I know better. I *knew* better." She balled her fingers into tight knots, like a tantruming child. "I hate my sister. There, I said it. I *hate* my sister." She exhaled once, then again, her gaze taking in the other detectives and finally coming to rest on Detective Hightower. "Detective, I'm so sorry about all of this. I'm sorry to have wasted your time."

"It's all right." Detective Hightower's tone had gone cool again. He rose, gesturing behind him. "Sure you don't want that glass of water, or a soda? I'm buying."

"No, thank you." Victoria turned to Brian, bristling with emotion. "Time to go, don't you think? Have I caused you enough embarrassment?"

Brian rose, his expression sympathetic, and he shook his head. "Don't worry about it, Vick. It's not in your control."

Jill rose, too, looking at Detective Hightower, in confusion. "I'm sorry, I guess we thought she was missing, but still."

"Still what?" Detective Hightower frowned. "I think that takes the wind out of your sails, don't you?"

"Not necessarily. It doesn't mean anything with respect to William." Jill tried to collect her thoughts. She was thrilled that Abby was safe, but what she'd learned today about William's double life only made her more sure that he had been murdered. She found herself thinking like a doctor, deciding that the new data didn't change her differential, but only confirmed it. "In other words, the fact that Abby's not missing doesn't mean William wasn't murdered."

"Oh please, Jill!" Victoria whirled around. "Do you really think even Abby thought Dad was *murdered*? She wanted you back in our life, and after Dad died, she saw a way to get it." Victoria still shook slightly, but the redness was finally leaving her cheeks. "It's totally weird that Dad had some kind of secret identity, but you know what, I shouldn't be surprised, and now that I think about it, I'm not. I know he was no angel. He played fast and loose with things. He and Abby, they're two of a kind. That's why they're so close."

Jill felt pained to see the jealous twist to Victoria's lips.

"Yes, Jill. Dad paid for art school for Abby, but not law school for me. Can you believe that? He had the money, but he wouldn't give it to me. He said he likes artists, but he hates lawyers. Funny, huh?"

Jill hadn't heard any of this before.

"I don't know what Dad was up to, but he wasn't murdered. He took one too many chances, sometimes with the wrong things. Didn't he, with you? Whether he cheated or you cheated, it all comes down to the same thing. He wasn't careful with anything, including *people*."

Jill couldn't say no.

"Dad could charm anything and anybody, but he met his match in a pill. You can't take chances with them, or they kill you." Victoria picked up her purse from the chair, threw her phone inside, and turned to Detective Hightower. "You don't think my father was murdered, do you?"

"No, I don't." Detective Hightower closed the manila file. "I'll talk with Detectives Reed and Pitkowski, but right now, I'm standing down."

Jill wasn't sure they could put it to bed so fast. "Just like that? So quickly? You're sure?"

"Dr. Farrow, I listened to you, as did two other detectives. We've given this matter more than enough of our time and resources." Detective Hightower touched his mustache. "Tonight was a fiasco. A murder investigation isn't a spigot you turn off and on."

"But you were convinced until Abby's call."

"Incorrect." Detective Hightower gathered the photo of William with the man in the polo shirt and slid it into the manila file. "I said I was going to follow up with Missing Persons. What you learned in New York isn't sufficient evidence to overturn a coroner's finding, or convert this case to a homicide. But I'll leave it to Detective Reed. He caught this case, and he's stuck with it." Detective Hightower handed her William's car registration. "Please, take this back. I made a note that I saw it."

"Thanks." Jill put the registration in her purse, and Brian moved toward the door, with Victoria behind.

"Good-bye, Jill," she said. "I wish you the best."

Brian nodded at Detective Hightower and Jill. "Thanks again for your time, Detective. Nice meeting you, Dr.

Farrow. Sorry I was so rough on you, before. Occupational hazard."

"Good-bye, take care, both of you." Jill watched them go, torn between pressing the matter and letting it lie, stuck between here and there. Suddenly she didn't know where she belonged, because she didn't belong anywhere.

Detective Hightower cleared his throat, in a pointed way. "Dr. Farrow, I've done all I can do."

"How will I know if they follow up with the girl-friend?"

"Call them. Not me." Detective Hightower softened again. "But, please, don't go chasing any more cars, and for what's it's worth, I don't think you're being followed. That SUV could've been anything."

"Like what?"

"He coulda been a guy waiting for a woman who's not his wife. He doesn't want to get caught by you, you could be one of her friends."

Jill tried to believe him, listening hard.

"You know, I've learned a few things, in twenty-two years on the job. People do strange things, every day. You meet them at different times in their lives, under the influence of whatever. Most of the time, people are straight-up *nuts*."

Jill nodded. "I guess."

"They're not criminals, they're idiots. Like your ex. The man's an idiot, I can tell you that, if he lost you."

Jill thought of Sam, bittersweet. "Thanks. I do appreciate all you've done."

"You're welcome." Detective Hightower extended a hand, and Jill shook it. "While I'm on a roll, you want some advice? Don't get caught between those two sisters. My wife has a younger sister, and I know how it goes. The baby of the family stays a baby. Period."

Jill wondered if he was right. She was an only child, with an only child.

"Now, go home."

"I will, thanks." Jill's heart went heavy in her chest. She turned and left, then realized suddenly where she could go.

## 44.

Jill told Katie the whole story, and she listened while she made a diorama. Magic Markers, construction paper, and overpriced modeling clay cluttered the kitchen table, and a shoebox sat on its side. Jill missed a lot of things about elementary school, but making dioramas wasn't one of them.

"I don't know what to think, anymore." Jill rested her chin in her hand, behind a mug of cooling decaf. "Why did William have a secret identity, and who the hell is the blonde with the Sephora bag?"

"She has no kids, this we know."

"How?"

"The eyelash curler. Really?"

Jill smiled. "I'm trying to talk about a murder."

"I bet she's young, like, an egg." Katie kneaded brown clay with her hands. "William was dating an egg."

"Still, Katie, not the point."

"Yes it is. You're the one missing the point." Katie held up the clay, which looked like a Tootsie Roll with pink spots. "How'm I doing?"

"What is it?"

"I told you, I'm making Winn-Dixie from the book *Because of Winn-Dixie*. It's a dog, named after the store."

"Oh." Jill was so distracted, she didn't remember Katie telling her.

"This is the body, but I can't get him skinny enough. Story of my life."

"What are the pink spots?"

"Bald patches, remember? Winn-Dixie had bald patches."

Jill didn't remember, and she was thinking of Megan, whom she should have called to tell her about Abby. She checked the clock—10:45. Megan should still be up. "Mind if I use your phone to call Megan? I can't believe I didn't when I first came in."

"Tell her I said hi, and don't beat yourself up. No teenager hopes her mom will call." Katie stuck brown legs on the dog body. "I don't know how they expect a second-grader to read a book and make a diorama, in three days. Why not ask him to juggle or take the SATs?"

Jill went over to the phone, picked up the receiver, and pressed in Megan's cell number. The call rang a few times, then went to voicemail, so she left a message. "Hey honey, just wanted you to know that we found Abby and all is well. Hope you're having fun. Love you. Call anytime, I'm at Katie's. Bye." Jill hung up. "Now what point did I miss?"

"Sam. Sam is the point. You love that guy, and you're about to lose him. Call him. Say you were wrong and you're sorry."

"But I wasn't wrong." Jill felt her gut wrench. "Abby behaved badly, but she'll be back, and I was right about the principle."

"Oh, okay, like *that* matters." Katie rolled her eyes, kneading the clay. "Abby was jerking you around, and her sister has her number. I'm with that detective. Call Sam and say, come home. You can use the phone in the living room, if you want privacy."

Jill put a hand on the receiver, but didn't pick it up. "I don't know."

Katie lifted an eyebrow. "You're really not going to call him?"

"I don't know what to say. He doesn't want Abby in our lives, and I don't like him telling me who I can love and who I can't." Jill felt her gut wrench. "I love Sam, I do. But I love Abby, too, and she's not in L.A. forever. She's just latched on to another, older guy."

"But Sam loves you, and he's worried about you. Call him and tell him the cops don't think you're being followed, at least." Katie frowned, her tired eyes pleading. "Tell him Abby's safe, too. He probably even cares about her. He's a caring guy."

Jill flashed on what Victoria had said, about William. *He wasn't careful with anything, even people.* "You're right. Sam is caring."

"So call him."

"All right." Jill pressed in Sam's cell number, and the phone rang. He didn't pick up, so she waited for voicemail to leave a message: "Hi babe, I just wanted to let you know that Abby turned up in L.A., and the cops don't think I'm being followed, so don't worry."

Katie was motioning to her. "Say you're sorry," she mouthed.

Jill said into the phone, "I'm sorry, and call me when you can. Try me at Katie's or later at home. Love you, bye." She hung up.

"Good girl!" Katie beamed. "Even if you didn't mean it, you sounded convincing, and that's all that matters."

Jill smiled, her mood lighter, which is what girlfriends were for. "Do you think the detective was right, that the baby of the family stays a baby?"

"Absolutely. Jamie is my baby, and I do more of his homework than the others. And don't think he didn't read *Because of Winn-Dixie*. He did, all of it. I'm the one who watched the DVD."

Jill's thoughts turned to Nina D'Orive. "Wonder how I can find out what his girlfriend does at Pharmcen? I know a Pharmcen rep and I could find him and call him, but it's a big company."

"Try Facebook."

"Right." Jill rallied. "Mind if I use your computer?"

"Go ahead, I'm already logged in."

"You use Facebook that much?" Jill went over to Katie's laptop, which was on the countertop, nestled among a stack of bills, catalogs, and school notices.

"Of course, don't you read your feed?" Katie flattened the dog body, but a leg dropped off. "I'm the Queen of Farmville."

Jill logged onto Facebook, went to the Search function, typed in Nina D'Orive, and there was only one result. "Got her. Good thing she has such an unusual name."

"What's her profile picture look like? I bet she's skinny. A skinny, skinny egg."

Jill clicked Nina's profile picture, which was a Welsh corgi puppy. "No, it's a really cute puppy."

"So she's either eleven years old or Barbie herself."

Jill clicked to Nina's wall, but the privacy settings must have been on the maximum. "Damn, I can't see her page. I'm not her friend."

"No, you're definitely not." Katie stuck the clay leg back on. "You're the psycho ex who's stalking her."

"Can I friend her, as you?"

"Sure, but why would she accept it?"

"I can send her a direct message with the friend request, right?" Jill thought a minute. "I'll say I work in a doctor's office. If she's a drug rep, she'll say yes."

"You can't do that, you're logged in as me." Katie walked over with Winn-Dixie. "My profile says I'm an at-home mom."

"I need to write something that will make her want to accept me." Jill found herself staring at the clay dog in Katie's hands. "We know she likes dogs. I'll say I'm looking for a corgi puppy for my daughter."

"You mean your sons. You're me."

"Oh, right." Jill got excited. "I'll tell her I thought her puppy was cute, and I'm curious who her breeder is. People love to talk about their dogs, and you don't see many corgis."

"It might work." Katie molded Winn-Dixie's other leg. "She's so young, she has a practice dog. Remember when you thought a dog was just like a baby, then you found out a dog is nothing like a baby?"

Jill clicked the box to send a friend request and typed a direct message: **Dear Nina, I think your puppy is super-cute. My boys would love a puppy like that. Who is your breeder? Best, Katie** She clicked SEND MESSAGE. "Think she's online?"

"Of course. Everybody's online at night, especially the hot girls. They talk to the men while the moms talk to each other."

"She is hot, the Realtor said."

"You jealous?"

"Of course not. I feel bad for her. God knows what scam he's running on her. She could be another drug rep, but if that's true, he's taking a big risk not using his real name. Someone could recognize him as William Skyler." Jill thought a minute. "I bet she doesn't know he's dead. She's probably wondering where he is."

"Unless she killed him."

"Aren't we dark, Winn-Dixie?" Jill glanced over, surprised, then her attention returned to the screen. "It can't be a coincidence that she works for a drug company. William targets women to use them."

"You know, I worry about you, girl. You fell out of love, but you need to fall out of hate."

"What?" Jill looked over again, and Katie's pretty features had fallen into troubled lines.

"I know you're not in love, but are you in hate? Because that's no good, either."

"What do you mean?"

"You didn't get closure on William, not really, because of the way it ended. You didn't see it coming. You're still emotionally involved with him."

"No, I'm not." Jill scoffed.

"Then why are we looking up Nina the Egg?" Katie cocked her head, and her reddish blonde bangs fell into her eyes. "You told me you cared if he was murdered because Abby cared, and I bought that. Well, now what? Abby's out, but you're still in."

Jill had to admit that it was true. "You're right."

"I know I am. I always am." Katie smiled. "So the question remains. Why do you care whether William was murdered or not?"

"I guess I do care, and maybe you're right." Jill shook her head, considering it. "I know I'm not in love with him anymore, but maybe I'm in hate. I'm not sure. But I *do* know that today, I got all the way up to New York, and I found all this out about his double life, and I felt like I was getting to the *real* him, like finding out what he was really up to."

"Yeah, so? Why does it matter to you, what your ex-husband is up to?"

Jill thought harder. "I guess that all this time, since what happened with the script pads and the way William left that night, I never knew what he was up to, in my own marriage. Under my own roof, under my own *nose*."

"Aww, honey." Katie's face fell into sympathetic lines. "Finding out what William was up to in New York isn't the same as finding out what he was up to in your marriage. That time has passed."

"Has it?" Jill looked up, questioning. "I'm still the same person. He's still the same person."

"Except for the dead part."

"It doesn't matter. Time doesn't matter. I want to know who William really is, or was. The *truth* of who he is, because I think it will help me understand the truth of who I am, or who I was in that marriage, and how I'll be the next time, if Sam comes around." Jill was finally getting some clarity, and she felt like it was her heart talking, now. "You can't go forward to the next step without figuring out the last one, right? It's like I'm trying to diagnose what went wrong in my own marriage, and part of me feels this will help. Because I really want my next marriage to last, Katie. Whoever I marry, Sam or no. I want it to work. I want forever, too, and I'm scared that this is my last chance." Jill felt tears in her eyes, and Katie put a warm hand on her shoulder.

"Okay, then. I get it, and I'll help you, whatever you need."

Suddenly the monitor screen changed, and both women turned to the laptop. Nina D'Orive had accepted the friend request, with a direct message: **Dear Katie, My puppy rocks! Check out my photo album to see more of her and her littermates! I love my breeder and she ships. Do you want the address? Thx for asking! Sincerely, Nina ox**

"Oh my God." Jill felt her heart pound. She couldn't believe she'd just made contact with William's girlfriend, when this morning she didn't even know he had a girlfriend.

"She uses the ox for someone she doesn't even know?

She's definitely Barbie." Katie set down the clay dog. "What's the *matter* with women?"

"I'm writing her back. I want to start a conversation with her, to see where it will lead." Jill clicked COMPOSE MESSAGE. "She could know everything about William, about what he was doing and why."

"Or, like I said, she could be the killer."

"Killers don't have corgis." Jill typed, **Dear Nina, I'd love the breeder's address and anything else you can tell me about your dog. I never had a corgi before and I'm on the fence. Are they good with kids? Best, Katie** Jill hit SEND MESSAGE. "See, I want her to convince me. I need to engage her."

"You sure this is safe?" Katie asked, her tone worried.

"Yes. Now, let's see what else we can find out about our new friend." Jill navigated to Nina's Info page, and her listed address was Hoboken, New Jersey. "That's funny. I had a Manhattan address for her. She must have moved."

"Jill, do you see what I see?" Katie pointed to PERSONAL INFO, and under STATUS, it read, **Married.** "Barbie's cheating on Ken."

"Whoa. That must be what happened with the address. She moved and married, but didn't change her name." Jill read down, noticing that Nina listed her employer as Pharmcen, but didn't specify her job. The page showed that she had sixty-three friends, twenty-nine in the Pharmcen network, and five others were family, including her husband. His profile picture was of an overweight guy in a sweatshirt, and his name was Martin Dunwilig. "See, the husband's last name is different."

Katie squinted at the husband's photo. "Dude. Unfortunate fashion choices. Also, hit the gym. Wifey's skinny for a reason."

Suddenly another message from Nina popped onto the screen: **Dear Katie, I see from your FB page that you**

**don't live that far from me, and your sons are adorable! If you want, you can bring them to meet my puppy Ruby! We can meet at the park! They'll fall in love! Sincerely, Nina Xo**

"Wow." Jill grinned, but Katie recoiled.

"You're not going to meet her, are you?"

"What do you think?" Jill hit COMPOSE MESSAGE. "Don't worry, I won't bring the boys. I'll just tell her I will."

"You shouldn't go alone, honey. Want me to go with you?"

"No, how can you? I'm you."

"I'll be me, and you be you." Katie screwed up her face. "Wait. I'm confused."

Jill laughed. "No thanks, I'll go alone. You don't know which questions to ask."

"She'll see that you're not me. We don't look alike."

"Damn." Jill paused, thinking. "What's your profile picture?" She plugged in Katie's name, and her Facebook page popped onto the screen. Her profile picture was of her boys, as was every other picture on the page. "No worries. The least-photographed person in the world is a mother."

"Wait, I think I have a shot of me in there. Let me check." Katie palmed the mouse, navigated to an album, and found a vacation picture that had a photo of her, but in a Phillies hat that covered her features. "Just one."

"Perfect. You can't see your face at all."

"Thanks. Also my hips are wider than yours."

"No, they're not, and she's a girl, so she won't notice."

"That's who *does* notice." Katie leaned over. "I don't think you should meet her."

"Why not?" Jill went back to Nina's page. "You don't mind that I'm using your name, do you?"

"No, but maybe it's dangerous. I think you should let it go."

"Luckily, you're not my mother," Jill said, typing away.

# 45.

The house phone started ringing almost as soon as Jill got home and closed the front door behind her. She dropped her purse on the console table and ran to the kitchen for the call, with Beef trotting after her, wagging his tail. "Hello?" she said, picking up.

"Hi, how are you?" It was Sam, still sounding cool, so Jill dialed down her expectations, like putting on jeans you knew wouldn't fit.

"Fine, thanks. You?" Jill flicked on the kitchen light and stretched the cord to take a seat at the island. She hit the mouse on her laptop, and the screen came to life, displaying her email inbox. She scanned the new messages to see if Rahul's bloodwork had come in, but it hadn't. The lab must've lost it somehow.

"Good. Busy. Met with Lee, then have to prepare for tomorrow. I'm glad they found Abby. I cared, even though it sounded as if I didn't."

"I know." Jill softened at the sentiment.

"Are you safe?"

"Yes."

"Good. I'm sorry, too, about everything," Sam said after a moment, but he wasn't as convincing as she had been.

"Thanks." Jill petted Beef, who put his head on her lap.

"I have to say, the past few days have been an eye-opener, in some ways." Sam sounded sad and, finally, like himself.

"In what ways?"

"In just how much Abby meant to you, and where Steven and I fit in with that."

"I see," Jill said, surprised at the chill in her own tone. She didn't want to have to choose anymore. She was sick of failing tests she didn't want to take.

"Will you do it again?" Sam asked, calmly. "When Abby comes back from L.A., do we all have to jump around? The entire house in an uproar, as we're led around by a child?"

*She's not a child,* Jill thought but didn't say, because he was right, in part. Abby did act like a child. "I can't say I have it all figured out. I can't plan everything that far ahead. But I know I don't want you to tell me that I can't love her, either."

Sam fell silent, on the other end of the line. "You can love her all you want, but what you do for her impacts me."

"Then we'll have to work it out as we go along."

"I'll have to think about that, for a bit. I don't know if that's feasible. I can't speak to that now, and I would like not to."

"Okay, thanks." Jill felt resentment calcifying in her chest.

"So you're finished then? Back to business, no more looking for your ex's murderer?"

"Not exactly." Jill petted Beef's soft head, watching the Microsoft flag flap across her laptop screen. She knew the answer Sam wanted to hear, but she couldn't give it to him. She knew what she had to do, and she needed the freedom to do it.

"What then? What's going on?"

"If I tell you, it'll sound worse."

"What is it?"

"William was seeing someone. She's married, and I'm going to meet her."

"Why?" Sam asked, his tone astonished.

"To find out if she knows anything about his murder."

"Why on earth would his girlfriend agree to meet with his ex-wife?"

Jill usually admired the way Sam asked questions, each one leading to the next, as if challenging and testing a scientific theory. But this time, with each answer, she felt as if she were hammering another nail into her own coffin, sealing the lid over her face. "She doesn't know I'm his ex-wife."

"You didn't tell her?"

"No."

"Then how did you get her to meet with you?"

Jill didn't know what good it would do to explain. "Honestly, you don't want to know."

"You're right, I don't." Sam sighed. "Are the police involved, at all?"

"No, but I did tell them everything I know."

"So why aren't they involved with this meeting?"

"They don't think William was murdered."

"But you do."

"That's what I'm trying to figure out. And what he was up to, and who he was, and who I was, too." Jill noticed that Beef had fallen asleep sitting up, his head still in her lap. The sight made her smile, even as tense as she felt, which was the special gift of a pet. Love, devotion, and no difficult phone calls.

*I'm not alone, I have Pickles.*

Jill remembered, all of a sudden. It was Abby talking, in their phone conversation after that first night. Abby had a cat, Pickles, but she hadn't mentioned him to Victoria, on the phone call at the police station tonight.

"Jill, are you there or did we get cut off?"

"Sorry, I was just thinking. Abby didn't ask Victoria or me to take care of her cat until she came back from L.A. Doesn't that seem strange to you?"

"Stop, please." Sam's voice went cold. "I can't talk about that girl or your ex-husband anymore. We're back where we started, but worse. I have to go."

"No, wait, Sam—"

"We'll talk later. Good-bye."

Jill hung up after a moment, wondering. She and Sam had been so happy, less than a week ago. She would never have believed they'd come apart so quickly, snapped apart like a suspension cable on a bridge, undone by winds unseen, pressures uncalculated, and stresses neither measured nor accounted for.

*You didn't see it coming.*

Jill didn't want Sam to leave her life the way William had, but she didn't know how to stop him. She hadn't known Abby would come back, William would die, or Victoria would both love and hate her. She didn't know that the past would come back to the present and obliterate the future. She'd thought she'd moved on, stepping over the human debris, but it turned out that her life was a morgue, and all the time she'd been surrounded by bodies, hidden away, to be dealt with later.

Some not even dead, but still very much alive.

# 46.

Jill bustled past the eye chart toward the lab, on the run. She still hadn't received Rahul's bloodwork and knew that something had gone wrong. She felt exhausted after a sleepless night, plus she'd had to be at the phone store early to buy a new BlackBerry and had stood in line forever. She'd listened to Abby's message on the way in, but it hadn't mentioned her cat.

Jill opened the door to the small lab, where their phlebotomist, Selena Grant, looked up from a full tray of blood samples, each standing like a soldier in its wire separator, with its rubber stopper labeled in her characteristically neat print. "Hi, Selena, did we get results for Rahul Choudhury? They should've been in yesterday, but I got no email."

"Choudhury?" Selena blinked, her dark eyes worried under a stiff curl of black bangs. She was small and slim, dwarfed in boxy scrubs covered with kitten faces, because she was a cat fancier. "I don't remember that name."

"He's a baby, a one-year-old? I ordered a CBC with differential. Mom is waiting for me in Exam Room B. He was in on Saturday."

"Oh no. I remember the baby, now." Selena's face fell into long, gaunt lines, and she looked much older than her forty years. "I messed up on Saturday. I forgot to send it in. I realized it late Monday, and I was going to tell you, then I forgot that, too. I'm so sorry, Jill."

"That's not like you," Jill said, surprised. "You're our rock."

"I know, but my mother, they moved her to hospice." Selena's eyes filmed. "They called me Saturday, and I left work, upset. I forgot everything." Her hand went to her cheek, pressed flat against it. "I'm at such a loss, I can't keep track of anything. They say she has only a week or so."

"I'm so sorry." Jill felt terrible for her and touched her shoulder. She had known that Selena's mother had stomach cancer, but not that she'd declined so quickly. "Is there anything I can do?"

"Pray."

"I will, but you don't have to be here. Go and be with her. Take the time off."

"I can't." Selena sighed, shaking her head. "I'm out of vacation days and all my other leave. I used it up, on her. Sheryl says I have to stay until Monday, when Linda comes back."

Jill knew that could be too late. She remembered the last week she'd spent with her own mother. It had been hell, and she still wouldn't have traded it for anything. "No, you don't have to wait until then. Go, now. You're finished for the week."

"For real?" Selena looked up, hopeful.

"Yes, go." Jill turned to the cabinet, found a cube of Post-its and a pen, and on the top paper, wrote LAB CLOSED. "I'll deal with Sheryl when she gets back from lunch."

"Thanks so much, Jill. But what about your patient?"

Selena grabbed her bag, and Jill picked up a phlebotomy kit.

"I'll take his blood. I've kept up my qualifications. We can all collect our own samples or send patients to Lab-Corp for a week."

"The docs will take their own blood?" Selena's penciled eyebrows flew upward.

"Yes, we're smarter than we look. Come on, let's go." Jill followed Selena out of the lab, stuck the Post-it on the door, and took off down the hall with the kit.

"Thanks again, Jill. So much." Selena waved good-bye, and Jill opened the door to Exam Room B, went inside, and set the phlebotomy kit on the counter. She faced Padma and Rahul, who sat on the examining table in his diaper, playing with a set of Acura keys.

"Padma, I'm sorry, but we lost Rahul's blood sample." Jill hated watching Padma's face fall, and there was new tightness around her lips. "That's why we didn't get his results yet. I'm so sorry. I'll take another sample myself, after I examine him."

"Oh no." Padma ran a hand through her glossy hair, stopping at the ponytail. She looked more stressed than usual, and her sweater was unusually wrinkled, for her. "I hate to do that to him again. He cried so much."

"I know, and I'm very, very sorry." Jill slid her stethoscope from around her neck and went over to Rahul. He'd been weighed by the nurse, and he'd lost another half a pound. Jill thought his *gestalt* wasn't any better, even after three days on amoxicillin. "How is your mother? Any better?"

"Yes, thanks. My brother thinks taking a blood test is overkill for an ear infection."

"I know, but I think it's important. Hey, Rahul, what do you say there?" Jill tickled his bare tummy, which felt warm to the touch, and he didn't smile as much as before, though another tooth nugget was popping through his pale pink gums. "Two teeth now? Good for you, big boy!"

"Gsmssm," Rahul said, producing bubbles, so at least he wasn't dehydrated.

"Let's get a listen." Jill warmed the stethoscope on her palm and placed it against the baby's tiny chest, then put it in her ears and listened to the stepped-up pace of his heart, then the noises of the infection in his chest. His temperature was 101, and he'd had it for too long.

"My nephew, he gets them all the time, that's why they had tubes put in." Padma tucked a glossy strand of hair into her ponytail. "You're positive that this is necessary, to take blood from him, twice now?"

"I'm sorry, but I do." Jill looped the stethoscope around her neck, then felt his glands at his throat, which were still swollen. She looked into his ears, nose, and throat, and it was still purulent. Most pediatricians would say that Rahul was failing the amoxicillin, but Jill hated that jargon. The medicine was failing the baby, not the other way around. "He's as sick as he was Saturday. I'd like to switch him to another antibiotic and see if that helps."

"Whatever you think."

"We'll put him on Augmentin then." Jill lay him down and palpated his belly, spleen, and liver, then sat him up and felt the glands under his armpits, all of which were swollen.

"My sister-in-law was over to dinner last night, and she said we should just get the tubes, too."

"Let's discuss it after we get the results, okay? I'll order them stat, so we'll know tomorrow." Jill checked his skin, and his patch of eczema was the same, no worse. "Is he drinking and eating?"

"Yes, but not so much."

"Sleeping?" Jill checked inside his diaper, which was dry, so she sat him up, and Padma took over, steadying him.

"Same as before."

"Let me write that script." Jill went back to the laptop, logged into Epic with her password, and found Rahul's file, then printed out a script for Augmentin and handed it to Padma, who slid it into her back pocket. "Okay, I'll need to take some blood. This time, I swear it won't go missing." She went to the kit and prepared a syringe. "Would you hold him or would you prefer that I get a nurse?"

"No, I'll hold him." Padma picked up the gurgling Rahul, cuddling him protectively, and he shook the keys. "He cried so hard, last time. I hate to do it all over again, for no reason."

"I understand, but we're doing it for a reason. It's good to be thorough." Jill knew that Padma was trying to do what was right for her child. "I'm trying to get to the cause of these infections."

"They all get ear infections, some more than others, isn't that so?"

"Yes, but it's the frequency of his that concerns me, and don't forget that he had pneumonia."

"My nephew got *eight* ear infections his first year. He was on amoxicillin all the time. They called it his bubble-gum drink."

"Your nephew isn't Rahul. We know that it's an ear infection, but it's always important to ask, what's behind this? We can't stop at the short answer."

Padma shook her head, holding the baby. "I just hate to do this to him again."

"Isn't it better to be on the safe side? We don't want to call off the search just because we have an answer, if it's not the right answer." Jill met Padma's dark eyes and could see that she was getting through to her. "We call that diagnosis momentum, which is a fancy way of saying that once you arrive at a possibility for a diagnosis, it sticks, when it shouldn't. Okay?"

"Okay," Padma answered, satisfied. "I know my family influences me, a little."

"That's okay, that's what family's for. Hold Rahul, and I'll make this fast." Jill wiped antiseptic on Rahul's arm, tied a tourniquet, attached a butterfly needle to the syringe for use with babies, and inserted it into a vein.

"WAAAAHHH!"

"I'm so sorry, Rahul." Jill pulled back the plunger, collected the blood, then loosened the tourniquet, extracted the needle, and put a cotton gauze on the wound. "Good boy!"

"It's all right, honey." Padma held Rahul close as he cried.

"Padma, well done, and thank you for assisting." Jill stuck a stopper on the test tube, labeled the sample, and set it down, then took a piece of adhesive tape and put it over the gauze on his arm. "I'll see you back here tomorrow, and I'll have his results. When can you come in?"

"The morning is best, while his brothers are at school." Padma wiped Rahul's tear-stained cheeks, and his little chest heaved a baby sob.

"Poor little guy." Jill touched his cheek, wet with tears. "Okay, see you at nine. I'll tell Donna you have an appointment. Thanks so much."

"Thank you." Padma smiled.

"See you tomorrow." Jill left the room and went down the hall to the appointment desk, where Donna was just hanging up the phone, pushing back a puff of dark hair. "Donna, can you please put Rahul Choudhury in at nine tomorrow? I'll come in specially to see him."

"You mean the cutest baby ever?" Donna hit a few keys on the computer. "Of course."

"Thanks, that's my girl." Jill smiled, and Sheryl came striding over from the office. The staff must have seen that Selena had left, because they were all sneaking glances from their computers, files, and phones, waiting to see what would happen between Jill and Sheryl.

"Jill, did you really close the lab?" Sheryl asked, her voice low, so that the full waiting room couldn't hear.

"Yes." Jill matched her soft tone. She didn't want to make a scene, and she'd never get along with Sheryl if she embarrassed her. "Selena's mother is very ill, and they should be together. I know you must feel the same way."

"I do, but we have a business to run."

"I'm not trying to interfere with that. I can take blood, and so can any doc who's kept up his qualifications. Let us do some work for a change, eh?" Jill smiled, and so did the staff.

"I'll take this up with John." Sheryl edged backward, frowning. Donna studied her desk, hiding her smile, and so did everybody else.

"Great, thanks." Jill turned on her heel, went back down the hall, slid the file of the next patient from the holder, and went into Exam Room A. It took only two colds, another ear infection, and a broken toe for John Gilbert, the senior partner, to find her between patients. He was a preppy internist in his fifties, in horn-rimmed glasses, a red-and-blue rep tie, and a pressed lab coat with his name embroidered on the breast pocket. He took her aside in front of his office.

"Jill, can I see you inside, a sec? This'll be quick." John opened his door, and Jill followed him into his office. "Jill, what happened with Selena?"

"Her mom's in hospice, and I sent her home. We're doctors, and if we don't have compassion for suffering, then who does?"

"This isn't about compassion." John frowned. "Sheryl handles personnel matters, not the docs."

"I know, but Selena is so distracted that she lost a sample for one of my patients. Do you want to make Sheryl happy or do you want to get sued?"

"Good point, but I'm not about to take blood myself. I haven't taken blood in nine years, I don't have time. None of us do, you know that."

"Then send your patients to LabCorp. It's not far."

"They're not accustomed to that inconvenience."

"It's the suburbs, John, nothing's *that* inconvenient. They probably have drive-through blood." Jill thought of Rahul. "Listen, please, help me get my new bloodwork stat, would you? You have privileges at Phoenixville, don't you?"

"It's not that easy."

"It has to be. I'm worried about this patient, and with babies, you don't get the margins that you do with adults. They go downhill fast."

"Enough, okay." John put up a hand. "Tell Donna to call Charlotte. She'll make it happen."

"Thanks. Gotta go." Jill hurried out to the door, with no time to reflect on whether she'd pissed off her boss. She had a slew of patients, and she had to be out of work on time tonight.

To go see about a corgi puppy.

# 47.

Jill stopped on the main drag of Hoboken, where low-rise apartment buildings and older brick townhouses stood with storefront bodegas, gourmet coffee shops, Greek restaurants, and hip boutiques. A constant stream of people filled the sidewalks, heading home from work or bubbling up from the PATH station, like a people geyser.

"You have reached your destination," said her GPS.

Jill spotted a parking space, slid into it, and cut the ignition. She'd never pretended to be anybody else before, and she wondered how William had done it, maintaining two identities at once. She retrieved the Phillies cap and popped it on. Oddly, it helped her play her part, like a costume for a role. Jill got out of the car and spotted Nina D'Orive across the street. She was a pretty, petite blonde in pink sweats and she was standing with her husband, in running clothes. A fawn-colored corgi puppy was tugging on his sneaker laces.

"Hello, Nina!" Jill waved, thinking of a way to get Nina alone. She crossed the street and extended a hand. "I'm Katie Feehan, from Facebook."

"Hiya!" Nina shook her hand, flashing a pretty smile. "This is Martin, my husband."

"Thanks for meeting me." Jill shook his hand. "I know I said I'd bring the boys, but I had second thoughts. I want to decide about the dog on my own, then make it a surprise."

"Oh, too bad." Nina glanced at her husband. "Martin wanted to meet them. He's all about kids."

Martin grinned. "I want my own baseball team. Go Mets!"

"Go Yanks!" Nina said.

"Go Phils!" Jill chimed in, and they all laughed.

Nina said, "Sorry we have to meet here, on the street. Martin didn't think we should meet you at home, since we don't really know each other."

"I get that, and you have to be careful." Jill bent down to pet the puppy, an adorable round-eyed little dog, with ears as floppy as a baby bunny. "She's so cute! I love that face."

"Isn't she something? Corgis are actually dwarf dogs, bred to herd sheep. Let's go for a walk before it rains." Nina and Martin started walking, and Jill fell into step with them.

"So, Nina, tell me a little about yourself. I saw on your Facebook page that you work at Pharmcen."

"Yes. I'm in Pharmacovigilance."

"Is that even English?" Jill knew what it meant, but she wanted to get Nina talking.

"I know, I get that a lot." Nina smiled. "Pharmacovigilance keeps track of adverse events of drugs, for reporting to the FDA. There's almost fifty people in the department, and I just became second-in-command. I'm a VP now."

Martin snorted. "They gave her a title, but no raise."

Jill let it go. "Congratulations, Nina. A promotion counts for a lot, in this economy."

Nina beamed. "I think so, too. If they have to lay people off again, I won't be one of them, I hope."

Martin checked his watch. "What do you need to know about the dog?"

"Right, of course." Jill didn't want to arouse suspicion. "Was she hard to housebreak?"

"She's almost housebroken," Nina answered, warming to the topic. "I crate her, but she hates it. Sometimes she cries in her crate at night, which breaks my heart, so I take her out, love her up, and put her back in. Martin doesn't want her sleeping with us."

Martin rolled his eyes. "I'm the bad guy."

Jill held her tongue. She could see the fissures in their marriage easily, though she had missed so many in her own.

"I keep the feedings and walks regular, and I crate her when I'm not playing with her. I walk on a schedule, three times a day. She even pees in the same places."

Jill smiled. "You've got this down to a science."

Martin laughed. "That's Nina to a T. She's the one who wanted the dog, not me, but I went with it. Only problem, it sheds like crazy."

Nina elbowed him. "Don't tell her that."

Jill saw her opening. "Martin, what other bad stuff can you tell me? I want the truth."

"You got it!" Martin turned to her. "She bites your heels when you walk."

"She *bites*?" Jill feigned worry, and Nina gave him a playful shove.

"Honey, go for your run, get! You're giving her the wrong idea."

"Does she really bite?" Jill asked, with ersatz concern. "I don't want a dog that bites."

"She doesn't bite." Nina turned to Martin, nudging him again. "You, get going!"

"Okay, okay." Martin shook Jill's hand. "I only do one lap, or I have a heart attack. Nice meeting you."

"Nice meeting you, too. Thanks for the tips."

"Take care." Martin gave Nina a kiss on the cheek, then took off, jogging, and Jill waited until he was out of earshot.

"Nina, I really came to ask you about someone we both know. Neil Straub."

"What? Who?" Nina blinked, and recognition flickered through her lovely blue eyes. "I don't know any Neil Straub."

"I know you do. I'm his ex-wife and I knew him as William Skyler."

"I don't know what you mean." Nina glanced down the sidewalk, where Martin was lost in the crowd.

"Yes, you do. I saw your Visa receipt in his car, from Sephora. Please talk to me before Martin gets back."

"No, really, I don't know any Neil Straub."

"I'm sorry, but I have bad news for you. Neil died last Tuesday in Philadelphia, and I think he was murdered."

Nina gasped. "What? How? That can't be true."

"So you do know Neil Straub."

"Wait, no, yes." Tears sprang to Nina's eyes, and her tone turned pleading. "Please don't tell my husband. He can't suspect a thing. He gets so jealous."

"I won't. The coroner says Neil died as a reaction to a mix of prescription painkillers, anti-anxiety drugs, and alcohol. But I don't think so."

"Drugs, Neil?" Nina asked, bewildered. "He never took anything like that."

"Do you know anybody who would want to kill him, and why?"

"Is this really true? He's really . . . gone?" Nina's eyes brimmed with tears, but she wiped them away, and Jill's heart went out to her.

"Yes. I'm so sorry."

"I haven't heard from him in about a week." Nina sniffled, trying to stay in control. "I called and called, but he didn't return my calls. I was so hurt, so angry. Oh my God, I thought he was ditching me, but all this time, he was . . ."

"I'm sorry." Jill wanted to be sympathetic, but she didn't have much time until Martin came back. "He hasn't been back to the apartment, but they don't know he's gone, either. They don't know him as William Skyler. They know him the way you do, as Neil Straub."

"He *is* Neil Straub."

"You didn't know he had a double identity?"

"No, of course not." Nina flushed.

"Do you know why he did?"

"No."

"What did he tell you he does for a living?"

"He's a real-estate investor." Nina wiped her eyes with a shaky hand.

"How do you know that?"

"He showed me buildings he owns, in the city."

"He lied."

"No, this can't be. I *love* him." Nina's voice broke, and Jill knew exactly how she felt.

"I know, I'm so sorry. I loved him, too, but he used me. I don't mean this to sound hurtful, but I suspect he might have been using you, too. Can you think why? Did you give him money—"

"He wasn't using me, he *loved* me." Nina's eyes spilled over with tears, and she wiped them away again as a young couple passed.

"How long have you been seeing him?"

"Why should I tell you?"

"If you loved him, it can help find his killer."

"What do the police say?"

Jill didn't have time to go through everything. "Please,

just tell me. It could help, and your husband will be back soon."

Nina paused, weepy. "Four years."

Jill reddened. Another thing she hadn't seen coming. She'd only been divorced for three years. So cheating was proven. She masked her shock. "Where did you meet him?"

"At a Starbucks." Nina frowned, recovering. "Wait a minute. Were those little boys on your Facebook page his sons, with you?"

"No, we had no children together. Did you give or lend him money?"

"No. He had plenty of money."

"Did you introduce him to anyone important?"

"No, of course I didn't. We kept everything on the down-low. It was just the two of us, always."

"Did you help him contact people at Pharmcen, like higher-ups? Give him names of people he could call, to sell them something or take something from them? He used to be a drug rep."

"Neil wasn't a drug rep." Nina shook her head, recovering her composure. "He doesn't know anything about the drug business."

"He told you that?" Jill was trying to piece the puzzle together.

"Yes, he told me that, and he used to listen when I talked about my job. He cared about me. He *understood* me."

Jill guessed that cheating wives felt as misunderstood as cheating husbands, and maybe they were. "What else did he tell you about himself?"

"None of this makes sense." Nina forced a smile for a woman pushing a stroller across the street. "Wait, stop. That was my next-door neighbor. We can't talk here."

"Look at this." Jill dug in her purse, pulled out the photo of William with the man in the blue polo shirt, and pointed at William, just to double-check. "This is the man you know as Neil, right?"

"Yes, that's Neil." Nina's eyes filled anew. "Oh my God, it's so hard to see him, now. I can't believe this. I don't believe it."

"Who's this other guy, do you know?" Jill pointed at the mystery man.

"I think that's Joe Z."

"Joe who?"

"Neil's friend, Joe Zeptien."

"Did you know him?"

"Not really. Neil talked to him on the phone all the time, and I met him once." Nina wiped tears from her cheeks, getting her bearings. "I was leaving the apartment one night, but I forgot my earrings, so I went back, and he was going in. Neil introduced him to me."

"So who is Joe Zeptien and what did he do? Did he have any reason to want to hurt William? I mean, Neil?" Jill slipped the photo back into her purse. "I'm wondering if Joe Zeptien is the man who killed him."

"No, never." Nina shook her head, tears returning to her eyes. "They were tight."

"How do you know?"

"Neil told me, and like I say, they talked all the time."

"How do you know he was talking to Joe Zeptien? You only know what he told you. It could have been anyone."

"No, I knew it was him. I answered Neil's cell once, by accident, when we were together. We both have Black-Berrys and we kept them by the bed, because I had to answer in case Martin called, and Neil always had to answer his email. I picked his BlackBerry up when he was in the bathroom, and it was Joe calling."

"What did they talk about, usually?"

"Hold on, here comes my husband." Nina looked left, stricken, and Martin was running down the block, breathing hard. She wiped her eyes, cleared her throat, and backed away. "End of discussion. I have to go. You have to go. We can't talk here—"

"What did they talk about?"

"I don't know. He always took the calls out of the room, so Joe wouldn't hear that he was with me. Neil was careful that no one find out about us, to protect my marriage."

Jill figured that William must've been protecting himself, so Nina couldn't hear his calls, not the other way around. "Where does Joe live?"

"I don't know. In the city, I think."

"New York? What did he do for a living?"

"I don't know that, either." Nina panicked as Martin got closer. "Stop. We're done. I want to know more, but we can't talk here. Did you get the police involved? Do they know my name? Are they going to contact me?"

"I can explain it all, but you have to meet me. Tell me where and when, tomorrow."

"I can't. I have work."

"I'll meet you there. How about noon, for lunch?"

"No, the only time I'm free is in the morning. I'll message you a place to meet me, on Facebook." Nina tensed as Martin got closer, panting and puffing, his T-shirt dark with perspiration. "Go now. I'll tell Martin I cried because I twisted my ankle."

"Wait, what time in the morning should I meet you?"

"Ten o'clock. I'll say I have a doctor's appointment."

*You do,* Jill thought, but didn't say.

It was until she was back in the car that she remembered:

*Rahul.*

# 48.

A thunderstorm broke on the way home, the rain pounding on the roof of the car, and Jill struggled to hear on the cell phone. "Padma, are you there?"

"Yes, hello?"

"I'm so sorry, but I have to cancel our appointment tomorrow morning." Jill cringed. She hated doctors who canceled, and now she was one. "I'm so sorry. Can you meet me later in the day? How about noon tomorrow?"

"I can do that."

"Good, let's make it then. I'll have the bloodwork. How is Rahul?" Jill switched lanes, keeping an eye on the rearview. Behind her was a FedEx truck, and the traffic was heavy, moving fast despite the fact that visibility was poor, the sky prematurely dark, and everything grayed out with rain.

"About the same. He's sleeping now."

"Fever?"

"Yes, but low."

"Eating and drinking?"

"Still not so great."

Jill made a mental note. "Okay, hang in. See you at noon. Again, my apologies."

"Good-bye," Padma said, hanging up.

Jill fed the car gas and checked the rearview, but the truck behind her had moved, showing a gray sedan. She pressed END, then M, to call and check on Megan, who would be home from practice by now, probably foraging in the refrigerator. Jill kept her eye on the road while the call connected, then said, "Hi, honey!"

"Hey, Mom, I was just about to call you."

"What's up?"

"I'm not home, I'm at Courtney's. We have to do our scene tomorrow, and we're almost ready, but I need to stay over one more night."

Jill groaned. "No. Megan, it's too much. It's an imposition on Carol."

"I knew you'd say that, and she's right here. She wants to talk to you."

"Good, put her on." Jill heard a shuffling on the other end of the line. "Carol, that you? Don't you need a break?"

"No, not at all." Carol sounded bright and cheery. "How have you been?"

"Fine, busy, and thanks for letting my daughter take up residence."

"Not at all. She's a dream, you know that. Let her stay here tonight. They're working so hard, you'd be proud of them, making costumes and all."

Jill felt so guilty. "But you're even doing the driving."

"You've done your share, plenty of times before. Don't worry about a thing, I swear. I'll be out of town next week, and you can be the chauffeur then."

"Okay, thanks." Jill felt grateful. "You're a saint."

"Aren't we all? Take care, and here's Megan. See you." There was a pause, and Megan came back on the line. "Okay, Mom?"

"Okay, honey. Don't forget to thank her for everything, and get some sleep tonight, okay?"

"I will. Love you."

"Love you and miss you, too. Bye-bye." Jill pressed END and set the phone aside, spotting the gray sedan, still behind her. Its driver was a shadow of a man, and the sedan stayed to her left, on her bumper.

She accelerated, and a minute later, so did he. She didn't like to drive fast when it was raining, so she decelerated. So did he. She switched to the slow lane and let her speed decrease to fifty miles an hour. So did he, which set her heart thudding. She hit the gas and picked up her phone, in case she had to call 911.

Suddenly a sign came up for the service area, and the gray sedan split off, taking the ramp leaving the highway. Still, Jill didn't let off the gas, her hand holding the phone, and she sped all the way home in the storm.

# 49.

It was dark by the time Jill got home, and she let Beef out in the backyard and lingered at the door. She scanned the privacy fence for anything suspicious, but there was nothing, and Beef was acting normal, burying his muzzle in the wet grass. Mist wreathed the air, which smelled musty and thick, and steam curled from the pool. It had stormed here, too, leaving the night sky oddly bright in patches, with particles of light hidden in the dark clouds, like vermiculate in potting soil.

Jill stood in the doorway, and her silhouette stretched across the lawn, a human taffy pulled out of shape, taut enough to be dangerously brittle. Sam hadn't called her, and she thought about calling him, but she still couldn't tell him what he wanted to hear. Her head was swimming since her meeting with Nina. Beef trotted out of the gloom, his movement fluid as a daisy-cutter, even at his age. Jill opened her hand at her side, and he slipped his head under her palm, which was their secret routine. His skull felt furry and damp, and she scratched behind his ears, where there was a knot.

Suddenly her phone started to ring, and she reached for

her pocket and slid out her new BlackBerry. The screen showed KATIE FEEHAN, and Jill picked up. "Hi, girl."

"What happened with Nina?" Katie asked, nervous. "Are you okay? Why didn't you call?"

"I had to talk to a patient, and the rain was bad all the way home, so I stayed off the phone." Jill was about to start the story about Nina when the boys started yelling on the other end of the line, at Katie's house. "What's going on over there?"

"Fight Club at the Feehans'. The two little ones are overtired, and they both want to be on the computer at the same time. It's not pretty."

"Uh-oh." Jill remembered when her house was full of girls, fighting over eye makeup and borrowed sweaters. She never thought she'd miss those days, but she did.

"God, these kids," Katie moaned, exasperated. The background noise surged, and the boys yelled louder. "I'm trying to let them work it out themselves. How long does sibling rivalry last? Oh, right."

Jill smiled. "Katie, if it's a bad time, I can call back."

"No, I'm dying to hear, and I got a Facebook message from Nina, saying to meet her at the Starbucks on 60 Weehawk Avenue at ten o'clock tomorrow. I'll email it to you, so you have the address. Hold on, Jill. Boys, take turns!" Katie covered the receiver, muffling her voice. "Jamie, let him use it, then you can get back on. Log out. Log out right now, okay, honey?"

"You have your hands full."

"Tell me about it. They use the same computer, so one has to log out before the other gets on, but Tommy isn't being patient. Hold on a minute." Katie covered the receiver again. "Tommy, give him a second. You know he's not that good with the mouse yet."

Jill imagined the two tow-headed Feehan boys,

pushing each other out of the way, in front of the kitchen computer. She knew the log-in, log-out system because they used it at work, for the Epic program. The docs and nurses shared the computers in the examining rooms, and each had his own user account, with a separate password. Jill's was Megan0112, because January 12 was Megan's birthday.

"Hold on, Jill. Tommy, he's logging out, right now. Tommy, he's littler than you are!"

Jill's mind raced ahead. She didn't know why she hadn't thought of it, earlier. She had searched William's laptop before, and it had been clean, suspiciously so. Back then, she'd thought he had only one identity, but now she knew he had another identity. She wondered if there was also a user account for Neil Straub, set up in the same laptop.

"Okay, Jill, I'm back. Whew! I'd buy each kid a computer, but a week later, they'll be obsolete. I mean the computers, not the kids."

"Let me ask you something." Jill felt newly energized. "Do you have different user accounts in that computer, one for each boy?"

"Yes, three for the kids, plus Mike and I each have an account. So we have five user accounts."

"In the same computer?"

"Yes. Mike also has his own laptop for work, but I use the kitchen computer all the time, like for Facebook. You saw. It was logged in for my account, and it has all my settings."

Jill didn't care about the settings. "When the computer reboots, does it show all the user names? And then you choose yours and log in as yourself?"

"Yes, sure."

"Ours don't do that, at work. The screen is blank, and we log in with a password."

"It depends on the software, I'm sure. The interface. They all work the same way, it's just a question of what you're shown on the screen at start-up."

"I see, so it's just programmed differently." Jill had rebooted William's laptop when she got it home from Abby's, but hadn't seen any choices of user accounts. "Katie, who set up those user accounts for you?"

"I did."

"You?"

"Sure, it's easy. I'm the administrator. Who better?"

Jill smiled, with admiration. Never underestimate the power of a mother. "Let me ask you this. Could you hide those user accounts, do you think?"

"You mean so they wouldn't show up on the start-up screen? Sure, if I wanted to. I could probably set it to show only a few of the names, or just the boys."

"And if you can hide them, can you find them?"

"Sure. Why?"

"I'm thinking of William's laptop. If he had a secret identity in life, couldn't he also have one on his laptop?"

"He could," Katie answered, catching on. "If he has a secret user account as Neil Straub, I can tell you how to find it on his laptop."

"Really?"

Katie snorted. "Did you forget, I'm the Queen of Farmville?"

Half an hour later, Beef curled up on his bed, and Jill was sitting down at the kitchen island in front of William's laptop, next to a cup of hot coffee and a printout of Katie's instructions. She got busy, and after one more phone call to the Queen of Farmville, Jill was ready to reboot the laptop and see if William had a second user account, for Neil Straub.

She turned off the computer, hit RESTART, and waited, and the screen came to life, first with the Microsoft logo, then a dizzying array of spinning numbers, like a slot machine. They finally stopped, the screensaver went black, and the screen read, PASSWORD.

Jill felt a frisson of excitement, as well as fear. She remembered that all of William's passwords were a combination of exotic cars and his birthday, because he always said he wanted an exotic for his birthday. His go-to shopping password was P9110701, for a Porsche 911 and his July 1 birthday, so she plugged that in. The message came up, PASSWORD INVALID. Jill knew he used JAGXKE0701 for their joint bank account, so she plugged that in, but the message came up, PASSWORD INVALID, again. Next she tried MB6000701, for the top-of-the-line Mercedes-Benz he coveted, but it came up PASSWORD INVALID, too.

Then she remembered the exotic that he always called his holy grail, and what he'd always said about the car: *I want to be buried in an Aston Martin DB9.*

Jill typed in AMDB90701 and hit ENTER. Instantly, the screen changed to the default screensaver, an idyllic sky and grassy hill, Microsoft heaven. Her heart beat faster as she moved the mouse, clicked, and read the screen:

WELCOME, NEIL!

# 50.

Jill clicked on the list of William's Microsoft Word files, and the first two were RESEARCH and NOTES, created the same date, September 9, three years ago. She clicked RESEARCH and almost fell off her chair. The file contained hundreds of files, each with a drug name, in alphabetical order: Abata, Akasin, Aormil, Aresta, Aritil, Aromytec, all the way to Zertax. She recognized many of the drugs, and they all treated different maladies: headaches, hypertension, gout, bipolar depression, skin cancer, psoriasis, nausea, aplastic anemia. There was no logical link between them that she could see.

She clicked on the first file, for Abata, which she knew treated asthma in children. The subfile was a PDF of the drug circular, with prescribing information for physicians and a description: "Abata is a hydrochloride salt of quinapril, the ethyl ester of a non-sulfhydryl . . ." She looked through the rest of the Abata file. One subfile was labeled PRESS, and she clicked on it, revealing a list of newspapers and blogs, next to dates and links. She clicked on the first link and it opened to an article in *THE OREGONIAN*, dated June 3, some eight years ago:

Moise Yakowicz, 6, of Portland, almost died today
at the Young Pioneers picnic, as a result of anaphylactic shock, which his parents claim was attributed
to Abata. The drug, manufactured by Pharmcen . . .

Jill thought a minute. Abata was made by Pharmcen,
where Nina worked. She didn't know if it was coincidence,
but it didn't feel like one. She navigated out of the article
and clicked the next, which was from the *Bucks County
Courier Post,* in Pennsylvania:

Today was a tragic day for the family of Paulina Ma,
10, whose memorial service was held at Kaybock's
Funeral Home, in the driving rain. Ma died last
week, the result of anaphylactic shock that her
mother claims was caused by Abata, a drug mar-
keted by Pharmcen . . .

Jill went to the next drug file, Akasin, and it followed
the same pattern: the prescribing information for physicians, then articles about the drug and its side effects,
from sources all over the Internet. She clicked the next
three, for Aormil, Aresta, and Aritil, and discovered a
common thread. All five drugs were manufactured by
Pharmcen.

She minimized the Word document, went to the web,
and clicked BOOKMARKS. The list stretched the length of
the screen, again, it was entirely drug names, starting with
Abata. It looked as if William was making himself an expert in the adverse side effects of Pharmcen drugs, and
she put that together with the fact that he was in a relationship with Nina, who worked in Pharmacovigilance at
Pharmcen, a department that collected complaints about
the adverse side effects of Pharmcen drugs.

Jill sensed she was getting close to the bottom of his

scheme. Drug manufacturers had a legal duty to collect complaints about the adverse reactions of their drugs and report them to the FDA if the reactions were serious, life-threatening, or unexpected. The complaints could come from anybody, most came from doctors. Pembey Family probably over-reported because of Sheryl and her lawsuit phobia, and Jill's old pediatric group was more typical, in that they didn't report as often. They couldn't always be sure if the drug had caused the adverse reaction, and it took time to fill out the paperwork, even electronically.

Jill logged out of the Internet and back to START, looking for an email server. She spotted the email account and opened to the Inbox, only to discover the oddest emails ever. The list of senders and recipients were all the same: Neil Straub, and the subject lines were all drug names. It was easy to see what was happening; William had been emailing himself about various drugs. Jill scanned the dates the emails were received, and the email stopped the day before William died, on Monday, and she opened it.

The subject line was Memoril, and she knew she'd heard about that drug somewhere, then she remembered. It had been in the waiting room at work, when she'd run into Elaine Fitzmartin and her mother, Mary.

*We're fine, thanks. Much better now that Mom's on Memoril.*

Jill figured that Memoril was an Alzheimer's drug, and she opened the email, which read in its entirety:

2, tot 4

Jill wasn't sure what it meant. She clicked the previous email, also with the subject line Memoril, and it read:

total 4 or 5, will check

Jill went to the earlier email, also with Memoril in the subject line:

1 more

Jill went to the previous email and the one before that, and they were all only numbers, as if William were counting. She went back further and found one that read:

One more. E worried

Jill didn't get the "E." It sounded like an initial, and she made a mental note, then closed the email and checked the times and dates that William had sent them to himself. Some were two days apart, some three. Then she realized something. Not one was sent on a weekend.

*He always had to answer his email.*

Jill put it together. The timing of the email must have corresponded to William's meetings with Nina. He must have been getting information from her about the number of complaints coming in on Memoril, then emailing the count to himself, so he kept track. He'd told Nina that he was answering his email, but really he'd been emailing himself.

Jill took a gulp of cold coffee and tried to understand why. If she assumed that William was counting Memoril complaints, she had to ask, how could that benefit him, or pay off? Then it hit her. Jill played a hunch, went back to the folders, and scanned the list. STOCK INFORMATION, read one folder, and she clicked. The file opened into another long list of folders labeled ANNUAL REPORTS, FINANCIALS, STOCK CHARTS, DIVIDENDS, SPLIT HISTORY, SEC FILINGS, CEO/CFO CERTIFICATIONS, ACQUISITIONS, and so on.

She clicked through one, then the next, confirming her

suspicion. It was information about Pharmcen stock, only. Pharmcen was publicly traded, and if William knew which of their drugs had the most complaints, he could predict which, if any, would be recalled. Drugs got recalled, or safety letters issued, more often than the public realized, and it could easily affect the manufacturer's stock price, especially in today's volatile market. Even a minor recall, a Class III, would affect stock price, and a Class I recall could send stock prices plummeting.

Jill felt her heartbeat quicken. If William knew that a major drug was about to be recalled, he could make money by selling Pharmcen's stock short, betting against its value. It would explain how he could afford his homes, cars, and double life, and it was just what he had done with her, except on a bigger scale.

She navigated back on the Internet to confirm her theory, but William hadn't bookmarked any stock-trading sites like etrade.com, schwab.com, or tdameritrade.com. It shot her theory. She looked elsewhere in the computer, for some sort of trading files, but the omission was obvious. William had inside information but wasn't trading on it, which made no sense, especially for a man like him.

Jill felt stumped. She navigated out of PROGRAMS to the START menu, to see what other programs William had. The only one she hadn't seen yet was Excel, for financial spreadsheets. She clicked, and the program opened to a list of spreadsheets, dating from three years ago. She clicked on the first one, and it blossomed into a sheet that showed dollar amounts, in large chunks: $20,000 on June 6, $20,000 on June 22, and another $20,000 on June 29.

Jill's eyes opened wide. Somebody was paying William for something, and it had to be inside information about Pharmcen drugs, and which were potential recalls. He wasn't trading on the information himself, but he must have been selling it to someone who did, and Jill bet that man was Joe Zeptien.

She sat back, amazed. She had figured out his plan, and all of it was contained in his laptop, hidden in his secret identity, behind his stupid little password, AMDB90701. Then a thought struck her, like an epiphany. Her own passwords were about Megan and Megan's birthday, like Megan 0112, or Megan and her old nicknames, like Miggy0112, or Megan and Beef, MGBF0112. Jill's passwords were about what she loved the most, and that's why she'd remember them the easiest; they were what came first to her mind, at all times. Jill guessed that lots of mothers, and fathers, were the same way, and a password could speak volumes about a person, like a modern-day key to the soul.

Jill blinked, eyeing the screen. William's passwords were about himself and cars, not Abby, Victoria, or anyone else he loved, because deep in his soul, he didn't really love anyone. So it wasn't that he didn't love Jill, it was that he simply wasn't capable of love. It simply wasn't in the man. She had wanted to know what he was really up to, and the answer had been before her all along. It was right in front of her face now, on his laptop.

Money. He had wanted money, not for what it bought, but for what it said about him, as a man. It was as simple as that, because the wish itself was nothing, as substantial as an electronic transaction. Money was nothing but a construct ultimately, a collection of paper and ink, printed at will, no longer backed by anything, and signifying nothing. We all agree that money has value because we all agree that money has value, and William was the same way. Inside, he felt valueless. And so, he was.

And suddenly, as soon as Jill thought about him that way, she understood William a little better. She wasn't as angry at him, or as hurt. She just felt sorry for him, going through his life, so hollow, so empty, feeling absolutely worthless. Oddly, the fact that he was dead now was beside the point. He was dead to her, beginning right this minute. It had taken Jill a long time to heal, but she had done it, finally.

*Physician, heal thyself.*

Jill smiled at the revelation, then set up a plan. She'd work all night to get this information together, and she'd meet with Nina tomorrow to fill in the details, tell her what was going on, and answer her questions. Then Jill would turn it all over to the police, and they could decide whether to talk to Nina, find Joe Zeptien, or figure out if William had been murdered, why, and by whom. Something must have gone wrong with William's scheme, and the police would figure it out. Jill had figured out what she wanted to know.

The truth about William.

It was awful, but it had set her free.

# 51.

The next morning, Jill waited for Nina at the Starbucks, dressed in her sweater, jeans, and loafers uniform, feeling surprisingly fresh after an all-nighter spent going through William's laptop. Her theory about William's scheme had proved correct, and now she had the financial details. He'd had two big paydays with Deferral and Riparin, equaling about $1 million over the last three years, and he'd also been paid another $500,000 for a stream of smaller insider tips. Memoril looked as if it was going to be his biggest score of all, and he'd already been paid $1.1 million for information about it. Jill had with her a manila folder that contained printed emails and spreadsheets, in case Nina needed convincing.

She checked her watch. It was 10:15 A.M. Nina was running a little late, although Pharmcen's sprawling complex in Parkertowne was just down the street, a series of brown brick buildings with a campus that boasted a man-made pond, a walking track, and an employee parking lot surrounded by manicured hedges. Jill had never been to central New Jersey before, but she could see the appeal, with lovely horse farms still managing to coexist with strip malls and corporate centers.

Jill checked her email for Rahul's bloodwork, but it wasn't in yet. She sipped her coffee, which was strong and hot, and looked around. The baristas worked quickly behind the counters, amid the squishy noises of espresso machines, and a long line of customers stood waiting to order, business people wearing laminated corporate IDs, young girls in black yoga pants, and moms with strollers, negotiating around kiosks with breakable logo mugs.

*I met him at a Starbucks.*

Jill wondered if this was the Starbucks where Nina had met William. It would make sense. He could have met Nina, started the affair, and after all that pillow talk, realized there was money to be made from the information and hatched his scheme. Or maybe he had even preyed on Nina, choosing to hang at a Starbucks near Pharmcen, hoping to meet a young girl who worked there, knowing he could charm her out of anything, including inside information.

The door of the Starbucks opened, and Jill looked up, expecting Nina, but it was two van drivers in Pharmcen blue uniforms, laughing and talking. She checked her watch—10:30. Maybe Nina had trouble getting out of work. The door opened again, and Jill looked up. Two young women, more Pharmcen employees, entered the Starbucks, but they were distraught, their eyes puffy and makeup streaky. Customers in line turned at the sight, and baristas craned their necks.

"I can't believe it," the one woman was saying, as they both sank into the first empty table. "It's so sudden. It's crazy."

The Pharmcen truck drivers walked over, and one asked, "What is it? Another round of cuts, in Corporate?"

"No," the woman answered, rubbing bloodshot eyes. "A

girl we work with was killed. Her husband shot her, then committed suicide."

Jill felt thunderstruck, in shock. Her hand flew to her mouth.

"Jeez, that's awful," the driver said, taking off his blue cap. "Was she a friend of yours?"

"Yes, and she was really sweet. Nina was the best girl ever."

"No, no, it can't be," Jill blurted out, stunned. She stood up, but went weak in the knees, and the Pharmcen employees turned to her, astonished.

"Miss, you okay?" asked the truck driver, in confusion.

"No, sorry, this can't be." Jill tried to recover, walking over, stricken. "Was it Nina D'Orive who was killed?"

"Yes," the woman answered, teary. "Did you know her?"

"Yes, I know her, I knew her. What? How? When did this happen?"

"Late last night," the woman answered, her throat thick. "She didn't come in today, and she's always on time, so Elliott called her at home, and the cops told him."

"Elliott?"

"Elliott's our boss, in Pharmacovigilance. He just called us all into the break room and told us."

Jill thought of the E in the emails, fighting a wave of nausea. Her mind reeled. She prayed she hadn't been responsible for Nina's murder. That Nina hadn't been crying over William's death and Martin had caught her. Or maybe Nina had confessed to the affair, and he killed her for it. It couldn't be a coincidence, after last night.

Jill felt her gorge rising, panicked at the frowning faces and puzzled stares, then grabbed her purse and manila folder, bolted for the door, and ran out of the Starbucks, reaching the edge of the parking lot just in time.

She bent over and vomited.

# 52.

Jill hit the gas and steered out of the Starbucks parking lot onto Weehawk Boulevard. Traffic was light, which was good, because she was in no shape to drive. Tears filled her eyes, bile coated her teeth. She felt wretched and horrified, and wherever she looked, she kept seeing poor Nina, so happy to show off her cute little puppy.

*Corgis are dwarf dogs, bred to herd sheep.*

Jill stopped at the traffic light, across from the blue-flagged entrance to Pharmcen's campus, with its PHARM-CEN sign and globe logo, in trademark blue. She thought of the laptop in her trunk, full of information about how Pharmcen's confidential information had been bought, and after what had happened to Nina, she felt the need to talk to someone at Pharmcen, find out whatever she could about Nina, tell them what was going on in their own company, and show them the laptop.

The traffic light turned green, and Jill took a left into the parking lot, followed the signs to the visitors' parking lot, and parked the car, cutting the ignition. She blew her nose, wiped her eyes, and grabbed her purse, then got out of the car, retrieved the laptop, and hurried to the glass entrance. She went inside and walked to the reception desk, a massive granite banquette with a panel of telephones and computer screens.

"May I help you?" The pretty young receptionist smiled, but Jill was too upset to smile back.

"My name's Jill Farrow and I'd like to see Elliott, the head of Pharmacovigilance. It's important."

"Do you have some kind of appointment with Mr. Horton?"

"I'm a friend of Nina D'Orive's. I need to see him, about her."

"My condolences on your loss. It's a terrible tragedy." The receptionist gestured at a seating area on the right, which held a group of well-dressed businessmen and -women. "Please, have a seat in the waiting area, and I'll call Mr. Horton."

"Thanks." Jill went over to the waiting area and sat down in a blue-patterned chair. She put the laptop and her purse on her lap, composing herself. The receptionist picked up the phone receiver, pressed in some numbers, and started talking in a low tone, then hung up, gesturing to Jill, who walked back to the desk with the laptop. "May I see him now?"

"I'm sorry, but Mr. Horton is unavailable at this time."

"Can I see someone in security, then?"

"What's this in reference to?" The receptionist glanced past Jill, to a black security desk on her right, at the back wall of the lobby.

"I'd rather not say. Can't I please speak with someone in security? This is a matter of corporate security."

"Please, relax." The receptionist motioned to the security guard, who was already on his way.

"Hello, may I help you, Miss?" The security guard had

a soul patch, which looked out of place with his Pharmcen blue uniform and billed cap. He wore a laminated ID, but his embroidered patch read BARRY RONAT.

"Yes." Jill introduced herself again. "I need to talk to your boss. It's a matter of corporate security."

"And what would that be?"

"Can I just see him?" Jill could feel the heads turning, the men in ties and women in low heels eyeing her. "It's not for public consumption."

"I'm sorry, I can't do that."

"I'm a friend of Nina D'Orive, and I was supposed to meet her this morning, about an important matter."

"I'm sorry, Miss. May I escort you outside, to your car?"

"No, thanks." Jill could see it was useless. She didn't know what she was thinking anyway, coming here. She'd let the police handle it. "I'll go myself."

"I'll escort you, Miss," the security guard repeated.

"Okay, thanks." Jill walked to the entrance, sticking her hand into her purse for her cell phone. She went through the doors, found her BlackBerry, and walked to her car while the security guard stopped in front of the entrance and folded his arms. By the time she was in the driver's seat, she was already pressing 411, for information.

"In Philadelphia, Pennsylvania," Jill said into the phone. "Please connect me to Central Detectives."

# 53.

Jill stopped at a red light on Weehawk Boulevard, holding her cell phone to her ear, waiting for the call to connect to Central Detectives. She felt sick at heart and flashed on Nina, smiling up at Jill, with pride at her new promotion.

*I just became second-in-command. I'm a VP now.*

The phone call connected, and a male voice said, "Detective Ramallah speaking."

"My name's Jill Farrow, and I'm calling about my ex-husband's case, William Skyler." She had to remember which detective to ask for. "I spoke last with Detective Hightower."

"Wait, I just saw him. I'm going to put you on hold."

"Thanks." Jill waited for Detective Hightower, still upset about Nina. The traffic light turned green, but the cars barely moved because of a commotion, up ahead. White municipal trucks were on the scene, and water bubbled from the street, sloshing from a broken water main. Cops were diverting traffic off Weehawk Boulevard, using a trio of parked cruisers as a blockade, their lights flashing. Jill heard a click on the cell phone.

"Yes, this is Detective Hightower."

. "Detective, thanks for taking the call." Jill fed the car gas as the traffic eased up, and she turned left in front of the waving policeman, driving slowly through the spreading water.

"Dr. Farrow, I thought we understood each other."

"I need to bring you some new information. How long will you be there?" Jill didn't have time to see Detective Hightower before her noon appointment with Padma and Rahul, and she couldn't postpone that again. "I have to see a patient first, but that won't take long."

"I'm here all day unless we get a job, you know that we closed the case on William Skyler. Correction, we never opened one."

"No, please, listen. My ex-husband was selling inside information on Pharmcen drugs, to the tune of two-and-a-half million dollars." Jill followed the traffic left, then right, and the scenery changed almost instantly, from corporate campuses to wide open spaces.

"Do you have proof of this?"

"Yes, I do. He was using his girlfriend, who works there, and I have proof, in his laptop." Jill passed a white clapboard farmhouse, with bay horses that grazed in a pasture near the road, their heads down and their black tails switching at unseen flies.

"Who is this woman? Is she coming with you?"

"No." Jill swallowed hard. She drove straight on the road, but everyone else turned right. She would have followed them if she hadn't been upset and distracted, on the phone. "She was just murdered, last night."

"What are you talking about? Who said it was a murder?"

"The Hoboken police, I assume. She lived in Hoboken. Her husband killed her, then shot himself."

"Oh, no. My apologies." Detective Hightower paused. "Dr. Farrow, where are you?"

"Parkertowne, New Jersey." Jill's thoughts raced ahead. It did seem coincidental that Nina was killed the night after her visit. What if it wasn't what it seemed to be? What if it had to do with the scheme? With William's murder? What if somebody else had killed Nina and made it look like Martin did it?

"Dr. Farrow? Did we get cut off?"

"No, sorry, I was just wondering if her murder wasn't what it seemed and—" Jill didn't finish her sentence. She didn't have any evidence and she didn't know if she believed it herself. "I'm on my way back home and I'll see you as soon as I can."

"Fine. I'll see you this afternoon, please, hang up the phone. Drive safely."

"Thanks." Jill hung up, then put the phone on the passenger seat. She didn't know the route to Philadelphia that well from here, so she started the GPS, selected FROM MEMORY, and pressed HOME, because it was quicker and close enough. She drove straight while the GPS calculated the route, and the farms spread out, surrounded by sun-dappled pastures. Tall oaks lined the street, which narrowed to one lane, the yellow line vanishing.

The GPS said, "Turn left in fifty feet."

Jill drove on a back road, and her fingers gripped the wheel, her body understanding something before her brain did. If Nina and Martin were murdered by someone else, it could mean that she had been followed to Hoboken. It could mean that she was being followed, even now. She checked her rearview mirror, and there were two cars behind her, a gray sedan and, behind that, a silver one.

The GPS said, "Turn left in twenty-five feet."

Jill drove with her eye on the two cars. The gray sedan looked like the one she'd seen the other night, but she couldn't be certain. The cars were driving in tandem, one close behind the other, as if they were together. She told herself it didn't mean anything. Many drivers tailgated, and people got confused when there was a detour.

The GPS said, "Please turn left."

Jill turned, and so did the silver and gray sedans. Her heartbeat picked up, but she told herself to stay calm, that all the cars had to turn, there was nowhere else to go. The GPS was taking them all back to the main road, with her in front.

The GPS said, "Continue on the road for five miles."

Jill felt her mouth go dry. The road ahead was a long straight stretch of asphalt lined with old trees. She told herself that it was a beautiful drive in the country, that there was nothing to worry about. That nobody got killed in broad daylight, in New Jersey horse country. Suddenly the silver sedan sped up, closing in on her rear bumper, with the gray car, right behind.

Jill's heart leapt to her throat. She reached for her Black-Berry. The silver and the gray cars were trying to run her off the road. She pressed 911 and hit the gas, going sixty-five miles an hour, then seventy.

The silver car accelerated, almost on her bumper. The gray car pulled up beside it. They both raced after her, riding her bumper, spraying gravel from the roadside.

Jill sped up to seventy-five, then eighty. She needed both hands to drive. She held the BlackBerry against the steering wheel with a thumb. The call connected, and she yelled, "Help me! I'm being chased by two cars! They're trying to kill me."

"What is your location?" the emergency operator asked, calmly.

"I don't know!" Jill looked frantically for a street or route sign but there wasn't one. She checked the GPS screen but couldn't read it this fast. "I'm near Parkertowne, in Jersey! Can't you find me? I have GPS! I'm in a white Volvo. Help!"

Jill whizzed past cows and horses. The steering wheel jerked and bobbled. A tractor in the field stopped as they flew by. She gritted her teeth and squeezed the wheel to keep the car on the road. One slip and she'd crash into a tree.

The silver and gray sedans formed a solid wall, racing to meet her.

"Help!" she screamed. She needed her hands and dropped the phone. She couldn't hear the emergency operator. Whatever happened was going to happen in the next five seconds. The cops couldn't get here fast enough.

She sped up to ninety-five, then 100. Her heart was in her throat. She began to scream and didn't stop. She'd never gone this fast in her life. The road swallowed her alive. Everything was a blur. She squeezed the life from the steering wheel. She aimed straight ahead with all her might.

The silver and gray sedans rode her bumper at lethal speed.

She floored the gas pedal, screaming at the top of her lungs. She couldn't hear the operator. No one could help her now.

*Help me, God, I have a child who needs me.*

# 54.

*BOOM!* Suddenly Jill's car was rammed from behind. The impact whipsawed her against the shoulder harness. She screamed and lost control of the steering wheel. Her car went spinning and spinning down the road. Her tires screeched in her ears. She whirled and whirled forever, like a nightmare amusement ride.

*WHAM!* The front of her car slammed into a fence. Her air bag exploded, shoving her back into the seat. She couldn't see anything but plastic. Couldn't smell anything but rubber. Felt dusted by a smelly powder of some kind. Her air bag deflated as rapidly as it had exploded. The car kept spinning in crazy motion, whirling off the road backwards, skidding sideways. A low-lying branch punched through the window on the passenger side.

"No!" Jill screamed, flattening herself against the seat. Glass flew everywhere. The end of the branch stopped inches from her head. Twigs and leaves raked her face. The car skidded, finally stopping.

The GPS said, "Please, make a U-turn. Make a U-turn."

Jill sat in the seat, stunned. Her skull throbbed with

pain. Blood dripped from her forehead. She put up a shaky hand to stop the flow. Warmth leaked between her fingers. She shuddered as adrenaline dumped into her bloodstream. Her heart thundered. She scanned her legs and arms. Nothing was broken. Her left hand bled from a cut. Blood and broken glass lay everywhere. Her head hurt like hell, but she couldn't see any other injuries. She was alive.

*Thank you thank you.*

The engine shook, then went silent. She couldn't see through the leaves and the shattered windshield. She looked around to orient herself. The car was facing backwards on the road. She heard people shouting, then realized with a jolt that the drivers could still be after her.

She twisted wildly around, ready to get out and run for her life, but she didn't have to. The silver sedan was disappearing down the road. The gray sedan had crashed into a tall oak on the other shoulder. Its passenger side was buried in the tree trunk. Broken branches fell onto its roof and hood. The fence around the pasture lay in splintery pieces. The horses galloped away toward a barn on the hill.

Jill could see the driver of the gray sedan, slumped over his deflated air bag. The sight brought her to her senses. He didn't look like he was moving. The impact must have been horrific. She had to save him. He'd tried to kill her, but she couldn't let him die.

"Miss, are you there?" said an urgent voice, emanating from somewhere. "Miss?"

Jill realized it was the emergency operator. She was still connected to 911. She didn't see the BlackBerry. She moved the air bag aside, spotted it on the floor, and picked it up. "Hello, yes?"

"Miss, can you speak to me?"

"Yes, I'm fine. The other driver is still in his car. Please send an ambulance right away. I'm going to check on him now." Jill edged out from under the air bag. Shards of glass fell off her forearms. She reached for the door handle and pushed, surprised to see that it still worked.

"Miss, please don't attempt to treat the other driver. Wait for the EMTs. I have your location, and an ambulance is en route."

"I'm a doctor, it's fine." Jill eased herself out of the driver's seat. Glass tinkled as it dropped to the asphalt. She smelled gas and burning rubber. It hurt her arm to hold the phone to her ear. "I have to go."

"Call if you need me. I'll hang up and clear the line. Thanks."

Jill hung up and slid the phone into her pocket. She hustled to the sedan, almost falling, but kept going. Blood dripped from her forehead. She reached the sedan and opened the car door.

The driver lay face-down on the air bag. She could only see the back of his head, and his neck wasn't broken. A gash split his scalp, and he bled profusely from the wound. Blood soaked his hair and ran in rivulets down to the front of his face.

"Sir?" she said, reaching for him. His hands were pinned under the air bag, so Jill probed his carotid for a pulse. "Sir, are you all right? Can you move? I'm a doctor."

"Ooh," he moaned, slumped over.

"Can you move your legs, sir?" Jill didn't try to wedge him out of the driver's seat because the dashboard had crumpled, pinning his knees. She couldn't tell if his legs were broken, but it looked possible. His eyeglasses lay cracked on the deflated air bag. Shards of windshield littered the seat. Oddly, he had on a suit.

"Sir, can you move?"

"No," the driver answered weakly, turning to her.

Jill gasped. Blood leaked from cuts on the driver's face

and pooled around his nose, but she recognized him instantly. It was Brian Pendle, Victoria's friend.

*"Brian?"* Jill said, aghast, just before his eyes rolled back in his head.

# 55.

"Thanks," Jill said, shaken, as the brawny EMT helped her step up onto the shiny, corrugated floor of the ambulance. Two more EMTs were on the scene, extricating Brian from the gray sedan. Another ambulance idled near him, ready to go, and the police stopped traffic, staking the street with smoking flares and flashing cruisers.

"Please, sit down slowly." The EMT steadied Jill as she sat on the gurney. "Now, lie back."

"Okay, got it. Thanks." Jill leaned back, and the EMT eased her shoulders down, lifted her feet, and placed them on the gurney.

"Good job." The EMT fastened wide orange straps over Jill's body. "We need to get going. I'll get your vitals and stop that bleeding on your forehead. You have a wound there, but it looks superficial."

"Thanks, I agree, I'm a doctor." Jill tried to collect her thoughts, but flashes of the high-speed chase burned into her brain. She was still sweaty from sheer terror. It boggled her mind to think that Brian was trying to kill her. She had no idea why he'd do such a thing, or who he was in cahoots with. Was he the one in the black SUV? Was his cohort? Jill didn't know, but she was damn sure going to find out.

"Robbie, here's her belongings," called a police officer, hustling to the ambulance. He tucked Jill's purse against the gurney, then turned to her. "Miss, somebody will come to the ER to take your statement. The tow truck is on the way for your car. I kept the ignition key and I'll give it to them."

"No, wait, my laptop." Jill tried to get up but could only lift her head. "I have a computer in my trunk. I can't leave without it. Can I go get it, or can you get it for me?"

"No, you have to get to the hospital. Your car is a wreck, your trunk won't open, anyway. You're lucky to be alive, Miss."

"But I need it, I can't leave it here. It contains evidence of a crime." Jill struggled to get up, straining against the straps, but the EMT pressed her back down.

"Please, stay down. We have to leave, and I have to treat you."

The police officer leaned in. "Miss, you can claim your laptop later, don't worry. Nobody can get inside that trunk. Robbie, you're good to go." He closed the ambulance doors, and the EMT rose and hurried to twist the handle into a locking position.

"Jenny, locked and loaded!" the EMT called to the driver. He turned and fetched a Rowbotham dressing kit from a cage in the wall, then the ambulance lurched off.

"I'm sorry, I have to make a call." Jill freed her hand and managed to reach into her pocket for her BlackBerry. "Somebody has to meet me at the hospital. Where are we going?"

"Shood Memorial, in Parkertowne." The EMT zipped open the kit, yanked out some cleanser, and swabbed the wound on Jill's forehead, applying pressure to stop the bleeding. "You okay?"

"Yes, thanks. Excuse my rudeness." Jill scrolled for Victoria's number, pressed CALL, and tried to gather her wits while the call connected.

"Hello," Victoria answered the call, testy. "What now, Jill? I can't talk, I'm driving to class."

"I have some bad news, very bad." Jill watched the EMT tape gauze to her forehead, then he rose and took a blood-pressure cuff and thermometer from a wire basket on the wall. "It's about your friend Brian. He was injured in a car crash when he and another car tried to run me off a road. They were trying to kill me."

"*What?*" Victoria gasped. "Are you serious? Is this a joke?"

"It's no joke. I'm in an ambulance now, and so is he."

The EMT didn't bat an eye as he checked Jill's blood pressure, and in any other circumstance, she would have remarked on his professionalism.

"Jill, what are you talking about?" Victoria answered, her tone still disbelieving. "You mean my friend Brian Pendle? It's not possible."

"Victoria, tell me, why would Brian try to kill me? How long have you known this guy?"

"A year, but it can't be him."

"He's a lawyer in New York, right? What firm does he work for?"

"Creed and Whitstone, but what's the difference?" Victoria asked, insistent. "You must be mistaken. It can't be Brian."

"It is, I saw him. Victoria, what does he do there, what's his field?"

"He's a securities lawyer. You could be wrong. It wasn't him. You barely know him."

"I *recognized* him, Victoria." Jill was trying to think, she still felt upset. The ambulance didn't use its siren, but it seemed louder inside than she remembered from when she went to the hospital with Megan. Its powerful engine seemed to roar, its wide tires rumbled, and the cab in back creaked mightily, the scrape of metal against metal. "So Brian works as a securities lawyer. Does that mean he knows stockbrokers and guys like that?"

"Yes, but—"

"Did he know a man named Joe Zeptien?"

"I don't know, why?"

"Did he ever mention anything about Pharmcen or Memoril?"

"No, is this real? Is it really him? He was in an accident?"

"Come and see. We're being taken to Shood Memorial in Parkertowne. He has a head wound and was unconscious at the scene."

"My God!" Victoria cried. "I'm turning around. I'll be there in half an hour, max."

"Let me ask you, did Brian know your Dad?"

"They met once or twice. Jill, what's going on? Why are you asking me all these questions? What's going on?"

"Hell if I know. I'm trying to figure it out. Did you ever hear Brian and your father talk about the drug business or Pharmcen?"

"No, of course not, just golf," Victoria answered, in bewilderment.

"Then what is Brian up to? Why would he try to kill me, do you have any idea?"

"He didn't do that, he would never. I have to go, I'm driving, and there's traffic. I'm on my way."

"Okay, good-bye." Jill hung up, more confused than ever, and her gaze fell on a digital clock embedded in the stainless steel side of the cab, which read 12:30. She thought of Padma and Rahul, and her heart sank. "Oh no. I was supposed to see a patient, half an hour ago."

"Hey, accidents happen." The EMT held the thermometer bulb to her ear. "Please, stay still a sec."

"Okay. One more call, sorry." Jill waited a beat, then pressed P for Pembey Family.

"I'm done here, your vitals are good." The EMT put the thermometer and cuff back in its basket, then stowed the dressing kit and flashed Jill a thumbs-up.

"Thanks," Jill said, as the EMT climbed up to the passenger's seat, and her phone call connected.

"Pembey Family, may I help you?" It was Donna, and Jill warmed to the friendly voice.

"Hi, it's Jill, and I'm calling because I was just in a car accident, in New Jersey. Is Padma still there with Rahul?"

"Oh no! Are you okay, honey? We tried to reach you."

"I'm fine, but I'm going to the Shood Memorial ER, in Parkertowne. Is Padma still there, with Rahul? Can I talk to her?"

Donna hesitated. "She left, but don't think about work now. Take care of yourself."

"No." Jill felt awful. "What time did she go?"

"You missed them by five minutes, but, well, Padma asked for Rahul's file, and I had to release it. She's leaving us. She said her family wasn't very happy after we lost the baby's bloodwork. But, Jill, but don't think about that now. Just get better."

"Oh no." Jill felt like kicking herself. She hated losing Padma and the boys, and she wouldn't rest until she checked Rahul's results. "Did Rahul's bloodwork come in? I need to see it."

"Yes, the hospital emailed it to us. I printed it out and put it in the file."

"Would you forward me the email?"

"Sure, right away."

"Thanks. I'll call Padma when I get the results. Can you email me her cell number, too?"

"No problem."

"See you tomorrow."

"Jill, you can't come in after a car accident. I'll start calling your patients."

"No, don't, please. It's nothing. I'll be in."

Donna lowered her voice. "Okay, but just a heads-up, Sheryl wants to talk to you when you get in. I think it's about Padma leaving."

Jill figured as much. "I'm *so* looking forward to that conversation."

Donna laughed. "Take care, Jill."

"You, too. Bye." Jill hung up, navigated to email on her BlackBerry, and scanned the senders, who were all patients. Donna's forwarded email about Rahul's bloodwork wasn't there yet. She felt a pang, thinking she wouldn't see Padma or the boys again.

But she wasn't worried about Padma.

She was worried about Rahul.

# 56.

Jill waited for the police in the examining room and eyed her reflection in a wall mirror. There was a new gauze bandage taped to her forehead, and tiny red cuts on her cheeks glistened under Neosporin. Another bandage covered her left palm, wrapped around the back of her hand. She smoothed her hair back into its ponytail and felt almost normal, except for the dried blood spattering her sweater.

Jill checked her BlackBerry for the third time, and the email with Rahul's results had finally come in, so she pressed OPEN ATTACHMENT. The attachment downloaded, but when she opened it, the numbers were too small to read. She pressed the button to magnify them, but it was still impossible to see.

"Dr. Farrow, here we go." The nurse slipped past the privacy curtain, returning with an Advil packet and a paper cup of water in hand. She looked young, with an easy smile and a long brown braid. "Your discharge papers will take a bit, though. We just got super busy. You slipped in right in time."

"Thanks." Jill took the Advil and cup, swallowed the

pill, and tossed the cup. "Can I ask you a big favor? I need to get some bloodwork results printed out. May I email them to you and you print them out for me? It's important."

"Sure thing. Want my email?"

"Thanks. Go ahead, tell me." Jill typed in the email address while the nurse told it to her, then she forwarded Donna's email. "Thanks again, so much. Also, how's the other driver, with the head injury?"

"I probably shouldn't say. You know, it's confidential under HIPA."

"Please, just give me the headline. I want to prepare his friend, and she'll be here any minute. She's my stepdaughter."

"Oh." The nurse blinked. "Well, I can tell you that he's in the OR, and they called in the best docs."

"When will the police come for me, do you know? The cop at the scene said to expect them."

"I heard they're on the way, and I'll bring them in when they get here. I guess I can open this now." The nurse swept the privacy curtain to the side, revealing a modern ER unit ringed with examining rooms around an octagonal station. Doctors, physician's assistants, nurses, and orderlies scurried this way and that, bearing meds and paperwork. Jill used to dream about working in a place like this but dedicated to children's emergencies.

"Don't mind me, I'm having ER envy."

The nurse smiled. "I'll be back with the printout and your discharge papers."

"Can I make a call?" Jill gestured at the NO CELL PHONES sign. "I have to arrange for my daughter to be picked up."

"Okay, but you didn't hear it from me." The nurse winked, then left the room.

Jill sat down, and the movement made her realize how much her neck and back ached. Megan would be in school, then practice, so she texted Katie. **Can u pick up Megan at the pool at 5:45 and take her to your house? Fill u in later.** It only took a second for Katie to answer: **OK. Love you. Making funfetti cupcakes. Shoot me now.**

Jill smiled, then thought of Sam, feeling a sudden urge to talk to him, whether it was mutual or not. She pressed S and waited for the call to connect, eyeing the bustling ER. "Honey?" she said, when she heard a clicking sound.

"Hi, how are you?" Sam asked coolly, and Jill felt her throat thicken. She hadn't realized how upset she was until she heard his voice. She almost felt like crying, the stress and the fear hitting her all at once, but she kept it together.

"I'm okay, but something bad just happened. I was run off the road by two cars. One got away, but the other was driven by Brian, Victoria's friend."

"*What?* Where are you?"

"An ER in New Jersey. The cops are on the way."

"How *are* you?" Sam sounded like himself again, full of concern. "My God, honey!"

"I'm really fine." Jill stifled a sniffle. "The car's totaled."

"I don't care about the car. You could have been killed."

"I think that was the general idea."

"What the hell? Why does Brian want to *kill* you? This is insanity!"

"God knows."

"And so does Victoria."

"What do you mean?" Jill asked, surprised. Just then she noticed Victoria, entering the ER area, standing out in a fashionable cropped jacket, skinny jeans, and fancy boots, with her hair in its sophisticated blonde twist. She was looking around for a nurse, but there was only one, talking on the phone at the station, behind her monitor.

"Jill, think about it," Sam was saying. "Victoria must

be the one who wants you dead, not Brian. He doesn't even know you. He must be acting at her behest."

"What are you saying?" Jill recoiled at the very notion, even on the phone. She couldn't believe what she was hearing. "Victoria is my *daughter,* or, at least, she's like my daughter. We may not be getting along that great now, but she still—"

"Babe, follow the money. William had a huge insurance policy, and maybe Victoria killed him for it, or had her friend Brian kill him for it."

"Victoria kill William? That's absurd." Jill watched as Victoria waited for the nurse to get off the phone, drumming her fingers. "She would never, ever do such a thing."

"No, it isn't. Think about it. Abby got you involved in solving William's murder, and you wouldn't let it drop. Victoria and Brian could have been worried that you were going to find them out, so they wanted you dead."

"That's *impossible.*"

"Jill, you don't know Victoria anymore, not the real her. You thought Abby didn't drink, remember?" Sam's tone grew more urgent. "Babe, you have to see these girls for what they are today. You said two cars ran you off the road. Who was driving the other car? Could it have been Victoria?"

"Sam, no, that's crazy. We drove a *hundred* miles an hour." Jill motioned to Victoria, to catch her eye at the nurses' station. "It wasn't her car anyway. She drives a white BMW."

"We know she has anger issues, from the scene she made at the memorial service. What if she got angry enough to kill him? I don't know how she got those drugs in his blood, but she has keys to the house. I'm getting on the next plane. This ends *now.*"

"Thanks, so much." Jill felt a rush of gratitude and love

for him. "But nothing in the world will make me believe anything that awful about Victoria."

"Jill, think without emotion." Sam's voice rose, alarmed. "You sound like those news reports where they interview the mother of the murderer, and she says her son was a good boy."

"I know what I know, Sam, and I know that child." Jill spotted Victoria waving back, her pretty face frowning with anxiety. "I can't talk anymore. Victoria will be here any minute."

"No. Stay away from her, honey."

"I hear you, but I'll be fine. Don't worry." Jill watched Victoria hurrying toward her exam room, bypassing the nurse.

"Please, stay away from her, honey. Don't be alone with her."

"I'll be careful. I have to go. Love you. Thanks, bye." Jill hung up the phone just as Victoria entered the examining room, distraught.

"Jill!" she cried, throwing open her arms. "Are you okay?"

# 57.

"What's going on? Are you sure you're okay?" Victoria released her, and up close, Jill could see that her eyes were bloodshot, and her mascara had been reapplied, so she'd been crying. "You look okay, kind of."

"I am, I'm fine." Jill managed a smile, warmed by her concern. "But I can't figure why Brian did that. It's appalling, I'm shocked."

"I know." Victoria swallowed, hard. "And they won't tell me anything about him. I called his parents but they're in Europe."

"The nurse said he's in surgery, and they have the best docs working on him."

"Oh God, please." Victoria sank into the chair. "Would he really do this? Is he going to be arrested?"

Suddenly Jill and Victoria turned as the nurse came into the examining room, leading two middle-aged men in dark suits. The taller man stepped forward, seeming to take the lead, and he was well-built, with a lined, craggy face and dark hair in a short brush cut.

The nurse gestured to him. "Dr. Farrow, this is Special

Agent Donator and his partner, Special Agent Cohz, of the FBI."

"Thanks for coming," Jill said, surprised. "I was expecting the local police." She extended her good hand, and Special Agent Donator shook it, firmly.

"Dr. Farrow, nice to meet you." Special Agent Donator glanced at the nurse. "Nurse, would you excuse us for a few minutes, please?"

"Of course. I have one last thing." The nurse handed Jill her paperwork. "Here's the bloodwork you requested and your discharge papers, to be signed."

"Thanks, I know the drill. Any headaches, go to my local ER." Jill accepted the envelope, scribbled a signature on the discharge papers, and handed them back.

The nurse turned to go. "Please don't stay long, folks. We need the bed."

"Understood, thank you." Special Agent Donator nodded as the nurse left, closing the privacy curtain, then he turned to Jill, with a stiff smile. "You've had quite a day, Dr. Farrow. Do you feel well enough to be standing up?"

"Yes, thanks." Jill gestured to Victoria. "This is Victoria Skyler, my stepdaughter, uh, my former stepdaughter."

"Hello." Victoria shook each agent's hand, but her manner gave off a chill. "I'm a friend of Brian Pendle's, and I have already called him a lawyer from Creed & Whitstone. So don't even think about questioning him when he gets out of surgery."

Jill felt taken aback, and Special Agent Donator stopped smiling.

"Ms. Skyler, excuse me, but you don't have all the facts—"

"I have all the facts I need," Victoria interrupted. "I'm not a lawyer yet, but I know that attempted murder is a state law crime, not federal. The FBI is federal. So what do you have to do with this?"

Special Agent Donator pursed his lips. "Ms. Skyler, the attempt on Dr. Farrow's life was part of a dangerous, active criminal enterprise, involving the breach of federal securities laws and other illegalities. We explained to the local police that we have jurisdiction, and they agreed after some discussion, hence the delay." He turned to Jill. "You have some idea of what I'm talking about, don't you?"

"Yes," Jill answered, finally validated.

"But you were wrong about one thing, Dr. Farrow." Special Agent Donator seemed to soften, his face falling briefly into sharp lines. "Brian wasn't trying to kill you. He was trying to protect you. He's one of us."

# 58.

"Pardon me?" Jill asked, uncomprehending. "Brian is with the FBI?"

"No, he isn't," Victoria said, incredulous. "He's a lawyer, not an FBI agent. He went to Georgetown Law Center."

Special Agent Donator faced Victoria, his expression grim. "Ms. Skyler, Brian has been a federal agent since he graduated from Georgetown. His law degree makes him invaluable to us in the field, and he's been working undercover. He blew his cover saving Dr. Farrow's life."

"Save me? What do you mean?" Jill flashed back to the silver and the gray cars, riding side-by-side, like a moving wall. "He was trying to run me off the road, with another car."

"No, the silver car was trying to run you off the road. Brian was in the gray car, trying to run *them* off the road. We were in communication with him during the chase, right up until the crash."

Jill blinked, shocked. "Then who was following me?"

"The man in the silver car, and we were following him. We have been, for some time. Successful prosecutions don't get built overnight, no matter what you see on TV, and they don't happen without dedication. Brian is one of the best young agents we have."

Jill couldn't process it fast enough. "He was trying to stop them? Why didn't he try to shoot their tire, or them?"

"Shooting a tire in a residential area is too risky, at speed, and we can't authorize the use of lethal force where non-lethal force can be employed. Brian trained in defensive driving techniques at the academy, and he assured us he could handle it. Unfortunately, he lost control of his car."

Jill remembered the scene, just before she was hit. Special Agent Donator was right. "The silver car *was* the one tailgating."

"Yes, and the silver car was the one that hit your bumper. It may have looked as if the two cars were working together, but they weren't. Brian risked his life to save you, and by all accounts, he behaved in an exemplary fashion. We're all pulling for his speedy recovery." Special Agent Donator glanced down, working his jaw, and Special Agent Cohz cleared his throat. He was shorter, but equally fit-looking.

"Is Brian going to be okay?" Victoria asked, stepping over. "What do you know about his condition?"

"Not much we can share, at this point." Special Agent Donator answered. "We'll discuss it further after he gets out of surgery."

Jill felt a wave of guilt. Her head throbbed, and exhaustion swept over her. She prayed that Brian would recover, quickly and completely. She couldn't bear it if one more person died because of this scheme, or because of her. Then Jill realized that Sam had been wrong. If Brian hadn't been trying to kill her, it meant that Victoria wasn't involved with William's death.

"Dr. Farrow, we'll need to debrief you and take a

complete statement. The investigation is being run out of
D.C., but the team is waiting to meet us in New York.
Please, get your things and come with us."

"Sure." Jill picked up her bag and slid the envelope inside, to look at in the car.

"I'd prefer to stay here," Victoria said, flatly. "I'd like
to see Brian when he gets out of surgery."

Special Agent Donator turned to her, his brow knit.
"Ms. Skyler, there are two special agents detailed to protect Brian as soon as he gets out of surgery, and he won't
be having any conversations, with you or anyone else.
Countless manpower hours, federal dollars, and hard work
went into this investigation, much of it from Brian himself. He's going to get a commendation. He's been undercover for a year."

"Wait, hold on." Victoria frowned. "That's when we
met. Is that a coincidence?" She faced Jill, in bewilderment. "Why did you ask me when we met, and how?"

Suddenly a minor commotion arose next door, on the
other side of the patterned curtain, billowing to accommodate a wheelchair. "Oooh, my leg, help me, oooh, please,"
wailed an elderly man in distress, as nurses tried to calm
him, wheeling him into the examining room and lifting
him onto the bed.

Special Agent Donator turned to Jill and Victoria.
"Ladies, let's go."

"But, this is so awful," Victoria said, shaken. "Brian
lied to me? For a year?"

"Ms. Skyler, we'll debrief you at the office." Special
Agent Donator pushed aside the curtain, Special Agent
Cohz led the way, and Jill led Victoria out of the examin-
ing room.

"We'll figure this all out together, honey." Jill put a
gentle arm around Victoria, but the girl didn't reply,
avoiding Jill's eye as they fell into step, walking down the

glistening hallway. Jill wanted to know the whole story about William, Zeptien, Nina, Martin, and Brian, though she felt terrible that it would bring Victoria's world crashing down on her head.

But first, Jill wanted to know about Rahul.

# 59.

Jill opened the envelope as soon she got in the backseat of the car, and Rahul's bloodwork confirmed her worry. His white-blood-cell count showed a major bacterial infection, at 18,000 when it should have been between 5,000 and 15,000, and his smear explained why. Rahul didn't have cancer or leukemia, but he had an immune deficiency that made him unable to fight infection properly, which was why he got so many ear infections and the pneumonia. Normal babies had four immunoglobulins, IgG, IgM, IgA, and IgE, but Rahul was missing IgE, which governed allergies, consistent with his family history.

"Oh no." Jill moaned, scanning the rest of the results. The numbers showed that Rahul's neutrophils were already shifting left, which meant they were leaving his bone marrow to fight infection before they were even mature cells. Jill felt a bolt of fear for the baby she adored, but went into emergency mode. Her plan was to hospitalize Rahul immediately and treat him aggressively with IV antibiotics, or the ear infection could spread to his bloodstream and turn septic.

Victoria looked over. "What's the matter?"

"I have a very sick patient." Jill caught the eye of Special Agent Donator in the rearview mirror. He was driving, and Special Agent Cohz was in the passenger seat, looking at some papers. "Gentlemen, I have to call the office now. We can talk afterwards."

"Go right ahead." Special Agent Donator nodded. "I'd rather wait until we get to the city to take your statement, anyway. The team needs to hear it, and you won't have to tell it twice."

"Good, thanks." Jill was already scrolling through her BlackBerry. She found Donna's email, pressed SELECT on Padma's cell number, and hit CALL. It rang and rang, then went to voicemail. "Padma, it's Dr. Farrow. I need to speak with you right away. It's about Rahul's bloodwork. Please call me immediately." She left her cell number, then hung up and called the office.

"Pembey Family," answered a woman's voice. It was Sheryl.

"Sheryl, it's Jill. I can't reach Padma on the cell, and I see a major problem with Rahul's bloodwork. I need her emergency contact numbers. Her husband's in Afghanistan."

"I know why she won't take your call, I spoke with her. She fired us today. Is this how you grow the pediatric practice?"

Jill bit her tongue. "Now, I need—"

"I heard you were in a car accident, but I'll have to dock you if you don't come in tomorrow. I told Donna to tell you to call me, to discuss this."

"She did. Sheryl, please give me the numbers." Jill tried to keep her temper, glancing out the window, where the traffic was congested. They were approaching Newark Airport, and a line of silvery planes hung in the sky as if suspended on an invisible string, their wings glinting in the sun.

"Padma's switching to Dr. Benson's group. She asked that all future results be sent to him."

"I don't have the time to discuss this, Sheryl. This is an emergency. Get me numbers."

"How dare you speak to me that way!"

Jill couldn't take it another minute, and she raised her voice to say, "Tell you what, give me the numbers, and I won't speak to you ever again."

"You have to. You're an employee."

"I'm not an employee, I'm a *doctor.* And I quit. Now give me the numbers."

"Fine. You're required to give two weeks' notice—"

"Give me the damn numbers!" Jill shouted. Victoria jumped, startled, and Special Agent Donator's eyes flared in the rearview mirror.

"Be that way, Jill. I'm emailing them to you right now. I have an office, home, and cell for her father-in-law in Seattle. His name is Frank McCann. But I don't know if he can reach Padma, because she left for Mumbai with the kids. Her mother had a heart attack."

"Oh no." Jill felt her heart race. "Mumbai, India?"

"No, Mumbai, Ohio. Yes, of course, India."

"When did she go?"

"She left from here."

"She can't go to Mumbai with Rahul, that's a twenty-four-hour flight. His system can't take it, he's already weak."

"Really?" Sheryl asked, suddenly hushed. "She was worried it would hurt his ears, but she said she had to go. She said she'd give him some Tylenol."

Jill thoughts raced. "The problem isn't pain, it's sepsis. In that amount of time, he could go into shock. They won't be able to treat him on the plane, and he needs to be admitted. He could die."

"Oh my God, oh my God," Sheryl said, panicky. "What do we do?"

Victoria looked over, her hazel eyes wide. Special Agent Cohz glanced back at Jill. Special Agent Donator slid on aviator sunglasses.

"Sheryl, get a grip, and we'll both call. We have to stop Padma. She can't get on that plane. You hear me?"

"Oh my God, this is awful. What if he dies? What do I do? I don't know what to do! The nurses are all gone, they're all gone! I'm the only one here! What do I do?"

"Do what I say. Do it now. I will, too. Go and do." Jill hung up, scrolled to email, found Sheryl's, selected the father-in-law's cell number, and pressed CALL. The cell rang and rang, then voicemail connected. "Mr. McCann, this is Dr. Farrow, Rahul's pediatrician. Please tell Padma *not* to get on the plane to Mumbai. Your grandson has an infection that could prove fatal. This is a medical emergency. Please call me immediately." Jill left her cell number and hung up, as Victoria turned to her.

"Jill, can I help?"

"Yes, you have your iPhone with you, don't you?"

"Sure, yes." Victoria started digging in her large black bag, bulging with stuff. "It's in here somewhere. I use the same bag for classes, so I travel heavy."

"Look on the Internet. See which airline has direct flights from Philly to Mumbai this afternoon. Get the flight while I try to get Rahul's grandfather."

"Okay." Victoria pulled out a round hairbrush, a white earphone cord, and a zipped makeup case. A stick of cream blusher rolled out like a shiny black log, then a hot pink tube of mascara, her EpiPen, and her iPhone. "Here we go." Victoria started tapping the touch screen. "Then what do I do, when I get the airline and flight?"

"See if you can find a phone number for the airline, then give me the phone." Jill pressed Frank McCann's work number, since that was a better bet than his home number at this hour. Outside the car, the traffic inched along, and a plane flew so low overhead that Jill almost ducked, reflexively.

Special Agent Donator leaned over to Special Agent Cohz. "We'll never get there, this traffic keeps up," he said, in low tones.

Special Agent Cohz shook his neat head. "Mick, take the way I showed you, to the tunnel. The exit's up ahead."

Jill held her phone while the call rang twice, then connected. "Is this Granger Accountants? My name is Dr. Jill Farrow, and this is a medical emergency. I need to speak with Frank McCann."

"Sorry, he isn't in," a receptionist said. "What's the nature of the emergency?"

"I treat his grandson Rahul, who I understand is flying with his daughter-in-law Padma to Mumbai, today. Rahul could go into septic shock during the flight, and I need to reach Padma as soon as possible and tell them not to get on the plane. Can Mr. McCann be reached? I tried his cell but he didn't answer."

"Oh no," the receptionist said, alarmed. "He's at a conference. All I can do is try his cell, too."

"How about the hotel? Is he staying at a hotel? Where is the conference held?"

"I can't give you that information, but I can try and get a message to him. I'll try, I swear, but I can't promise anything."

"Please try, right away. Have him call me if he has any questions, but it's imperative that he stop Padma. It's a matter of life and death, for his grandson." Jill left her cell number and thanked her, then hung up.

Victoria looked over at Jill, with strain showing all over her young face. "Jill, I have the flight, but it's boarding in half an hour. It's Continental, Flight 440."

"Oh no." Jill felt her pulse pick up. "Got a phone number?"

Victoria tapped away on the touch screen. "I see phone numbers for reservations and customer service."

"Call reservations, press 0, and give me the phone when you reach a human being."

"Okay." Victoria pressed a number, then held the iPhone to her ear. "Damn it. I'm on hold, a ten-minute wait."

"That's too long." Jill shifted forward toward the front seat. She had to try something else, fast. "Special Agent Donator, can you help me? The plane is about to board at Philadelphia airport, Continental Flight 440. Can you call TSA? Or can you call the Philadelphia police, or the airport police, and tell them not to let Padma Choudhury and her son board? Or can they hold the plane?"

"That's not procedure, Dr. Farrow." Special Agent Donator pursed his lips, and his sunglasses obscured his thoughts.

"Please, a baby's life is at stake." Jill leaned forward, ready to beg. "It couldn't be more important."

"Understood." Special Agent Donator steered off the turnpike at the exit, then turned to Special Agent Cohz. "What do you think, Pete? It's not kosher, but we could always call Sean, at the Philly bureau."

Special Agent Cohz nodded. "It's a baby, for God's sake, and the Dad's in Afghanistan. Call Sean. He'll know what to do."

Jill's heart leapt with hope. "Yes, please. Call Sean. Do it, please!"

"All right." Special Agent Donator reached his hand to the backseat, palm up. "May I use your phone, Dr. Farrow?"

"Sure." Jill handed over her phone. "Thanks so much."

"You're welcome." Special Agent Donator took her

BlackBerry, but instead of pressing in a phone number, he slammed it against the dashboard, where it splintered with a loud *crak*!

"What are you doing?" Jill asked, horrified.

But the next thing she knew, Special Agent Cohz had twisted toward her, and his fist was heading straight for her face.

# 60.

Jill regained consciousness in the backseat, slumped against the corner of the car, her head lying on its right side. She tried to understand what was going on. The two men in the front seat weren't FBI agents, they were killers. They were going to kill her and Victoria. Rahul was on the plane to Mumbai. He might already be dead.

Jill fought to suppress a rising terror. Her face and head throbbed with pain. Her nose was bleeding. She heard a soft bubbling sound, her own blood leaking from her nose. Her right eye felt loose, warm, and wet, so she knew her orbital bone had been hit, maybe broken. She heard the sound of quiet whimpering.

*Victoria.*

Jill felt the sensation of movement, a slight jostling. There were no other car sounds, no passing trucks. The rate of speed was low, maybe fifty miles an hour. There was only road noise, and weeping.

Jill lay still, forcing herself to think, and function. If her right orbital had been hit, her eye would look like a sunken and bloody mess. Nobody could tell it was open. The two men would think she was still unconscious.

She kept her left eye closed and looked around through her right eye. It wasn't easy but she could see well enough. Victoria was hunched over, crying and shaking. Her hands covered her face. Blood dripped through her slender fingers. Her phone and purse were gone. Her blusher and hairbrush lay scattered on the backseat.

"I gotta take a leak," said one of the men, up front, and from the direction of the sound, Jill guessed it was the driver talking, Donator or whatever his real name was. He must have shown ID to somebody at the hospital, but it must have been fake. Jill hadn't even thought to ask, she'd been so preoccupied.

"Make it fast," said Cohz, or whoever. "This chick is making me mental, with the boohooing."

"So pop her again."

"It just makes it worse. Hurry up."

Jill felt the car slow down. She couldn't let anything happen to Victoria. She felt a rush of love and terror, in almost equal measure.

The car pulled over to the side of the road, and Jill could see thick woods. No houses. No people. No cars. No help. She and Victoria wouldn't get far if they ran for it. The men had to be armed, and there were two of them. It was late afternoon, still daylight. One man would go after her, and the other would hunt Victoria down.

"Be right back," Donator said, braking. There was movement on the floor of the car as it stopped. Something rolled out from underneath the seat, an orange color that caught Jill's attention.

*Victoria's EpiPen.*

Jill knew it was a syringe of epinephrine, or adrenaline. In case of an allergic reaction, it would restore breathing, but injected into the muscle of a healthy person, it would have almost no effect. It would only increase the heart rate, cause nausea and tremors. It would have no effect in a vein.

*Unless it was the right vein.*

Jill didn't know if she could do it, but she and Victoria were dead, otherwise. She heard the sound of the car door opening, then a beeping that signaled that it had been left open. She couldn't see the driver, but she heard the crunch of his foot on the gravel road, then his footfalls disappeared.

She imagined him walking up a distance, then turning away from the car. His back would be to the roadside. She'd have to wait until then. It would buy them extra seconds.

It would be her only chance. *Their* only chance.

She stilled her heart, listening. Counting.

*One, two, three.*

*Go.*

# 61.

Jill swooped down, grabbed the EpiPen, tore the cap off with her teeth, then lunged forward and plunged its long, thick needle directly into Cohz's carotid.

His eyes flew open. His lips parted in shock and pain.

Jill clamped her other hand over his mouth to stifle his cry. The EpiPen wouldn't kill him, but it would immobilize him long enough to give them a head start. "Go, go, go!" she hissed to Victoria.

"Oh!" Victoria sat upright, teary and shaken, then reached for the door handle and shoved the door open with Jill right behind her, pushing her outside.

"Run to the woods! Go!"

"Help!" Victoria screamed, but Jill didn't have time to tell her that screaming was the worst thing to do.

"No, stop!" Donator shouted, from up the road, behind them.

Jill grabbed Victoria's hand. They crashed together into the woods, running as fast as they could. They tore through the trees, tall and thick. They ducked low branches.

The trees grew denser. There was no room to run in between. They let go of each other's hands, running together, racing with all their might. Bark scraped their legs. Their hair caught on branches. They leapt over dead limbs. The temperature cooled. The sun vanished.

Victoria panted as she ran, her arms pumping. Her legs churned. Her jacket caught on something and ripped.

Jill's breath went ragged. She put up her hands to shield her face. She was too adrenalized to feel pain. They twisted and threaded through the trees, trying not to trip on vines and undergrowth. Twigs, stones, and dry leaves covered the ground. There was no path or trail. No room to run side-by-side.

"HELP, HELP!" Victoria screamed.

*Crak!* a gunshot fired, close behind them.

Jill ducked, on the run. A jolt of sheer horror shot through her system. Donator was after them now. She knew what she had to do. They couldn't keep this up. She turned to Victoria.

"Go left," Jill shouted, gasping for breath. "You go left, I go right."

"What? Why?"

"Go and shut up. I'll draw him."

"No!" Victoria reached for her, but Jill slapped her hand away, though it killed her to do it.

"Listen to me! Go left! Do it! We have to separate! We can't both make it!"

"No, I'm not going!" Victoria met Jill's eye for a split second, panting hard, tears streaming down her cheeks, as heartbroken as she was terrified, and in that instant, Jill could see that they had become mother and daughter, once again.

"I love you, honey. Now, go! Get help!"

"No!"

"Yes!" Jill turned right and bolted away from her, screaming at the top of her lungs, to draw Donator. "Help! Help, police! Somebody!"

*Crak!* went the gunshot, closer.

Jill knew it had worked. She was on her own now.

She put her head down and ran for her life.

# 62.

*Crak!* went another gunshot, even closer.

"Help!" Jill put on the afterburners, running faster. Raising her hands to clear her way. Keeping her knees high so she wouldn't fall. Ducking when the branches got too low. She sweated and bled. She had no idea where she was. She didn't know if she was running straight or in a circle. She knew only that she was running *away*.

Her chest heaved with each breath. Her legs ached, and she started to stagger. Thorns sliced her palms and forearms. She tripped on a vine, yanking it to free herself. She didn't know how much longer she could keep going. Donator would catch up with her. Cohz would regain consciousness and join him.

Then she saw it. Up ahead, through the trees. It looked oddly lighter, like a clearing. She didn't know what it was, but she ran for it. Civilization lay ahead.

"Help!" she hollered, with hope.

*Crak!*

Jill felt the heat of the bullet, whizzing past her head. She bolted in terror through the woods toward the clearing. She had to get to help before Donator got to her. She didn't know how many bullets he had. The promise of the clearing gave her new strength. She got a second wind.

She raced ahead. She cried out when a branch sliced her cheek, its end pointed like a steak knife. She ran and ran, knocking dead limbs out of the way with her arms. Beyond the trees was a brightness. The sun shone through. She spotted rooftops and glimpsed houses.

"Help me somebody!"

*Crak!*

"No!" Jill cried out. Her left shoulder burned like it had caught fire. She'd been shot. Her arm flew instinctively to grip the wound, but it slowed her pace and she let go. She reached the clearing like crossing a finish line.

It was a housing development, unfinished. The trees had been cut down, making a circle of dirt and clay around a few Cape Cod houses, then a row of bare wooden frames for houses. They sat on an unfinished paved street, part of a larger asphalt grid. Tattered orange flags marked the building lots. RUNNING HORSE REALTY, read the faded sign, with a peeling overlay that read MODEL HOME.

"Help!" Jill yelled. Tears of relief ran down her face. She sprinted toward the model home, then noticed something, on the run.

There were no people, no cars. No toys in the front yards, no swingsets in the backs. No trash cans or recycling bins. Everything was quiet and still. It was a suburb that never happened.

Her heart sank, her hope vanished. Still, she ran on and on. The development had been abandoned. The Cape Cods stood empty and unoccupied. The unfinished houses were skeletons, their Tyvek skins flayed by the elements, their plywood bones bleached by the sun.

She ran past the model home, guessing it would be

locked. She scanned on the fly for a place to hide. There
were no open garages. No gardening sheds. No sewer
pipes.

She ran down the street past the finished houses. They
had to be locked, too. She felt exposed and vulnerable.
Donator could pick her off here with ease. Her breath
came harder and harder. She couldn't keep going much
longer. Her shoulder was killing her. Her heart pumped
hard, she was losing blood fast. She had to get out of sight.

She gulped for breath. She ran for the last frame house
in the row, which was almost complete. Plywood sheets
formed its front wall. She tore through the rubble and red
clay to the threshold. It had no door.

She whirled around, looking for a place to hide. It was
a see-through house. Wood frames stood where the walls
would have been, their studs at regular intervals. All the
rooms were open except one in the back, intended to become a garage. A cinderblock wall blocked her view.

She raced for the cinderblock wall and ducked behind
it. The garage was open to the back, facing the woods. The
floor was poured concrete.

She looked around for something she could use for a
weapon, left by a construction worker. A two-by-four, a
hammer. A boxcutter, a pipe. There was nothing. It had
been picked clean.

She faced the front of the house, her eyes glued to the
threshold for Donator. Then she saw something that sick-
ened her.

Drops of her own blood dribbled along the plywood
floor, leading to her hiding place. She was bleeding from
the shoulder wound. She should have thought of that. She
couldn't hide here, she couldn't hide anywhere. She was
bleeding, making her own gruesome trail of crumbs.

Then she realized. She hadn't heard a gunshot in a

while, and that was the only thing worse than hearing a gunshot. It meant that she didn't know where Donator was.

She rose silently, trying to slow her heart, quiet her breathing. Maybe he was out of bullets. Maybe he'd given up. Maybe he'd gone back to his car.

Suddenly she heard a shuffling behind her, and she turned.

# 63.

"You bitch!" Donator roared, running at Jill, his hands reaching for her throat.

"No!" Jill raised her arms, but he was already upon her. His strong hands caught her, pushing her off her feet, crushing her Adam's apple under his thumbs.

She gagged. She tried to breathe but couldn't. She tried to pry his fingers off but they closed tighter. She tried to kick him but he kept coming, knocking her off-balance.

She lost her footing. He dragged her backwards by her neck, scraping her heels across the plywood floor. She couldn't breathe, he'd sealed her windpipe with his hands. Still, she kept hitting, prying, and kicking, fighting for her life. Her shoulder exploded in agony.

"Give it up!" Donator yelled, his face crimson with rage. He bared his teeth like an animal. She fell backwards, her head hitting the floor, her arms flailing at him. Donator fell on top of her, tightening his grip, strangling her.

She felt dizzy, she saw stars. She was out of oxygen. She writhed and twisted, trying to wiggle away. She tried to knee him but he weighed her down. She tried to move but couldn't.

Her strength started to desert her. Her arms fell backwards. Her shoulder was agony. Her legs flopped open. She couldn't fight anymore. She couldn't form a single thought. He had choked the life from her.

"Good girl," Donator whispered, his hot breath in her face, his grimace an inch from her lips. He was killing her and he was enjoying it, she could see. Then she didn't want to see anymore.

Jill closed her eyes. She heard her own, final choking sounds, pathetic and fading.

Then, she heard nothing.

The last sound she heard on earth would be her own silence.

# 64.

*Wham* was the sound, then a loud *thud,* and a man's agonized shout.

Suddenly Jill was gasping for oxygen, her chest heaving, her body bucking up and down, her autonomic system kicking into gear, the organism trying to survive before its brain could process what had happened.

Victoria was standing at her feet with a two-by-four, and Donator wasn't on top of her anymore.

Jill gasped for breath, sputtering, trying to come back, wanting so much to stay alive. She rolled her head to the side, choking and coughing.

Donator lay still on the floor beside her, face up. Dead. His eyes stared fixedly at the exposed rafters. His mouth was open, his lips a shocked circle. His arms lay at his sides. Blood poured from a gaping wound in his temple, pooling on the concrete floor around his head, like an infernal halo.

"Jill? Jill?" Victoria dropped the two-by-four and rushed to her side.

Jill could feel her heartbeat pounding, her gasps wracking her body, and her lungs beginning to function.

Her throat hurt so much, and she tried to speak, but couldn't.

Victoria bent over, gathered her into her arms, and hugged her close. Jill looked up into Victoria's eyes, which shone with a tenderness they'd never held before.

"Are you okay?" Victoria asked, with a weepy smile. "Are you hurt?"

Jill shook her head. She managed a smile. She couldn't say a word, but she knew what she thought, in her heart.

*I was hurt, before this very moment. I've been hurting since the last time I saw you.*

*But I'm fine, now.*

# 65.

Jill was only vaguely aware of everything that happened next as she faded in and out of consciousness, in and out of pain, in almost continuous motion. There were police, ambulances, then being strapped into a gurney with EMTs looking down at her with concern. They attached her to monitors, an IV bag, and at one point she cleared her aching throat enough to ask what she had to know:

"Can you call, about Rahul?"

"This is no time to worry about the office," the EMT answered, then they were hustling her out of the ambulance and to the ER nurses in their patterned scrubs, all of them looking down at her with even more concern as they whisked her inside through the automatic doors.

Jill kept saying, "Call somebody, please. Please, call about Rahul."

But they didn't listen, either.

# 66.

Jill sat up in the hospital bed, stitched, bandaged, medicated, and finally safe, in the company of real, ID-producing FBI agents, Special Agent Anthony Harrison and Special Agent Gordon Kavicka. The bullet wound to her shoulder wasn't deep, sutured with only a local anesthetic, and some pain meds had made her comfortable enough to meet with the FBI. The two special agents sat in chairs at the foot of her bed, dressed in dark suits, with striped ties and short haircuts. Victoria sat next to Jill on the bed in her torn jacket, and the cut on her cheek had been butterfly-bandaged.

"Can anybody tell me what just happened?" Jill asked, her throat aching. "Who was Donator, where is Cohz, and did somebody reach my office to ask about my patient, Rahul Choudhury?"

Victoria added, "Also, was my father murdered, and what did Brian have to do with it, if anything? Is he really undercover with the FBI, or were they lying to us?"

"Hold on, one question at a time." Special Agent Harrison raised a hand, his expression grim. He was a tall, lean man with smallish brown eyes, deep crow's feet, and a prominent cleft chin. "Dr. Farrow, we have a call in to your office, and we'll let you know about your patient as soon as they call back. Now, as for what happened, I'll answer as many of your questions as I can, on a need-to-know basis."

Jill felt taken aback. "We need to know everything. We were almost killed."

"Let us finish our jobs, then we'll explain everything. You have found your way into an ongoing federal investigation. We're within hours of making major arrests and indictments, and we cannot jeopardize anything. An investigation as large and important as this one requires countless man hours, budget dollars, and hard work."

Jill didn't interrupt him to say how much he sounded like the fake FBI agents.

"For now, we'll tell you only the information you need to know, and we expect you to treat the matter in complete confidence. Beyond this circle, we depend upon you to say nothing to any friends or neighbors, and explain your injuries by saying that you were in a car accident. Dr. Farrow, your fiancé, when he arrives, must also keep it confidential."

"He will." Jill hadn't spoken to Sam, but evidently the FBI had.

Victoria leaned over. "Special Agent Harrison, can you please tell me about Brian? Is he out of surgery, and is he one of you or not?"

Special Agent Harrison cleared his throat. "Brian works with us. He's awake, and we expect a full recovery."

"Thank God." Victoria brightened, and Jill touched her shoulder.

"There's good news."

Victoria nodded. "But who is he, really? Is he even a lawyer?"

"I can't answer that, yet."

Jill thought back to the ER room, with the fake FBI agents. "Cohz and Donator knew he was undercover. How did they know?"

"I can't answer that, at this time."

"So who were Donator and Cohz and why did they try to kill us?"

"I can't answer that, either."

"Don't we have a need to know that?" Jill tried to keep her temper, but it wasn't easy. "What if Agent Cohz, or whoever he was, comes back to try to kill us? Or did you catch him?"

Special Agent Harrison hesitated. "Dr. Farrow, the man who told you he was Special Agent Cohz is dead."

"What? How?" Jill asked, shocked. "The EpiPen wouldn't have killed him, even in the carotid. It's only epinephrine."

"Apparently, he had a heart condition, and it caused a heart attack."

"Oh no." Jill flashed on the scene in the car. "I didn't know, he was so young. It wasn't supposed to kill him."

"We've already discussed this with the local authorities, and you won't be charged, of course. Either of you. It was self-defense."

Jill felt stunned. "But I'm a doctor."

"He would have killed you both without a second thought."

"Maybe, but that doesn't make it right, for me. I took an oath." Jill felt a wave of guilt, and Victoria took her hand.

"I killed a man today, too."

Jill looked over, feeling for her. "But you saved me."

"We saved each other," Victoria said, squeezing her hand. "We'll help each other through this, like you said. We'll get through it, together." She turned to Special Agent Harrison. "Was my father murdered?"

Special Agent Harrison pursed his lips. "I can't answer that. I'm sorry. You don't need to know that—"

"The hell I don't," Victoria snapped. "I *do* need to know that. My sister needs to know that. He's our *father*."

"I'm sorry, but I can't share that information with you at this time." Special Agent Harrison glanced at Special Agent Kavicka, then back at Victoria. "When this is over, you'll see why."

Victoria squeezed Jill's hand. "I don't understand any of this. Why did my Dad have a double identity, and why was Brian undercover? Was it because of my Dad? Was Brian just pretending to be my friend?"

Special Agent Harrison cleared his throat. "Ms. Skyler, you can discuss that with Brian yourself, but not tonight. We need to debrief him."

Victoria turned to Jill, abruptly. "Oh, no, we didn't call Abby. Should we call her and tell her to come home?"

"No, not yet," Special Agent Harrison interjected. "She's safer out of the picture, and you must wait until after we've made the arrests to tell her anything."

Jill thought of Megan, stricken. "Is my daughter in danger? She's with a friend of mine."

"We know exactly where she is, and she's in no danger. We have a team stationed at the Feehans' house to protect her."

"How do you know where she is?" Then Jill realized something. "Have you been following me? Are you the ones with the black SUV?"

Special Agent Harrison shook his head, his lips a flat line. "Again, I can't explain that to you, at this time. When everything is resolved and things become public, all of your questions will be answered."

Jill couldn't take no for an answer, not after today. "Did Nina's husband really kill her? Or was she murdered by Cohz and Donator?"

"Again, after the grand jury meets and the indictments come down, I will meet with you and explain everything."

Jill felt sick at heart. "Did I lead them to Nina, can you tell me that? Did I get her and her husband killed?"

"Again, I can't answer."

Jill had too many questions that couldn't wait. "Let me tell you what I figured out, and maybe you can confirm or deny. My ex-husband, William Skyler, also known as Neil Straub, was getting inside information from Nina D'Orive about upcoming Pharmcen recalls and selling it to a man named Joe Zeptien, who sold the stock short and made a ton of money." Jill glanced over at Victoria, whose face was downcast, her emotions clearly in turmoil. "They did it on the Deferral and Riparin recalls and they were about to make a fortune on Memoril. But somehow it all fell apart. Why? Why kill anybody? How?"

"I won't confirm or deny. You don't need to know."

"But it's all in the laptop, oh, wait." Jill remembered, with a start. "The laptop and my notes are inside my car."

"Don't worry, we've already obtained the laptop. It took some doing, out of the wreck, and we think we can get it operating again."

"Good." Jill looked over at Victoria, but she sat slumped on the bed, crestfallen. Jill turned back to the FBI agents. "Special Agent Harrison, can't you tell us if William was murdered, and who did it and why? It may be a case to you, but it's Victoria's life, her family. She *needs* to know, in the truest sense of the word." Jill heard herself talking and realized that she was talking about herself, as well. "She's going to spend years trying to figure out who her father was. That process is healing, but if she doesn't know the truth, she can't heal. I know, I've lived it."

Special Agent Harrison paused, his dark eyes shifting to Victoria, his expression less guarded. "Ms. Skyler, I'll make you a promise. As soon as this is over, I'll explain everything. You lost your father, but there are other victims, and more potential for danger. Look at what happened today, to you both. Let us finish our job, and it will all become clear."

"Okay," Victoria said, after a moment.

Jill gave in, only reluctantly. "But what about our safety? Are you protecting us all?"

"Absolutely. We already have a team outside your house."

"How do we know that? Will we see them?"

"No, not if they're doing their job correctly. Trust me. We have you covered."

Suddenly there was a knock on the door, and a young FBI agent stuck his head inside the room. "Special Agent Harrison, sorry to interrupt you."

"What is it?" Special Agent Harrison turned to him.

"You wanted to know if a call came in about Dr. Farrow's patient, Rahul Choudhury." The young FBI agent held out an open cell phone. "This is it."

"Yes," Jill answered, her heart in her throat. "Please, let me have that phone."

# 67.

"Is it someone from my office?" Jill held her out her hand and tried not to notice it was trembling.

"No, it's a woman," answered the young FBI agent. "She's crying, and she has an Indian accent, so it's hard to understand."

*God, no.* "Please give me the phone."

"Okay?" The young FBI agent looked at Special Agent Harrison, who nodded, annoyed.

"Give it to her, would you? It's her call." Special Agent Harrison rose and walked to the door, and Special Agent Kavicka did the same, following him. "Dr. Farrow, we'll leave and give you some privacy."

Victoria looked over. "Jill, should I go, too?"

"No, please, stay, it's okay." Jill took the phone. "Dr. Farrow speaking."

"Oh my God, oh my God," said a woman, talking fast, her voice choked with tears.

"Who is this?" Jill asked, stricken. "Who am I speaking to?"

"Oh my God, it's Arami, Rahul's auntie, oh my God, oh my God!"

Jill braced herself. "What happened to Rahul? Please, tell me."

"Rahul is at the hospital now, Padma didn't take the flight." Arami cried happy tears. "He's in stable condition, now. He'll recover from his infection. He'll *live*."

"Thank God." Jill felt a gratitude and joy spreading through her very bloodstream, a sensation she couldn't medically explain.

"Yes, yes, Padma is with him, she just called me. My sister, her mother, is fine, too, in Mumbai."

"What happened? Did Rahul's grandfather reach Padma?"

"No, no, no one could reach her, she had turned her phone off, for the plane." Arami started to calm down, her words slowing and her tears subsiding. "Padma boarded the plane with Rahul and the boys. They were going to take off!"

"Who stopped them?"

"Someone went to the airport, they *drove* there. They got pulled over for a speeding ticket, then they got a *police escort*. They got Padma and the baby off the plane, right before it left for Mumbai."

"Who did that?"

"Your office manager, Sheryl."

"*Sheryl?*" Jill asked, astounded.

"She's wonderful woman, that Sheryl. A *wonderful* woman."

"She is?" Jill caught herself. "I mean, yes, she is."

"I must go, talk to you later. Thanks again, so much."

"Thanks for calling, and please tell Padma to call me, if she wants." Jill hung up just as there came a knock, on the door.

# 68.

"Honey, are you all right?" Sam gathered Jill in his arms, and she hugged him back, her eyes brimming, her heart full of love.

"Yes, I'm fine."

"Don't cry. I'm here now, it's okay now." Sam held her close, and Steven stood behind him, looking like a mini-Sam, complete with thick hair, sharp blue eyes, tortoise-shell glasses, and tan Dockers.

"Thanks for coming home." Jill wiped her tears and got in control, and Sam released her, his pained gaze appraising her injuries.

"What did they do to my girl? My God, it looks like it hurts, so much."

"No, it's not too bad."

"I've got nothing left to kiss."

"My lips are fine," Jill blubbered, but the words weren't out before Sam gave her a soft, sweet kiss.

"I love you," he said softly.

"I love you, too." Jill realized suddenly that she hadn't introduced Victoria and Steven. "Victoria, this is Steven Becker. Steven, Victoria Skyler." She hesitated.

"Stepson, meet ex-stepdaughter. Oh, whatever. Kids, meet each other."

Victoria smiled. "I'm not an ex-stepdaughter, I'm a step-daughter."

Steven snorted. "And we're hardly kids."

Sam laughed. "You're both kids, to us. Forever." He turned to Jill, leaned over, and kissed her again. "Let's go home."

"Yes." Jill thought they were the sweetest words ever. "Let's."

"Victoria?" Sam straightened up, turning to her. "You're coming home with us, I hope. We can all have dinner and try to decompress. I'm sure Megan would love to see you again."

Jill felt tears brimming again. She appreciated that Sam made the offer, but she was old enough to know they were still at an impasse. Sam would feel the same way, and it remained to be seen if they could agree on how to make a new family. If they couldn't, there wasn't going to be a wedding. Jill had come to understand that love didn't answer the question of whether they should marry, but merely asked it. Love wasn't the end, but the beginning.

Victoria was beaming at Sam. "Thanks, but what do I do about school? I have class tomorrow."

"I think we can get you a doctor's note," Sam answered, with a crooked smile, then looked down at Jill.

"Done," she said, smiling back. She felt an overwhelming yearning to see Megan again and get everybody safe under one roof, her roof.

On second thought, her greatest wish would be that someday, it would be *their* roof.

# 69.

Jill was cleaning up after take-out pizza, in the kitchen with Sam, Steven, and Victoria, all of them waiting for Katie to bring Megan home. It was raining hard outside, another spring storm, making Beef shudder on his bed. Victoria had showered and changed into an old T-shirt and sweatpants that belonged to Megan, and Jill had on a pink cotton sweater, jeans, and clogs. Except for the bruises, bandages, and pain meds, she felt like Mom again.

"Mom?" Megan called from the entrance hall, then entered the kitchen in her yellow sweats, gasping when she saw Jill's face. "Mom! What happened to you? Your eye and forehead? Mom, oh my God!"

"Come here, I'm fine." Jill smiled, opening her arms for Megan, who came running to her like when she was a little girl.

"Are you okay?" Megan hugged her tight. "What happened? Katie said it wasn't that bad, but it is. You look like you got really hurt."

"I'm fine, and so is Victoria. We had a long day, but now it's over."

"Nice face, Jill," Katie said with a smile, coming into

the room. She met Jill's eye, and in one look, told her that she loved her.

"Back at you." Jill smiled. She had already told Katie everything on the phone. Not even the FBI could come between best friends.

"Hello and good-bye, all." Katie waved to everyone. "I gotta go. Much love!"

"Bye and thanks, honey." Jill kissed the top of Megan's head as Katie left. "Want some pizza? I can microwave it."

"No, I ate." Megan looked up, shaken. "Nothing can ever happen to you, Mom."

"It won't." Jill knew what she meant. "I love you."

"I love you, too. So what happened? This is so weird! It's like everything's gone crazy all of a sudden."

"Go and sit." Jill let her go, and Megan went to her stool at the kitchen island, setting down her cell phone. Sam and Steven stood by the counter, and Victoria sat next to Megan on the island.

"Megan, it's so good to see you," Victoria said, giving Megan a hug. "I missed you."

"I missed you, too." Megan smiled, worriedly. "Does your head hurt? Did you get stitches? This is so random. Jeez!"

"I'm fine. We both are."

"Mom?" Megan turned back as her phone chimed a text alert, but she ignored it. "What happened to you guys? Tell me, I can't even deal!"

"The bottom line is that Victoria and I met up with some criminal types, and we got a little hurt, but we're fine."

"What criminal types? Did they steal from you, like you were mugged?"

"No. It was about William, but I'm not sure how yet." Jill poured Megan a glass of water and set it down in front of her. "The police know all about it, and we'll know more in a few days."

"Did somebody kill William?" Megan asked, then seemed to stiffen, bracing herself for the answer.

"Honestly, I don't know. The police will tell us as soon as they can."

"Where's Abby? Why isn't she home? Does she know?"

"No, and she'll be home soon."

"Jeez." Megan turned to Victoria, touching her arm. "I know you feel sad about your Dad. I'm sorry."

"Thanks, and I'm sorry about the way I behaved at the memorial service. I know you loved him, too. We're in this together, now." Victoria offered her hand, and Megan accepted it, with a smile. Her cell phone chimed again, but she still ignored it.

"I love you, Vick."

"I love you, too, Mega."

Jill watched them, touched. "One last thing, Megan. We have to keep this a secret. If anybody asks, we have to pretend that I was in a car accident and that's how I got hurt. Don't go into school tomorrow, and I'll write you a note."

"I have a meet this weekend, on Saturday, but maybe we shouldn't go." Megan's brow furrowed suddenly, and Jill thought her reaction was strange.

"No, we can go. Don't you want to? You've never missed a meet."

Megan hesitated. "Mom, there's something I have to tell you." Her phone chimed again, but she ignored it again. "You can't do anything about it, though. Anything you do will only make it worse."

"Okay," Jill said, surprised. "Tell me what happened."

"That boy I liked from swim club, Jake? He asked me to send him a picture of myself, so he could show his friends at his school. He said I was his *girlfriend*." Megan picked up her water glass and took a gulp. "So I sent him a normal picture that Courtney took of me, but he photo-shopped it to make it look like I was naked, like I sexted it to him."

Jill felt anger flare, but kept a lid on it. "How did he do that?"

"He cut out my head and put it on a naked body and he sent it to all the guys on the boys team, and then all the girls got it, and now the whole club thinks I'm a slut."

"No, they don't, honey." Jill felt terrible for her. "No one thinks that."

Victoria added, "What a douche."

"I know, right?" Megan turned to Victoria. "Sorry, I feel so bad for you, about your Dad, and I have all this dumb stuff going on. It's not as important, and I'm just so, well, lame."

"No, you're not lame at all." Victoria smoothed back Megan's hair. "I can't believe he did that. We're in this to-gether, right? We just said."

Megan looked back at Jill. "Mom, I'm too embarrassed to go to the meet because everybody knows. It's a big, big mess, and I can't even go back to the team. And they need me to win."

Jill was trying to get the facts. "Wait. When did this happen?"

"Sunday, right before the meet. I think that's why I had the panic attack, but I just didn't want to tell you. I knew you'd want to call his parents or Coach Stash, and that would make everything worse. I'm sorry, I know you were all worried about me."

Jill blinked. She had assumed the panic attack was be-cause of William's death, Abby's reappearance, and her own absence, but she had misdiagnosed her own daughter.

"What do I do, Mom? I can't go to the meet, and I can't *not* go to the meet."

"I can't talk to Coach Stash?"

"No, you can't. It's embarrassing. The more you do, the more it's a bigger deal, and the naked picture will go everywhere and everyone will think I'm a *total* slut."

Jill cringed for her. "But if I call his school—"

"No! That only makes me look dumber, don't you see?"

"Yes," Jill answered, because she did, finally. It was a no-win.

"I have to deal with it myself, and I hate myself for hiding and running away. It *sucks, I suck*! I'm the best swimmer on the team and I almost *drowned* because I'm so *stupid and lame*. I don't want to be *that girl* anymore!"

"You're not that girl, honey."

"Yes, I *am*!" Suddenly Megan jumped to her feet, almost knocking over the stool, and before anyone knew what she was doing, she ran out of the kitchen. Beef lifted his head from his paws, and Jill started to go after her, but Victoria rose and put a hand on her arm.

"Jill, wait. Let me go. No offense, but sometimes you don't need a mother. Sometimes you just need a friend."

"You're right. Go." Jill knew it was true, and Victoria left the kitchen and hurried upstairs.

Sam came over to Jill and embraced her, gently. "This, too, shall pass," he said, his voice deep and soft at her ear.

Jill was about to respond when she heard someone calling her outside, in the storm. She looked up at Sam, wondering. "Do you hear that?"

"What?" he asked, but Beef was already up and scampering to the front door, his toenails clicking on the hardwood floor.

"You know who that sounds like?" Jill let Sam go and hurried from the kitchen just as the doorbell rang. Sam and

Steven were right behind her, and she opened the door wide.

Standing at the threshold was Abby, next to Special Agent Harrison, who held a pet carrier.

"Abby!" Jill cried, throwing open her arms.

# 70.

Jill, Victoria, and Megan embraced Abby as Beef ran around them all in excitement and the entrance hall became a whorl of hugs, wet eyes, and wagging tails. A smiling Sam and Steve stood wisely off to the side, next to Special Agent Harrison, who set down the pet carrier on the floor.

"I'm so happy to see you all again," Abby said, with a teary grin. "I missed you guys!"

"We missed you, too." Jill grinned, but she was bewildered. "What are you doing with Special Agent Harrison? Did he pick you up at the airport?"

"No, he's my new best friend, along with Special Agents Tella, Leonard, and Palumbo." Abby counted off on her fingers. "I've been living with FBI agents for the past week."

"*Real* FBI agents?" Megan's eyes popped. "Like on TV?"

"Better," Abby answered. "They're women FBI agents and they even make quilts, for fun. They call themselves the Needle & Gun Club, and they meet every Monday night. How cool is that?"

"What? Why?" Victoria asked, confused, and Special Agent Harrison turned to Jill.

"We picked Abby up for her own protection. We've had her in a safe house with some of our female agents." Special Agent Harrison paused, glancing at Megan. "This may not be the right time for details, but I will fill you in."

Abby turned to Victoria. "I'm sorry, you were really worried about me, weren't you?"

"Of course I was." Victoria's eyes brimmed, too. "I love you, you idiot."

Jill was slowly coming up to speed. "Abby, does this mean you weren't in L.A.? And there's no Brandon?"

"Right." Abby nodded. "None of that was true. But you believed it, right?"

"Yes," Jill answered, secretly relieved.

Victoria nodded. "Totally."

Abby pursed her lips. "I knew what you'd expect to hear, so I said it, and you know what? It taught me something. I don't want to be like that anymore."

"Aw, Abby." Victoria embraced Abby again, and Jill held Megan close to her side.

"Anyway," Abby said, "know what I decided? I'm going back to college, to study criminology. I really loved the agents, and it might be weird to say now, but I think I'm good at it."

"That's wonderful, honey." Jill felt bittersweet, sensing why Abby had made that choice. "I'm so proud of you."

Sam came over, putting his arm around Abby. "Great idea, kid. If there's any way we can help you, let us know. We're here for you."

"Thanks, Sam." Abby grinned. "You guys are the best, and I think I'll be fine."

Victoria smiled. "Of course you will. We already decided we're all going to be fine. We have each other."

"Right," Jill added. "Family is forever, and so are pets."

She gestured to the pet carrier. "And that, I bet, is Pickles. I knew it was strange that you didn't mention him."

"Oh, I almost forgot!" Abby bent down and opened the wire door, and out of the carrier flew an adorable corgi puppy, scampering around like a bunny rabbit out of hell. Everybody laughed as Beef gave chase, barking.

"Wait, don't I know that puppy?" Jill asked, astonished. "It looks like Nina D'Orive's dog."

"It is." Special Agent Harrison nodded. "We were on the scene that night, and I noticed the puppy. The locals wanted to bring it to a shelter, but I knew my wife would love it, except that our son turned out to be allergic."

Abby smiled, sadly. "So I took her, and I call her Hobo, short for Hoboken. I named her in memory of Nina."

"Way to go." Jill patted Abby on the back, touched. "I'm proud of you."

"Thanks. Now here's Pickles." Abby went over to the carrier, cooing, and just then an orange tabby crept out, meowed loudly, and bounded off. "Great. Good-bye, Pickles."

Special Agent Harrison turned to Victoria. "Ms. Skyler, I made you a promise that I'd answer your questions, and I always keep my promises."

"I remember." Victoria turned to him, her smile vanishing. "I'm ready, if you are."

"Let's all go have that talk, shall we, folks?"

# 71.

A thunderstorm raged outside, but Jill, Sam, Victoria, Abby, and Steven were safe and warm, if not exactly happy, in the family room, gathering on soft couches and chairs with Special Agent Harrison, watching the eleven o'clock news. The screen showed men in suits being led in handcuffs from an office building on Wall Street.

The voiceover was saying, "The FBI made arrests late today in Operation Hedge Clippers, for alleged acts of insider trading and securities fraud by an individual and a manager at Piper, Flanagan, one of the largest hedge funds on Wall Street. The Justice Department says that the indictments will begin to clean up illegalities on Wall Street, in the wake of the Galleon Group case and wave of Occupy Wall Street protests. And in other news . . ."

"Okay, we've seen this twice now." Jill aimed the remote to turn off the TV and put her arm around Megan, who sat with her, Victoria, and Abby on the couch. "Special Agent Harrison, can you explain what's going on?"

"Of course." Special Agent Harrison straightened up. "Before I begin, you asked me to confirm or deny your theory in the hospital, and now I can confirm it. You didn't have the whole picture, but you had a piece. Nice work, for a doctor."

Sam winked. "That's my girl."

Abby smiled. "She's Dr. Watson."

Megan looked up at Jill, her eyes shining. "Wow, Mom."

Jill waved it off with a smile. She hardly felt like celebrating, after all the people who had died, including William.

Special Agent Harrison continued, "Operation Hedge Clippers started a few years ago, when the SEC notified us that Piper, Flanagan was showing a suspicious trading pattern, short-selling Pharmcen stock before recalls of two drugs, Deferral and Riparin. We investigated whether Piper, Flanagan was engaging in insider trading, and we learned that the trades in question were made by the same fund manager, Skip Priam, who was indicted today. We investigated and were able to gather sufficient evidence that Priam was trading on the information that he bought from Joe Zeptien."

Jill asked, "Was Zeptien a drug rep?"

"No, he's a former stockbroker." Special Agent Harrison turned to Victoria. "We then were able to connect Zeptien to your father, as a result of visual surveillance at Zeptien's homes and electronic surveillance on Zeptien's cell phone. We gathered evidence that Zeptien was buying the inside information from your father, whom he first knew as Neil Straub. Zeptien was paying your father with money he got from Skip Priam."

Only Abby seemed calm, maybe because she had been living with the truth. Victoria's eyes glistened, and Megan remained quiet, her lips over her braces. Jill suspected that Megan wasn't understanding much, except that it was bad for William.

Victoria shook her head. "Our Dad really did this? So it's true?"

"Yes. You may be wondering why your father didn't trade on the information himself, and we believe the answer is, because he wouldn't have made as much money that way, as he obviously lacked the capital that a hedge fund can commit, and also, it wouldn't have been possible to hide it from the IRS." Special Agent Harrison paused. "In addition, by merely selling information, your father wasn't technically in violation of federal securities laws, because insider trading is only unlawful if the trader is a fiduciary. The classic case, as you may have learned in law school, is of someone overhearing a tip in a bathroom. The listener can trade on that information, legally."

Victoria nodded, and so did Jill.

Special Agent Harrison shifted in his red-checked chair. "We were uncertain, however, as to how your father was obtaining the information, and we didn't as yet have his New York apartment under surveillance. We needed to learn more, so we placed Brian as a securities lawyer at Creed & Whitstone, because it represents Piper, Flanagan, and at the bar downtown that night, in order to meet you, Victoria."

Victoria looked stricken, her hands clenched together in her lap. "Why me? I'm not the one who lived with Dad. Why not Abby?"

"Frankly, Abby already had a boyfriend, at the time. You introduced Brian to your father, and they began to meet, without your knowledge, and they developed a relationship."

"Why did my Dad do that?" Victoria shook her head, dazed.

"Your father wanted to expand. He knew that Pharmcen could only have so many drug recalls, and he told Brian that he wanted to find other hedge funds to which he could sell inside information about other drug companies." Special Agent Harrison tempered his tone, knowing he was on difficult emotional ground. "Nor did your father want to be tied to Zeptien. The two men disliked each other, and we know this because we have Zeptien telling Priam as much. Zeptien told Priam that he suspected your father would eventually go off on his own and find other middlemen and other hedge funds."

"You know that by wiretap, on Zeptien's phone?" Victoria asked.

"Yes. So Brian offered to serve as the new middleman and let your father know that he had significant contacts at other hedge funds and investment banking houses."

Jill could imagine how much the prospect would appeal to William, and she realized that he wasn't evil incarnate. That gave him too much credit, and power. Ultimately, he was merely an opportunist, and he denied the harm that he caused as a result.

Special Agent Harrison continued, speaking mainly to Victoria, "That plan would have cut out Joe Zeptien, and we believe he may have found out about it, or that the friction between the men became too much. We know Zeptien feared losing control of your father, whom he viewed as a potential loose end, and we believe Zeptien murdered your father." Special Agent Harrison paused, and the family room went silent. "Unfortunately, we can't prove that, so we didn't include that in the indictment. We didn't have your father's house in Philadelphia under visual surveillance that day, or from the start. Your father did an excellent job keeping his identities separate, and our best information is that even Joe Zeptien didn't know he was William Skyler, until a little over a year ago, which is how we learned it."

"But how could you not know that?" Victoria gestured to Jill. "She figured it out in a week."

Special Agent Harrison leaned forward. "You have to understand the way we really work. Like any government agency, we're tasked with a mission, in this case, to investigate a Wall Street hedge fund. We have resources and budgets to expend toward that mission, but they're not infinite. On the contrary, they're limited, especially now, in view of the sluggish economy and the demands of domestic terrorism. So we direct all of our resources toward our mission. Piper, Flanagan was our priority and we started there. We maintained visual surveillance on Skip Priam's office and his homes in the Hamptons and Greenwich, Connecticut, as well as on Joe Zeptien's office in New York and his homes in north and south Jersey."

Jill understood. The FBI couldn't be everywhere at once, but it wouldn't be easy to explain that to Victoria.

Victoria's eyes narrowed. "So my Dad falls through the cracks? And Zeptien gets away with murder?"

"No, not at all." Special Agent Harrison frowned. "Joe Zeptien is going to jail for a long, long time. Our case against him for insider trading and tax evasion is rock solid. Believe me, he'll be punished, and we don't need to make a deal with him, so we won't."

Abby turned to Victoria, shaking her head. "He's right, Victoria. Zeptien will rot in jail, and that's all I care about. I wish I knew how he did it, but I saw how hard the FBI works, with my own eyes."

Sam looked over, from his chair. "It's like those Mafia cases, isn't it? The government doesn't charge mobsters with murder, it charges them with tax evasion. Either way, they're in jail for decades."

"Yes, exactly." Special Agent Harrison turned to Victoria again. "In addition, you have to put this in a proper time frame. Your father was killed only a week ago. No murder case gets put together that quickly, even if we weren't involved. In fact, we did liaise with the Philadelphia police, and they still don't believe it was a homicide."

Victoria nodded, mulling it over. "Okay, I guess I see your point."

Jill felt the same way as Victoria, vaguely unsatisfied, but she kept that to herself. "Special Agent Harrison, I have a different question. Did Zeptien kill Nina and her husband, or did Nina's husband really do it?"

"Neither," Special Agent Harrison answered. "We believe that Zeptien and Skip Priam hired contract killers to do it, named Richard Deyaz and John Hutcheson. Deyaz and Hutcheson were the ones who posed as Special Agents Donator and Cohz."

Victoria glanced over at Jill but said nothing, undoubtedly for Megan's sake.

Jill turned to Special Agent Harrison. "Did I lead them to Nina?"

Special Agent Harrison shook his head. "No, they already suspected she was the source. We knew it, too, by that point. It took us some time, because your ex-husband dated a number of women as Neil Straub, and he and Ms. D'Orive had an interest in keeping their relationship under wraps."

Jill thought that made sense. "Did you indict Zeptien and Priam for those murders?"

"No, to be precise, the indictment against them would have been for conspiracy to solicit, because they didn't commit the murders themselves. But, again, we kept the indictment as clean as possible, with only the insider-trading allegations, and of course, Deyaz and Hutcheson are dead."

"Who was following me, all this time?"

"Deyaz and Hutcheson, and we were, too. That's why we all came together today, in Parkertowne. We think Deyaz was following you in a black SUV until you spotted him in Manhattan, then we believe he switched vehicles."

Jill masked her shudder. "Why follow me, at all?"

"We theorize that Zeptien got wind that Abby was asking questions about her father's death. We believe that he thought she was a loose end, so he hired Deyaz and Hutcheson to follow her. When she came to your house, they started to follow you. They were together in the silver car that tried to run you off the road."

Jill was processing the information. "Deyaz and Hutchison told us that Brian was undercover. How did they know that?"

"They saw him. Brian blew his cover to save you, and that's why we indicted so quickly tonight, before Piper, Flanagan started erasing computer files and shredding documents. The Bureau tends to move slowly, like any government agency. We at the Philadelphia office call it Eastern District time." Special Agent Harrison smiled, briefly. "We were going to take Mr. Skyler's computer when we picked up Abby, but she had already given it to you. You actually helped us, though you were at great risk."

Megan nestled against Jill's side, and Jill gave her a reassuring pat.

"Piper, Flanagan made $75 million short-selling Pharmcen stock over the past three years. If Skip Priam decides to cooperate, which we believe he will, we'll likely issue an indictment against the top dogs at Piper, Flanagan." Special Agent Harrison leaned back in a final way, as if he were about to conclude. "We're trying to clean up Wall Street, to bolster the nation's economy and get the public investing again. That's what Operation Hedge Clippers was about, from day one."

Victoria raised her hand halfway, almost as if she were in class. "I have a last question. Did Brian pretend to be my friend? Because of my Dad? Is that the way you work, undercover?"

Special Agent Harrison puckered his lower lip, slightly. "Brian's job was to get close to your father, but his friendship with you was genuine. He felt conflicted about having to deceive you, and he'll explain that to you. You can visit him tomorrow in the hospital, if you wish."

"But who is he, really? Is he even a lawyer?"

"Yes, he is, and it aided us immeasurably in this operation. His real name is Brian Prendergast. We usually choose a name close to the original, in case he gets recognized on the street."

Abby looked over at Victoria with a sly smile. "And guess what? He doesn't really have a girlfriend in Paris. They made that up, because he wasn't allowed to get in a relationship with you."

"Oh, *there's* a silver lining." Victoria rolled her eyes. "Brian's a liar, but he's single. Count me out." She returned her attention to Special Agent Harrison. "Why did my Dad have a double identity?"

"I'll tell you what I know, because you may find it some comfort." Special Agent Harrison's expression softened. "He told Brian that he wanted to protect you and your sister, in case things went wrong. He wanted you completely screened off from trouble. He loved you both and he didn't want you in danger."

Victoria's face fell, and Jill got a lump in her aching throat, not knowing if it were true but sad just the same. For a minute, nobody said anything, giving William a moment of silence, all of them lost in his or her own thoughts. Megan looked down, playing with her fingers, and Victoria sat motionless, her eyes filming.

Sam was the one who broke the silence. "We'll help each other through this, as a family. That's *my* promise," he said, simply.

# 72.

Jill was in her nightshirt, listening at their bedroom door, which she'd cracked open so she could hear what was going on in Megan's room. Victoria and Abby were in there with Megan, and the girls hadn't emerged except to let Beef join them. Jill couldn't help but wonder what was going on.

"Honey, they're fine." Sam was in bed, reading, his glasses perched at the end of his nose.

"But what are they doing in there?"

"I think they're dealing with it, and they'll be fine."

"This is the week from hell, for Megan." Jill stayed at the door. "And I haven't been the most attentive mother."

"Megan knows you love her."

"Now she's the one who needs triage." Jill felt achy, bruised, and tired. "I can't believe I was wrong about her panic attack. I blew that, big-time."

"No, it was all of a piece. She had everything going on, all at once. The text photo was only a part of it."

"Not to a thirteen-year-old."

"Come here, love. Come to bed." Sam took off his glasses and set them and his book on the nighttable, and

Jill shut the door, went to bed, and slipped under the covers, lying on her good side. Sam reached for her, stroking her arm. "How do you feel? Does your eye still hurt?"

"A little." Jill edged over, giving him a kiss, then another, sweeter one. "I love you."

"I love you, too, and I have something to say." Sam met her eye, growing serious, and Jill sensed it was time for their reckoning.

"I guess we have to figure this out, huh?"

"Yes, and one of us already has."

"Okay, go ahead," Jill said, trying not to be nervous.

"I'm sorry I acted like a fool. It's not that I don't want the kids, it's that I wanted more of you. You see the difference?"

"Yes." Jill felt touched. "I'm sorry, too. I should have talked to you more. I don't want it to be about the kids twenty-four/seven, either. I really don't." She gestured down the hall. "I'm not listening at Megan's door, for example. That would be *crazy*."

Sam laughed. "Good point. That's progress."

"See?" Jill smiled, then it faded, and it was her turn to get serious. "But what are we going to do about Abby and Victoria? You see them, they're down the hall, one door from Steven, and I like it. I *love* it. All of us, under the same roof. This is going to happen, from time to time, if I have things my way. What do you say?"

"You know what, I'm fine with it."

Jill scoffed. "Come on. Really?"

"Really." Sam nodded, apparently happily. "I'm fine with it now. I'm educable, for an academic."

"What changed your mind?"

"A few things. First, losing you. It scared me, to think about losing you. It put everything in perspective. All the fighting, and all the disagreements, they're stupid. Life is short. Too short." Sam touched her cheek. "And second, and more importantly, I finally understood what you had been saying about Abby."

"How so?"

"Remember when you said that if something happened to me, and Steven needed you, what would I want you to do?"

"Yes."

"Well, that wasn't the hypothetical that convinced me. The hypothetical that convinced me just happened." Sam paused, his jaw working, and even the trace of a smile vanished. "Because if something happened to you, if I lost you, I realized that I would never stop being there for Megan. I realized that I'd always love her and I'd always feel like her father. No matter what, no matter who. Forever. I'm *hers*."

Jill could have cried with happiness. "Sam, that's lovely."

"You taught me. Of course, you almost had to get killed to teach me, but I came around." Sam smiled, touching her face. "So. Again. Will you marry me?"

"Yes. Please." Jill kissed him softly.

"Good. Thank God that's settled. I can't function. You should've seen me, in Cleveland. Worst paper I ever gave."

"I doubt it."

"No, truly. Lee put me on the plane. He practically said, good riddance."

Jill laughed.

"Now, let's get some rest. You must be exhausted. I'll get the lamp." Sam reached over and switched it off, so the bedroom was dark and still. The only light came from the moon outside the open windows, and a cool breeze ruffled the sheers. The rain had stopped, having washed the world, and the air smelled fresh, clean, and most of all, like home.

"This is nice." Jill shifted over and fitted her body to his side, finally exhaling.

"It sure is. We made it. We *survived*."

"Yes, and all that is over now."

"Yes it is, all over now," Sam repeated, and Jill lay still while he fell asleep, not five minutes later.

But she didn't fall asleep. She couldn't. Her head pounded, her throat ached. Her shoulder bandage made it hard to get comfortable. She tossed and turned, but couldn't shut out her thoughts. So much had happened in such a short time, and her mind crackled as if it were electrified. She'd been in two different ERs in one day, as a patient, not a doctor. And she'd quit her job at Pembey Family.

*I'm not an employee, I'm a doctor.*

Jill didn't regret her words, rash as they were. Even if Pembey wanted her back, she wasn't going. She was already thinking she might try to get a job in an ER at a children's hospital. She could put her triage mentality to good use there, and maybe she'd work full-time, now that Megan was older. Maybe the next chapter of her life wouldn't be so bad. The future could be better than the past. Maybe, after all, there was a forever.

She turned over but still couldn't sleep, so she got up and went downstairs. The house was dark and quiet, except for the sound of crickets and bats coming through the screens. Jill turned on the kitchen lights, went to her laptop, sat down, and moved the mouse to wake it up. Its bright screen light made her squint, but her eyes adjusted, and it was still open to the last document she'd worked on, the file she'd made of her notes from William's laptop. She'd copied all of his files, too.

*Nice work, for a doctor.*

Jill couldn't feel pleased with herself, not after such a bittersweet day. After all the people who died, and at the end of the day, the ones she felt sorriest for were the girls. Victoria would need time to understand her father, and Abby had her work cut out for her, starting over in school.

Jill thought of Megan, with a pang. They would have a lot more conversations before she understood what had happened, and Jill felt terrible for being wrong about her panic attack. It's true that more than one thing could have caused it, but she'd lost touch with Megan this week. She'd been guilty of diagnosis momentum, with her own daughter.

Jill mulled over the events of the day. The only bright spot was Rahul. That hadn't been an easy diagnosis, and she thanked God that she hadn't stopped asking what was behind Rahul's ear infections. That's where the truth lay. Behind. Under. Hidden.

Jill's gaze fell on her laptop screen, aglow with the all the files William had made, about tons of drugs. He had made tons of money, too, but he wanted more, and that had gotten him killed. She eyed the screen. Something felt wrong, but she couldn't put her finger on it. And she found herself wondering.

*What's behind this?*

# 73.

"Sam, wake up," Jill whispered, giving him a quick kiss on his grizzled cheek. She'd showered and dressed as if on fire, then made him a mug of black coffee, and its aroma scented the air. "Wake up, I have something to tell you."

"What?" Sam shifted over, groggy. "What's got into you?" He glanced at the clock, its digital numbers glowing in the dim bedroom. "Babe, it's five o'clock in the morning."

"I know." Jill rubbed his back in the thin T-shirt. It was still dark outside, but dawn was on the way and there was no time to lose. "We have to hurry. We have to leave."

"Okay, okay." Sam edged up in bed, blinking, his hair ruffled. "What's happening?"

"I figured out something. The diagnosis is wrong." Jill switched on the lamp, and Sam squinted against the light, putting up a hand to shield his eyes.

"What are you talking about?"

"We stopped asking, what's behind this? We mistook the first answer for the right answer."

"What diagnosis? Wrong about what?"

"Okay, well, here goes." Jill handed him his coffee and

launched into telling him what she'd figured out last night, and he drained his cup while she finished. "And now that I know the truth, I'm going to do something about it. This morning. Are you with me?"

Sam blinked. "You really want to do this?"

"Yes. Absolutely."

"Then I'm with you, all the way." Sam smiled, shaking his head. "I figured us out, you know. I'm a thinker, and you're a doer."

"So what are you waiting for?" Jill smiled back. "*Do!*"

Sam threw off the covers, and Jill ran for his clothes.

# 74.

Jill approached the Pharmcen building, walked through the glass entrance, and strode past the security desk to the granite reception banquette, with its phones and monitor screens. The pretty young receptionist was the same one as yesterday, and she hung up the phone, recognizing Jill.

"May I help you?" she asked, already wary.

"Yes, hello, I don't need an appointment, but I have some documents for Elliott Horton." Jill handed over a manila envelope, which contained copies of a few of William's emails to himself, without the identifying information. "Can you get these to him, as soon as possible?"

"Yes," the receptionist answered, but her attention shifted to the right, and Jill guessed that the security guard was coming up from behind, so she turned around and saw that he was the same one, too, with the funny soul patch.

"Hello, Barry," Jill said, with a smile.

"How may I help you today, Miss?" he asked, coldly.

"I'd appreciate it if somebody could take these documents to Elliott Horton."

"Documents?" The guard eyed the envelope with suspicion. "What kind of documents?"

"It's only paper, and he'll want to see it." Jill lifted the flap, showing him. "Okay?"

"Fine." The guard nodded at the receptionist, who extended a hand, and Jill gave her the envelope.

"Thanks so much. Please give those to Elliott as soon as possible. I'll be leaving now." Jill turned and walked to the entrance, with the security guard on her heels. He stood watch outside the building while she went to Sam's Lexus, got inside, and drove away.

She had reached the first traffic light on Weehawk Boulevard before her cell phone rang. She checked the screen. She didn't recognize the number, but she knew exactly who was calling her.

"Hello, Elliott," Jill answered, bracing herself.

# 75.

Jill waited on a wooden bench in the corporate park behind Pharmcen, with her purse and BlackBerry beside her. The park was beautiful and quiet, a several-acre tract of open space for company picnics and softball games, bordered by willow trees, boxwood, and hedges. There was a man-made pond on the left, and a mallard duck landed on the pumped-in water, its wings extended, showing bright blue stripes. The only other people in the park were a young man and a woman a few benches away, their heads bent together.

Jill straightened up when she spotted Elliott Horton entering the park. He came stalking toward her across the grass, his head down and his thin, white-blond hair catching the sunlight. He looked to be in his forties, tall and skinny, in a white oxford shirt and dark blue pants, and he was frowning deeply. He hadn't even reached Jill before he started firing questions at her.

"Is this some kind of joke?" Elliot's voice was on the high side, and his diction precise. "Who are you and where did you get that information?"

"Sit down and I'll explain."

Elliott remained standing. "That information is confidential, the property of Pharmcen. It's a massive breach of company security."

"Yes it is." Jill thought a minute. "Yet you came to meet me alone, and it couldn't have been easy to get away this morning, with Pharmcen in the news. The government indicted the biggest hedge fund on Wall Street last night, for insider trading in Pharmcen stock, specifically with respect to recalls. I would think somebody would want to interview you." Jill cocked her head. "Come to think of it, how did you get away?"

"Our PR department handles all that, and I didn't think this would take long. Now who are you, and where did you get that information?"

"Oh, I guess I was wrong. I was thinking that your bosses and maybe some security types told you to come out and meet me, to see what I wanted."

"No, not at all." Elliott's eyes widened slightly, a wan blue. His skin was as pale as a lab rat's. "Now answer my question. Who are you, and how did you get our data?"

"My name is Jill Farrow, and my ex-husband was William Skyler, who was Nina D'Orive's lover. That's how I got the data, from my ex's laptop. You might not know who I am, but your bosses do. I've been to Pharmcen twice this week, I talked to the security guard both times. Barry Whatever, with the soul patch." Jill met Elliott's eye. "Your bosses aren't leveling with you. They're playing you. They know who I am. You're the only one who doesn't, and oddly, I'm the only one on your side."

"I don't know what you're talking about." Elliott lowered himself onto the bench, his bony fingers linked in his lap.

"You know, somebody's going to have to take the fall for what just happened. Poor Nina passed on some very valuable information, and you were her boss. You even promoted her to VP." Jill rested her bandaged hand on the back of the bench. "I know it's not fair to blame you. You oversee fifty employees in Pharmacovigilance, and you can't be accountable for everyone."

"How do you know all this?"

"They will ruin you, Elliott. Not in the foreseeable future, while they still need you. But in the end, you'll get fired, and you'll have a helluva time getting a job anywhere else, given the scandal. I know that part, I lived that part."

"What do you want?"

Jill could see he was choosing his words carefully. "First, let me tell you how I figured out what was really going on. My ex's scheme started about three years ago, with Deferral. How'd that sell, by the way, before it was recalled?"

"None of your business."

"Okay, I'll tell you. It sold well. I saw online, it was used by two million allergy sufferers in the U.S. alone. My ex also sold information about Riparin, a diuretic that interacts with enzymes in the digestive track. How'd that sell, about the same?" Jill didn't wait for confirmation that she wouldn't get. "Both Deferral and Riparin had about the same number of complaints, and they were recalled."

"How do you know that?" Elliott raked his thinning hair. "The number of complaints per drug isn't public information."

"I know. My ex got the raw data from Nina. I gave you only some of it, like an appetizer."

"That can't be true." Elliott shook his head, and filaments of his fair hair caught the sun.

"It is. You may have noticed that none of the raw data I gave you is in the federal indictment. The government doesn't know it yet. That's why I said I'm on your side." Jill shifted toward him. "Now, as I was saying, the next drug up is Memoril, but now, there's a twist."

"What's the twist?"

"Correct my facts, because all I had to go on was the Internet. Memoril is a new Alzheimer's drug, and about five million people in the U.S. have Alzheimer's. Other major diseases like stroke, breast cancer, prostate cancer, even AIDS, they're all on the decrease. But not Alzheimer's. It's up 66 percent."

"Yes, I know all that. Alzheimer's is huge."

Jill winced at his callousness, but wasn't surprised. "Memoril was approved a year ago, and it has great potential, given that there are so few drugs like it on the market. I even knew a woman at my old group, Mary Fitzmartin. She was on Memoril, with good results."

"What's your point?"

"I studied the data that Nina was supplying my ex, and I found the same proportion of complaints for Memoril as for Deferral and Riparin. In fact, the men who were indicted were waiting for Memoril to get recalled or withdrawn, but it wasn't, and I know why." Jill met his eye, calmly. "Pharmcen isn't reporting those complaints to the FDA. They're deep-sixing them. They're covering them up to keep a very lucrative Alzheimer's drug on the market."

Elliott's eyelids fluttered. "That's not true."

"Oh, please. I'm on your side, Elliott. The government believes that those Wall Street types killed my ex because he was trying to expand to other hedge funds and middlemen, but I thought there was something else behind it, and there was." Jill tried to collect her thoughts. "The complaints on Memoril were coming in, but they were being covered up. By you, at your bosses' behest. Nobody at your level does that alone. They told you to do it, and they used you. They played you. I think my ex-husband figured it out, because he had the raw data from Nina, and I think he tried to blackmail you. And you killed him."

Elliott recoiled.

"Am I right or am I wrong?"

"You must be crazy." Suddenly Elliott reached over and yanked on Jill's sweater, almost tearing the neckline, but she made herself stay calm, raising her hands.

"Frisk away. I'm not wearing a wire. Go ahead, you're a doctor. Kind of."

"You don't know what you're doing." Elliott patted down her sides, then her chest, his eyebrow twitchy. His gaze fell on her bandaged hand. "Let me see that hand."

"Fine, allow me." Jill unpeeled the gauze, showed him her purplish cut, then covered it back up. "Satisfied?"

"Give me your purse." Elliott grabbed her purse, rummaged inside, and tossed it aside, then rose to go. "This is ridiculous, I'm leaving."

"I wouldn't do that yet. You didn't hear how I'm on your side, and you're going to wish you did. Because, sooner than you think, you're going to have no job and no money and no career. Or you're going to end up dead. Either way, you're going to wish you'd stayed."

Elliott turned, then sat back down, saying nothing.

"Your bosses aren't very nice people, Elliott. The government thinks that the Wall Street guys hired two killers to kill Nina and her husband, but I think your bosses did it."

"No, that's wrong." Elliott blanched, shaken. "Nina's husband killed her. He was abusive. We all know that."

"Did you really buy that? It looks like you did. No, your bosses had Nina and her husband killed, I assume so there wouldn't be any loose ends. Then *I* became a loose end, and they sent the killers after me. But I guess they kept all this from you, for some reason." Jill eyed him, wondering. "Oh, did you like Nina? That's too bad." Jill let it go. "Well, to get to the point, your bosses sent you out here, so they know what I have and they can guess what I want. Money. I just quit my job, and it'll come in handy."

"How does that benefit me?"

"You know there's a fortune in that building, Elliott. Enough for us both, and we're not as greedy as they are. Tell them I want to be paid, but let's share it. We can set the figure together. I say five hundred grand? Six?" Jill paused to let it sink in. "Let them pay us, and we'll split the money. You collect it from them, and deliver half to me. Three for you, three for me. No one has to know but you and me. I want to be paid, and I'll keep quiet about your lousy drug."

"Memoril's a *great* drug," Elliott said, suddenly animated. His light eyebrows flew upward, and his cheeks mottled, with new emotion.

"Not if there's that many complaints about it."

"You don't know the first thing about Memoril. All you did is read our website." Elliott snorted. "You have no idea how much R&D, clinical trials, time, money, and superb chemistry went into that drug. It was *nine years* in the making."

"All for naught. Memoril's a terrible drug, Elliott. Admit it, it doesn't work."

"Yes, it *does*. You said so yourself, it helped someone you knew."

"Until it kills her. Memoril doesn't work if you have to lie to keep it on sale."

"I *don't* have to lie." Elliott flushed, angering. "The regs don't require me to report a complaint to the FDA unless it's serious, life-threatening, or unexpected. They're open to interpretation, and I interpret them. That's my job."

"Oh, please. You don't *interpret* anything. You find the wiggle room in the terms to prop up your bad medicine. You fudge the data. You *cheat*." Jill could see he loved his drug and he was protecting it, like a mother did a child. Or even like Megan, who didn't like it when people said Beef was fat. Suddenly, Jill knew how to get to him. "It's a bad drug and a bad plan. Pharmacists can report adverse effects directly to the FDA. So can any consumer, online. It's only a matter of time before the world finds out that Memoril is *poison*."

"No, you're wrong," Elliott shot back. "The numbers will be far lower if we don't report, and it's the total numbers that trigger their attention."

"They're the FDA, not the IRS." Jill forced a cocky smile. "They go by the severity of the adverse event, too. Deferral and Riparin were only Class III recalls, but Memoril works on brain chemistry, so it's probably causing strokes, even fatalities."

"Who can say that any given death is linked to Memoril, especially in a geriatric patient? They get so decrepit, they would've died anyway, from a myriad of causes." A cruel smile curled Elliott's upper lip, and Jill felt her stomach turn over.

"You can't hide those complaints forever."

"I can, and I *have*." Elliott lifted his chin, defiantly. "Memoril helps more people than it kills. It's a true scientific advance."

Jill realized he'd just shown his hand, but she couldn't stop now. "You're making a monumental mistake. If you don't get me that money, I'll go to the media and I'll sell them the story. I'll tell them all about Memoril and what you're doing."

"Don't you *dare*." Elliott jumped to his feet, leaning over her, his features contorted with anger. "You and your ex are two of a kind. You think you know everything. Well, did he know everything? Where is *he* now?"

"You don't scare me, and you can't stop me." Jill could see he was about to explode, so she provoked him. "I'll get my money one way or the other. I'll *kill* your drug."

"I'll kill *you* if you do, and don't think I'm not capable of it!" Elliott's eyes flashed with a zealot's madness. "I killed your ex-husband! He was easy to fool. I let him think we were going to pay him, told him I was coming over to negotiate the deal. I told him he drove such a hard bargain, I needed a drink. It only takes a second to dump a test tube in a drink. You think I don't know how to mix drugs in solution? Add a masking agent, for flavor? I'm a *chemist*!"

Jill didn't know what to say, and suddenly she didn't have to say more, or get Elliott to say any more.

"FBI, hands up!" shouted a squad of FBI agents in dark windbreakers, racing from the treeline, lead by Special Agent Harrison. "FBI, get your hands up!"

"Don't shoot!" Elliott froze, raising his hands, his eyes popping as Special Agent Harrison and the other FBI agents grabbed him, patted him down, and handcuffed him.

Jill hustled away, as she'd been instructed, and the man and the woman sitting on the bench, both FBI agents, sprinted toward her and whisked her aside.

"Great job, Dr. Farrow!" The female FBI agent thrust out her hand. "I'll take the device now."

"Here you go." Jill handed her the BlackBerry, which had been specially outfitted as a recording device. "Thanks for protecting me."

"Jill!" Sam yelled, and she turned to see him running toward her, his sport jacket flying open. The sight lifted her heart, and she hurried to meet him.

"Sam, he admitted it, did you hear? Did they hear?" Jill met him, and Sam hugged her close.

"Way to go, babe. They've got the murder charge against him ready to go, and next they're going after Pharmcen." Sam smiled, looking into Jill's face with love. "I hope this gives the girls some real closure, too."

"So do I." Jill hugged him, finally at peace. "*Now,* it's over."

# 76.

It was dark by the time they got to Shood Memorial, and Jill and Sam exchanged looks as they walked down the glistening corridor. Megan and Abby were behind them, chatting with Steven, and Victoria brought up the very rear, her head down, her thoughts to herself. It had been Jill's idea to visit Brian tonight, but neither she nor Sam knew which way it was going to go, between Brian and Victoria. Victoria had confided in Jill that she was nervous about seeing Brian again, but she'd wanted to go, so Jill felt some trepidation as she led everybody into the hospital room.

"Hello, Special Agent Prendergast." Jill smiled, relieved to see that Brian was well enough to be sitting up in bed, reading a sports magazine. A bandage was wrapped around his head, making his brown hair puff in odd directions, and an older-looking pair of glasses perched on top of the gauze over his ears.

"Hello, hey, nice of you to come, Dr. Farrow, everybody." Brian grinned gamely, setting down the magazine. His color was good, but his face showed a few cuts and some bruising. His blue eyes were weary, but they came to life when Victoria finally walked in. "Vick, it was nice of you to come, too."

"It wasn't my idea," Victoria shot back, standing stiffly at the foot of the bed, and Jill stepped over to his bedside, to smooth things over.

"Brian, meet my fiancé, Sam Becker, his son, Steven Becker, and my daughter, Megan." Jill gestured at them, and Sam came over to shake his hand.

"Good to meet you, Brian."

"You, too." Brian nodded, acknowledging them all with a smile. "Hi, everybody. Good to meet you. Hey, Abby."

"Hey, Brian," Abby said, walking over. "How are you feeling?"

"Fine, thanks. Nothing's broken. I lucked out."

Jill felt her throat thicken as she thought about what she'd come to say. "Brian, I want to thank you for saving my life. I don't know how to say thank you for something that huge, other than just to say it, so thank you, so much, from the bottom of my heart." She managed to hold back her tears. She didn't want it to become about her. "I owe you, everything."

"No, you don't." Brian smiled, modestly. "It's my job."

"Maybe so, but it's quite a job, where you risk your life for other people." Jill flashed on the memorial at the police station in New York, with the plaques to the officers who fell on September 11. "I think you deserve at least a thank-you, a commendation, or whatever medal they give you. To me, you're a hero."

"To me, too," Sam said, nodding gravely.

"Yep," Abby added, and Megan nodded, staring at Brian, thrilled to be in the presence of a real FBI agent.

"Well, thank you, all." Brian turned to Jill, cocking his head. "By the way, Dr. Farrow, I heard you were quite the undercover agent today. Wearing a wire, the whole nine? Way to go, rook."

Jill blushed, still too moved to laugh, but next to her, Sam chuckled.

"I know, my wife is 007 now. You should've seen her. She kept him talking like a pro."

Jill nudged him, embarrassed. "Hardly, Sam." She gestured at Brian. "*This* man is a pro. He tried to drive bad guys off a road, at a hundred miles an hour. I'll never forget that day. I've never driven that fast in my life."

"I have, except for the tree." Brian laughed, and so did everybody else, except Victoria. "Doc, you're a tough cookie when you want to be. I tried to warn you off, remember? When I threatened you with the restraining order?"

"Oh." Jill smiled. "That only made me madder."

Brian laughed, turning to Sam. "Dude, you've got your hands full. Good luck."

Sam burst into laughter. "You can say that again."

"What's the secret, with these women, bro?"

"It's easy. Do what they say, when they say it."

Everyone laughed, except for Victoria, again. An awkward silence fell, with everybody wondering about the elephant in the room. Brian looked over at Victoria after a moment, clearing his throat.

"Vick, I'm sorry for deceiving you, I really am." Brian winced, and it wasn't from the scratches on his face. "It's part of my job, too, but it's, hands-down, the *worst* part of my job."

"Then congratulations on a job well done." Victoria's tone was heavy with sarcasm. "Way to go, Operation Hedge Clippers."

"Go ahead and yell at me." Brian frowned, his regret plain. "I deserve it, and you know you want to."

"Yell at you? I wouldn't stop at yelling. If you weren't already in a hospital, I'd put you in one."

Jill cringed, looking down.

Brian said, "Victoria, I really am sorry."

"You made friends with me just to meet my father."

"But then we became friends, you and I. The time we spent, that was real. We're real friends."

Victoria scoffed. "No, we're not, not anymore."

Jill stiffened, uncomfortable, but she didn't interfere, as much as she wanted to. She knew it wasn't her place, and since she'd been deceived herself, she could understand Victoria's reaction. On the other hand, she felt for Brian, who was only doing his job, and was obviously crazy about Victoria, job or no.

Abby rested a hand on the bedrail, her young face falling into prematurely sad lines. "Brian, I'm not mad at you. I got to know some of the other FBI agents and I understand why you did what you did, with Victoria. I even get it, about Dad. I love him and I always will, but I know that he was the one doing wrong, not you."

"Thanks, Abby." Brian frowned, in a sympathetic way. "I know this is hard for you, for both of you, and just so you know, your Dad talked about you guys all the time. He loved you both." Brian turned to Victoria, again. "Victoria, I really am sorry. I'm sorry I deceived you. I want you to know that I mean that, whether we stay friends or not."

"We've known each other for a year, and you lied to me every day." Victoria shook her head. "You lied about what you were doing, where you were going, even who you are. What am I supposed to do about that?"

"I had a job to do, and I did it, but I'm really sorry."

"But still." Victoria exhaled, frowning, her eyebrows sloping down, as anger gave way to hurt. "It's just that you lied to me about everything, even your name."

"Not everything. I care about you, that was real."

"How do I know that?"

"I'm telling you, now."

"But you told me before, when you were lying." Victoria tilted her head, pained. "And what about your imaginary girlfriend, in Paris?"

"I had to say that, it was part of the cover. What can I do to convince you?"

"I don't know. That's your problem, not mine."

"What if I proposed?"

Victoria blinked. "What?"

Brian smiled, a new smile, one full of feeling. "Will you marry me, Victoria? I love you, you have to know that."

"What?" Victoria asked, astonished.

"Please, marry me. I don't have a ring and I can't get down on one knee, but I love you, and I've loved you every day for a year." Brian's voice thickened, suddenly. "And when I thought I might die in that car, you were my last and only thought. *You*. Marry me. Please. That is, if you love me, too."

Victoria's mouth dropped open. Her eyes filmed, but she didn't say anything.

Everybody held his breath, all equally amazed. Sam and Steven exchanged glances. Jill felt tears on the way. Megan's eyes popped with delight.

Abby interjected, "Yes, yes, yes! She loves you, she's crazy about you! She told me she wants to marry you, a million times! Yes, already!"

Victoria burst into teary laughter, rolling wet eyes. "Abby, shut up, please, and let me think."

"Victoria, say yes! You know you want to!"

"Abby, please. This is my business, not yours."

"Tell him!" Abby gestured at Brian. "He's waiting!"

Jill couldn't believe these girls. She stepped in and separated them, smiling. "Girls, don't fight, not now, okay? Abby, please be quiet. Victoria, you have the floor."

"Thank you, Jill." Victoria turned to Brian, trying to

compose herself. Her eyes filled with tears, and she pursed her lips, but she didn't answer.

Brian's eyes stayed glued to her, a steady blue, but his face began to fall, and his smile slowly faded. "Vick?"

Victoria smiled sweetly, her lower lip a little shaky. "Brian, please understand, I love that you asked me. But don't you think we should go on a date before we get married?"

Brian laughed, a little sadly, then he nodded. "Okay, if you want, I guess we could do it that way. It's somewhat conventional, but I can work with that."

"Wonderful." Victoria smiled, her eyes shining, and she stepped over to his bedside. "But I can tell you this, I love you, too."

"You do?" Brian asked, grinning again.

"Yes, I do, so much." Victoria leaned over and kissed him, once, then again.

Sam and Steven clapped, and Jill burst into happy laughter, proud of Victoria.

Abby squealed, and Megan chanted, "Victoria's in love! Victoria's in love! Victoria's in love!"

Victoria straightened up, breaking into a huge grin. Her face flushed with happiness, and she turned to Megan. "Mega, can you wait a little longer until we go dress-shopping?"

"Yes! Yes! Yes!" Megan squealed, running into Victoria's arms. "Yes!"

# 77.

Saturday afternoon swim meets always drew the biggest crowds, with parents home from work and siblings off from school, and the pool gallery was packed to bursting, with the crowd talking, laughing, and joking around. The meet was held at Sequanic High, and the last time they were here, Megan had had that panic attack. Jill prayed that today wouldn't be an instant replay as she and Sam made their way down the row to Victoria, Abby, and Steve, who had driven separately in Steve's rental car, taking Megan.

Jill and Sam waved hello to the Cohens, the McGraths, and Bill Roche and Jenny Zeleny, then sat down on the hard wooden bleacher, where Jill turned to Victoria. "How was Megan on the ride over?"

"Fine, and we gave her lots of support."

"It has to be hard for her to see that boy again. I hope she'll be okay."

"I know she will. We gave her a pep talk in the car."

Steve turned to Jill, grinning warmly. "I drove and pretended not to hear anything."

"Way to go. I do the same thing, all the time." Jill

smiled, then caught sight of the boys' team, grouped on the far side of the pool, against the sunny window. She squinted at the swimmers. "Which one is he?"

Victoria pointed. "The blond in front."

Jill spotted a skinny kid with curly blond hair, and almost growled. "Is his mother here? Can I deck her?"

"Down, girl." Victoria looked over. "Megan's stronger than you think. After all, she's her mother's daughter."

Jill smiled, then eyed the pool deck for Megan. A flock of yellow bathing suits and matching swim caps clustered behind the starting blocks with Coach Stash, and Megan stood at the periphery, looking up at the bleachers the way she always did. Jill raised her bandaged hand. "Hey, honey!"

Megan broke into a grin, waving back. "Hi, Mom," she mouthed, which she had never done.

"She looks happy," Sam said, waving.

"She really does." Jill felt a rush of relief.

"Jill, Jill!" Rita motioned from down the row to Jill, who leaned over. "Victoria and Steven told us about your car accident, in Jersey." She gestured at the bandage. "Are you okay?"

"Fine, thanks," Jill answered.

"I heard what that little jerk did to Megan. How is she?"

"She was upset." Jill knew it had to be the talk of the swim moms, but they'd all be on Megan's side.

"She's fine, you'll see," Victoria said, smiling mysteriously.

Jill turned to her, puzzled. "What, is something going on?"

"Yes, and it was all Megan's idea. Watch."

Jill and Sam craned their necks at a sudden commotion, taking place poolside. Coach Stash had walked away with his clipboard, and Megan and the rest of the girls swarmed like yellowjackets, flying toward the boys' team. Megan grabbed the blond swimmer by his one arm while Courtney nabbed his other.

"What's she doing?" Jill asked, confused. Sam and Steve looked over at the scene, and Victoria and Abby pointed in delight. Heads turned in the gallery as Megan, Courtney, and the rest of the girls whisked the boy to the edge of the pool and pushed him into the water.

"Yay! Yay!" Megan, Courtney, and the girls burst into laughter, applause, and cheering. The boys doubled-over with laughter, shoving each other in glee.

Victoria, Abby, and Steven cheered, and the Valley West parents stood up, clapping, as the blond swimmer swam to the side of the pool. The girls crowded around a grinning Megan, jumping up and down, hugging her.

"Way to go!" Sam laughed.

"Good for you, Megan!" Jill stood up, clapping loudest of all. Her throat caught as she realized that her daughter was growing up, right before her very eyes.

And it was a beautiful sight.

# Acknowledgments

I've written eighteen novels, and in each one, my goal is to write something that's true. That doesn't mean true in the literal sense, at all. It means emotionally true. A novel doesn't connect unless it's emotionally true, and when it's emotionally true and does connect, what happens is magic.

To write a novel that's emotionally true, I have to go within. For it to reach your heart, it has to come from mine. I dug deep for *Come Home,* because in my own life, during my second marriage, I was a stepmother of three girls, in addition to my own daughter. The first point I need to make here is in the nature of a disclaimer: the stepdaughters in this novel aren't my real stepdaughters, nor are they based on them, in any way. The characters herein are completely fictional, and the same is true of the second husband in this book. But the emotional truth of being a stepmother, and an ex-stepmother, I know that. I lived that, and so I'm free to write about it, and I hope it informs the novel and gives it an emotional truth.

That said, you don't have to be a stepmother or even a mother to recognize the feelings or have them strike a chord in you, because that's the way it is with truth. It rings true, for everyone.

And, of course, the other point to be made is a big thank-you to my (former) stepdaughters, for the years we spent together, and for letting me into their lives. I love all three of you, and always will.

Now to the thank-yous, where I get to thank all of those experts who helped me, and make clear that any and all mistakes herein are mine.

I needed a dynamic duo of pediatricians to help me understand how they think and work, and for this, I am indebted to Dr. Carol Actor, in private practice in Phoenixville, Pennsylvania, and Dr. Eileen Everly, of the Children's Hospital of Philadelphia. Both women took valuable time to answer all of my questions, and I could not be more grateful to them for their kindness, expertise, and guidance—and more important, for all they do for children.

For the intricacies of the Federal Bureau of Investigation, I turned to my dear friend and former special agent Linda Vizi, and thanks so much to her. I am so grateful to Linda for her time and expertise, as well as all of the years of service she gave to the FBI to take care of us all. And yes, there really is a Needle & Gun Club of female FBI agents, and I'm proud to have one of their quilts hanging in a place of honor in my home.

Thanks to the police officers at the Sixth Precinct in Philadelphia, as well as the police officers of the Sixth Precinct (a coincidence) in New York City, for their help, and again, their service to us all. Special thanks and a big hug to Detective Kenneth Baker of the NYPD for answering all of my questions.

Thanks to Tom Melvin, genius accountant, who helped me with the financial details herein, as I have math anxiety. Thanks to Mary McMahon, swim mom extraordinaire.

Thanks to Danielle Bersch, Elaine Gondek, and Veronica Mendina, too.

Thank you to the gang at St. Martin's Press, starting with the terrific John Sargent, Brian Napack, Sally Richardson, Matthew Shear, Matt Baldacci, Jeanne-Marie Hudson, Brian Heller, Jeff Capshew, Nancy Trypuc, Kim Ludlam, John Murphy, John Karle, Sara Goodman, and all the wonderful sales reps. Big thanks to Michael Storrings, for an astounding cover design. Also hugs and kisses to Mary Beth Roche, Laura Wilson, and the great people in audio books. I love and appreciate all of you.

I want to take a special moment to thank my editor, Jennifer Enderlin, to whom this book is dedicated. I came to Jen when my writing life was well-established and my habits somewhat entrenched (if not ossified). But getting to know her, to listen to her suggestions, and to watch her approach to my work has opened my eyes, and heart, in so many ways. A great editor has the talent and power to bring out the best in a writer, and I feel Jen doing that for me, encouraging me to go deeper, and truer, with each book and even each sentence. Jen, I can't thank you enough, and this dedication is only a start.

Thanks and big love to my incredible agent and friend, Molly Friedrich, who has guided me for so long now, with her expertise, brilliance, humor, and heart. Thanks, too, to the amazing Lucy Carson and Molly Schulman, for all of their comments on this manuscript. Thanks and another big hug to my dedicated and wonderful assistant and best friend, Laura Leonard. She's invaluable in every way, and has been for over twenty years.

Thanks, too, to my girl pack of Nan Daley, Rachel Kull, Paula Menghetti, and Franca Palumbo. We're all moms of daughters and they're all we talk about, and always will be. Thanks, ladies, for being yourselves, and for helping me, every day.

This is a long way of saying thank you very much to my amazing and brilliant daughter, Francesca, a wonderful writer in her own right, to my mother, Mary, and to my late father. I love you all, and you've taught me everything about everything.

Thank you, always and forever.

Read on for an excerpt from Lisa Scottoline's novel

# DON'T GO

Available in trade paperback from St. Martin's Griffin

# 1.

Chloe woke up on the floor, her thoughts foggy. She must have fallen and knocked herself out when she hit the hardwood. She started to get up, but felt dizzy and eased back down. The kitchen was dark except for pinpoints of light on the coffeemaker, TV, and cable box, like a suburban constellation.

She tried to understand how long she'd been lying here. The last thing she remembered, she was rinsing the dishes after lunch, eyeing the sun through the window, like a big, fresh, shiny yolk in the sky. Yellow was her favorite color, and she always tried to get it into her painting. Chloe used to teach art in middle school, but now she was a new mom with no time to shower, much less paint.

She heard a mechanical *ca-thunk,* and the Christmas lights went on outside. Red, green, and blue glimmered on the wetness underneath her, which seemed to be spreading. Her gaze traveled to its edge, where her Maine coon, Jake, sat in silhouette under the table, his ears translucent triangles, backlit by the multicolored lights.

Chloe reached for a chair to pull herself up, but was oddly weak and slumped to the floor. She felt cold, though

the kitchen had a southern exposure and stayed warm,
even in winter. She needed help, but was alone. Her sister,
Danielle, and her brother-in-law, Bob, had come over for
lunch, then Danielle had taken the baby Christmas shopping and Bob had gone to work. They didn't have children,
and Danielle had been happy to take Emily to the mall by
herself.

*We can pick out Christmas presents for you and Mike!*

Chloe closed her eyes, wishing her husband, Mike, were
here, but he was a reservist in the Army Medical Corps,
serving in Afghanistan. He'd be home in a month, and she
was counting the days. She'd prayed he wouldn't be called
up because he was thirty-six years old, and when the de-
ployment orders came, she'd taken it badly. She'd simply
dissolved into tears, whether from sleep deprivation,
crazed hormones, or worry.

*Mike, please, I'm begging you. Don't go.*

Suddenly Chloe realized something. The Christmas
lights were controlled by a timer that turned them on at
five o'clock, which meant Bob and Danielle would be back
at any minute. She had to hide the vodka she'd left out on
the counter. Nobody knew about her drinking, especially
not Danielle. Chloe should have been more careful, but she
was a beginner alcoholic.

She reached for the chair and hoisted herself up partway. The kitchen whirled, a mad blur of Christmas lights.
She clung to the chair, feeling dizzy, cold, and spacey, as
if she were floating on a frigid river. Her hand slipped, and
the chair wobbled. Jake sprang backward, then resettled
into a crouch.

She put her hands on the floor to lift her chest up, like
a push-up, but the wetness was everywhere. Under her
hands, between her fingers, soaking her shirt. It didn't
smell like vodka. The fog in her brain cleared, and Chloe
remembered she'd been loading the dishwasher, and the

chef's knife had slipped, slicing the underside of her arm. Bright red blood had spurted from the wound, and she'd fainted. She always fainted at the sight of blood, and Mike used to kid her.

*The doctor's wife, who's afraid of blood.*

Chloe looked at her left arm in horror. It was covered with blood, reflecting the holiday lights. Blood. Her mouth went dry. She'd been bleeding all afternoon. She could bleed to death.

"Help!" she called out, but her voice sounded far away. She had to get to her cell phone and call 911. She dragged herself though the slippery blood to the base cabinet, clawed the door for the handle, and grabbed it on the second try. She tried to pull herself up but had no strength left. She clung to the handle.

Chloe spotted her laptop to her right, on its side. She must have knocked it off the counter when she fell. Her best friend, Sara, was always online, and Chloe could Gchat her for help. She slid the laptop toward her and hit the keys with a slick palm, but the monitor didn't light up. She didn't know if it was off or broken.

She shoved it aside, getting a better idea. She would crawl to the front door and out to the sidewalk. The neighbors or someone driving by would see her. She started crawling, her breath ragged. The front door lay directly down the hall, behind a solid expanse of hardwood and an area rug. She dragged herself toward it, smearing blood across the kitchen threshold.

Hope surged in her chest. Her arms ached but they kept churning. She pulled herself into the hallway. She kept her eye on the front door. It had a window on the top half, and she could see the Christmas lights on the porch. She had put them up herself, for Emily's first Christmas.

The door lay thirty feet ahead, but Chloe felt her legs begin to weaken. Her arms were failing, but she couldn't

give up. She was a mother. She had a precious baby, only
seven months old.

Chloe moved forward on her elbows, but more slowly,
like a car running out of gas. Still, she kept going. The
front door was only fifteen feet away. Then thirteen, then
ten. She had to make it.

*Go, go, go. Nine, eight, seven feet left.*

Chloe reached the edge of the area rug, but couldn't go
another inch. Her forehead dropped to the soft wool. Her
body flattened. Her eyes closed as if they were sealed. She
felt her life ebb away, borne off on a sea of her own blood.
Suddenly she heard a noise, outside the house. A car was
pulling into the driveway, its engine thrumming.

*Thank God!*

She heard the sound of a car door opening and closing,
then footsteps on the driveway. They were slow because
the driveway was icy in patches, the rock salt melting it
unevenly.

*Hurry, hurry, hurry.*

Chloe remembered the front door was unlocked, a lucky
break. She was supposed to lock it behind Danielle, who
had been carrying Emily, the diaper bag, and her purse,
but she had forgotten. It would serve her well, now. Whoever was coming could see her through the window, rush
in, and call 911.

The footsteps drew closer to the door, but Chloe didn't
recognize them. She didn't know Bob or Danielle by their
footstep. It could be anybody.

*Please God hurry*

The footsteps reached the front door, and Chloe heard
the mechanical turning of the doorknob. The door un-
latched, and she felt a vacuum as it swung open. Frigid air
blasted her from the open doorway. Her hair blew into her
face, but she couldn't even open her eyes.

*Help me help me call 911*

She heard the footsteps walk to her, then stop near her head. But whoever it was didn't call her name, rush to her side, or cry out in alarm.

*What is going on why aren't you calling 911*

She heard the footsteps walk back to the door.

*Wait don't go please help me*

She heard the sound of the front door closing.

*No come back please help I'm*

The latch engaged with a quiet *click*.